Reluctant Hero

Reluctant Hero

Book One of the Seeded Saga

Vanessa MacLellan

Cover design by Khalid20

ISBN-13: 978-1-7377157-3-3
First Edition
First Printing, July 2024
The text of this book is in Georgia.
www.vanmaclellan.com

This is for all the Gamers
Keep dreaming up the Heroes

Inset 1
Wikipedia Article

Seeded

From Wikipedia, the free encyclopedia

Seeded, also termed evols, mutants, or gumps, are a group of individuals who have gone through the Genetic HyperMutation Phenomenon (GHMP) and have developed the deinde gland, also termed a Seed. A Seeded individual almost always has pale eyes, sometimes in unusual colors, e.g., pink, yellow, or purple. Eyes that are not pale are instead abnormal, e.g., oddly shaped pupils, lack of sclera, and other anomalies. Approximately three percent of humanity is thought to have the Seed based on eye color alone, though only an MRI test can confirm the presence of the deinde gland. Based on the TransHuman poll performed by the Whitcomb Medical Facility, less than ten percent of Seeded exhibit a power or ability. These powers can range from something that a standard human in excellent condition could achieve, such as holding one's breath for extended periods, to powers that break the laws of physics, such as personal flight or creating matter from nothing.

The Seed was first discovered by Doctor Erin Molinsky of the Reicher Institute, during a study to explain odd eye color in a broad array of volunteer test subjects. The first power was presented by....

CHAPTER 1

Martha

Martha, aged more by crap circumstance than her actual years, raised her ratty sign higher as the traffic slowed for the red light. Her sign used to say *Will Work for Food*, but that saying stank, and she'd dropped that old, battered phrase inked out on that old, battered cardboard. Now her sign, written in black block letters that grew smaller and smaller as her space ran out, read *Anything Will Help. God Bless.* You always added the God Bless; it made people feel guilty if they didn't give you jack.

Even with some undiscovered power trapped inside her, she was one of the freesteaders—without means, a car, a home, a future. Scanning the drivers with her failing eyes, her gaze grasped for anyone to look at her. The light switched green; the cars sped by. Her grubby shoes squeaked as she shuffled to her backpack, stashed behind a nearby bush, to pull out some water. The plastic bottle crackled as she brought it to her lips. The weather had been dry, sparing her from rotting socks, but the shoes had a definite odor that even turned the rats away.

All these milk-fed cows, driving by in their sleek electric cars, they probably never had to wear rotted shoes. She wanted to rattle them, show them what rotted shoes was like—that would be a nice superpower, pushing her world on others. If only it would manifest. Her eyes were unnaturally pale, tagging her as having the Seed, and therefore she had to have a power. Too bad she had no clue what it was. It certainly wasn't the superpower of having daisy fresh feet.

These bling-bling peacocks didn't even glance her direction, to see her eyes. Maybe she was invisible and didn't know it. That could be her secret Seeded special ability. Her magic. A load o' cock and bull, really. All the other freesteaders saw and talked at her just fine; only the one-percenters wouldn't piss on her if she was engulfed in flames.

Martha muttered to herself, scratching where her invisispec's arm pressed into her left temple. The arms of the VR-glasses were much tighter than the old sunglasses she used to wear and always dug into her face. Another car zipped by. The specs reported the make and model and how much it cost new.

That could be her power. Invisible to those with money.

All the potential of the universe and no idea how to flip on the switch.

She'd tried all the tricks folks yammered about to make one's power manifest. Usually, it was all about putting yourself under stress, like near-death experiences. Martha lived on the streets of Portland. Near-death experiences were a daily occurrence, and she still couldn't fly or make her skin turn to steel or burp lilac scent. Nothing.

Rush hour traffic oozed by at the clogged intersection she'd staked out in front of the empty gas station at the off-ramp. An old, rusty heap, still fueled by gas, backfired, letting loose a black fart of acrid smoke. Martha ducked behind the light post while she coughed up the heavy, burnt lungful, scanning the sky for drones. Two of the air spies zipped by. Maybe police drones, or those for traffic. None swooped down to harass the puker. Or her.

A sedan slowed to a silent stop beside her, pulling her thoughts back to the reason she stood at the stoplight that early evening: money to buy shoes and food. The window lowered and a middle-aged dude handed her a five. A five. Just a five?

"Thank you so much," she said in that self-deprecating tone all the freesteaders offered these bastards.

The bastard nodded, not even smiling, and rolled the window up as he sped up to pass through the intersection.

By the end of rush hour, Martha's pocket sung to the amount of forty-seven dollars. A spit in the pot for her shoe fund. She used to make more. Get a twenty here and there. Someone had tossed her a pack of cigs, though, so she puffed one out as she wandered to the bus stop and back to the Portland waterfront.

RELUCTANT HERO

A ring of space surrounded Martha as she climbed on the bus and paid the fare with coins, one coin at a time. Nobody said anything to her face, but the hems and haws and teenage-dramatic sighs were certainly aimed her way. Screw 'em! The man behind her swiped his phone over the reader, paying his fare. The bus was half full after the 6 p.m. surge, most with their invisispecs down, tuning out the world. Her eyes flicked to the camera mounted above the windshield before she planted herself onto a seat with a woman—student type, earbuds in, specs down, mitted hand twitching as she accessed her specs, hints of music slipping out. The woman's nose scrunched, and she leaned away from Martha. Internally, Martha crowed. The snobby bitch deserved a snoot pounded by rotting shoes.

Several girls were nattering on behind Martha, talking about the latest Seeded media whoring. Not that all Seeded were attention slaves—Martha certainly wasn't—but their TV shows and their magazines and their prizefighting and their online feeds were all about them them *them*.

"And the government is pushing for the Certification of the hero groups. Won't that be awesome if Portland gets a Certified hero group?" one teen blathered.

"Who do you think it'll be?" another asked, then started belting out a song about touching herself, causing the other girls to giggle.

If they didn't watch it, some of the men would want to touch *them*, flaunting themselves like that. Martha looked around, glared at the bastards not specced in who watched the girls. Filthy lechers. One met her eyes, his own going wide, and and then found the floor damned captivating. She captured his image on her spec. If she'd had a good power, she'd take a knife to 'im. Right in his nads. Thinking bad bad thoughts about little girls. Sick fucks.

The girl's solo ended and another of the girls, voice authoritative in the ways Martha remembered from her own girlhood, said, "I think it will be the Bullet. Check the Saturday line-up on the SW1 feed. He was promoting Certification. Says it will give their group validation and direction on where they are most needed."

One snorted, while another mooned on about how fine Bullet was. Martha sneered to herself. As if. Like the second most powerful Seeded in America would want to be a Certified guardian.

"The Bullet's in New Orleans, what would he want with Portland?"

"Well, Portland's a hub, like New Orleans. Why not Portland?"

"Nah, it will probably be someone local. Maybe that cop. Geier."

"He's lame, doesn't even have a cool name."

"He talks about it all the time. Did you check his feed? Protecting Portland with his group. What're they called again?"

Martha knew. O.G.R.E., or something like that. Like a big monster. John Geier talked a lot, walked the streets of Portland on and off duty. Talked to people like Martha. He wasn't a bad sort, for the fuzz. Not like some of them other pigs who harassed the freesteaders, kicking in their tents, throwing dirt on their sleeping bags. Evicting them from public property. It's public, for God's sake! They had a right to set up tents there.

According to John Geier's lip service, he didn't like the drones, either.

What Portland needed protecting from was itself.

Martha climbed off the bus, leaving the nattering girls behind with one final glare at the letch and walked towards the waterfront where her friends camped under the Steel Bridge. She'd tucked her money deep into her shoe, under the stinky insole that was disintegrating into little pieces of foam and rubber. She'd go to the Mission later and get a meal. Hoped salt wasn't the main flavoring tonight.

At the bridge, traffic lined up tail to nose along Naito. Camps had been tossed and garbage strewn everywhere: all signs the cops and the city road warriors had come through and rounded up the freesteaders. Her quick scan didn't see any pigs on patrol, but it was probably better to leave. She didn't fancy an ass search. Time to hit the backup location: the Firehouse.

Overhead, a drone buzzed by. Martha shadowed her face with her hair. People disappeared from the streets out here. She didn't wanna get pegged by any of those spies.

One had to be careful going into the Firehouse because the Ghost haunted the upper level. A bit of a crazy—crazier than most of the other freesteaders. A kid, under twenty certainly. He talked to himself and had a tingle for dead things. Found out every time any of them kicked it and ran off to fiddle with the corpse. He set her skin crawling.

That, and his eyes were totally white. No pupil. No iris. Nothing but white.

Same with the rest of him. Albino or something.

Still the place was dry and usually safe. Martha just had to make sure she came at it from the north side and avoid the watch dogs: cops, drones, and pushers. On alert with her head kept down, she rushed along the street, keeping to the darker side versus the side lit by streetlamps. The smell of piss and burning garbage mingled in the cooling air. She stepped over trash, dog shit, and legs, and around groups of people talking, sharing a smoke and other, more rancid things.

"Martha, hey baby. Wanna join us?" Greg, another freesteader, tapped the breast pocket of his thick flannel jacket. Martha shook her head. She wanted no part of that kind of fun. Last three years, that poison spread across Portland's freesteader population like a plague. Meth was as shitty as a half-full Chinese food takeout box sitting out for a week. Matoro, out of Japan they said, was that box in the sun, under a heat lamp, with a wad of spit from the local infectious disease center. It tore a person apart. Beat down freewill. Took it away. Left you a zombie. Since it didn't make the user violent, nobody cared. She was sure some jackass government agent brought it to the streets. On purpose. Drugs were all legal here. She remembered when they weren't. Before, you got rounded up for using, now they just let you wallow in your own piss. They handed out mind-drugs at the Betterment Stations, why not brain friers on the streets? All needful things. For some, Matoro took away the cravings for other drugs, took away their mental teeters, but it took away their choices, too. Their desires. It took the person away.

Martha offered Greg the bird. "Not interested in lala land, Greg. Toss it in the river." She left the losers and rounded a corner, still looking over her shoulder at Greg and his friends, when she bumped into someone.

The someone, a man, sneered at her like he'd just stepped in shit. Bastard. Then his normie eyes locked onto hers, and his lips twitched into a not-so-friendly smile. Instinct honed from street living pecked at Martha's brain, causing a shiver to squirm up her spine. That smile was dangerous. Predatory. From a normie, when she had the Seed. "Sorry," she muttered, ducking around him, making herself small to rush away.

Run. Run, her instincts roared.

The man grabbed her, spun her to face him. Slowly, slip by slip, his smile grew. "Pale eyes, I see."

She bared her teeth. "Yeah, and you better let go, or I'll show you how to ride a hockey stick, long side up."

The man laughed, a purely mean sound. "I think not."

A tiny voice told Martha that she'd had a good run, but now, with the hard gaze of the man before her, she knew she'd hit the end. She pulled. Yanked her arm, but her strength could never match a man's. He wound up his fist. Ducking her head, she tried to protect herself. A strike pounded her back, then her head. Smacked into her face.

The end swooped down on her as her body hit the ground.

CHAPTER 2

Nekoka

N*ekoka, go right. I'll bust around the next block and take him.*

Nekoka sent an affirmative thought to Jenni, who telepathically picked it up then shifted into Speed Racer mode, dashing through a mass of tourists filtering out of Mona Lisa Pizza. Nekoka tucked her bag full of beignets protectively under one arm as she ran at her own human-normal speeds after the purse snatcher, her long cat tail trailing out behind her.

Sheesh. The two friends had been enjoying a leisurely day looking for a birthday gift for their friend Zack—Nekoka basking in the adoration of her fans and Jenni McGuire ignoring all the people staring—when some idiot tore a woman's purse off her arm and fled. Seriously, in a Seeded hub city?

When God was handing out smarts, He beat this guy with the amoeba stick.

New Orleans adored the Seeded, unlike those MAAD cities, and so she and her Usual Suspects resided here. Not that squatting in Zack Silversmith's plantation mansion wasn't a strong incentive.

Nekoka zigged and zogged through the early evening foot traffic in the French Quarter after the thief. She'd gotten a partial of his face and, using *kokogyo,* sent her memory to Whisker, her super sexy tiny computer docked on her arm since she was currently wearing the shape of a catgirl. Through Whisker, Nekoka used SPYme, a program she developed with threads into all data, public and private, offering up specific details on everything she witnessed.

SPYme took only seconds hunting the thief's stats. He was a mouse, her prey, both physically and information-wise. With both Nekoka and Jenni after him, this would-be crime lord had no chance of escaping. Mentally skimming the relevant data on Jason Olman, nineteen, a few arrests, she discovered he was Seeded. Pale blue eyes. Nothing noted on his power. Probably one of the dominant duds who had no obvious ability manifestation.

Not everyone was as lucky as Nekoka, who had two powers, although this fact was kept on the down-low. Only the Usual Suspects knew of *kokogyo*, her secret swanky power of ill-gained means, as Eugene liked to call it, though another adequate name would be technomancy. Alter Shape was her public power, the ability to morph her body in a variety of ways, with anything feline-related coming with shameless ease.

Frustratingly, this jerkoff was managing to pull away from her. She bared her canines, letting the predator in her surge forward. She wasn't a slouch, even if she wasn't boosted with stacked strength like Jenni. The bastard was *pulling away*. Maybe he did manifest a power, was a little stronger, a little faster than the norm. An undersized version of Jenni's physical boosts.

Nekoka made a quick note in her ever-expanding database on every Seeded she came across, then mentally withdrew from her computer to focus on the chase.

Jason hit the end of the block, and Jenni T-boned him from the cross street, sending him flying towards vehicular traffic, until Jenni—with her juiced-up reflexes—seized him from the air and yanked him back securely to the sidewalk. Nekoka pounced. So, she hadn't caught him first, but some instincts you just couldn't curb.

"*Kusoyaro*!" Nekoka snatched the purse from the snatcher, handing it to Jenni. "That's not yours." The guy stared up at her, then at Jenni, and all his fight slipped from him with a gusty sigh.

Nekoka climbed off him and brushed her tabby-striped fur down with her palms. Sometimes the chase got her a little ruffled. Around her she was aware of the clicking of phones and the watching eyes of VR-glasses. This close, the tiny computers sang to her cyber-senses, telling her exactly what they were doing, whispering to her, drawing her attention like happy kittens. She straightened her spine and put on the badass Scratch persona the press knew.

She smiled, toothy and cocky, and tossed out the V sign. Cliché? Maybe, but she was Japanese and a catgirl. She'd learned to own this long, long ago.

"Is that the shape-changer, Scratch?"

"What other catwomen are you aware of?" someone responded in a lowered voice, then louder. "Scratch! I love you!"

"Fiann! Nice catch."

"Scratch, can I pose with you?"

"You guys are awesome."

"They're not guys, Rick."

"Fine, fine.... You *ladies* are awesome."

The crowd grew. Jenni, largely disregarding them, focused on the thug, while Nekoka posed and purred. Let a little girl pet her tail.

The snatcher cowered at her feet like a bug.

"Hey Scratch," one guy in skinny jeans and thick-rimmed glasses called out. "What do you wear under your fur?"

Nekoka popped her eyebrows once, giving her lips a little flirt. "Nothing." Really, she was a shape-changer. Why would she have anything under her fur? Clothing was for mundanes.

Nekoka, quit teasing. Is the purse owner here? Jenni asked, mind to mind, searching the crowd.

Nekoka didn't see the purse owner, so she stepped past a newspaper box and leaned against the traffic signal. Those same cyber-senses that could feel all the eager computers in phones, specs, and watches sank into the light pole's innards, greeting the tiny computer controlling the traffic light and the watching cameras. The system was broad, citywide, but Nekoka's thoughts skipped along from one camera to the next, skidding through the system, until she found the woman in a few seconds, a half a block away, trotting towards them.

On a whim, Nekoka checked out the New Orleans city info feed through Whisker and saw herself and Jenni from seven different angles. News of the capture streamed through the feed. An announcement that the city police were already on their way popped up under a great shot of Jenni tackling the criminal. Nekoka pulled her mind back to her body and noticed a lozenge-shaped drone hovering overhead. Nekoka scowled at it.

Scoped by individuals' invisispecs was one thing, but government drones caused her ears to hug her skull.

"Purse-lady's coming this way," Nekoka said, hopping up to sit on the newspaper box.

"Fiann," a woman asked Jenni, using Jenni's alias, "is S-Force going to go Certified?"

Nekoka's fur rose at the question, obviously spiked by overdoses of reality TV and sensational news. The idea of Certification was stupid. It would force the Seeded to act without any say, and to hold back even if they felt action was the best path. Cities had to request assistance and could demand it as well. Someone else made the decisions, not the individual. Just another type of registration the MAAD cities wanted to institute, but the hub cities also seemed on board with it. It was only a way to make the norms feel *safe* and *in power* and *free of Seeded domination.*

Why the masses thought the Seeded desired to rule anyone was beyond Nekoka. An individual might, sure, but that was an individual's problem, not the entire group's. Why throw out the whole cow for a few curdled jugs of milk?

The Seeded were special, the rules of the natural sciences did not govern them, and even those without a feed or a fanbase or any spectacular powers, just by virtue of pale eyes, drew attention. Sometimes positive, most often negative.

Luckily, Nekoka and Jenni existed on a completely different scale. They had important friends. Backing. Adoring fans. They had true power. No mundane government could leash them. Well, not without difficulty.

Not unless they gave up their power and freedom willingly.

Nekoka sought out her best friend.

For the most part, Jenni McGuire could easily pass in normal society. In her mid-20s, she was a woman of complete normality—if you ignored her pale green eyes—dressed in black from torso to toe: boots, jeans, T-shirt. She symbolized the Perky Goth back when it was trendy and had let it soften to a more comic book grim reaper with dark, tamed hair as she grew out of the desire to be "in".

Nekoka, on the other hand, would fit in nowhere. During her change—and wasn't she happy that git Carlson hadn't called it the

Sprouting or some other inane phrase—something occurred to her that only happened to a few of the Seeded: her entire physiology morphed into a form visibly non-human. Sure, Alter Shape could make her look human with effort, but it wasn't her default. Instead, she sported cat ears, tail, eyes, and a body covered in soft fur. She had impeccable control over her appearance; therefore, she never needed to bother with clothing. She loved her image and all its wondrous possibilities; why would she want to look *human*?

In the Caribbean, there lived a man who had grown tentacles and went by the name Davy Jones. One guy from east Sussex developed skin texture rough like a brick. The flesh of a woman from Russia had turned transparent, so her organs, veins, and bones were visible to the eye. Several had completely alien forms, such as multi-legged space spawn, or skinny, pulled-thin bodies that reminded Nekoka of an X-Files's Grey. A few turned into fish folk, bird men, other forms of animal transformation.

But of even more importance than their eyes, transformations, or feeds, Jenni and Nekoka were members of S-Force, a Seeded group of six based in New Orleans that contained the second most powerful Seeded known in America: Zackary Silversmith, aka the Bullet.

And his birthday was just around the corner.

Little did the world know that Zack was a huge beignet fan. Nekoka clutched her bag close, but not too tight. She didn't want to flatten them more than they already were.

On a regular basis, due mainly to Zack, Jenni, and Jenni's girlfriend, Gracie, they ventured out and did *good things*. People liked them. Nekoka didn't mind, because it was for her friends and boiled down to being her choice.

Choice, a very important aspect of her daily life.

To be obstinate, Nekoka called her group the Usual Suspects. S-Force sounded too...heroic.

An attractive Indian woman in her twenties jogged up to them and scooped up Jenni's hands, shaking them both. "Oh, thank you," she gushed. "I don't know what I'd have done if you hadn't stopped him." Sargati Panicker, twenty-four, residing in Baton Rouge with a permanent account on *Hero's Rise: Second Seed*. Regularly dosed with Soratall, the newest concentration drug from the dispensaries. Nekoka's attention shifted to Jenni and caught sight of the slight smile, the crinkle at the edges of Jenni's eyes. Jenni always liked the exotic, swarthy ones. Definitely Jenni's type, though there was no way Jenni would stray from Gracie. Jenni was a one-woman kind of woman. Crazy concept.

Jenni held out the purse. The woman took it with more thanks before she glared down at the thief. Her eyes went wide, and her frown deepened. Probably noticed the kid was Seeded. "And to think, we adore you all here in New Orleans and you do this to us. Bastard."

The crowd lingered until the police arrived and took Jenni's statement. Nekoka wanted to slip on her kitty skin and hide as the men in blue made their appearance, but Jenni wouldn't be pleased, so she stuck around and answered a few questions, too.

"Are you two Certified?" a cop asked Jenni.

Nekoka scowled, ears pulled back, as Jenni denied any Certification.

"Ray, they're Scratch and Fiann, of S-Force...might as well be Certified," said his partner, who had the purse snatcher on his feet in cuffs. "Thanks for helping out."

"We're not Certified," Nekoka said, ears still back. "We're not heroes." She hated being pigeonholed. Just because she was special, better than the rest of these people, didn't mean she owed them anything.

Jenni glanced over at her. *You keep protesting that and you're going to lose your fan base.*

Tough shit. I'm not someone's pet dog.

The woman cop, Heather Rodgers, on the force for seven years, native Louisianan, nodded. "Of course, Scratch." She said it with a kind of amused smirk that only razzed Nekoka up. Officer Rodgers peered into the thief's eyes, not usually a smart move, and asked, "What's your power?"

The thief dropped his gaze to the ground. "Don't got one."

The cop's own monospecs would have fed her the information on Jason Olman through a less robust app than Nekoka's SPYme called ISpy, but Nekoka wasn't about to help them with what she assumed was a minor strength power on this guy. He probably couldn't break away from the cuffs, anyway.

Several years ago, she'd developed the ISpy app the cops, government agencies, and anyone with invisispecs used, a facial and item recognition software that collected all the data available in public databases that wasn't behind safeguards. Anything on the individual's social media, what books he or she'd read, home address, place of employment, grocery shopping haunts. The advertising services loved it. Special apps connected ISpy feeds to each other and let people know if others were looking for a date, a jogging partner, a babysitter, or had some shoes to sell, and users could message each other through their personal feeds.

Everyone used ISpy, making Nekoka flush in cash.

Her personal version, SPYme, dug even deeper, into the dark web and skipped happily through onion sites. It cracked most security protocols. Credit card numbers, driver's license reports, medical records, police records, private video feeds. Nothing was a secret from Nekoka. The information world opened to her mental will and submitted.

Another drone joined the previous one, hovering overhead, sucking in vid feed. Nekoka wanted to hiss at it. Jenni touched her shoulder, lifted an eyebrow. "Ready to go on a rum run?"

"What about Zack's gift?"

"You already ordered him some stuff, and we got the doughnuts..."

"Beignets..." she corrected.

"So, I think we'll be good."

Nekoka nodded. Rum run, it was.

It was their secret lingo. Let's go, it meant, but really it meant: let's go together.

Nekoka just needed a nap and some cream. The entertainment room at home called to her. She imagined curling up between Minnie Mandalis and Gracie Bravo, letting her two friends pet her while she scanned her favorite boards and chatted with her net friends. Eugene Mayor would spam her with worthless texts, just to see if he could overwhelm her. Minnie had the best hands, her manicured nails providing the perfect scritch. They would sit together after training, Minnie most likely watching some gardening show on the overly large television, while Gracie did something productive on her tablet, Nekoka tucked between them as a cat.

They returned to the car, and Jenni drove them back to Breton House in Vacherie, Louisiana, the radio turned low on some '80s channel. Part of Nekoka scoffed at the idea of a house having a name, but the other part of her gleefully loved it. Her parents would have considered it pretentious, something above their station. Above Nekoka's station. Especially now. They'd approved of her time working for Dr. Carlson in the genetic lab, thinking it would give her some credibility as a Seeded scientist, as if her parents assumed that people wouldn't believe an evol capable of higher thought processes, even their daughter.

Her parents.... Nekoka sighed and leaned towards Jenni, assuring she was well within Jenni's reach. Jenni rubbed over Nekoka's head, soothing her.

It was an old wound.

As a *nisei*, Michiko Takaki had been born with her parent's bright expectations wrapped around her throat, a necktie of hope. From the first instant she had a computer under her fingers, everyone had declared that Michiko had a future in numbers and order and the bright cubicles of Silicon Valley. She entered Stanford at fifteen, developed a new facial recognition program, a data-mining worm, and designed an ultra-micro-computer. All of these things she put to use later, but initially, she'd just wanted to prove herself. Make her parents proud. It was a tired old song. With that necktie snug tight, her parents' single-minded intentions herding her like an eager collie, she excelled at doing all that was expected of her, as was right and proper for the daughter of Japanese professionals. Her path had been laid out from graduation, to job, to early retirement, until Michiko had turned seventeen, grown a furry tail, gave up university and rebranded herself as Nekoka.

Now, she'd been a fully powered Seeded for almost half her life and things weren't so neatly planned out.

But they were so much better.

Oh, she'd tried for a while. Done the song and dance at the Whitcomb Medical Facility with the good doctor. Patented and sold her inventions. Made a name for Michiko.

But then...she wasn't really Michiko anymore. Retirement was a farce, planning was boring, and responsibility was something for the lesser people. Nekoka was here to have fun and live life. Do *everything*. Have *experiences*. Once her Seed had developed, reality had changed for her. After she'd shucked that necktie, sending it through the shredder of denial, it was plainly obvious that the normal rules had no hold on her.

Her parents' rules, either.

If you rolled it all up into one simple statement of fact, once *Nekoka* was born, her parents had washed their hands of her. In their home, they held a little shrine with a portrait of her human face holding a prominent position, as if their only child had been laid to rest.

She checked her feeds as Jenni petted her, letting the rocking of the car lull her, wash the past away down a drain that led out into the ocean where it would all be diluted and worn down by the endless surging of waves. Her parents were old news. She had the Usual Suspects. They were her family now.

"We're home," Jenni said, gently patting Nekoka on the cheek.

Jenni parked next to two other cars, a month-old SUV and an older sedan of a modest beige, in the cobbled driveway arcing around the end of the east wing of Breton House.

Breton House stood like a sentinel amidst the sprawling pecan orchards, its two-stories basking in the golden glow of the setting sun. Flowing bushes, vibrant and thriving, grew along the white-planked walls of the plantation house. Tall pillars reached up from the ground, supporting a second-floor balcony that wrapped around the entire building. At the entrance, a massive oak door, polished to a rich mahogany hue, bore the weight of generations, beckoning guests with its timeless charm.

The driveway was shaded by a line of oversized oaks that cooled the house and yard in the deep heart of summer. In the Silversmith family for only a single generation, Zack couldn't claim southern heritage, but he grew up here and loved the people and the pecan farm that came with it. Nekoka had a more than mild hatred of the humidity, but luckily, they had Gracie, who, with her chanting power, could affect an area in a number of ways, including lowering the temperature or humidity. Invaluable.

Cradling her bag of pastries in hand, Nekoka called out, "*Tadaima*!" as she entered the side foyer, scraping her thick-soled feet against the mat left specifically for her. As she stepped on the tiled floor, she altered her soles, no longer needing their hardened bottom to protect her against walking on the ground, to something soft and subtle, like normal feet, only slightly furred on top.

Stepping into Breton House felt like crossing a threshold into another world. A peaceful world. The side entrance opened up into a modern kitchen with some holdovers from its previous era that showed off its opulence and history. A crystal chandelier, suspended from a lofty ceiling adorned with intricate molding, cast a warm, inviting light that danced across the gleaming marble floor. It was a place to entertain, and the guests from their many parties loved it. The air was redolent with the scent of cinnamon and baked chocolate. Soft music murmured in the background from hidden speakers that Nekoka and Eugene had installed. But most of all, beyond the grandeur, was Nekoka's friends. Her family. Who accepted her and her nonconforming ways.

From inside the house, Minnie called back, "*Okaeri*!"

The outside world slipped from Nekoka's shoulders.

Eugene waved a slicing knife at them as they entered the kitchen. "You want dinner?"

Sitting at the island bar, Minnie and Zack were going over some papers. Their coloring, Zack pale while Minnie was dark, contrasted as they leaned close together, thick in a heated discussion. Eugene, his blond hair a little mussed, was stationed near the counter—a pile of vegetables, some noodles in a box, and jars of sauce littering the countertop. An average kind of guy, his most striking feature, other than his straw-colored eyes, was his hair of similar light shade, usually very tidy and trim.

A cake was cooling near an open window.

"If you're cooking, then yes," Jenni said, setting her keys and purse down on the side table.

They'd just had a heavy lunch in the city, but both Jenni and Nekoka agreed, Eugene was their best cook, and while the duty was on rotation, their friend often took it upon himself to work his magic in the kitchen outside of his scheduled chore.

From his perch on the stool, Zack glanced over at Nekoka, then back down at the pile of papers.

"Hey, Birthday Dude! I got you yummies," Nekoka sing-songed, handing him the beignets. She warmed as his eyes suddenly brightened.

At six feet, Zack cut an imposing figure with his dark blond hair and piercing silver eyes that seemed to hold the weight of their collective adventures. His hair fell effortlessly, giving him an air of rugged charm that immediately eased and reassured those people he saved. For Nekoka, Zack's significance wasn't just in his heroic form but in the profound connection they shared, a bond that had weathered the storms of their extraordinary lives.

"Thanks!" He opened the bag and stuffed one in his mouth. For a rich, powerful man, he was such a kid sometimes.

His attention caught the piles of papers again, and his face suddenly went blank.

Zack smiled freely and joked with them all the time. With wide-flung doors, he opened his house to them, supporting them in almost everything they needed for day-to-day living. He was wealthy and could live life any way he wanted, but he liked having the team with him at his huge mansion. To him, it was his Seeded playhouse. He cherished it as much as Nekoka, both finding safety and comfort having their found family nearby. He wasn't shy and he wasn't withdrawn and that expression he was now wielding like a shield was not normal.

"What's going on?" Nekoka asked, ears alert, hairs suddenly all on end.

Gracie slipped into the kitchen in classy heels, dressed in a flowy dress with a Coach purse over one shoulder and shades perched in her curly dark hair. Avoiding looking at anyone, she grabbed Jenni's arm and squeezed. "I'm off. I'll be back after mass." They shared a quick kiss, then Gracie dropped her voice. "We'll chat then?"

"Yeah, see ya. Have a good time." Jenni watched her girlfriend leave, then swiveled around and eyed Zack and Minnie.

Minnie slapped her thighs and stood from the bar stool. Short with a bit of pudge, Minnie was an exemplary caregiver who loved wholly and willingly. Almost at the opposite end of Gracie's classy ensemble, Minnie was dressed for gardening, in loose jeans and a light shirt straight off the rack, her tight, black curls a floof around her head. "Oh, you know. I've tried. It's not like it's necessary, and I'm with Nekoka on this. Two against Four." She scowled at Zack.

"Hey, don't count me. I don't care. Whatever anyone else wants." Eugene snapped up a carrot and began aggressively slicing it on the wooden cutting board.

Jenni took a step closer to Nekoka. "You know, it isn't as restrictive as you're afraid," she said consolingly to Nekoka.

"What are those papers?" Nekoka demanded. The world had suddenly gotten hot, and with a ripple, her fur thinned out over her body. The blood was pounding in her ears as her gaze homed in on the papers.

They couldn't do this. They *wouldn't* do this.

They were her friends.

Her *family*.

"It's just a trial," Zack said, finally facing her, his silver eyes barely meeting hers. "Temporary. So, you can see how it won't be that big a deal."

Nekoka charged forward and snatched the papers off the tiled countertop.

Application for Hero Certification – New Orleans

"But..." Nekoka started, fur bristling. Everything went quiet for a moment, stretched out and thin.

Zack cupped her shoulder with one hand. He wanted so hard to be important, to be a hero, to help people. One of the strongest Seeded on the planet and he was being so gentle with her body.

Too bad he was so careless with her loyalty and heart.

"It won't change anything, really. Not much," Zack said. "We'll have sanction from the city. *Insurance* if something goes wrong. We'll be called in sooner if the criminals are too much for the police force, like with that bomber."

The pounding returned, louder and louder like an approaching drum corp.

"The police should be able to handle criminals." Nekoka's words started slow and quiet and increased in intensity as the pure betrayal unleashed her ire. "There are Seeded on the police force. They are the ones who should be upholding the law. You are going to be replacing people who *choose* to be police. And whether we are Certified or not, they can still call!

We'd *have to* jump when they call. What if you don't want to deal with a bank robbery—which the police can deal with—what if you wanted to do something about a trafficking ring but the police say hold on it because they've got their own agenda? You think the best way to shut a criminal organization down is judicially, but they want you to go in all silver and punchy. You don't get to *choose*." Her body bunched over as she yelled out the word.

"I told you," Minnie said, crossing her arms over her ample chest. "We can't do this without everyone's say so. Nekoka and I aren't certain this is the best path for us. It takes away our autonomy."

She'd told him. Told Zack she didn't want this. They'd *talked* about this.

"I know you think this is going to be some big Supervillain versus Superhero all-out war. That's ridiculous." Zack shook his head, then returned to staring at Nekoka, his silver eyes red around the edges, a sign of sleepless nights. A sign that this had been planned, and he had been worried.

"We have power," he continued, pleaded. "We've a *duty* to help people."

"No!" Then she took in a breath. The air felt stiff. "We do not." Her voice sounded hard, alien. Then words kept coming, flowing from her mouth. "We have a duty to ourselves. That's it. Bottom line. All else is simple *choice*." Everything went numb inside. "Listen, you go ahead."

Would her mouth stop talking? Would her friends not do this?

Her sour gut churned. Everything was hot. So hot.

"You go ahead," she said. "Go Certified. Do what you want."

She yanked her shoulder out of Zack's hold and walked away.

CHAPTER 3

Nekoka

When Zack had begun grumbling about the honor of Certification and how it would give them 'clout', 'status', and the 'legitimacy' to act, Nekoka had laughed. Right in his face. She might have even spewed her Coke on his clean-shaven cheeks.

"Zack, we are Seeded, nobody could stop us if we chose to act," she'd said simply.

That hadn't been an answer Zack had approved of.

It eluded her as to how her friends didn't understand the basic fundamental truth of how powerful they were. It was like when the hot guy at the theater didn't catch on that she wanted to fuck his brains out and wasn't just being friendly. Dude, he was hot, he should innately grasp when people wanted in his pants.

Things needed to stay the same. It was comfortable. Safe. The Usual Suspects saw something happening, and they acted. And if they didn't want to get involved, for whatever reason, that was okay, too. Sometimes people just had to figure things out on their own and didn't need a band of powered people to intervene. Sometimes the police needed to take action against the minor criminals, because that is what they were paid to do. Let people do their jobs.

But with Certification, Gracie had said, joining in on the argument that afternoon, it *would* be their job.

Gracie, as wonderful as she was, didn't get it sometimes.

Jenni did. Jenni always got Nekoka. But during that first discussion, she'd thrown her cards in with Zack. "If it will help us to help others, then I'm in."

She'd looked at Nekoka when she'd said that, eyes sad, almost regretful.

Well. It was a choice.

How she'd befriended such noble people, Nekoka couldn't fathom. Was she lucky, or cursed?

It was the first crack to a swiftly growing rift. The end result would see them donning that nobility as a work uniform, and Nekoka—who clutched onto her dear sensibility—would cherish having no reins and stay independent.

This was bound to happen. It was like a neon sign, glowing and flashing and warning her: Danger, Danger, Paths are Diverging.

She'd wanted to stick her head in the sand, though. Pretend things would be okay. And now...and now...

Minnie chased her as she stomped out of Breton House, her curls bouncing with each step. "Nekoka...you're being rash. Would you just stop for a minute?"

Nearby a great oak shivered where it was rooted in the ground, and Nekoka wondered if Minnie—code name Arbortia—was going to have that tree wrap its branches around her, trapping her in this place that was too fucking *hot*, not letting her go, not letting her be free.

Nekoka's freedom ranked second only to one other thing—her friends—and in this moment of isolation, a sense of abandonment clawed at her heart, as if she were stranded on a lonely stretch of deserted highway, sun beating down on her, sucking her dry.

It was practically tattooed on her forehead: she was nobody's hero. Why the hell was Zack, one of her best friends in the world, her family, pulling her feet out from under her, putting them to the fire, trapping her in bureaucratic vines just as Minnie could do with her plants?

"Well, Zack made his decision. He knew I was out, but didn't care," Nekoka droned.

"You don't have to leave. You can stay. It would only be the other four. You and I could hang out and play some old Zelda or that one with the carts. We could work in the garden and have cream and tea, and you could sit in my lap, and I'd pet you, and you don't have to *leave*." Minnie's voice cracked as she babbled, talking faster than Nekoka was used to. Minnie thought her words through like each one held weight, and now they tumbled out like a jumble of stones, falling on Nekoka's buzzing ears.

Nekoka halted and turned, pulling a small pack onto her back, readying to shift into a cheetah to abandon the plantation, escape into a city where she would rent a room for a while and wallow.

Minnie held her arms out, as if ready to embrace Nekoka, tears glistening in her eyes. "Don't leave."

Those tears cooled down the panic-heat that had washed over Nekoka. She tried to smile, to reassure her dear friend. "Minnie, I hafta go. I just.... I can't—" She didn't know how to finish that. Can't trust Zack? Well, he hadn't lied to her. He'd gone behind her back by getting those forms, but he'd always been excited about Certification. He'd always needed that validation, just like Nekoka needed to be free. Could she keep that from him?

She loved him too much. All of them too much.

"They gotta figure out if this is good for them," she told Minnie. "It's only a trial, Zack said...after that, they can tell me if it'll be permanent. I just," she shook her head, "I just can't. I need some air."

Recollections of college and projects and her parents urging urging *urging* her to work hard and define excellence stirred a cauldron of painful emotions within her.

One of the cars crawled up from the parking lot near the east wing. Jenni.

"Get in," Jenni said. "Let's go."

Nekoka blinked. Jenni was here. That tight presence in her chest loosened.

Nekoka's thoughts drifted to when she was twenty-three, recalling when she, Jenni, and Zack had met at a GUMPs of New Orleans meeting. Back then, GUMP had been one of the many names for the Seeded, a working of GHMP – Genetic HyperMutation Phenomenon – a term more despised by Nekoka than that of Seeded. Jenni and Zack had been so young, kids really, and Jenni and Nekoka hadn't initially gotten along. Nekoka, admittedly, was going through her wild phase, tearing through parties and men, getting into trouble, throwing caution and common sense into the fire. Done with her schooling, breaking off from her parents, having made beaucoup bucks on the early version of ISpy, she'd left the

Whitcomb Medical Facility in South Dakota and had made her way to New Orleans to mix with the large Seeded population there.

Every day had been a party.

She'd had to scrub the internet of the evidence of those years, making it disappear. Some things are better buried, like a hot steaming turd.

Gracie had been the one who'd inadvertently forced them to see each other in a different light. After a late night at the Spot Tavern with Zack and some of their GUMP friends, a beautiful Hispanic woman—Gracie—had raced into the bar, preceded by a terrible wrenching noise from outside. A tanker truck had overturned and crashed into a meat smoker. The police were on the way, but people had been hurt, and Gracie begged for anyone to come and help.

Nekoka had seen it in Jenni's face, that moment of instant attraction.

So, Nekoka realized that Jenni wasn't such a stick in the mud, she was just repressed. Perhaps not quite comfortable with herself. All of her scolding and judging made a bit more sense now.

Many of the Spot regulars joined them as they ran to the scene and helped contain the spreading fire and get people to safety. Zack, being fireproof while in his Bullet skin, saved the lives of two people trapped near the smoker during the hit. The fire truck wasn't too far behind them and the officials quickly had it in hand. Jenni had hugged Nekoka after that, a wealth of forgiveness and connection, and the next day the Usual Suspects had been four, with Gracie now in their inner circle.

Forged in flames and now sundered by a hero complex.

Nekoka ran to Minnie and squeezed her goodbye. "I'm not leaving you. I'll be back." She kissed her friend on the cheek before climbing into the car. Her heart rabbited in her chest, a sensation that wasn't at all comfortable. Her cat eyes didn't cry like a norm's, but they still watered, and now she blinked rapidly, making sure no wetness dropped. The car eased down the long drive to the road.

Relief so heavy pushed the strength out of Nekoka's bones. Jenni glanced over at her, eyebrow raised. Nekoka guessed she'd leaked some stray thoughts out loud to her friend. It wasn't unheard of.

"I can't force my decision on you. I know you have to do what you feel is best for you, but I can stick by your side," Jenni answered Nekoka's unspoken gratefulness.

"I don't mean to drag you along," Nekoka said.

"You so effortlessly charge into the unknown, Nekoka, how could I want to be anywhere else? So, where's this rum run going?"

"Portland." Nekoka gazed into the side-view mirror and saw Minnie standing there, watching them drive away. Guilt tore at her gut.

"Okay," Jenni said. Portland was a hub city, safe and welcoming for Seeded.

"What about Gracie?"

"I'll talk to her. She'll understand," Jenni said reasonably.

"Should we take Minnie?" Nekoka asked, hollow.

"Someone's gotta take care of the others. She's the best one we have."

Nekoka rubbed at her nose. Minnie was their healer, but also their mother hen. "I feel bad now. I hate feeling bad."

Jenni rubbed the top of Nekoka's head. "I know."

The drive to the airport took over an hour, and by then, Nekoka had bought their tickets and had everything set through Whisker. They stuck the car in long-term parking, letting Eugene know its location.

She'd escaped, temporarily, the hangman's noose. But she could still hear it creaking as it swung in the wind, waiting.

Nekoka had set her vote. It was up to the others now. A weasel of guilt gnawed at her about abandoning Minnie. Before the plane took off, she sent Minnie a text: Please forgive me. I will come back.

ABOUT FIVE YEARS AGO, Jenni, Zack, and Nekoka had traveled to the Caribbean. The Caribbean was a mixed bag. Some islands tolerated the Seeded, and others were a bit more hostile. And, of course, Nekoka was a freak who wouldn't tuck that freak flag away when dealing with the norms. She could go completely human if she tried very hard. But it was all effort with no gain, and as was common knowledge, Nekoka abhorred effort with no gain, so that was that.

They'd joined in on a distillery tour and the three had tried the rum at all its stages, from its nascent, raw, colorless base akin to rubbing alcohol, to the richly-flavored, caramel-colored final product after it had been aged in precious oak barrels shipped in from some far away countries, blessed by the Ministry of Rum, and let sit for an ice age. Nekoka still thought it tasted like rubbing alcohol, but with less bite.

"You hate this," Zack had finally realized, laughing, after their third distillery. He was laughing so hard, he had to lean against the serving bar. The server just kept watching them, unsure, as if he was waiting for one of them to start shooting off sparks.

Nekoka had her ears pulled back, her fangs half bared as she lifted the next shot glass. Her entire body was fuzzy. She couldn't even feel the tips of her tail or ears anymore.

"Nekoka, just stop drinking it. You don't have to try every one." Jenni tapped her hand over the small glass.

With a determined set to her shoulders, she lifted the glass, braced it against her lips, and downed the shot of rum from some rum makers who'd been brewing the paint thinner for so long they'd once served some real-life Jack Sparrow.

It burned. All the way down.

"I'm not backing out. We're on this rum run together." Nekoka slammed the shot glass onto the wooden counter and demanded the next one. She knew she didn't have to drink them all, but Zack and Jenni were, and she would stand by them, even if she hated it. It's just what one did for friends.

And Nekoka had kept true to that, or so she had thought. But now, she was abandoning them just like she felt they'd abandoned her.

It was all eye for an eye down here.

Inset 2
Metro Times Newspaper Article

Dr. Braydon Carlson Reveals Seeded Powers Not of Natural Origin

Thirty years ago, a physical anomaly began appearing within newborns of the human race that changed our world as we knew it. It was called the Genetic HyperMutation Phenomenon (GHMP). At first, it appeared that the only strange aberration to occur was abnormal eye colors and shades. Upon deeper study, a unique and previously unknown gland was found to have grown near the base of the brain, called the deinde gland. This anomaly, however, had another effect; it gave some of these pale-eyed individuals powers and abilities as seen only in comic books and science fiction movies. Some had telepathy and telekinesis, were physically enhanced, and some even controlled the elements of nature. Dr. Carlson of the Whitcomb Medical Facility in Sioux City, South Dakota, with the aid of specialists around the world, has recently come to the conclusion that this mutation is not of natural origins and the gland appears to have been planted within these special people by some outside source.

A picture, Dr. Carlson—dressed in a starched light shirt, dark tie, and a white lab jacket—gazed sternly out from the paper. In a box near the right corner of the paper was a list of other "Top Seeded Stories" which included: *Top Five Most Dangerous Evols, The New Era of Entertainment, Who Do You Want Protecting Your City?, Break Outs of Wolf Walker Institute,* and *Separatists: Terrorists or Nonviolent Dissidents?*

CHAPTER 4

Nekoka

There was an actual line for the Betterment Station in Portland's Waterfront Park. Nekoka had never seen a line before, nor this many homeless. At a Betterment Station, one could get any of the medications one needed, recreational or prescribed, easy peasy lemon squeezy. All that was required was a press of the thumb to the print reader, and it delivered the pill in a foil package from a chute, much like a kibble dispenser. She secretly wondered about the cleanliness of the station after watching one woman drop trou earlier behind a parked car to piddle.

"I don't need my pill," she grumbled to Jenni, because she didn't. There wasn't a *need*, she just liked the anti-anxiety meds because during their few days in Portland she couldn't sleep, couldn't think, couldn't relax unless she'd ridden someone hard or danced the night away.

"It will only be a little wait," Jenni said, checking her phone, "but there is another dispensary by a Safeway about a mile into the city."

Nekoka gazed at a pile of clothes ditched by the roadside, wondering about the story behind that, and nodded. The two women left the bustling mood dispensary.

All along the waterfront south of the Steel Bridge was an array of camps. Brightly colored camping tents, each one with piles of things around it. This must be where the clothing had come from. Many camps had a bike or three. Men and women were staked out before their squatters' homes, guarding their stuff, arguing or smoking. The air was full of a black miasmic smoke from a couple of railroad ties someone was burning in a scorched metal barrel.

No other tourists passed through this park, and Nekoka and Jenni drew more than a few watchful glares.

"Do you think," Nekoka asked as they watched some guys feeding their compact dog something that might have once been a hamburger, "that dog would benefit from a snoutectomy?"

Jenni tilted her head towards Nekoka, but kept watching the dog. "Why would you do that?"

"It's altruistic, really," Nekoka explained. "Take the snout from one dog and chop it into many pieces and plant them. You'd get multiple dog sprouts after that."

The dog wagged as the man gently rubbed its ears. Least those two had each other to watch over...Kinda like Nekoka and Jenni.

That probably meant she was the pet in this scenario. Okay, she'd own that.

Jenni hummed in thought. "So, like snoutenogensis?"

"I'd say so." Nekoka smiled at the happy dog. Though it was a dog, and dogs were obviously lesser than cats, it was nice to see it being so well looked after by someone who couldn't look after himself. "That's the magic of a snoutectomy. Oh, hey, it's that cop we met at Rain."

A tall policeman, shoulders broad and waist trim, with an unruly head of hair peeking out from under his blue cap, patrolled the walkway close to the Willamette River. He was Nekoka's age and had Jenni's unwavering sense of justice. With a boyish grin, he waved high overhead when he saw them.

Nekoka and Jenni waved back.

"Hey ladies," Officer John Geier greeted, tipping his policeman's hat. He had pale gunmetal blue eyes. A Seeded officer. Gotta love hub cities.

Any Seeded could expect one of two kinds of city. The hub cities: places where the normal population accepted and even adored the superpowered Seeded, and the Municipal Autonomy Act (MAA – or better known as MAAD) cities. MAAD cities resided within the nine circles of hell, probably between the fourth and fifth rings if you followed Dante's map.

Nekoka's parents lived in one in Japan.

A man slipped from a tent and trotted over to John. "Hey, Officer Geier." He held out his hand, and to Nekoka's cringing astonishment, John shook it.

"Hey, how're things?" the officer asked.

"Well, Tina from Angels of the Road told me they were kicked out of the industrial district." The man shrugged, then scratched at his scraggly beard.

"By whom?" John asked.

The homeless man shook his head. "Just wondering if you knew about it?"

John touched the man's elbow, and Nekoka wondered how many germs crawled from the man's grungy shirt sleeve onto John's hand. She narrowed her eyes, attempting to spot anything.

Jenni elbowed her. Nekoka huffed. Her thoughts were leaking again. She wished he'd had her pill.

"No, but I'll look into it. Thanks for letting me know."

"Yeah man. Have a good one," the guy said and walked back to his tent.

By now, everyone was watching them. Normally, Nekoka basked in attention, but this didn't feel like good attention. She shrank into Jenni's side.

"So," John said to them, "just wanted to let you know that Rain's having a special Seeded Night."

Nekoka's ears swiveled towards the cop, intrigued.

"What's that mean?" Jenni asked, pressing her weight into Nekoka.

"Oh, well, I guess like a Lady's Night, cheaper drinks and no cover. Pablo'd love to have a Seeded only night, but you can't discriminate like that. Everyone's allowed, but more Seeded come on the second Thursday than other nights. Happens once a month."

Nekoka turned to Jenni. "I want to go."

"Yeah, okay. We can do that." Jenni smiled down on her, and it stunned Nekoka. Jenni had such a big smile when she was relaxed. She hadn't seen that easy joy much since they'd come to Portland last week.

"Great," John said, cheeks pinking, and scratched at the back of his neck. "I'll see you two there, then." He nodded as he walked up to a group of other street people, chatting with them.

Nekoka couldn't wait. There would be loud music and drinks and people to grind against on the dance floor. She felt Jenni's warmth against her. And Jenni would be there. By her side.

THAT THURSDAY, THEY made their way to the north side of Burnside where the club, Rain, was.

Jenni was flicking through her outdated phone, using the touch screen to type out a message instead of using a VR-glove. It was one of Jenni's many idiosyncrasies.

She laughed, then typed some more as Nekoka steered her friend past a crowd near an entire city block of food carts.

"What's funny?" Nekoka asked.

"You'd know what was up if you didn't have them on communication blackout."

Them, meaning the Usual Suspects, and Nekoka didn't have them on blackout, she just inwardly whimpered every time Minnie asked about her and none of the others had reached out at all. Nekoka's light mood grew heavy again, and she suddenly felt alone, which was stupid. She was in a city, surrounded by thousands of people, and Jenni was by her side. She wasn't alone.

"Apparently, Eugene stole someone's lawnmower and drove it over Jaworski's lawn, leaving a Heroes' Rise symbol on it."

"What? Why would he do that?"

Jenni's smile dimmed. "Gracie thinks he's acting out. Rebelling like a kid. I just think he's bored without you to taunt him."

Nekoka glowed in memory. She and Eugene poked each other just to get a rise. He'd curdled her cream once. She'd put Elmer's glue in his shampoo. All good times.

As she and Jenni neared Burnside, aiming for the Pearl District and the nightclub, Nekoka had a bright idea. They had a little time to kill.

"Let's stop by Powell's first." Nekoka gave Jenni big eyes. Orange and watery with just a proper bit of pleading to season her request. "Please."

Jenni shook her head, not even looking at Nekoka and her expertly needy eyes. "No, you were just there yesterday."

"But—"

"No." *I don't want to spend another three hours in there while you flirt with geeks. You get all the geek pheromones together and it's chaos,* she continued, mind to mind.

Nekoka's jaw dropped. "I do not flirt with geeks," she said out loud. Then closed her mouth, her jaw snapping audibly. *They get my jokes.* "Fine. I'll go later."

Jenni shrugged. "Fine by me."

They crossed Burnside into the Pearl as Nekoka checked out her inbox—both electronic and voice—and the reports from her spiders. Nothing on red alert. Though she did get an IM from Brian, a Powell's guy she'd met, asking for shag number two and a voice mail from Matt, a bartender at the Minnow she'd collected back on Monday, pretty much asking for the same. Neither was worth a second fuck, so she deleted their messages. No personal contact from Zack.

Soon enough they stood before an old building that crowed of a more artistic era versus the surrounding neighborhoods sporting new mid-level condos. Four stories tall, it nestled right in with all of the other brick buildings. Despite being somewhat nondescript, the front facade was dressed up in artful patterns of red, gray, and black bricks with little gargoyles peeking over the rim above the door. A neon sign of sky blue hung between them; the dripping letters spelled out RAIN in a drizzle. A set of stairs led up to a landing where double doors opened into the club. When Nekoka and Jenni had first arrived in Portland almost a week ago, Rain had been a major destination. Rain was the country's only establishment fully owned and staffed by Seeded. Owned and operated by Pablo Castile: aka sex on legs.

Jenni pulled on the door, sending it into a slamming swing.

"Ah, damn," Jenni cursed. "Sorry," she called out as she walked past the unattended coat check toward the open dance floor.

Nekoka skipped after, tail flicking through the air.

A placard waited near the coat check:

Seeded Night: Pales Eyes gets you in with half priced drinks. Party with the mutants.

CHAPTER 5

The World

Under the Eiffel Tower's scaffolding frame, thousands of people had gathered to either protest or support the Guardian Alliance's Certification, a group of twenty-three Seeded individuals who considered themselves Superheroes and wanted to do good for the world as a whole.

In languages from across the globe, homemade and professionally designed signs swayed side by side, held up high by long poles, thin slabs of wood and even just hands. Some people bounced them to the tempo of their chant, while others gripped them as burgeoning panic writhed around the edges of their eyes.

"Seeded Are Not God's Will," "No Freaks Wanted," "Hidden Government Agenda," and other discriminating and irrational slogans were taken up as rally cries and mottoes for their distress.

Not everyone was protesting the foundation of the Guardian Alliance. Many supporters brandished their own signs—"Seeded For Our Future" and "I Love Starburst!"—and more and more arrived as the summer day emerged from the dawn.

A huge banner held aloft by drones read "Guardian Alliance" and other drones cruised over the crowd, recording the entire announcement. A podium had been cordoned off with a line of suited men with little wires dangling from their ears, wearing dark invisispecs.

"Why don't you take off your shades so we can see if you're one of them?" A man shook his sign so violently that the board pulled away from the wooden stick to which it had been stapled. The guard didn't respond.

France was one of five countries worldwide where the Guardian Alliance was making their announcement. The United States, Korea, Peru, and Morocco were all hosting similar rallies of protest and support.

At 7:52 a.m. Paris time, the Parisians and their neighbors began looking up into the sky, pointing at a bright orange object that inched its way across the upper atmosphere. At first, it measured the size of a pinhead.

"Starburst."

Then a flea.

"Look, Starburst is coming."

Then the size of a grain of rice...

"The Witch of Fire!"

...a perfect rocket that came blazing with the power of the sun, growing in size as it flew down through the heavens. The now visible woman slipped through the metal frame of the Eiffel Tower, weaving like a falcon darting through the branches of the very oaks surrounding them.

And while the people's rapt attention focused on that blazing form as it settled on the stage before them, two other individuals moved into position, one on either side of the lady of flames as she touched down delicately, first with one foot, then the other, her fire dying out as she took her place between her teammates.

The chanting had fallen silent the minute Starburst had come into view, and the people stood in wonder and awe as she'd flown through the air. Now that she had landed, her deep, toothy grin overcoming her face, the boos and cheers erupted again amidst the horde.

Then the President of France strolled onto the platform, escorted by his ever-present security drone. His gray Zegna suit contrasted against Starburst's tight, fireproof and armored costume in solar colors, oranges, reds, and yellows, with a great GA embossed on the front over her chest. Her long wavy hair flowed down to her mid-back and, even though she wasn't the most beautiful of women, something about her smile, so open and honest, calmed people.

"Thank you for coming," the President said to a roaring crowd, and he waited, eyes focused ahead. Soon, the audience closest to the stage caught the hint and quieted. "To my fellow French and the World, over the last three decades, humans have been changing in ways that haven't been seen since we stood upright to hunt game. But even with this change, today we are more similar than ever before: our cultures embraced by all, our identities embraced by each other, and we also embrace those transformed by the Seed. For, we are all one species."

The President paused again. Cries of "propaganda" and "we are not the same" mixed in with cheers of "All For One, One For All," the latest slogan for Seeded acceptance since the Certified program was announced.

The three Guardian Alliance members stood sedately behind the French president. Next to Starburst was a rustic looking fellow with angry, light brown hair and thick-rimmed glasses. He looked unassuming in his jeans and button-down work shirt. On his feet were heavy boots that belonged on a factory worker.

"Today, we welcome three members of the first worldwide superhero Certified group. Starburst, Mozart, and Battle Axe of Guardian Alliance."

The President stepped away from the mic, clapping loudly as the factory worker came forward. In thick rural French, he addressed the assembly.

"Hello people of France and Europe. I thank you for coming to listen to me and my wife speak." He reached back and grabbed Starburst's hand. For a brief moment they looked into each other's eyes, and her grin grew wider and even more warm. Then he returned to his address. "...and my friend Murphy here." The other man, thick and over six and a half feet tall, nodded at the group. His hands were buried in the pockets of his jeans and more whispers coursed through the crowd when he stared at his feet. Those close enough to the stage could see a deep red spread over his crop of freckles and the clash of it with his washed-out pink eyes.

The speaker cleared his throat. "My name is Adrien Chevalier, though most of you know me best as Mozart. My wife is Starburst, but to me, she shall always be my Eliane. And I'm sure you all know Battle Axe from Ireland, Mr. Niall Murphy. We are some of the Seeded—" cries interrupted his speech, and he raised his hands up in placation.

"Please, let me continue." The murmuring became a low hum as the drones and VR-glasses recorded each word, and the flashes of cameras sparkled in the morning.

"It is our intention, as we establish and develop the Guardian Alliance, to protect the world, all aspects of it and every nation. We are not a mercenary group, and we do not answer to any one nation. We have members from France, America, England, Peru, Korea, and many other places."

Adrien stepped back and gestured towards his wife. Eliane, with a soft laugh, moved towards the mic.

"Hello."

A few cheers rose from the crowd. "Starburst. Starburst. Starburst," began on the east edge.

She giggled and faced the chanters. "Hello." She waved; hands waved back.

"I know that acceptance of the Seeded is not universal—" more cries, not all supportive, drowned out her words so she stopped and simply smiled until the crowd quieted. It suddenly became obvious that she used to be a kindergarten teacher. "But I want to assure you that Guardian Alliance's mission is to help in natural disasters, human accidents, and environmental catastrophes. It is each member's desire to make the world a better place."

"Yeah, sure," one woman screamed out. "But what about when your 'desire to make the world better' treads on our free will?"

Adrien Chevalier retook the mic. He stared hard at the gathering, his eyes going thin, a frown turning down the left side of his mouth. "When someone tries to hurt other people, we accept that that individual has given up his or her free will. Yes, some people are not going to be happy because we'll be staving off their free will to rob banks or hijack airplanes. The law will not be changed. Illegal will still be illegal."

Adrien stepped back, and the President came forward again. They did not meet each other's eyes.

"France is working with several world governments," he said as another man in a business suit came up to his side, "to establish guidelines for the events that would mobilize Guardian Alliance. Many of these governments have already developed a type of certification they have implemented. You can join the government feed to keep abreast of new updates to the certification process and submit your concerns and questions."

People demanded if driving a car was enough harm to the environment to cause an intervention, or if they would be called in for parents' punishment of their children.

The President did not respond, instead he turned to the newcomer. "Let me introduce you to Chief Aide Michael Samson to answer further questions. Thank you, and good day." The President followed the Guardian Alliance members off the stage, a security drone hovering a foot over his head.

The late June warmth had coaxed the oaks along the eastern edge of the park to leaf out in a splendid celebration, and as the breeze danced within the thinner branches, shafts of sunlight filtered through. When the sunlight hit just right, a dark, man-sized form of light and shadow came into view, sharp and contrasting in the morning's sun. Then another behind it. And another. The forms appeared to be watching the stage.

The breeze shifted, and the branch swayed a different direction, dowsing the earth beneath it once again in muted light. The forms disappeared, subsumed in the dim.

CHAPTER 6

Nekoka

Everything in Rain was tinged with a faint blue glow the same shade as the sign outside. Little LCD bulbs, held by wires thin enough to give the impression of hovering fireflies, hung above the booths that lined the walls and the few couples sitting intimately at them. Over the dance floor, more hovering globes flashed through a blue rainbow interspersed with harsh white; a group of four women were dancing with bachelorette abandon. Thick glass walls filled with bubbles and distortion partitioned the two-story club, offering some seclusion to the patrons in the dining area while still allowing them to be a part of the nightly party.

The stage was empty of performers and Heaven Sent crooned through the speakers. Nekoka instinctively sought out Zack. He always danced with her, sometimes mocking the fast beats with over-the-top body flailing. They would take over a vacant dance floor like this. Own it. Her tail dipped behind her. Zack was in New Orleans, probably saving puppies from a pool with backing from the local city council.

Behind the bar, backlit by a wall of blue water dripping between panes of reflective glass, Wilhelmina "Billie" St. Cloud waved a friendly hello at them. SPYme informed Nekoka that Billie was a member of O.G.R.E. and had bartended here since it opened. She bore the Seed but had no power on record. Must be something or she wouldn't be a member of the hero group. Whisker registered Billie's monospec, ready to receive any orders if Nekoka chose to abandon the use of her mouth and instead communicated electronically. Which wouldn't be atypical for Nekoka. Billie was also a bit of a bohemian, since none of her clothing registered through SPYme as a certain brand or from a certain store but were either homemade or special order because their details came up blank. Much of that information

Nekoka ignored, but just having such personal details on people or things gave Nekoka a tiny, private thrill.

Jenni glided up to the bar and requested a cranberry juice. Billie nodded at Jenni, simultaneously mixing a fizzing drink while reaching for a new glass. Her monospec was down, though she offered an amazing performance of not appearing to give it any notice.

"Is Pablo here?" Nekoka asked as she leaned against the bar's blue illuminated countertop. Her tail swayed through the space behind her. With everything shimmering, the effect gave the sense of being underwater. Just under the surface, holding the promise of air and light.

"Yeah, upstairs." Billie tilted her head towards the upper floor, her long brown hair shifting over her shoulders with the gesture.

Nekoka turned and felt a smile slip upon her lips without any command from her brain. There he was, a true *ikemen*, leaning casually against the chrome railing that protected the drunken patrons from plummeting to an unwelcome stop below. A tumbler of amber liquid on the rocks was held loosely in his hand. His keen, piercing gaze surveyed the bachelorettes dancing to the early evening canned music.

Then his eyes brushed over the two newcomers, and he smiled. Nekoka's heart stuttered in her chest. While mythical Helen of Troy's beauty launched a thousand ships, Pablo Castile was at least 0.5 of a Helen. Five hundred ships would sail for that face. Oh, those dimples. He was lickable.

She would never claim that this was love or anything so silly, she'd only just met him that week, but he was gorgeous and confident and exuded sexual charm. Nekoka liked sexual charm. And sex. She wouldn't mind a night with Pablo.

Of mixed race—half Asian and half African—he'd inherited all the desirable attributes of both. Not much on SPYme about his background or his power. He'd had his electronic history scrubbed, and Nekoka hadn't been the one to do it. A thatch of tight dreads a few inches long crowned his head. His eyes, the same pale icy blue as the neon sign, were slanted and piercing, and while Nekoka knew to be wary of eye contact with other Seeded, she couldn't help but be caught up in them.

Maybe that was his charm, his power. He could capture your heart, wrap you in a weave of desire, with just one glance.

He took a sip of his drink and strolled down the stairs. By some architectural trick, the steps looked as if they hovered in midair, making him appear to descend from a sky castle. Actually, he didn't walk so much as strut, chin held high like a regal head of state.

"Jenni. Nekoka," he greeted. His youth in the Caribbean delicately flavored his words. He raised his glass in salute and downed the rest in a gulp.

"Pablo." Jenni lifted her glass of cranberry juice. The blue lighting gave it the impression she was drinking down the essence of purple dinosaur.

"You're here early." He set his glass down on the counter, the rattle of ice barely audible over Lady Gaga, and Billie whisked it away. Stylish slacks hugged him tight, and a fitted button down highlighted all of his assets.

Whoa there, stablemaster. Don't push it. He did say no once already.

Nekoka pouted. He had, but that didn't mean she should give up. "No" yesterday did not always mean "no" today. Minds did change.

Jenni rolled her eyes and gulped down the rest of her drink. "Another please," she asked Billie, who promptly squirted more juice into the glass.

"Sure hitting the juice hard, aren't you?" Pablo asked as he slipped onto a bar stool, his back to Billie so he could inspect his establishment.

Jenni quirked a crooked grin. "Must chill out the nerves somehow."

"Nerves?" he asked, face angled her way with eyebrows raised.

Jenni tilted her head towards Nekoka, who ignored her friend and continued to dutifully gaze at Pablo. "Nekoka, she'll wear anyone out." Nekoka could pretend to be affronted, but what was the point?

Pablo chuckled, a deep, reverberating noise that caused Nekoka to melt a little bit more.

"Glad to know my mixers are better than the moods."

He had such awesome cheeks when he smiled. Nekoka stepped around Jenni to insert herself between the two and invade Pablo's personal space. Tonight. She'd bed him tonight.

"Did you see the article on Carlson?" Billie asked as she handed Jenni a toothpick with cherries on it. Jenni grinned in thanks and ate them in one bite. "Nekoka?" Billie asked in offer, and Nekoka shook her head. Fake cherries. Ew.

"Thank you, though," Nekoka said.

"The esteemed Dr. Carlson? No, what's he got to say?" Pablo asked.

"Oh, just his grand pronouncement that the Seed was inserted by someone, didn't evolve naturally. Some government experiment on toddlers or something, injected the same time as vaccines, I'm sure," Billie said with little inflection as she filled an order for a martini.

Planted by an outside source. Nekoka's ear flicked. So, they finally decided to make it public.

"Well, who do you think did insert it?" Jenni asked.

"The government," Billie said with a shake of her head, as if 'duh, Jenni, I just said that'.

Jenni laughed. "Thought you were kidding."

"Maybe it was another Seeded. The first," Pablo conjectured, spinning around on the stool to face Billie. "That individual's Seeded ability. We'll probably never know."

"Oh, I'm sure some brain trust is working on it," Nekoka said. In fact, she knew one was and had turned down an invitation to be a member.

Jenni knew Nekoka had been on Carlson's team as their computer expert a handful of years before she migrated to New Orleans and met up with the Usual Suspects and knew Nekoka's opinion on their origin. Back when Carlson's team had realized it could not have evolved naturally, the Seed was just too biologically different, theories had been tossed around. Aliens, maybe mad scientists, some ruthless government trying to create super soldiers but had no idea what cat—Nekoka snickered—they let out of the bag. Nekoka was certain it was aliens. It just seemed as good an answer as any.

Nekoka remembered those unpleasant months working on the research team, setting up situational computer models with the self-possessed jackass Dr. Carlson at Whitcomb, until his pomposity caused her to vomit her tuna. The development of advanced humans, or mutants—or evols as some called them—had nothing to do with hidden potential, nor was it a sign of environmental influences like radiation or pollution.

Her models tried to establish which individuals might or might not develop a Seed based on genetics and other factors. Well, as it so happened, it had no connection to genetics. Not at first. The initial batch of Seeded had been abducted by aliens and injected with a Seed. That was Nekoka's theory, and she thought Fox Mulder would toe that line with her. In essence, it was proven a small nodule had been implanted between the pons and the pituitary gland of the brain, tiny, like a seed, and from that it had grown roots affecting every system within the human host body.

However, the Seed was smart. Another discovery, not public yet but not too difficult to suss out, proved that the Seed could reproduce itself by using its host's own biology.

A Seeded individual's children had a high chance of being Seeded themselves. The population of evols would grow exponentially unless someone decided to sterilize them. And Lord knew some MAAD cities would love to do just that.

"And in other news, Guardian Alliance went official," Pablo said. "All twenty-three members signed on." Pablo watched their reflection in the bubbling glass behind the bar. "Going to be a big announcement today on Nuclear, probably CNN and BBC and the SW1. Think O.G.R.E. is going to as well."

Nekoka growled.

Pablo ignored her, causing Nekoka to puff out in annoyance. "How about you guys?" he asked Jenni. "Any news from S-Force?"

Whisker beeped at her—not a sound, but an electronic nudge—letting her know she'd received a text. Your day is about to change. Nothing is as it seems.

Jenni leaned her back against the bar and sighed. "They're going through a trial period. Nekoka told them in no small terms that she did not want to join. Another of our members didn't want to go Certified either. No idea what's going to happen."

Nekoka flicked her mind over the message and couldn't dig up where it came from. No delivery number. A ghost hacker, leaving no trace? Interesting. She'd have to scratch up the trail later.

"It is a lot of government oversight." He nodded in agreement with Nekoka, and she felt appeased, but her fur still didn't lie down. Jenni petted her back. "Paperwork and someone breathing down your neck all the time. But it gives you a lot of leeway if you wanted to do the whole superhero thing."

Nekoka grumbled, "'M not a superhero."

Jenni's hand landed on Nekoka's head, where she gently patted her hair. Nekoka leaned into the touch. "I know you're not a hero. Wouldn't dare call you one."

"Where do you sit?" Billie asked Jenni.

One of the dancers squealed, and the group burst into giggles as they made their way to a table.

Jenni shrugged, her small smile hinting at some personal mischief. "Actually, I'm pro. For several reasons, one being that collateral damage is covered if the team is officially called in to act. But honestly, I'm not going to change my behavior either way."

"Yeah, you will," Nekoka bit out. "You'll be doing a lot more paper pushing and having to respond to requests to act even if you don't want to, or not respond to those you do, and reporting your every minute action."

Jenni shrugged and sipped her juice. Her hand remained on Nekoka's shoulder, so Nekoka didn't feel too put out.

"Well, how are you enjoying Portland, then?" Pablo asked.

The tense bundle of knots in Nekoka's back relaxed, and she took a deep breath. Portland was a pretty nice place. Another hub city. They had good food and interesting people, and if Nekoka really thought about it, as long as she didn't have a car and didn't mind the smell of urine, she could stay here. Make a life for herself and not have to worry about her friends or anything. Maybe get the top floor on one of these high rises and stare down at the city below. Jenni could keep the crime in check. Nekoka chuckled warmly. Honestly, as long as Jenni stayed, she wouldn't need anything. Well, a daily milk delivery wouldn't be amiss. And a harem of willing men. She felt herself smiling over at Pablo. Jenni choked on a laugh.

Nekoka studied Jenni, then studied herself.

Hmm, she certainly felt happy right now.

"Pablo—?" Nekoka questioned. Sure, she was moody, but she typically didn't experience that stark of a swing.

"You feel better, don't you?" he asked.

"Did you just slip me an emotional jimmy?"

Pablo shrugged, then offered a little bow. "Sorry if I upset you. Going for the opposite. You were just pretty frustrated and since there's nothing you can do about it, thought you'd like to relax a little."

So, Pablo's knack was emotional manipulation. He was a smoother talker, a silver tongue. Nekoka updated her database, and though she normally would hate on anyone who screwed with her this way, she was still trying to get in the man's pants. Some indiscretions she could let fly. Plus, he was pretty enough and had said no, so she knew that emotion hadn't been manufactured. Perhaps she could use this...

She leaned up against Pablo, draped her arm around his waist. "I'll forgive you if you entertain me for a night."

"Sorry, sweetheart," Pablo said, his breath tickling the hair on her cat ear, "But I'm waiting for true love."

Nekoka scoffed, ready to tell him love and sex were two totally different states of bliss and that she wouldn't hold him to any fidelity, when the door behind the stage banged open with a boom and a "Fuck!"

Nekoka's nerves electrified, her Pablo induced good mood instantly gone. The fur on the back of her neck and shoulders bristled when she spotted who entered Rain.

"Oh my God, traffic was fucktastic. We've got only thirty minutes to sound check. Stab me with a spoon and throw my corpse off the Steel Bridge." Sepia Montgomery strutted in, carrying a large round object wrapped up in a soft-sided case. Guitarist and singer for the band, Ravenous Red Death, and member of O.G.R.E. A brown-haired man, about Sepia's height, trudged in behind her, a sound mixer cradled in his arms. Jasen Road. Originally from Georgia, he attended Washington State University and earned a bachelor's in philosophy. Now the drummer for Ravenous Red Death.

Well, at least he wasn't asking "do you want fries with that?"

"Chill out, Sepia," Jasen said, patting Sepia's shoulder consolingly after he'd deposited his cargo. "Just take the bus like the nice city planners want you to."

Sepia carefully set down the equipment she'd been carrying, then flung a glare at Jasen. "Fuck a pogo stick, Jasen."

Jasen raised his hands in surrender. "Time for a chill pill, Sepia."

Sepia straightened, standing proud with a bit of a hip tilt, gesturing at herself in a very Vanna White kind of way. "You think this is me, clean and clear?" She snapped her fingers. "Fuck. I'm on a blue as we speak. You think I'm this level-headed off my meds?"

Pablo snorted. Nekoka's ears pulled back.

Jasen shook his head and headed for the rear door. "Well, that *is* your natural state. On dope."

Sepia opened her mouth, as if to argue, but the so-observant guitarist finally noticed the group by the bar. "Well, it's either the government mandated moods, or mass homicide. You pick. Oh, eww. I thought I smelled something.... Look what the cat dragged in."

Nekoka unwrapped her arm from Pablo. "Why are you here, Sepia? Shouldn't you be out bullying small children for their lunch money?"

The new arrival sneered, the lighting over the stage glinting off at least a pound of metal drilled into her head.

Please don't start with Sepia again.

She's like a bulldog, Nekoka sent back. *Bark bark.*

Nekoka could hear the exasperated sigh in Jenni's thoughts, and generally, pleasing Jenni came second only to pleasing herself, but Sepia was one of those people that made your hair all go on end. Sylvia "Sepia" Montgomery, 27, founding member of punk group Ravenous Red Death and the bass guitarist and backup vocalist of said group. Member of O.G.R.E. Power: intimidation. A few misdemeanors, mainly possession of marijuana and ecstasy before the government legalized all drugs and handed them out free of charge at the Betterment Stations. Since then, her record had been clean. Not much else on her, other than her band's website, which noted a show tonight, at Rain.

Well, damn.

"Hello, Sepia," Jenni said.

"Oh, hey Jenni." The woman's face went through a complete refit as she dismissed Nekoka and greeted Jenni. Nekoka couldn't understand why anyone would want to be friendly with the pierced freak. The woman had dyed her hair a stunning shade of red with black roots, and it was usually done up in silly childish styles like pig tails or cornrows. Today she was wearing it in two balls, one on either side of her head, in an impression of a schoolgirl anime character.

Piercings covered every aspect of the landscape of her face: her eyebrows, nose, all the way round the edge of each ear, not to mention her lips and tongue. And, though Nekoka wasn't sure if they were glued on or not, what looked like rivets pierced her temple. Nekoka didn't want to think of those places not visible that might be rammed through with metal.

She had an impressive rack that would draw the eyes of most people, mainly due to their in-your-face nature, if she hadn't wrapped her boobs up in camo like a Salvation Army reject.

Plus, Sepia was loud.

They'd clashed the minute they'd met last Saturday. It seemed natural to hate her, like it was natural to love cream and being petted. Some things were just planned out from the origin of the universe.

Sepia planted her hands on her hips, then tilted her head towards the stage. "Pablo," she said at one-ten decibels, "Jasen's got some other crap lined up right after our gig. Any hope of storing our gear in the back room tonight?"

With a casual wave, Pablo gestured at the stage on the far side of the dance floor. "Knock your heart out. Do try to keep set up down, though. Some patrons are enjoying the music from the pipes."

Sepia gazed upwards at the ceiling, listening to Rihanna belt it out, then said, "No problem. Quiet as a mouse." She turned away and motioned wildly towards three men sharing beers on the other end of the bar.

"If mices were elephants, maybe," Nekoka muttered.

Jenni laughed. "Oh, Nekoka, please don't go all poofy. You know it takes forever for your fur to lie down straight again."

Nekoka snorted. She'd already gone poofy, and Jenni well knew that. Nekoka brushed her hands along her arms and hissed at her best friend.

Then an idea popped into Nekoka's head.

Jenni stopped laughing. "What do you have planned? You are not going to screw with her."

Nekoka stepped away from Jenni to make it easier to block her friend from reading her thoughts, and sent her mind into Whisker, which then connected to the cell phone in Sepia's pocket. She wasn't a telepath, like

Jenni, but her ability worked much the same way. If a computer had a hooked-up Wi-Fi or the data was on, Nekoka could use Whisker to connect with it, but that was pretty much simple hacking. Touching the computer always clinched her power's connection and allowed for complete access.

People were confusing, even the one person she knew best. Computers were straightforward, rarely lied unless they were very clever, and usually gave up everything to her.

Pablo laughed, drawing her attention to where he stood with the band. Howard, another guitarist with pink splashes in his spiky blond hair, tossed Pablo some drumsticks. Sepia hoisted a speaker up and carried it to the stage.

Nekoka scowled. Sepia had her damned Wi-Fi off. Probably didn't even have a smart phone let alone invisispecs with VR-glove.

In Jenni it was endearing; in Sepia it was just another failing to add to the pile.

Nekoka spun away in frustration. She felt grumpy again and wondered if she could get Pablo to juice her up. Better than a pill any day. She caught her image in the reflective glass behind the bar. Tabby. Her usual color. A little dull, a little plain. That could be the problem. Maybe tabby just wasn't the right color for today.

With a ripple of her fur, each of her hairs shimmered and changed to the browns and grays of a tortoise shell. She toyed with making her breasts bigger, but that was usually more of a pain than it was worth. Plus, she didn't like resorting to the typical feminine wiles to win her lovers. Surface modifications were easy, like shading her fur into the S-Force uniform when she was out officially as Scratch or hardening her feet. Trying to look human was hard.

The only thing she never changed were her eyes. She could do it, but it took so much concentration that she rarely did. They would always be cat eyes.

Jenni popped up one eyebrow. "You okay?"

Nekoka shrugged, but her tail whipped around behind her. She glared at it.

"Just bored." She wouldn't meet Jenni's eyes. Jenni didn't try to slip in any thoughts.

"Sepia or S-Force?"

Nekoka barked out a laugh that sounded a little like she was coughing up a hairball. "Both?"

Jenni nudged Nekoka with one combat boot, the black banal against the ever-present blue of the bar. Her shoelaces were laced up tight, though one of the laces was frayed at the end, missing its little plastic sheath. The aglet, SPYme informed her.

"Will you look at me?"

Nekoka slipped her attention to Jenni's face. What an odd pair they made. Jenni's dark hair hung just past her shoulders. Her clothing usually rested on the no-color side of the palette.

Nekoka tried to make up for that in her own coloring.

Truly, what a pair.

"Cool trick, Nekoka," Billie said with a smile. Nekoka forced a smile back. It was her public power, shapeshifting. She'd been caught on camera plenty of times changing her coloring and her shape into that of a house cat or even her battle cat form that gave her several feet, more muscle, and Ginsu-sharp claws and fangs. Another minor ability, not too distant from her first, was her affinity with felines. But her second power, the *kokogyo, that* made her an elite amongst the Seeded. A fat Seed. Multiple powers, like most of the Usual Suspects. *Kokogyo* wasn't publicly known, and Nekoka worked hard to make sure it stayed that way, scrubbing away any hint of it on the web, dark or white.

The door banged open. Officer Geier charged in. "Pablo, Sepia. Gotta go. Emergency!"

Pablo left the stage where he'd been helping Ravenous Red Death and their groupies set up. Sepia popped off the stage to join the officer. "Geier, what's up?"

"O.G.R.E.'s got a call. Big pileup on 84 east. ODOT's emergency equipment is already rallied, but they've called me to bring us in. Cruiser's outside."

"Well, let's go," Pablo said. "Sepia?"

Sepia tilted her head, chin down, eyes fierce. "So, you want to call in O.G.R.E. for a car crash?" she said. "It's a car crash. It isn't like someone did anything to make it crash. I mean, who do we have to fight? O.G.R.E. fights other Seeded, to even out the game. Isn't that what we said we'd do?"

The women who'd been dancing earlier had stopped and were staring at the four. The canned music blared out the technified mashup of Green Day's "When I Come Around" and 441 Gone's "Superfly".

"That shouldn't matter." The officer shook his head. "If we have the power to save people, we should!"

"Shit." Sepia threw her hands in the air. "This isn't what we agreed to, but yeah. I'll do what I can."

Nekoka snorted. Like bullying people could help them not die in a pileup.

Then Officer Geier, neophyte hero, noticed Nekoka and Jenni and lit up. "Hey, I know you're not O.G.R.E., but you'd both be really helpful. You've useful powers for this."

Jenni looked at Nekoka. Nekoka knew that look.

"People die all the time, Jenni. We can't save everyone. It isn't our mandate in life."

She smiled at Nekoka, a kind of sad acceptance that caused Nekoka's heart to squeeze. Jenni turned to John. "I'm in."

CHAPTER 7

Nekoka

Portland was a city of many names: City of Roses, Bridge City, City of Gridlock, Stumptown. Nekoka had come to Portland to get away from the emotional shit storm consuming S-Force and the monumental decision whether to form a Certified group or to keep their relationship on the unofficial but undeniably more favorable status of *nothing*. Nekoka wasn't blind. It was a done deal. The writing was splattered on the wall in hyper-glo print.

Nekoka enjoyed freeloading at Zack's New Orleans estate—big enough to house the population of the few rural eastern Oregon towns that still fought for incorporation. They'd screw around on the net and go out to eat and travel. Life was easy, and, after all that business with working with Carlson—and his demands and his order and his *focus focus focus*—she was ready for easy. And sure, so the Usual Suspects liked to go out and save the day once in a while, that was fun too. She loved seeing her friends in action, and yes, sometimes it was fun to save sinking ships and stop oil fires in the fields of Texas. It was fun when it was her choice. It was fun when there were no expectations.

So, her and Jenni's escape to Portland, Oregon, was a type of vacation from reality, though some questioned why they'd chosen P-town. Simple. Portland, even more than New Orleans, was also known as a city that worshiped the Seeded, and, as was common information to any who followed her feed, Nekoka loved being worshiped.

The place reeked of new age mumbo jumbo—even though over fifty percent claimed atheism as their tenet—Big Brother surveillance, and the scent of overripe homeless who'd staked out tent cities in the public areas, but even with the wack jobs and weirdoes, Nekoka had, in only a few days, felt some kinship in the west coast town.

And maybe it wasn't just this little glow of contentment that she felt, maybe it had to do with Sepia's disapproval about mounting the team for a simple accident, maybe it had to do with Pablo's torn expression or the urgent words from the policeman, but it was probably, mostly, the sad look Jenni had given her, that look of "I wish your soul wasn't quite so hard" when she announced, "I'm in."

Nekoka growled and thrust herself from the bar. In her own strut, she approached the gabbing group of O.G.R.E. members and said, "Death waits for no laggers."

Officer Geier eyed the gathered group of Seeded and nodded. "That's five for the car. Good thing you two are little," he said to Jenni and Nekoka, then spun for the door.

Pablo grabbed his jacket and followed Geier towards the exit. "Billie, the bar's yours."

Billie grinned and saluted Pablo and the other O.G.R.E. members with a fist in the air. "Got it," she said with a casual roll of her shoulders. "Go save some people. Give O.G.R.E. a name."

A little shiver tickled over Nekoka's fur. She would get to see Pablo in action. See what he could do. Curiosity proved to be one of Nekoka's other catlike features. Categorizing, listing, naming: all added elements of joy to her day. She collected the Seeded's dossiers like ten-year-olds collected Pokémon, and she doubted anyone had more accurate intel on them.

Outside in the narrow city street, a handful of people milled about the double-parked cop car with its lights flashing its distress. Two drones hovered overhead. Nekoka showed her teeth at the constant spies. They'd catch her doing a good deed and there would go her reputation. John Geier pressed his thumb to the car handle, and after it read his print, the door popped open.

"Thanks, I appreciate the help." His eyes darted to Sepia. "I know this isn't exactly what we'd agreed upon..."

"Whatever," the woman growled and yanked open the back door. Pablo moved to sit in the front. Jenni opened the other rear door, and Nekoka eyed the middle seat next to Sepia with wariness, checking for signs of an automatic restraint meant to trap her there indefinitely. She held her breath as she climbed in next to Sepia's larger bulk and venomous attitude. This could be a long ride.

The doors all slammed closed and auto locked.

John flipped up his specs and glanced over his shoulder, offering a broad grin, before he pulled into traffic, blaring the siren to disperse the gawkers. "This is good, good to show how we can help save lives." Nekoka caught the gunmetal blue of his eyes in his rearview reflection and nodded in acknowledgment, adding some notes about him to her database. Rabid Hero Dreams.

SPYme told her that John Geier had been on the force for 4 years and was a huge proponent for Certification. Speech after speech was available for viewing, on his own personal feed as well as other news feeds, where he talked about how it was the Seededs' duty to help those who needed it and be available to be called upon to aid the greater good. Nekoka rolled her eyes. His power on record was Life Sense, which Nekoka guessed meant he could determine if someone was alive or dead. Which seemed a lame power, but she wouldn't judge until she saw him put it to use. He also had boosted strength, like Jenni. On the nice hand, there were an awful lot of topless pictures of him out there. Apparently, the guy hated wearing shirts. That was something Nekoka could appreciate. The officer worked out.

Trapped by the early evening gridlock that even the siren had no sway to alleviate to any noticeable extent, Nekoka stared out the window at an unused lane separated from them by a line of white traffic pickets. Then a bicycle zoomed by. Then the lane was empty again. The cars oozed forward another four car-lengths, then stopped to idle again. News crackled over the cruiser's radio. A knifing. A robbery. The freeway catastrophe. Nekoka checked in with the police news through Whisker and found emergency vehicles had yet to arrive at the crash site. She hacked into the traffic drones' feed and saw no end to the nose to tail production of cars. Two bicycles tootled by, one powered by a Chinese woman easily tipping seventy with a basket full of groceries on the front and a private drone hovering at her shoulder like a trained sparrow.

"This is such bullshit," Sepia groused, then slouched lower in her seat. "This fucking city."

Nekoka returned to perusing pictures of John in various stages of undress. Her computer beeped. She'd received a text: I deliver the convergence.

"Seriously? Isn't there a two-lane road anywhere, so people can pull aside?" Jenni asked.

Convergence of what? Nekoka responded, as she checked the sent-from number. Nothing. Nekoka sat up in her seat. Another mysterious text?

John sighed. "It's inner city, bike friendly, car abhorred. Just wait 'til we get to the freeway. It's tolled, so pretty clear this time of day."

Plots. Nekoka tried to follow the trail, but no trail existed. Interesting. She kept at it anyway.

The instant John got to the freeway, he gunned it, driving half the way on the wide shoulder in his dash to get to Interstate 84 past 205. They cut down the Banfield, cars slowly slipping out of the fast lane of traffic, following a city firetruck that had just escaped its own cocoon of rush hour molasses. Smoke billowed from around a bend in the freeway, an easy target for them to home in on.

Why so much smoke?

Flames engulfed the crash, which looked like Godzilla had grabbed a few cars, a semi, and a tanker truck and mashed them together like Play-Doh.

Nekoka leaned over Jenni to stare at the devastation through the window, her throat closing up in horror. "*Yabai*," she muttered, slipping into Japanese. Siren screams churned the air into a froth of chaos. John slammed the brakes, and the cruiser jerked to a stop. He punched the off button and burst from the car, sprinting towards the burning mass in the center of the three-lane freeway. Jenni and Sepia popped out of either side door; Nekoka scrambled after Jenni. Together, a team of supercharged individuals hurtled towards the burning scene.

The scent of scorched blacktop, charred metal, and chemical foam assaulted Nekoka's nose, causing her eyes to tear up. All of her feline senses were overstimulated, sending her messages of death and danger and run. The undertang of panic and despair tasted sour on the back of her tongue.

Though it'd taken them nearly thirty-five minutes to get from downtown to the crash site, the flames' roar as it devoured the crunched pile of vehicles still crackled against the siren wails, and Nekoka felt disoriented, not sure what to do. She didn't savor the idea of jumping into a fiery freeway wreck.

Where was Zack and his fireproof body when you needed him?

Then she heard it, through the crackling and the screaming and the helpless pounding of her pulse, she heard words. Her ears tilted forward.

"Help me." The words were weak, so weak against the power of the destruction. "Help. Please, someone." Nekoka scampered toward a twisted minivan, thickening the skin on her feet and hands to add some protection against roasting her flesh on the hot ground and metal.

"Jenni, over here." In an instant Jenni was at her side, like she'd never been anywhere else, and the two Seeded dashed over to the mangled van.

When Nekoka focused, she heard scratching.

"Someone's over here!" Cries from other rescuers popped up in staccato all around her, and all Nekoka could do was shift her body over one car that had already been evacuated to climb onto another. The metal, hot from the blaze, scorched her fur until she simply removed it, replacing her fur with hard, scaled flesh, like a dragon, adding insulation from the heat. Jenni had found some fireman gloves and pulled them over her small hands. Nekoka grabbed at a piece of metal—how had it become so mangled?—and tugged. And tugged. It screeched as the metal ground against metal, then Jenni grasped it and yanked, and it came free.

A small pile of twisted metal and car parts grew behind her and Jenni as they dug for the person, throwing bits and pieces in a haphazard array. Jenni's superior strength helped move things along, but it seemed the age of dinosaurs had passed before they saw a hand, long pink fingernails chipped, one broken at a jagged line.

"Here." Jenni reached out to touch the fingers; Nekoka's heart didn't seem to be beating anymore. Everything had frozen, a spell cast upon time, but then the fingers reacted to Jenni's touch. Time jerked back into place as Nekoka realized the survivor *was* a survivor.

Jenni pushed herself up and grabbed at the rest of the pile that trapped the woman. In one huge heave, she threw a ball of metal thirty feet behind them. Nekoka quickly made work of the smaller stuff, pulling and tugging with little mind to her surroundings. She turned from the pile of debris to grab another chunk when she saw that the woman was freed.

The victim's dress slacks, once classy, were now torn and soaked with blood. The smell was sharp in the air, metallic, tangy. Nekoka didn't need SPYme to tell her who this woman was.

Eliza Silva, the spokesperson for Sapian True, one of the many anti-Seeded movements flourishing in the world. Nekoka was a little surprised to see her in Portland. Glenn Ryan of True News talked her up at every possibility. With a flick of her gaze, she realized Jenni recognized her as well.

The woman's voice, almost vacant, floated towards Nekoka's twitching ears. "Help...Please..." Then the anti-Seeded spokesperson finally recognized the status of her saviors. She pressed her lips together, and Nekoka saw the slow bob of her throat as the woman swallowed.

Though emotionally eviscerated, Nekoka almost chuckled.

Jenni leaned down and surveyed the survivor's body, searching for where she was bleeding. Nekoka checked the woman's neck, not that she was certain what she was looking for. She had little medical training, only a few lessons from Minnie. Minnie, who she'd abandoned, left behind back in New Orleans. She wasn't here now, and Nekoka could only rely on her own intelligence and common sense.

Intelligence she had in spades, common sense...not so much.

"You support her head, and I'll lift her body," Jenni said, and Nekoka nodded. "On three." Nekoka cradled the woman's head and neck. "One. Two. Three." They lifted Eliza, and a scream tore from her throat, the sound piercing and desperate. Nekoka almost dropped her, but soon propped her up, and they hauled her from the ruins of the van to a safe distance away.

A man and woman in paramedic jackets ran over to them with a gurney, taking over the care of their survivor. "Thank you," the man said with genuine appreciation. Before they settled her on the gurney, Nekoka collected a few photos of the Seeded hater with Jenni, the wreckage in the background a beautiful backdrop to the image. Adding a quick blurb about Jenni's heroics, Nekoka plopped the post on a few feeds as civilians, firemen, and Seeded alike pulled people free of the crash.

Dashing back into the chaos, Nekoka thought to Jenni, *Did you want to leave her? Maybe? Just a little?*

Nekoka. Jenni scolded.

Yeah, me too.

"Hey, Jenni, Nekoka!"

The two women turned towards John, about thirty yards away, who was supporting a chunky guy who hopped on one leg, his teeth gritted in a grimace of pain.

"We need more hands over here! The semi had people in it." John shook his head. "This man says twenty."

He set the wounded man down near a huddle of paramedics and jogged back towards the semi that had rolled onto its side. Fortunately, the fire hadn't reached the trailer. Nekoka wondered why people would be inside a semi, and the only reason that came to mind didn't make sense, they weren't anywhere near the southern border. As they drew closer, they spotted Sepia waist deep in debris, thick gloves stuffed onto her hands.

She'd have to send the local fire department a thank you gift for supplying the gloves to her team.

"Over here." John pointed into an opening made by two cars that led to the semi, that looked from this angle to have been twisted by giant hands. People had been in that? Nekoka's gut bubbled, and if she hadn't removed her fur, it would be all up on end.

"Eleven people towards the back doors and seven back towards the cab. The ones in the middle...." He frowned, and squished up his nose before he said, "Probably won't make it."

Life Sense. He must be able to find their beacon of aliveness and tell if one was going to die. Part of that just seemed really depressing.

"Shouldn't we get those first? The dying ones?" Nekoka demanded, already heading for the dark opening that would lead her to the back doors of the trailer.

There was a pause behind her, though she didn't stop her march to those trapped, and then John continued talking, his voice keeping up with hers. "Okay. The others appear stable, but I just want you to be prepared."

Nekoka dove into the tunnel entrance Sepia and John had created earlier, with Jenni only a few paces behind. This area had not been ravaged by the fire, so the scent of blood rose to the top. Nekoka sniffed deep, but couldn't pinpoint where it was coming from. "Go deeper, if you can," the officer directed. Around her, a twisted maze of metal enclosed tighter as she continued in.

"You okay?" she asked Jenni.

"'Course. Do you hear anyone yet?"

Nekoka shook her head and contorted her body to slip beyond a vicious-looking knife of a car hood that had somehow been wrenched away from the car body.

"Below you, to the left!" cried out John.

Nekoka glanced around. Spears of light cut through the dimness within the cavern of destruction. Going by John's directions, all she saw was the side of the trailer, squished and twisted. She searched some more and found a rip in the side. Inside, she caught weeping.

She wanted to just charge through and save these people, this person who was crying. Right there. Feet away from her, but she worked slow, moving small pieces while Jenni heaved on the tear to expand the opening.

When the opening was large enough for her dainty size, Nekoka pushed her torso through. When she saw the face, Nekoka had to swallow down her bile. Nekoka didn't have a weak stomach; she loved horror movies and sometimes ate things alive while trouncing around as a cat. But the man below her flipped her stomach, causing its contents to creep up her esophagus. This was a person, not a prop. Not a made-up actor. A heavy object had smashed into part of the face, crushing his cheek and embedding his specs into the flesh. Something else had skinned the lower half of that already brutalized face, taking part of his bottom lip. The flesh dangled, and a fly crawled over it, up along the blood coated teeth. Nekoka swatted it away.

His eyes were open and staring straight ahead. They were soft, pale gray. Seeded.

"Nekoka!" Jenni yelled, and Nekoka jerked, eyes tearing from the sick mask to glance at Jenni, farther away and no witness to the poor man's fate. "Geier says the life is gone. The person is dead."

Something sparked down Nekoka's spine. She scrambled back towards the hole. "What? No! No, he isn't. He's right here, Jenni. Right here and we can...we can still save him. I can *see him*."

Nekoka reached for another scrap of metal, yanking on it to pass to Jenni. Jenni didn't take it. In the background, Nekoka finally noticed John. "Come on, other people are still in there. Jenni? Nekoka! They still need your help."

Sepia roared out. "Can you get a clear path to the trailer's back doors? Come on!"

But he was right there. She could see him.

A buzzing filled Nekoka's ears.

Deeper within the trailer, someone spoke. "Hello? Hello, can you help us? Please?"

"Nekoka." Jenni touched Nekoka's arm.

Nekoka jumped. Her vision no longer full of a mutilated dead man but that of her best friend. Jenni's worried frown built a little dent in her forehead. Nekoka knew it well. Sorrow, and worry, but also determination. "Come on," Jenni said. "Let's get the others free. Sounds like there's some passage to the back now."

Nekoka nodded, not looking at the man. "Lead the way."

THE EVENING DRAGGED on, and they doggedly helped the mundane humans in every way possible. Nekoka slipped into tight places to seek out more survivors and more bodies of the dead. Jenni tore apart the pile of cars to get them. They were quite the team.

In the end, they were both disgusting, covered in soot and blood and automobile seat fluff saturated with fire retardant and tears. Jenni got a check-up from the paramedics—minor burns and abrasions. The two friends stationed themselves on the median's untouched stretch of grass; Nekoka sprawled out, arms and legs thrown in exhaustion—both physical and emotional. The scent of green grass fought the dust layer crusting her nose. Most Seeded were physically superior to the norms, but the entire ordeal had drained Nekoka.

She missed her chance to see Pablo in action, to watch him stretch some muscle, show off whatever powers he might have. She figured he must have a second, other than making people happy. Her files on the man would have to remain simple: Pablo Castile. Caribbean of African/Asian descent. Early twenties. Hot. Friendly. Could charm the habit off a nun. Emotional manipulator. Owner of Rain.

"So, that wreck. It wasn't...normal," Nekoka led.

"Yeah, too much damage."

Nekoka thought about that text. About how the informant said he'd deliver a convergence. "It was...ah, set up."

Jenni was quiet for a moment, and Nekoka listened to people talking and the slow movement of cars in the westbound lanes of the freeway.

"How so?"

"Well, I had this idea, and I checked out some of the cars, and someone took over the cars' autopilots for maximum damage."

"What?" Jenni sat up.

"Yeah, intentional collision." Or convergence?

"Could you do that?" Jenni asked.

"I could. I didn't. I wouldn't." She huffed.

"I know." Jenni patted Nekoka's belly, now comfortably furred again. "But, would it have to be someone like you, with *kokogyo*, or just a normal hacker?"

Nekoka thought about the informant's message and how she couldn't track it. It had no origin. "Um, maybe someone like me. Or close to. There are very good protections on the auto-drive, but it's not infallible. Nothing is if you've got the mad skills. And I think whoever did this has mad skills."

"There you are."

Nekoka looked up and saw her fellow Seeded. Though his clothing was ripped and stained, Pablo still exuded a certain magnetism, and just the sight of him soothed something twisted in Nekoka. John was jacketless, and shirtless—and wasn't that a nice, furry chest—with a long cut splitting the skin of his forearm. Sepia had black smeared all over her left cheek, her hair all fucked up in a mad housewife kind of way, but she didn't appear injured. All of them looked exhausted.

"Here we are." Nekoka pulled herself up to sit with a grunt. She really needed a nap. "You should get that fixed," Nekoka said with an upward nod towards the cut on John's arm.

He glanced down at his injury and rubbed his hand over the layer of blood pooling along the skin. It smeared into a pattern of flames. "I'll be okay. It's just a scratch. Anyway, I wanted to thank you guys. I don't think we would have saved as many people if you four hadn't come with me." His face was solemn, but his lips were relaxed enough to look pleased.

"No problem," Jenni said. She was jacketless as well, though she wisely kept her shirt on. "Guess who was in the crash."

Sepia's face lit up. "Oh, someone important? Was it Billie Boyd?"

Jenni laughed. "No, better. Eliza Silva."

Sepia's hopeful delight crashed into disgust. "Shoulda let her burn."

Nekoka laughed this time. Bloodthirsty, that one. Bark bark. In that, she could approve. Sepia scowled.

"She was burned and cut and bloody, if it makes you feel better." Nekoka thought at her computer. "I just sent you some info on it." She smiled innocently at Sepia. "Just think, when you all go Certified, you'll be forced to help horrible people like her every day."

"Lots of people were burned and cut and bloody," Pablo said, his seriousness sapping Nekoka's moment of mirth as the image of a torn and busted face surfaced in her mind.

"So," John began. "Those people in the semi, it's believed they were all Seeded."

Nekoka's memory couldn't drag itself from that face. She looked away from John, down to her lap.

He cleared his throat. "They all claimed to have been kidnapped."

"What the hell?" Jenni said, pushing herself to her feet.

"Most were homeless, too. Many claim to have been attacked on the streets, a few just woke up in the semi...those ones were high, or on some medication that made them less reactive."

"Zomboys?" Sepia asked.

"Matoro's everywhere, so...probably. I can tell they are messed up on something," John tapped the side of his head, "but I couldn't tell you what they're messed up on."

"Who would take them?" Sepia asked, scowling.

John shook his head. "Don't know yet. We'll look into it."

"Too bad Minnie isn't here," she said, looking up into Jenni's face. "Or Gracie. Gracie could increase everyone's pain tolerance until Minnie healed them." Though this was probably too many people for Minnie to heal in one go; she'd burn herself out.

Jenni's lips twitched, not into a fond remembrance, but instead into an instant of something sorrowful, then was gone. She must miss Grace, Nekoka thought. She filed that away to take up later, when the others weren't around.

"You have a healer *and* someone who can reduce pain...in multiple people?" Pablo asked, pursing his full lips.

"Minnie Mandalis and Grace Bravo," Nekoka said, her eyes flickered over to Jenni. Jenni's whole air seemed dejected. Nekoka decided not to add the bit that Gracie was Jenni's girlfriend. "They're back in New Orleans, though." And that might be why Jenni suddenly turned moody. But Nekoka didn't really think so. "Gracie is awesome. She chants and affects a variety of things, like air temp or things concerning the body, but she's not completely mastered that. She's like one of those Buddhist monks in fantasy games."

Pablo's eyes widened with an appreciative nod. "That's handy."

Nekoka shrugged. "We have a good team back there." And she'd left them behind. She was so stupid. Her heart ached for her friends.

Why did this have to happen? They wanted to sign up as saviors of the world, a true group of heroes.

Nekoka blinked away her surge of emotion. She couldn't keep Jenni from them for long. That wasn't fair.

"Can I give you a lift back?" John asked as he turned and surveyed the diorama of loss.

Pablo nodded, then said, "That would be great. I'm ready for a bath, need to soak these old bones."

Jenni stood and pulled Nekoka up to her feet. "Old," Jenni said with a snort. "You're barely twenty."

Pablo shrugged as they all turned towards the police car and began tramping through the grassy field. "Mid-twenties, thank you." He rubbed his fingers over his sooty cheek. "Got the best skin mixture of all the races."

Nekoka looked off into the sunset, the colors layered in abyssal hues. She sighed. How many bad decisions could she make concerning her friends? She should send Jenni back, stop breaking apart her friends' happiness. Now, though, she just wanted some hot chocolate, a bit of a scrub, and that overly comfy pillow-top at the hotel.

CHAPTER 8

Martha

The vehicle was rolling along at rattling speeds, the interior black like hell and sin, an absence of light she never experienced in the city. Martha squinted to make out three other hunched over shapes, one next to her and the others on the opposite side of the van. Everything was fuzzy, spinning. The jackass that'd clocked her upside the head must've slipped her some Matoro before stuffing her in this van. Filled her veins to overflowing with it, 'cause her body burned. A hazy swirl of memories and dreams, tied up with that song, "I Touch Myself", fluttered around in her head on half a wing.

Getting hit. Getting drugged. Losing time. Now, she was driving at demon speeds in the back of a van with three other prisoners. Kidnapped. Abducted.

And her pants were cold and damp. She sniffed. Piss. She smelled piss. And her specs were missing.

A dry tick crackled as she struggled to swallow, her throat a parched, raw tube that dumped into her empty stomach. Her tongue stuck to her mouth.

"Hey," she said, though it didn't really come out as a word, more of a grunt from the bottom of her belly. She tried to get her saliva flowing, lick her tongue around her mouth, but she couldn't coax any spit into action. What had they done to her?

What were they *going* to do with her?

After a moment, she examined her situation. Her hands were cuffed with thick plastic cable ties attached to a metal bar at her crotch. Her feet were similarly attached to a bar near the ribbed sheet metal floor.

The van rocked along for hours. Must be on a freeway. She twisted and shifted and worked on her hands. Her wrists slicked up with blood, the cuts stinging but the sensation barely there, hidden below the damned hammering of her heart. The van slowed, stopped, and turned left, picking up speed again. Off the freeway, taking her to somewhere far, far away from home and freedom. Far, far away from everything she knew. Goosebumps tingled over her skin.

Day came on, light seeping through seams around the back door and a few holes that punctured the metal sides and ceiling of the vehicle. Two of the people emerged under the dawning light into women, the third a man. Worn clothing, unkempt hair. Over the smell of her own body, she guessed they, too, were freesteaders.

The man had awakened. He leaned as far forward as he could, a shaft of light slicing his face. He had pale yellow eyes.

"What's going on?" he croaked. Guess he had more saliva than she did. She only shook her head.

By the time the van roared onto a gravel road, all four of the prisoners were awake, sharing hissed questions and worried looks carved in deep shadow. One woman, a dark stain of something down the side of her face, was talking to the man. Short clipped "where are we?" "what's happening?" as if the man had any better clue. Martha was stuck with a bunch of cattle, mooing in distress.

Obviously, the one-percenters found a solution for the unsightly homeless problem. Didn't want to face what their righteous society had done to the poor on the streets. Just wanted to shut them away, put them in huge warehouses. Maybe, they were going to be sent to the ovens, like the Germans did to the Jews in the forties. Cook them all up and send them out through the cement stacks to fertilize the fields.

Is that what she amounted to? What human life amounted to? Fertilizer to feed the next generations?

The van came to a stop. Her bladder throbbed as the doors swung open, and she struggled not to let it loose again as men in black military gear cut their bindings and yanked them out the back.

No one said a word. The prisoners gasped, hissed in pain, whimpered. Their abductors kept silent in their dirty work.

Martha, momentarily blinded in the full brightness of day, stumbled as a man dragged her along a gravel parking lot, her shoes scraping divots within the rock, through a single door to an elevator. At the bottom, the doors opened to a corridor so bright it washed out all other color, giving each of the people a faded, worn look. Much like the eyes of the Seeded.

Another man, an Arab with dark brown skin, came forward. Was this all a terrorist plot? But that made no sense. Since they'd left behind the need for oil, peace with those countries was more the norm. So the feeds said.

"Clean them up," the Arab said. "They go to Bay 4. Any power that you've observed?"

"No, sir," said the guard holding the taller women. "Just low-level spunks."

If Martha could get her tongue to work, she'd cut him down, put the bastard in his place, the jack-booted, dark-eyed piece of nobody! Tear him apart with her mind, if only she could figure out how to make her power work.

They were led to a room with shower heads and little cubbies available to stow their clothes like the showers had at the YMCA. The room could easily have fit twenty people. Martha glared at the closed door and up at the video cameras housed in boxes skulking in the corners of the room like vultures waiting for the delivery of their corpses.

She turned to the showers and cranked one on, cupping her hands under the stream to finally curb her thirst. The water was cool and chlorine flavored, but all the sweeter for her thirst. The others followed suit, one woman invading Martha's space—the tall one, with short scruffy hair that looked hacked at by a two-year-old. A line of blood down her forehead stained her cheek. She scrubbed at the blood. Her eyes were those of the Seeded, pale tan, nearly off-white.

"You know we're all going to die," said the last woman, fat packed into polyester shorts with boobs that could knock someone flat with the right heave. "Why else would they—"

"They ain't gonna kill us. They spent time and green to get us to wherever we are. Maybe forced labor or something. Make us work in a meth house or somethin'," said the one man of their group, a crusty bastard with rotting teeth and wandering eyes. No way was Martha dressing down in front of this guy.

None of them truly showered. They washed their exposed parts—the man taking his shirt off and scrubbing at his pits and chest—and waited. Waited until the SWAT team returned, each of them with a baton and a scowl and a grip that the powerless Seeded couldn't fight.

Martha was third in line as they were dragged down another hall, then out into a huge auditorium. The ceiling hung above them, full of pipes and fire sprinkler heads. Huge lights blazed down, and across the floor of the room were cages, like the ones you'd imagine circus animals had been housed in back before the bleeding hearts wanted animals to be treated better than humans. There were no animals in these cages. These cages were full of people.

A guard opened the door to one of the cages and threw the man in. Then the woman. And Martha was the next to join them.

Inset 3
Code of Federal Regulations

Title 24 CFR Part 35.91.001

Powers and duties of municipalities to control the rights of Seeded residents (Municipal Autonomy Act)

The legislature finds that local governments working towards providing a violence-free city is beneficial to the public health, safety, and welfare. The legislature is aware many municipalities' local police forces cannot handle the rash of violence Seeded individuals may bring into a city. The legislature is also concerned about activities and provisions that serve to bar a person with a deinde gland from obtaining viable housing or employment regardless of other factors that may indicate a Seeded may be violent.

(1)(a) Except as provided in (b) of this subsection, a local government may adopt and implement a violence-free Seeded registration program within its jurisdiction in accordance with this chapter.

(b) A violence-free Seeded registration program adopted and implemented by a municipality is applicable only to Seeded individuals with valid MRI results.

(2) Except as provided in subsection (3) of this section, a violence-free Seeded registration program must provide for housing and employment possibilities for Seeded individuals.

(3)(a) A local government may require a landlord or employer to participate in a violence-free Seeded registration program upon meeting specific parametric limits a municipality deems important to a violence-free city. Instances of parametric limits include, but are not limited to, distances to schools or daycares, interaction with children eighteen and under, or population density.

(b) Seeded individual restrictions may include, but are not limited to:

(i) Right to assembly;

(ii) Ownership of business;....

CHAPTER 9

Thomas

With a left-handed drive, Thomas Hallaman slammed the small rubber ball off the back court wall and watched his opponent swing high and miss. The ball bounced, hit the front wall, and after two consecutive bounces to the floor, Thomas won the racquetball match.

He smiled genially at Scott Oak, and the two shook hands.

"Great game, Thomas," Scott said, running his fingers through his sweat-streaked short hair. "Bastard. That backhand of yours should be banned. It's your size. If you didn't have the reach of Godzilla..." He leveled his racquet at Thomas. "But trust me on this, old pal, I'll get you eventually."

Tall, broad, and exuding an athletic prowess hinting at a disciplined life, Thomas Hallaman was an imposing figure in the world of business and recreational sports. His presence demanded attention in boardrooms and galas alike.

"Scott, I'm sure after extensive training and years of dedication, you might attain such perfection." Thomas twirled his racquet against the palm of his hand and then snapped it from the air to lean over his left shoulder. Scott rolled his eyes, as Thomas knew his companion would. "Let's hit the showers and get some lunch before the board meeting."

The two men retired to the locker rooms and a half hour later emerged in tailored suits: Thomas in his favored charcoal, Scott in a dark blue.

"Goodbye Mr. Hallaman, Mr. Oak. See you tomorrow," called out the receptionist.

"Yep, see you later, Candy," Scott said. Thomas simply waved.

With briefcases in hand, they left Atlas Sports Club and climbed into Scott's classic gas-powered Mercedes, waiting for them at the front pull out. Scott slipped a bill to the valet. The engine was already purring.

Thomas fit his large frame into the car. "How's Mary's latest show going?" he asked Scott. They'd gone to university together at Columbia twenty years ago, and Mary had been Scott's sweetheart in school. Thomas always teased his friend about his fairy tale life. Scott took it all with poorly-hidden happiness. Mary owned an art studio, Soliel, on Halsted and had been hosting a series she'd called "Crying Out". Every artist hosted was one of the growing homeless plaguing the Chicago streets, many of them being nuls. The Chicago Municipal Autonomy Act disallowed Seeded jobs where they would have direct contact with the public. However, many other labor jobs were available for those with the lack of education. And there was always the option of moving out of town.

Scott revved the engine and pulled his Mercedes out in between two closely spaced cars. Thomas tried not to watch but lauded himself for not scrambling for the grab handle above the door. "Well, Mary believes she's boosting awareness, and most of her proceeds go to the Mission Gospel, so that makes her feel good."

Thomas chuckled. "Well, anything to keep up domestic bliss."

Scott snorted, flipped his blinker on to take a right, waiting for a gaggle of office workers crossing the street. Drones hovered ahead, monitoring traffic and observing for crime. "Well, I support her studio. I just wish she wouldn't give all that money away. You know how much the real estate on Halsted costs?"

Thomas did. He was a developer and liked to keep his eye on Chicago's markets as well as those in other major cities. His business was currently booming on the west coast.

Thomas had attended "Crying Out's" grand opening four months ago and praised one photograph of a dead crow resting on a boardwalk with Lake Michigan in blurred focus in the background. The feathers had been mussed, as if an animal had tried to eat it, but decided other nourishment would be better found elsewhere. He wondered how the hell someone who claimed to be homeless had an adequate camera or even everyday specs to take a sharp enough photo to enter in a gallery. These people were all beggars, standing on roadsides with signs claiming despondency when they probably made double minimum wage tax free from the bleeding hearts that handed out fives and tens with little thought to the effect it would have on those people's lives. Why work when society would pay you to be pitiful? The country was being ground down under the tread of those who'd rather sit back and let others clean up their mess.

Soliel's celebration for the homeless had attracted a large audience and received extensive publicity, and Thomas had made a show of purchasing the piece with the dead bird, titled 'Hope,' saying something about how it reflected the plight of the homeless and how people should look out for their fellow man. He'd even been quoted in the paper.

Though he'd never actually admit it, Thomas had hoped the portion of the sale that went to the photographer would help him get back on his feet. Sometimes, people just needed a break. He got that.

Scott and Thomas obtained their usual table at Pearson's Steakhouse, where lunch consisted of rare steaks and two martinis and plenty of superficial chatting men called networking. If he were in a lower tax bracket, it might be called bonding, but he wasn't the type to bond. It was important for Thomas to keep good ties with Scott and many of his other contemporaries. His network was vast.

Scott sipped his martini. "What's wrapped your brain up, Thomas?"

Thomas thought about the rows of tents lining the back streets of the city, where the drones didn't patrol. "Oh, the problems our city is facing. Not sure Mary's art show is going to save the day."

Scott's eyebrows rose in sympathy as he nodded. "You remember Roco?"

Thomas gave Scott a blank stare. Scott's lips quirked in a half-chuckle as he said, "The *artiste* who submitted 'Hope' to Mary's charity show?"

"Oh, was that his name?" Thomas asked, slicing through the last portion of his steak to dip into the red wine sauce.

Scott snorted, leaning back in his chair. "Mary told me he overdosed on Matoro and was kicked out of the show." His neutral expression momentarily degraded into exasperated expectation, then it was washed away by neutrality once again.

Thomas' heart sunk, just briefly, then he tucked the disappointment away. He should have known better.

"How many of the show's...artists have been kicked out by breaking her rules?" Thomas didn't expect many of the participants of "Crying Out" to want to hold to any rules.

Scott sighed before smiling fondly, his blue eyes lighting up at the thought of his wife. "You know Mary. I think at least half have broken the drug rule, but she likes to give them a second chance. Unless it's Matoro, then she gives the Zomboys their final payment and cuts them out." Scott gripped Thomas' gaze, and Thomas saw the man's jaw muscles flex. "Sometimes I worry about her being around these people on drugs."

Thomas felt his entire body go numb. "Yes, I can understand." His deep voice flat to his own ears.

But that wasn't helpful. He was a problem solver, not a wallower. And Lord knew he didn't want Mary to get hurt, either. They needed to protect the ones they loved. This was a law of life. "At least she has a security drone."

Saying their goodbyes, Scott dropped Thomas off at Arnold and Hallaman Development housed in the Inland Steel Building.

Stephanie, his secretary, greeted him and gave him his messages. Her sharp eyes, shielded by a pair of thin glasses, flicked over the computer screen.

"Mr. Hallaman, you have a 2:30 with a gentleman, a Mr. Rodwerd of Tillman Real Estate. He wanted to discuss the Portland, Oregon waterfront area."

Thomas frowned, shuffling through his mental life planner that was nearly as good as the electronic one on his phone or the one Stephanie was referring to, then nodded. Rodwerd was scheduled for tomorrow, not today. "Set him up in the small conference room when he comes in. And make him wait ten minutes before you call me."

Stephanie's jaw flexed, but she only nodded in response.

"And bring me a coffee, please."

He pushed through the stout door into his office and quietly closed it. He pinched the bridge of his nose and discarded his calm mask, his 'outer face' as he called it. Hard lines of annoyance etched ridges across his features. He'd have to reschedule another meeting to fit Rodwerd in. People never stuck to their promises.

He pulled out his phone and noted the address of the tent he'd seen off South Lake Shore and called Winston "Bucky" Buckland at the City.

"Thomas," Bucky said, a smile evident in his voice. "How can I help you?"

"Hello Bucky, how is Heather?"

Bucky laughed. "Great. Still trying to lose those last ten pounds, though—"

"—you keep telling her you think she's the most beautiful woman in the world," Thomas finished.

Bucky laughed again. "Well, she is."

"I won't argue that," Thomas said, letting warmth seep into his voice. "Listen, Bucky, I got another tent for you. Not sure how the drones miss them."

"Well, you know the city's policy—unless it's in specific neighborhoods, we don't evict unless there's a complaint."

Thomas bristled at the term 'evict' as if these people had any right to tenting in property designated for the public's enjoyment. Families can't visit the park if it's become a homeless tent city decorated with all of its refuse. "We should keep our city grand and make sure the kids are safe."

"Of course, of course. Sorry about your sister."

Thomas gritted his teeth. Every damned time Bucky brought her up. He needed a new contact at the city code enforcement who knew nothing of his past. "It was twenty years ago," was all he said. Back when his sister was a senior at the University of Chicago and he a sophomore at Columbia.

While returning from her part-time job to campus, Kathy had been knifed to death by a man in a public park, his handmade cardboard sign begged the good citizens of Chicago for help, guilting them with the name of God. He'd been high, claimed mental health issues, and had gotten off with only forced rehab and community service.

Slap on the hand. For murder.

What a grand country this was. Everyone got a second chance. Everyone, except his sister.

CHAPTER 10

Nekoka

Something sharp was poking Nekoka's thigh.

"Nekoka, get up. We've got to eat."

Nekoka rolled over, pulled the pillow over her head.

"Nekoka. I'll go without you."

"Fine," Nekoka whined. "I'm not hungry."

Her stomach gurgled. Well, never let it be said that Nekoka could be mighty in self-denial. "Bring me something back."

"No," Jenni said. "You come with me and get your own food or go hungry." Jenni's voice carried that annoying flat tone to it that suggested she was getting fed up with Nekoka. Nekoka huffed.

"Fine. Fine." She sat up, and the room spun around her. She flopped back down. "I can't move."

Dead weight had been attached to her limbs. She hadn't felt this trounced upon since she'd become a Seeded. Since she'd *sprouted*. Normal, everyday exertion didn't touch her. But pulling car wreckage off trapped people obviously did. Testing her head, she opened her eyes again, to look into the faded green of Jenni's.

"You okay?" Jenni asked, and Nekoka smiled. Jenni always took care of her.

"Just dizzy. Sore. You?"

Jenni shrugged. "Knackered. But, I'm starving."

Sleep and food were the best ways to fuel an over-clocked body.

Nekoka thought at Whisker and saw that it was nearly 8 p.m. She'd slept all day. News of the freeway crash, pictures of Nekoka, Jenni, and the O.G.R.E. members flooded her feed. Eliza Silva gave a speech that Nekoka would need to listen to later. Lots of PMs from her net friends, asking for more details. She groaned as her stomach grumbled. They could wait. She didn't have the focus for interaction and information right now.

"We've slept the day away," Jenni said. "Come on. I could eat a horse." She pulled the covers off Nekoka.

"Horse is a bit tough," Nekoka said, sitting up with care, and when the world didn't unbalance, she threw her legs over the edge of the bed to stand. "And you might have to do some searching to find a place that serves horse. We could visit Japan; they eat horse there. I've had it at fancy places." Nekoka's shoulder clenched in a cramp. She rubbed it as best as she could. "Let's just e-order and have it delivered."

"No, I want to go somewhere, sit at a table, and read an actual menu."

Oh, Jenni, Nekoka thought to herself, not broadcasting out to Jenni's telepathy. Such a crotchety old lady at times. Instead, she mumbled, "But we'll have to deal with people." Nekoka didn't possess the moxie to be friendly right now.

A message popped to her phone that was integrated with Whisker. Wow, nice save, Nekoka and Jenni!

The text was from Minnie. Nekoka immediately responded.

Thanks. The local group asked for an assist and we joined up. The image of the man's face surfaced into her head again. Crushed and torn. When would it ever leave her be? It was pretty horrible.

Well, I'm sure the people you helped appreciated it. How are you?

Okay. How is Gracie? Is she holding Jenni's escape from NO against her, or me?

Escape? Dramatic much?

Nekoka could easily envision Minnie's stern expression. It made her smile.

You been called yet, since you're temp Certified now?

No. Nothing's changed. Just. Come home already.

Nekoka noticed that Minnie dodged answering about Grace's reaction to Jenni's exodus, and Nekoka realized she really should send Jenni home.

"Minnie says hi, and good job," Nekoka said as Jenni walked past Nekoka to the window and opened the double layers of curtains. They didn't overlook some night landscape of the Portland skyline, but instead opened on to an interior atrium of their hotel. A high ceiling crowned the atrium and three stories below them was the seventh floor, a lounge area with a bar and upscale restaurant. The floor was packed with scantily clad women. Nekoka had wondered if they'd wandered into a hooker convention when they'd first arrived.

Jenni smiled and grabbed her phone to send her own text.

Gotta go. Jenni is going to eat me if I don't feed her soon.

Ha, that sounds like that should go the other way round. Have fun.

Say hi to everyone. Nekoka wasn't ready to talk to Zack.

Will do.

"We could just eat here," Jenni offered, stuffing her phone in her back pocket before she sat on the edge of the bed. Jenni was clean and dressed in jeans and a satiny dark shirt that looked oddly classed-up and feminine on her grounded friend. Though she still wore her leather boots, which was a relief. Nekoka didn't know what she would do if Jenni strutted about in strappy heels.

The two friends left their room and made their way around the corner to the elevator bank. Nekoka sneered at the gaggle of women surrounding the elevators, squawking like hens, with vacant expressions and ruby red lips. The minute they noticed the two newcomers, the group grew quiet, openly staring at Jenni and Nekoka.

With narrowed eyes, Nekoka studied the women. Nancy Yontz, a nurse at Oregon Health Sciences University, plastered her feed with her three children, Julian, Demask, and Joey. Must have had some body work with a flat belly like that. Becky Johns, a recent divorcee, was a model for High Rose cosmetics line. Nekoka SPYed the rest, to see if any were interesting, but honestly, they were just normal women, out on the town, all early to mid-twenties, slim, attractive. All five shots to the wind, at least. A few of them weren't standing upright without the aid of the wall. They'd have been more interesting if they were hookers.

One woman, a leggy brunette, smiled at Nekoka and asked, "Are you one of those super types or do you just have a cartoon fetish?"

To her side, Jenni began to say something, but Nekoka interrupted. "Are you a prostitute, or are you just pretending to be one in hopes of getting laid?"

"*Nekoka*," Jenni thought, her tone scolding as the women all pretended to be insulted. Nekoka found that amusing, as if they had any pride to insult.

The elevator arrived, and the seven women piled in. They smirked as the doors closed, and Jenni and Nekoka were left in the hallway. Nekoka smirked back.

The minute the elevator doors closed, another arrived, and the two friends walked in. Every wall was reflective and Nekoka leaned forward and stared at her face, plain in her tabby stripes. She never wore make-up, never tried to pretty herself up. No short skirts or high heels or low-cut shirts highlighted her body. She wore what was essentially a natural furry bodysuit, no clothing at all. While attractive in form and face, the fur, ears, and tail were all odd enough quirks that a lot of men didn't consider her with any interest.

Some were repulsed. Nekoka was sure they were just repressed.

Which was a crying shame. Nekoka enjoyed men. They scratched an itch, alleviated her persistent worry better than any pills available from the dispensaries. And she was very considerate with those she enjoyed.

"Nekoka."

She stopped staring at herself and shifted her attention to Jenni's reflection, whose arms were crossed over her chest, her head tilted to look down at Nekoka, though they were close to the same height.

Nekoka didn't say a word. She could be very patient if she wanted to.

"Did you trap those women on that elevator?"

Nekoka's eyes opened in shock. "Why Jenni, I'm surprised you would think of me as such a monster, to trap those kind ladies in a small, enclosed space for hours on end. How horrid do you think I am?" Her ear twitched.

With a tremendous roll of her eyes, Jenni dropped the verbal conversation, but tossed off, "*Don't leave them in there too long*," as the elevator descended.

When they got to the restaurant, the maître d' caught a glance of Jenni's jeans and boots and pulled on his mask of polite refusal, until his specs must have registered that Jenni wasn't just anyone in jeans. Plus, she was with Nekoka, who was obviously one of *those* types of people, and he seated them after parading them through the entire dining area where everyone else was dressed in social finery.

Sitting near the window with a view of Portland's brightly lit skyscrapers, Nekoka scanned the drinks list. With a scowl, she said, "Jenni, there's no yummy drinks."

"Just ask for cream."

"You think they'll give me cream?" Nekoka asked and caught a young man, blond and tall, walking up behind Jenni. His long waiter's apron almost met the floor, and his shirt was starched and white. Posture upright, chin level, a contented half-smile on his face, his bearing and manner reminded her of gentry. His eyes, specless like all the wait staff in high-class eateries, were focused on Nekoka. He winked and continued on.

Cyrus Anderson, 23, waiter for Blue Stripe restaurant, made a good wage, too. Lived in the Hawthorne District and was owned by a calico and a gray tabby. And would you look at that...he was one of Nekoka's followers on her feed. They have, as she mind-dashed over his past comments, interacted a few times. He'd told her, in fact, he was quite skilled at petting and followed the line with a winky. Promising.

She sent him a text: Hey Cyrus, Whatcha doing tonight?

"Nekoka." A bit of bread stick pinged her between the eyes.

"What?" She tore her gaze away from Cyrus' retreating shoulders.

"Were you even listening? Do you have our debit card?" Jenni's eyebrows rose in frustration. "I don't want another *Le Remo* incident."

One time. Years ago. *Le Remo* actually didn't take cards, and they hadn't had enough cash to pay for dinner. Jenni was still pulling her whiskers for it. Now, few places took cash, and everyone accepted e-pay of some sort.

With a show of teeth a magician would have been proud of, Nekoka opened up a flap of skin near her waist where she'd created a safe pocket for Whisker, and pulled out the card. They didn't need a card; Nekoka could pay through Whisker, but Jenni had this thing with tangible objects. "We could have just ordered through Whisker and e-paid, you codger." She handed it over the table to Jenni. "If you're so worried about it, you keep it."

Jenni's expression softened, and she shook her head. "No, you keep it. I just wanted to make sure."

Nekoka prickled inside. Then sniffed, and looked away, up into the ceiling like a martyr. She knew she could always get Jenni when she pulled the martyr card. "You just don't trust me."

Jenni snorted. "About as far as I can throw you."

Nekoka purred...Jenni had a mean right arm.

"Can I help you ladies?"

Their waiter, not the cute blond who reminded her of English nobility, gave them a welcoming smile. Sam Gould, 36, married, an avid hiker who loved to plaster his feed with pictures of him and his lab by every waterfall in the northwest. Jenni ordered asparagus truffle risotto, and Nekoka picked the plank-baked salmon, both ignoring the high price tag of their meals.

"Oh, and a large glass of cream, please."

"Of course, ma'am, anything else?"

"A coke, please," Jenni said, and he nodded before he retreated to turn in their order.

An elderly woman came up, dressed impeccably with gray hair pulled up in a fancy twist and a deeply lined face. "I just wanted to thank you ladies for helping the police and firemen at the accident yesterday." She gave them a brief nod and returned to her seat. A few other patrons clapped for a moment before going went back to their meals.

Nekoka beamed. "I think I like this place."

Plus, the salmon was excellent and the cream thick.

I cannot believe Scratch is at my restaurant. I can be free, totally, finally came a reply as they nearly completed dinner. I'm off at 2am.

Where would you like to meet? I'm staying at this hotel.

I know. ;)

Oh, you've done your homework.

Just a little.

My friend won't want us messing up her sleep. So, meet downstairs at the entrance at 2:15?

See you then.

Pleased, Nekoka sent her thoughts back to her inbox and saw another message she'd missed while she was eating. Her brain went from pre-sex anticipation to uncomfortable resignation.

Found signs of autodrive system malfunction in cars at crash. The message came from Officer Geier. *You were right.*

Sorry, eating. More details...? she responded, then quick as thought added, *please.*

Cyrus sashayed up, his long apron swaying with his stride, and gave Nekoka and Jenni each a plate with a slice of cheesecake. "On the house," he said in a low purr, eyes half-lidded and suggestive. Nekoka nearly laughed. She so enjoyed it when they tried to seduce her. But really, there was no need.

"I added some whip to the side of yours." Dimples lined his cheeks, he grinned so hard.

Nekoka purred. "Thank you, Cyrus. I'll see you tonight."

He smirked confidently. "Tonight." He sashayed off again to help another customer.

"New friend?" Jenni asked, not really sounding shocked. "He's maybe twenty."

"Twenty-three. And he's so pretty," she said with longing, leaning her chin on one hand as she stared at his shoulders, back, and ass, her tail tip twitching. "He says he's good at petting. We've got a date. But," her gaze shot back to Jenni, "more importantly, the crash was orchestrated, the drive systems had been compromised. The police proved it, so it's not just my word."

Jenni stilled. She took one sip of water and set the glass down.

What the hell? No expression on her face.

Waiting for more news from John. Just found out. Missed the text earlier.

Their waiter came up with the paper bill, and while Nekoka slipped him their card, she forwarded John's message to Jenni, who pulled out her phone to read it. Jenni hated wearing glasses and gloves, unless they were stylish shades and those were not wired. The idea of being so disconnected gave Nekoka the heeby jeebies.

Nekoka's phone pinged her. John's response popped into her inbox. *Police models suggested the cars were all set on specific courses to converge on semi, including gasoline tanker. Our tech guys confirmed the compromised systems. Silva and several others explained their cars were unresponsive.*

Nekoka forwarded it to Jenni and responded to all with her next text. So, Silva stuck in a mess of hacked cars. With the semi truck with those kidnapped Seeded.

Going to be a media circus, John texted followed by a link.

The link led to a clip of Eliza Silva, looking worn around the edges, a bruise on one cheek and a bandage over her temple hiding her full, dark hair:

"The horrifying event took many lives. Portland is in mourning, as are many families and friends of the victims of the ten-vehicle pile-up on Interstate 84 just east of Interstate 205. It was through the heroic efforts of emergency personnel that I and many others survived the fires. To them, I say thank you. But most of all, I thank God for protecting me during my pass through Hell."

She's thanking God? Why not the heroic SEEDED who pulled her ass out of that mangled sardine can?

What do you expect? John replied. And your previous pics are all over the place. She can't hide that she was at least with Fiann at the crash.

Nekoka's tail flipped in irritation.

"Nekoka, it's not important," Jenni said.

"It is!" she said, drawing more attention to herself than she'd already earned. She dropped her voice and leaned over the table, cheesecake forgotten. "You have these people who hate us, just because we exist. Just because some alien plugged our brains with a magic superseed. And *we* are better than them. That's what I don't get. Why the attitude, when they are obviously the lesser?"

"They're afraid," Jenni said, contrite. She reached out and stroked Nekoka's head. Nekoka instinctively pressed into it. "You're too ferocious for them. Too big and amazing. They don't know how to deal with it." She ceased petting, probably conscious of even more attention. They were cooler than supermodels or NBA players.

Nekoka felt a smile pull apart her frown, even though she'd given a smile no permission to cross her face. "Yeah, she sucks. Gracie would totally subdue her with scripture recitation for using God as some sort of evol shield." Nekoka never liked the deep religious beliefs of Jenni's girlfriend, but she was Puerto Rican Catholic, so Nekoka couldn't really hold it against her.

Jenni was staring down at her plate. Nekoka nudged her with a toe under the table.

"Have you talked to Grace recently?" Nekoka asked, knowing she could peek into Jenni's phone to find the answer, but she tended to ask first when it came to her friends. Secrets were her catnip, but she'd learned to respect privacy through the gentle but firm scolding by those who had the patience to deal with her. "I know this isn't easy for you. And, ah," she cleared her throat, "I appreciate you coming with me, I mean, it means everything, but I know you need to go back, because you can't just up and abandon your girlfriend, and, umm..." Her friend remained silent. "It'd be okay if you wanted to go home." Nekoka could read the struggle on Jenni's face, trying to remain passive, to be calm, but warring with another matter altogether. She was always the stable one, the one in control, and Nekoka knew something wasn't right in the love bed of Jenni and Grace.

Before she could ask—and really, did she want to dredge up bad feelings right now?—another message came in. Nekoka automatically read it. Go to Washington and Third. The tarnish mutes the bright city. Help her.

Nekoka checked who it was from. A cold sliver of uncertainty dribbled into her vast vat of ego. It was that informant again. No address, no trail. Nekoka dove her mind into Whisker and tore through the metadata. Finally, she found some code, and she sniffed after that, but the trail was dead. Whoever left the message was good. Either an excellent hacker, or someone like her, a *kokogyo-nin*, someone with psychic power over computers.

Her ears perked up. She'd never met another like her.

But what if this person was the one who'd sent those cars smashing into each other? Her ears pulled back to her skull.

"Jenni." Jenni looked at Nekoka, the emotional display disappearing due to whatever she saw on Nekoka's face. "We need to go. Something happening a few blocks north."

Jenni crumbled up her napkin and tossed it on her cheesecake plate. "What?"

Nekoka pressed her lips together. She needed to filter through her own info, search for any proof of her secret informant, and intel, before she told Jenni. A computer whiz that left nothing for even Nekoka to find...even pre-Seed Nekoka was a force when it came to computers. No, she'd tell Jenni later, when she had it all figured out and could dazzle her friend with her brilliance.

"Not sure. Someone needs our help, I think."

Jenni cocked one eyebrow. "Don't you have a date?"

"Yeah, but that's hours away." Nekoka scooted her chair back. "Come on. This is about saving people!"

"Oh, well, why didn't you say so?" *This better not be a geek chase, or some random naked jogging event you found on Living It Up.*

No, it's a tip about someone needing help. Honestly, I've no info on the validity. Let's get to a street camera so I can hop the vids and see if we can find anything.

Okay, if you say so. "Shall we?" Jenni pushed her chair back and stood, drawing attention with the simple act of standing. Eyes drew towards Jenni like bees to a flower. The women left the restaurant, though Nekoka made a point to wave at Cyrus.

Nekoka watched her friend. She seemed to have perked up after their non-discussion of Grace. Jenni liked to help people, and any prospect of doing so gave her purpose. She was one of those genuine heroes that some thought all of the Seeded should be. Those who grew up on comic books and science fiction expected that if you have a superpower, you should save the world. They didn't realize that most people just want to live and let live. Or enjoy the fame and fruits of being famous, but didn't really want to put any effort into actually doing anything to earn it.

Jenni was different. Jenni *was* a hero, without even thinking about the fame and riches. Nekoka couldn't give a rat's ass whether people thought she was *good* and *heroic*, but Jenni was her friend, and she would always help Jenni.

Wading through the people on the ground floor, they popped out into the late evening, still alive in downtown Portland. Nekoka walked toward the river three blocks, then turned north as a man wearing a Darth Vader outfit tottered by on a unicycle, blowing on some bagpipes.

"Hey, you wanna share the force with me?" Nekoka called, but Jenni was already moving. Another few blocks north, flashing lights and a flock of drones pinpointed the 'altercation'. Nekoka trotted to catch up.

An ambulance and three police cars lit up the side street not a block away from Huber's Cafe, Portland's oldest, and perhaps loudest, restaurant. Two women stood behind the police line and watched as a bagged body was loaded up into the ambulance. Soon, more people joined. Jenni sniffed the air while Nekoka listened hard, both with her ears and with her mind that was tuned into the chatter of the computer systems singing all around her. She slipped over to a street camera-light and began filtering through block by block to see if anything jumped out. She wished she could get to the recordings on file.

Nearby, a young black woman said, "I didn't kill anyone! Let me go," twisting and turning her wrists held tight by metal cuffs. Nekoka couldn't get a good line up of her face through the gathering crowd, so SPYme had nothing to report.

A policeman walked the herd of onlookers, and as he approached Jenni and Nekoka, Jenni asked him what was going on.

Sergeant MacRoe lifted his chin. "Police business. Why don't you ladies just move on?"

Nekoka took issue with the way the man said 'ladies' and decided she didn't like him. "Who died?" she asked, leaning over the yellow tape towards the man. He took a step back, his hand going for his nightstick.

"Remain where you are, evol." Sergeant MacRoe's voice held firm, and Nekoka leaned back, her body poised to dart either left or right if he chose to attack. The party line was that people in Portland loved the Seeded. They had special Seeded parades and hosted SuperCon. This *kusoyaro*. He ruined Portland!

"Officer, perhaps we can help," Jenni, ever the diplomat, offered. "We've had some experience in aiding the police in crimes in New Orleans."

"Well, that's the south. We do things by the book here."

Nekoka wanted to inform him that they'd saved over a dozen lives earlier by aiding a Seeded member of the Portland police but didn't. Bringing attention to John might not make his position on the force any easier.

"I found the body, damn it! Why do you think I killed him? Asshole, let me go! You've no proof. Where's my due process?"

Jenni introduced herself as Fiann, said she could read the woman's mind to validate her testimony, when Nekoka caught the woman's face. Dana Schultz, 17, Seeded. With a little search, Nekoka found she swallowed fire: hot coals, burning torches. She was an entertainer and fire dancer and there were masses of vids of her performing.

"Keep back, witch. If you continue to hamper this investigation, I will arrest you."

Nekoka hissed, then immediately texted John Geier about the situation, noting who the cop was. Guess she was going to make it difficult for him, after all.

Shall we break her out? Nekoka thought at Jenni.

No, leave the police to it. Theoretically, if the woman they are arresting isn't guilty, she will be let go. We don't want to mess with a police investigation.

Nekoka cocked one eyebrow. Oh, her sweet, naïve Jenni.

Well, Jenni might have faith in the law, but Nekoka snapped a shot of Sergeant MacRoe and began a deep background scan on him.

CHAPTER 11

Berlin

Berlin Fischer leaned forward on the park bench, the sidewalk between him and the Willamette flush with walkers and cyclists even at the early hour. The left pointer finger of Berlin's glove was gone, ripped open before he'd even found the gloves at a free handout by Sisters of the Cloth. The white flesh of his finger stood out against the pale off-white of the newspaper he'd saved from the trash. Something pink and gooshy had spread a stain along the upper right-hand corner, but it didn't make it unreadable. People hurried by as he muttered under his breath, squinting at the lines from the newsprint with some effort. His eyes weren't that good.

"Mommy, that man is white."

Berlin peered through his plastic shades into the face of a little girl, pig-tailed and sweet. He smiled. She shielded herself with her mother's legs as the older woman dragged her daughter away, refusing to look at him. "Leave that boy alone," she said. Behind them wandered the gray blur of an old ghost, long gone to pattern, all memories of its past self dissolved.

It was just one ghost of many he spotted throughout his day.

He dropped his gaze back to the print, the words blurry. He knew what people thought when they looked at him. Kept their kids away. Gave him extra space as they walked by. He never, ever asked for handouts. Never even talked to anyone. He knew what he looked like. The other homeless called him the Ghost, because of his albino skin, but he was nothing like the formless fog that made up most of the dead.

The buzz of a drone set him skulking deeper into his jacket. He wasn't laying on the bench, and he didn't have a cart or bag nearby, so it shouldn't tag him as homeless and then squeal out its high-pitched alarm. He held his breath until the drone moved on down the park towards a large lawn where children were screaming and chasing the geese.

Maybe he should just go.

He blinked, scrunched up his nose while he waited for his emotions to pass. No good letting people think he was a wino. So, he cracked the paper with a sharp flick and held it open wide. The sun was blinding, even through his sunglasses, so he tilted the newspaper to avoid the harsh light trying to char his sensitive retinas.

"Seeded Save the Day at Interstate 84 Pile-up," the headline read. Below that was a picture of five people walking away from the charred wreckage and a pile of metal debris off to the side. Berlin ran his pale finger over the faces of each one. First was a black man with tiny dreads sprouting from his head. His face, though pinched, was suave and attractive. He had an air of confidence about him that Berlin found off-putting. He knew men could do terrible things with that kind of power.

A woman walked beside him, taller than the other two women farther down the line, but no skyscraper, on the heavy side. The camera caught her in mid-stride, giving her a sense of defying gravity. She scowled, a model of put-upon frustration, though her hair was styled in a way the little girl would have enjoyed, if it was mussed.

Next was a man Berlin recognized, the officer that sometimes talked to the homeless and asked them how they were. Berlin never spoke with him, but he'd heard through whispers on the streets he was a nice guy, though the pushers and hustlers hated him. Taller than the rest, he had a bush of hair caught in the frozen time of the photograph. He looked like he came from some magazine ad, with his jacket tossed over his shoulder and his head held high.

The next person was a woman, with shoulder-length hair, the color indistinguishable in newsprint, though it looked darker. She was brushing a hand across her brow, her jeans torn and dirty, maybe with blood, maybe just the soil, Berlin couldn't tell.

And finally came the oddity. The woman as fantastical as the furry art he'd used to browse on the internet when he'd had a home. She was short, a little shorter than the woman next to her, and practically dwarfed by the policeman. She had a sharply featured face with a dusting of fur on it—he could tell even through the grainy photo. Cat ears perched on the top of her head, peeking out of her long dark hair, and a tail swished behind her. Her hands and feet were normal, but her entire body was covered in that fur. Dark fur, so opposite to his own pale abnormality. She looked off into the distance, towards the crash site, her face awash with the betrayal she was feeling, as if in awe that catastrophes actually happen.

Investigators blame faulty autodrive systems in the I-84 pile-up.

Berlin skimmed the rest of the text until he reached the information that interested him.

Officer John Geier, a Seeded member of the newly announced Oregon GUMP Response (O.G.R.E.) arrived with four other Seeded to help in the rescue attempts. Pablo Castile, member of O.G.R.E. and owner of a popular dance club in Old Town called Rain, and Sylvia "Sepia" Montgomery, member of O.G.R.E. and guitarist for local band, Ravenous Red Death, aided in the rescue as well as two Seeded from New Orleans, Fiann and Scratch.

Scratch. Berlin laughed. He'd always thought it a silly name. He squinted at the photograph, studied the cat woman's eyes, two-dimensional and flat. "Scratch," he said reverently, running his finger over the picture several times. "You're a freak like me. I'm going to find you. Don't you worry."

CHAPTER 12

Nekoka

Cars cruised by during one of those magical slivers of time after the morning rush and before the lunch crowd charged in. Nekoka was making her way back to her hotel room with quite the swing to her tail. Cyrus had been deliciously athletic, willing, and creative, and she gave him the thumbs up to contact her again, suggesting another hook up—or two—before she departed, whenever that was.

She'd left him sprawled out on his cramped twin bed in his studio—larger than some apartments in the high-density towers she'd visited—a bit scratched up but totally blissed out. "Before you leave," he promised as she waved, closing the door behind her, feeling better than she had since her last romp. Until she checked her inbox and found an update from John.

Kid arrested last night was let go, though marginally battered. No evidence she had any connection to murder. She's got a record now. Hampering investigation and violence against an officer. Also, blaming the crash on Seeded. Nobody came forward about it yet. Keeping it out of the news.

Blaming it on the Seeded? Which Seeded? The guesstimate offered up a population of 210 million Seeded in the world—who would their culprit be? The anchor on Nuclear! News? The barista at the Dutch Brothers by the airport? Most likely Samantha Fontos, the Queen of the Endless Night, the voice of Seeded superiority and leader of Xenofontos. Maybe one of her minions?

Nekoka had to agree with Fontos' viewpoint; she gave a good argument. Those with power have more valuable than those without. Just common sense. But why would she have caused the crash? Nekoka thought it out. Okay, so Eliza Silva was there. And a truck full of kidnappees. Plus, there was that text.... Okay, maybe they weren't all *bakamono*.

With a spring to her step, she popped onto a local bus to get back to her hotel. Let's chat. Meet at Rain? she texted John, unsure of an answer this early, but one came before the near empty bus crossed the river.

Sure, I'll have Pablo open it for you. Lunch time?

Okay, see you then.

Upon her return to the hotel room, she pounced on Jenni, rolling her friend over as Jenni tried to beat her with a pillow.

"Evil. Foul. Wicked," Jenni groaned. Nekoka dodged under one pillow strike, but then another caught her in the chest, and with a burst of foam, she was flung off the bed.

She sat up, grinning.

"Oh, for all the.... Keep your cheer to yourself." Jenni rolled over, giving Nekoka her back.

Nekoka frowned. She should have brought some coffee.

"Fine, grump. I didn't get much sleep either." She waited for some rude comment, but Jenni didn't say anything. "We're meeting John at Rain at noon. 'Kay?"

"Fine," Jenni said into the pillow.

Nekoka crawled across the bed and curled up behind Jenni, wrapping an arm around her friend's waist. Jenni grabbed her hand and squeezed. Nekoka relaxed, purring a little before she fell asleep.

NEKOKA AND JENNI PUSHED through the doors of Rain, escaping the real rain outside that had slurped into the city with familiar ease. An unexpected silence wrapped up the establishment. Nekoka shook her entire body, propelling droplets all over Jenni and the floor. Jenni stiffened, then wiped her wetted hands down on her jeans, not even bothering to give Nekoka a glare-powered scolding. A quick scan revealed no sign of John. Billie lounged at one table, her invisispecs down and the mitted fingers of her right hand twitching away as she accessed her specs, drinking coffee with her free hand. Propped against the railing of the second level, Pablo smiled down at them. Nekoka waved as he descended the stairs.

With Pablo's every stride and strut, Nekoka's inner hot bod aficionado purred deeply. Cyrus was lovely, but Pablo oozed desirability. *Damn.*

"Pablo, looking lickable today," Nekoka said with a husky burr.

"Oh, a licking. Is that why I had the bar opened early?" he asked with a smirk, leaning against the bar with one hip, the long lines of his body on display, the cheeky grin holding promises and secrets. There was always an element of grace and fluidity to Pablo's movements, and it wasn't any surprise to Nekoka that every pose, every posture he presented, cast him in an elegant light.

How could he simply lean and look sexy? And not be attainable? It wasn't fair.

"Your fault if you lead her on," Jenni warned.

Nekoka laughed, then slipped on her sexy smirk. "Well—" Nekoka stalked over to him, one foot delicately placed before the other, letting her own sensuality slip into every contraction and relaxation of her muscles "—not the original reason, though we could totally shift purposes." Nekoka reached out with the intention to run her fingers over his chest, which was deliciously wrapped up in tight silver satin that contrasted beautifully against his skin. Oh, she could just run her tongue up—

Jenni popped up on a stool and asked, "How many feeds are you watching, Pablo? Billie—?"

Billie flipped up her specs. "Checking out some of the fubar right now."

Nekoka dropped her hand, catching Pablo's raised brow. They'd play this cat-and-mouse game later, now there were other mouses afoot.

"Okay, spill, what's up?" Pablo said.

"I'll just send you the important ones." Nekoka scooted onto the stool beside Jenni and zapped a few feeds and articles over to Pablo and Billie.

Pablo pushed himself off the bar with a press of his hip and pulled a phone out of his back pocket. "Well, I did see the articles on the car crash. Not really surprised you didn't give them your real names."

Jenni shrugged. "We're used to that. We always use our Seeded names in New Orleans."

"Secret identity?" Pablo said, tilting forward and dropping his voice with exaggerated conspiracy. "Since I know who you two really are, does that mean I'm a select member of a small group or that your secret's not all that secret?"

Nekoka laughed, her tail switching over the edge of the stool. "It could mean that we're going to have to kill you."

Pablo stood straight, blinking in mock confusion. "Well, if that's the case, who are you people, and why are you in my club?"

The doors pushed open, letting in a stray gust of moist wind and John, looking bedraggled with his misted hair and rain jacket. "Hey, guys. Thanks for coming." He rubbed his hands through his hair, brushing off some of the water and poofing up the entire mess.

"No prob. So, why the impromptu meeting at my bar?" Pablo asked, strolling forward to give John a friendly handshake.

"Well," John pulled out a VR-glove from an inside jacket pocket and slipped it on, "I was hoping for lunch." He beamed at Pablo. "But, as you might know, there are some interesting things happening. I messaged the whole crew." He glanced around. "Missing Trior, Sepia—Chandler, you here?"

"I'm here."

Nekoka nearly leapt to the ceiling to hold herself upside down by her claws. Her gaze skipped across the dance floor, the tables, the booths in back. A man sat at a table just behind Billie. Totally nondescript. Standing, he nodded at John, stuffing his hands into his jeans pockets in such an 'ah shucks' kind of way. His shirt boasted a huge ax on a green background with *Portland Timbers* scrawled over the bottom. He came across as a total non-threat. Nekoka blinked. He hadn't been there a few seconds before.

"And you are?" she asked. Though as she focused on him, SPYme told her exactly who this was, sometimes it was polite to ask.

The man, light brown hair, simple clothing, plain face, ducked his head. "Chandler." He approached them with his hand held out, and Nekoka examined it from afar, before Jenni came forward and shook it.

"Jenni, that is Nekoka."

"I know." Chandler sat back down. Nekoka narrowed her eyes. She would have to keep her eyes on that one.

"He can't help it," Pablo said, smiling over at Chandler, narrowing his almond-shaped eyes—the new guy was a dull yin to Pablo's bright yang. "His power makes him completely unremarkable."

Nekoka's ears perked forward. "Oh, really. That could be..." *dreadful* "...useful. So, you have this...what, Overlook ability?"

Chandler smiled, totally friendly, and Nekoka warmed to him in an instant.

"I like that name," Chandler said. "Better than Notice-Me-Not. Do you mind if I use it?"

"Oh, no, by all means." Her ego inflated. Contrary to Jenni's speculations, it did have room to grow. She loved naming powers and Seeded. She updated her database.

"Trior said he'd be a little late, and we should start," Billie said, throwing her long hair over her shoulder before she pulled her specs down again. "And I'm ordering pizza from next door. Everyone good with that?" She got agreements all around.

"All right then." John grabbed a chair and sat at Billie's table. The rest all grabbed chairs or scooted into the circle. "Let's start with the crash."

"The crash caused by someone very skilled hacking the autodrive systems in multiple cars that crashed purposefully into a truck full of kidnapped nuls as well as a car carrying one of the spokesmen for the anti-Seeded movement," Nekoka babbled, to make sure everyone was onboard. She thought back to that text: Your day is about to change. Nothing is as it seems, and wondered just what that meant. Did it mean the crash in general? Dealing with Eliza? Or that truck full of Seeded with little to no powers stuffed in it without their say so? The biggest mystery: who was it from?

"Do they have any suspects yet?" Jenni asked. "Other than speculation, but real solid suspects?"

Nekoka, what have you found?

Working on it.

Who could hack that?

Honestly, any number of people. I'll send you a list I've collected so far, but these are just people with good skills, not really suspects. I'll search some more. Watch me.

Nekoka disengaged her consciousness and dove into Whisker, effectively turning the dial of her brain to a different frequency and tuning the room out. With Jenni guarding her body, she wasn't as nervous about the psychic dive. She had to be careful of her surroundings. Back home, Eugene had died her fur pink when she'd been prowling the e-streams. Not that it stayed pink once she realized it, but still. Some people just couldn't be trusted.

Thought-quick, she modified an existing search program to gather all information pertaining to the crash. That wasn't a challenge at all. The real challenge was when she slipped into Whisker's Wi-Fi and transported herself *out there*. Away from her body. Directly into the police department's mainframes. She never ever did this without Jenni nearby. It left her body defenseless, her mind open to attack by aggressive programs as if she were a program herself. But it was fast and thorough.

After a little study of the security code, she snipped lines, replacing commands with a version she rather approved of. Not with anything that would compromise the system to an outside attack, but the new code would now let one little kitty slip through. Kitties were not very large and in fact, it only took her about three minutes and a half page of tweaks, and she was in. And when she was in, she released her search program...her little squirrel.

All of this had to be tiptoe quiet. Whether she hacked it remotely, or from within the very system she was compromising, some anti-virus could still catch her actions. She never liked fighting software while vulnerable and skinless in their domain.

Her squirrel scurried around the police reports and dug for nuts of info. Nekoka lovingly imagined it gathering up important information in its cheeks, but really it just shuffled data out through the security breach back to Whisker, the file on Whisker growing by each millisecond.

Theoretically, Nekoka could leave the squirrel to it, and it could scurry out when finished, but she waited to close her little door. No reason to leave any proof of an unexpected visitor.

Though, now that she was inside the police records, she had another fish to filet. Sergeant MacRoe.

And wasn't he a piece? Several profiling complaints against evols, falsifying evidence for search warrants, and a bent for brutality. As Nekoka dug deeper, she felt a nudge in her mind. A fluttering of thoughts against her own, but words didn't come through. Nekoka focused on the touch, ascending from the police mainframe, until words began to form.

How are things?

At this distance, Nekoka got no sense of emotion, no urgency, no worry. *Need me?*

Been gone a while.

Had she? Well, Nekoka checked her squirrel and found its search was complete. With another quick mind jump, she searched for MacRoe's most recent arrest of Dana Schultz, fire dancer, and erased the young woman's record and began pulling herself from MacRoe's files until something interesting caught her attention. Most of the complaints against him were filed by Officer John Geier. And Officer John Geier had been put on crap duties, mainly dealing with casing the homeless sector, kept off of homicide, which he'd applied to several times, as well as the narcotics team.

Hub city, maybe. Hub police department, no way.

When she surfaced her mind from the morass of the electronic telecom waves and settled back into her body, an elephant weight of lethargy pressed down into her. She mewled and checked the time. One hour! She sucked in a shuddering breath and felt a hand run down her head, along her neck and spine, soft and caressing. The scent of melted cheese and pepperoni curled against her nose. She opened her eyes.

Jenni stroked her long hair again, and Nekoka wanted to shift into her other skin and crawl into Jenni's lap, but she was too damned tired. "I'm toast," she said and leaned her head on Jenni's shoulder.

"Did you get anything?" John asked.

Nekoka's eyes shifted to John, who had doffed his raincoat and jacket and was lounging in the bar chair in a white T-shirt a shade too tight, his hairy arms showing off their bunches of muscle. Nekoka licked her lips; John pinked but offered her a half-smile. His hair had dried in a haze of brown and as he ran his hands through the mess again and again, Nekoka finally knew how it got whipped into such a froth. Next to him was another man she didn't know. Trior Juaire, from South Carolina, owner of Taste of Heaven distillery in the distillery blocks of the Pearl District, about ten blocks away from Rain. O.G.R.E. member number six.

"Oh, is she back now?" the newcomer asked, his voice a custard of Southern charm. "I'm Trior, and it is a pleasure to meet you." He stood and took off his trilby hat, revealing his black hair reaching past his ears, and pressed the hat to his chest as he bowed. Every inch of his suited frame declared plantation gentleman. Zack would have loved him.

"Nekoka," she managed before a yawn cracked her introduction. "And the pleasure is all mine." She attempted a seductive purr while her eyes roamed over his body—too hidden under the layers of linen—but all she could manage was a toothy smile.

Trior chuckled and added, "With such skill and beauty, my dear, I am certain you offer the greater pleasure."

Oh snap! That got Nekoka's attention on all channels. Jenni patted her indulgently on the head.

I've got the time, if you've got the interest. Perhaps we can discuss sharing such pleasure, she sent to his specs, never one to lose an opportunity.

His white dress glove twitched, and she received a message. Time...how about the energy? He winked across the table at her, and she huffed out a chuckle. Right now, she didn't even have the energy to lick herself.

"I got stuff," she said wearily. "I'm organizing it right now, and then I'll feed it to each of you."

"How long with that take?" Pablo asked.

The bar phone rang, and Billie went to go get it while Nekoka assessed the time for her program to have completed its cataloging of data. Jenni kept up a steady rubbing that had a purr rattling through Nekoka's chest.

"Did you want some pizza?" Jenni asked.

"Yeah, when I'm done." Her belly rumbled. She gave Jenni a sheepish grin.

"Pablo." The tone in Billie's voice drew everyone to look towards her. "It's Jasen. Say's Sepia is missing. She was supposed to meet with a recording agent early this morning. The agent said she'd never showed." She put her hand over the receiver. "Jasen's pissed, but it's not like her to miss something this big. He wants to know if it was an O.G.R.E. call that made her miss."

Pablo's dark skin had taken on an unhealthy sallowness, even though his voice remained steady. "No. Not that she told any of us. And she's not the kind of woman to flake on something this big. This was their chance. Trior?"

Indigent glee bubbled up inside Nekoka, popping out as a snort. "She probably found herself a nice camo party where coon hound breeders gathered to guzzle homebrew swill and compliment each other's piercings and forgot about the meeting."

Everyone ignored her. Trior's fingers began twitching as he sent a message.

"No, Jasen," Billie said into the phone. "Of course. We'll let you know. Thanks for calling." She hung up, pale eyes crinkled in concern.

"Think she's hurt? Anyone call the hospital?" Jenni asked, pulling out her own phone.

Though still totally steamrolled by her latest dive, Nekoka did a simple search in the local 'missing persons' and 'found persons' catalog available on the police department's website. None were Sepia. She let Jenni know. She could hack into the hospital's database to see if Sepia had been admitted at each hospital, but she didn't have the gumption for that.

"I'll make some calls," Chandler said, startling Nekoka again. It was just creepy, how he faded away.

"Nekoka, can you find her car?" Jenni asked, forcing Nekoka to open her eyes again. The bar seemed really bright.

"I can—"

"She doesn't own a car," Trior interrupted. "She transits everywhere, and when she needs a car, she uses mine, and she doesn't have it now."

"Maybe it was that asshole, MacRoe," Nekoka suggested, nestling up against Jenni again, practically sitting in the other woman's lap, though there wasn't much room. "Maybe he bashed her upside the head and kidnapped her."

This time, apparently, they listened.

"MacRoe," Pablo said in near enough growl that Nekoka found it worth her while to pry open her lids and catch that blaze of fury lighting up his eyes. "He's an ass, but why would you say that?"

Nekoka only shrugged.

"Well, there is always the option of kidnapping," John said grudgingly. "Though I'd be impressed by anyone facing down Sepia. It is possible, especially if it was some powerful Seeded."

Nekoka's ears twitched. She gave her mind two seconds to mull that around, then nodded. "You'd think that with her kind and loving nature, that nobody would want to do her harm."

Below her head, Jenni's shoulders shifted, maybe a sigh, maybe a shrug. "Looks like you might be the next target then," she said.

Nekoka laughed. Ah, Jenni. She nuzzled in closer.

"So..." Nekoka said. "Don't care about the hijacked cars anymore now that little miss sunshine has gone for a prolonged, drug induced holiday?"

The room went quiet; Nekoka decided to open her eyes. Everyone was staring at her.

Nekoka...

What? Everyone's so sensitive.

Trior had a stunned expression; his hand paused in mid-message. Pablo stood, a very unfriendly, un-Pablo like frown turned his beauty into something cruel. "Nekoka, you are new here, and I don't know you well, so I will give you the benefit of the doubt that you are not always a cold-hearted bitch."

Nekoka flinched.

"Sepia is our friend," Pablo continued. "She's saved my butt more than I can count, and I would do anything for her. She's loyal and dedicated and helps people. Something I don't think you've any notion about."

Something inside of her felt as big as a gnat, something inside of her felt *ashamed.*

"Sepia is *my* friend." Nearly a roar, Pablo's lecture sank into Nekoka like a narcotic. "Now, keep your bitter words to yourself and either leave or help. I would appreciate any help you can give us, but not if all you're going to do is hen-peck my friend because you can't get over your own inadequacies and self-esteem issues." Pablo walked away, his feet colliding with the wood facade of the dance floor. Nekoka watched him, her heart shame-shattered, as he stomped up the stairs and slipped beyond her view.

Deep down, she knew she was selfish. Actually, the thought wasn't even that deep down. It was simply who she was. Weren't most people selfish, human-norm or human-special alike? Everyone was. Even altruism was selfishness...doing nice things because you wanted people to acknowledge your deed. But never before had she seen that as a bad thing. Nekoka cast a glance at Jenni, but her face came through blurry. Nekoka blinked, certain she saw a storm cloud of disappointment churning through that blur. Wondering if this time Jenni would be fed up with Nekoka and would leave her behind.

Someone said something, but Nekoka couldn't quite parse it out from the repeated mantra of 'you're not worthy' and 'you suck' playing on auto-cycle through her mind.

She wasn't very helpful, either. She just got in everyone's way. Totally *kuradanai.* She should just leave, so nobody had to suffer her presence again.

Slowly, she pushed back her chair, the scraping of the feet against the wooden floor barely registering, and walked towards the door. Behind her she could hear people talking, Billie with her kind voice, Jenni, her own words disgusted. The street was busy, an endless line of cars inching along, horns bipping. She didn't know where she was going to go, what she was going to do. Did it matter? She'd go somewhere and keep out of people's way because she was only a nuisance.

"Nekoka."

Nekoka turned right, towards the river, and started walking.

"Nekoka!" *Nekoka.*

Something buzzed in her head, but the sound of thoughts slumped under the truth of what she amounted to. Nothing.

She was nothing.

Nekoka's body changed, slipped down into the small form of a cat, and she slunk away, slipping through pedestrians' legs and under the cars struggling down the clogged street, tail low and tucked to her rump.

Rattling through her mind was Jenni, screaming, *Nekoka! Snap out of it. It isn't real, it's Pablo!* but soon enough the distance cut her words off.

NEKOKA SLUNK FROM ONE dark place to another, her belly dragging along the filthy, damp streets. They all hated her. Everyone. Her parents hadn't cared about anything but what she could accomplish. Her friends in New Orleans didn't care about her and were going to go Certified, the label as heroes more important than one single friendship. Pablo thought she was trash.

Jenni didn't care. Jenni was always disappointed in Nekoka. Disappointed in how horrible she was.

Something in her chest broke.

Years ago, before Nekoka had been born and she was just Michiko, she and her parents were visiting family back in Japan. It was spring, she remembered, and the cherry blossoms covered everything, the sidewalk, cars, the roads. Little pink petals, as delicate as spun candy. Michiko had won some programming fair prize for grade schoolers, and her parents had been very nice to her. That trip was part of their approval package.

The small family was passing through one of the JR stations, and Michiko had somehow gotten separated from her parents. There were so many people. She was little, and they were adults, and they were packed in, and Michiko couldn't find *haha* or *chichi* and she was very, very afraid.

Lost and alone and with nobody there for her.

Nobody to care for her.

Her parents hadn't found her for what seemed like hours, though it was probably only a little over thirty minutes, but still. Michiko had clung to her mother's skirts, shivering but not crying, while her parents scolded her for getting lost. And she knew she'd done wrong, wandered off, not paid attention. But she still wished they'd found her faster, kept a more watchful eye on her. Protected her better.

Now, she was just as alone, surrounded by an army of uncaring eyes.

She padded along the pavement, her tail trailing low behind her. Tires squealed; a chime rang as she slunk across a street. The smells of the neighborhood, the shops squatting on the edge of the road, the construction, the strip of bushes planted before multistory condo complexes were all a bombardment of information that her refined cat senses attempted to categorize, but her brain was too busy mulling and dwelling that soon enough, she was lost.

She found herself at a city park: brown grass worn down to dirt in places, jets of water spurting out of a brick fountain set level with the ground. The jets would dance, shooting forth in an easy pattern. Without intention, Nekoka felt a twitch in her rear, her chase instinct clicking on through her gloom, and she burst from her spot under a bush and dashed after a beam of water.

It pumped from one hole in the red and gray bricks to another hole about ten yards away, and Nekoka leapt through the air, splashing her paw to break up the stream, splattering herself in chlorinated water. It was then that she remembered she hated getting wet. With a yarl, she raced to hide under a park bench.

The scent of rat urine tickled her whiskers. She peered in the bushes for beady eyes.

"Hey there, little kitty."

Nekoka slunk lower to the aromatic cement patch underneath the bench. A hand was reaching for her. All she could see was an arm in a stained jacket that had probably once claimed waterproofing and a gloved hand, one uncovered finger sickly white, like something that had been dead and underwater for far too long.

"Come on, kitty. I won't hurt you."

Yeah, right, Nekoka thought. Probably some homeless guy who wanted some fresh meat. She'd seen them catch the pigeons back home, deft hands snapping necks before they gutted the birds and tossed them onto a fire.

The man clicked his tongue in an almost enticing way, but she wasn't really a cat, and she wasn't really curious. Well, that was a lie, but she didn't want to go to this crazy, smelly man.

"Okay, I'll just sit here and talk to you." The hand pulled away, and then legs approached the bench, and finally he sat on the bench. Nekoka knew she should just run away, but she was intrigued. And a little lonely. Not to mention lost. He wore jeans and white running shoes, and the smell of the ensemble caused Nekoka to turn her head away.

"I know who you are." Nekoka's body went cold. "You're special. A beautiful Abyssinian who doesn't deserve to be on the streets." His voice was young, gentle, yet eager with a soothing cadence. She twitched her skin, flicking her short, reddish-black fur. "You're noble—directly descended from the cats of Egypt. Perhaps I should build a shrine to you and bring you the choicest tidbits of the day." Nekoka liked that idea. "I would pet you and scratch behind your ears and keep you warm. Keep you clean and beautiful. Because you are beautiful." His soft voice lulled her, and she crawled out from under the park bench to look into the man's face.

She blinked, surprised that the paper white color of his finger spread to his face. A wide brimmed straw hat you'd find someone named Farmer John wearing shaded his head. When he saw her peek her head out from under the bench, he smiled hugely, a picket fence of large teeth. Nekoka strolled out from the shelter of the bench and sat with her tail curled around her paws. Through half-lidded eyes, and with a casual lick of her paw, she studied the man.

Youngish, upon further study, solidly landing in the late teens category. White hair, white skin. His sunglasses were like those Jenni would wear, just for hiding the eyes, not jacked-in at all, but were chosen for maximum coverage. He took off his gloves and crammed them into a pocket. White hands. Nekoka wondered if his eyes were pink like an albino lab rat's. He could be a natural mutant as happened in every living thing, or another Seeded, who'd picked up more of a physical oddness than most.

With his face half covered, she couldn't get a good read for SPYme.

His voice was pitched low, in that 'soothe the animal' way she'd heard from all sorts of people who wanted to touch her. How could she blame them? She was a perfect specimen of a cat. She had a knack for picking the right colors, ear tuffs, shading. That's what Jenni had said, anyway.

At the thought of Jenni, a surge of melancholy hit her. A vast universe of nothing rooted itself at the core of her belly. She shook her body, her skin rippling over her flesh, and jumped up on the bench. The solid shape of Whisker bulged slightly at her middle, tucked away inside her flesh pocket. She briefly considered texting Jenni, but a sneeze overtook her when she neared the guy, forcing her to cover her nose with a paw.

He laughed and said, "Well, you don't get many showers when you've got no home. I'm sorry my smell is distasteful to you, Aby." She cocked her head at him. "You don't mind if I call you Aby, do you?" Nekoka blinked at him, swished her tail. "Good," he said.

The guy finally fell into silence. Two kids—a toddler and a boy about five—ran through the fountain, soaking themselves as the mother watched on, eyes bouncing between her children and the albino man watching them. Other people passed by, laughing, couples leaning in towards each other, an old woman walking a terrier. Some gave the homeless man and his cat some distance, others passed by as if they were invisible. Notice-Me-Not. At this time, Nekoka liked that, being invisible.

Didn't want anyone else to see her, and judge her, and deem her worthless.

CHAPTER 13

Berlin

Berlin fiddled with the gloves in his pockets, running his fingers over the rough fabric. He wasn't one hundred percent certain, but hot damn if this kitty couldn't possibly, maybe be none other than Scratch, the mutant Seeded, a complete oddity like him, who was currently in Portland. Maybe it was wishful thinking, but this kitty didn't quite act like a simple cat.

And he was a near expert on Scratch. She was special.

It was hard to keep his shoulders hunched, to make himself small as he walked among the tourists and homeless with Scratch by his side. He strolled down Davis like a ringmaster in his own circus. He imagined African elephants decked with head dresses and horses with pretty ladies standing on their backs marching behind him.

Though he had his ambition to find her and was quite determined, he also hadn't, in his inner soul, believed it could happen. Had one of the ghosts instructed Berlin to write up a list of people he'd expected to show up at the park in the late morning of a Friday, his list would be lined with simple folk more likely to waltz right by instead of Scratch.

That shelter worker who sometimes played chess with him, the pigeon training bum from Burnside, Ethyl the crazy bag lady, maybe even Desere, his girlfriend from junior high, or the Mayor of Portland himself. All more likely than Scratch. She was a hero, saving people from crashes. She wouldn't have time for a stroll through the park.

Behind Belgian Bagels, Berlin had once met a singer from a folk band handing out free bagels to anyone who wanted one. For publicity, probably, but free food was free food. He'd been killed by an overdose two months ago, and *he* was higher on the list than Scratch, but then death wasn't a barrier to Berlin.

Though Berlin no longer had invisispecs, he had subscribed to Scratch's feed when he'd had a home and parents who took care of him. On her feed, she claimed to be a cat. A Japanese catgirl extraordinaire, he remembered her saying in a vid. Now, she was walking by him in kitty skin—his own lion ready to jump through a burning hoop. He loved being so close to his hero in her secret identity. It was his honor, and he would cherish it with all the other secrets he'd been given stewardship to.

He crossed through Old Town, the drones here rarely harassing the homeless like they did in the Pearl and Northwest, to the Firehouse. The street was a symphony of car horns, the pedestrian accompaniment of men and women shouting, arguing over who had what claim on the sidewalk, made it all feel lived-in. Familiar. Some of the others who camped on the streets saw him coming and grew quiet, dropping their gazes and their arguments and stepped away. Berlin's imaginary elephants and horses twisted into monsters with gnashing teeth and pestilence. He became a dark angel that passed through, and all who looked upon him feared to rot from within.

The perk in his step vanished.

"1913" had been carved into a stone monument above the Firehouse door on the small second-floor balcony. It always amazed Berlin that a building over 100 years old still existed in the city that had been knocking down anything with character and replacing it with shiny and new. The Firehouse was constructed of beautiful red bricks, now rough and splotched with dry, black mold eating away the mortar with tiny mildew mouths.

His stomach rolled around, clawing in annoyance. He'd grown used to hunger pains. The hospitality place gave out three meals a day, but the lines rapped around the block. Sometimes a group of vegans came by and handed out food, and it was good stuff, though some of the others turned their noses up at it.

Scratch trotted along, tail held high, and her large ears perked in attention.

The tight yoke unleashed its hold on his chest. He could get used to this, having a friend.

Tucked under the Glisan Street ramp, on the backside near the tracks, hid the door all the squatters slipped through. Pressing the makeshift door of plywood and corrugated metal with his shoulder, it opened with a metallic scream that echoed through the building. Scratch shook her head at the noise, and he muttered an apology. But the rickety squeal-door was intentional; it gave everyone the chance to scatter if they needed to, if whoever was entering didn't belong.

A pair of eyes blinked at him from the swaddling of a filthy blanket.

"Ghost," the old man greeted, his voice something closer to a frog's call than a human's.

"Good evening, Gregory," Berlin said with a little bow to the Middle Eastern man. He was perhaps a hundred years old and could still scramble as well as any of the teens from the gangs who descended on the homeless. With him watching the doors, Matoro and its pushers never slipped in. Some of the other inhabitants of this building called it the Hagia Sophia, because Gregory always talked about Allah and the Garden of Heaven, where every wish was fulfilled. Berlin thought that place sounded lovely.

"Allah be with you," Gregory said as they passed him. The little cat paused a moment before the man, then trotted to catch up to Berlin.

"And to you, sir," Berlin said.

He ascended the back stairs, skipping the second and sixth. Someone, years ago, had tried to repair those with two-by-sixes and two-by-fours that had since lost their attachment to the stair's frame and slipped if you put any weight on them.

Scratch kept tight to his feet as he moved between the piles of junk the bereft had collected as treasures. Her head swiveled this way and that, her ears in constant, erect attention. Then, with a burst of speed, she raced under a pile of cardboard boxes full of metal pipes. He heard a few thumps and then a high squeak. Seconds later, Scratch pranced out, batting at a limp rodent, sending it across the dirty floorboards to bump into Berlin's tennis shoe.

He caught the black, beady eyes of the dead mouse. A flood of images swarmed him, blotting out the Firehouse and the piles of old clothing and the scent of rot and mouse piss. A fierce beast with fangs and claws came at him, slicing through the air as it raced for his life, his blood, seeking to kill him. His little heart fluttered in his chest, faster than hummingbird wings. Death descended. Slashing. Pain, sharp and swift. Darkness.

Berlin blinked the death vision away; he was sitting on the floor with his back to the hall's wall and his hat a few feet to the side. A gray haze shifted above the tiny corpse laying between his sprawled legs. The spirit: fresh and new and strong. He closed his eyes again. Berlin gentled the spirit and helped send it on its way.

Scratch sitting near, eyed him with intensity. Her tail swiveled about as if attached to a string.

"I'm okay," he said in a small voice. Gregory said he had a gift, an ability to help the restless spirits, and Berlin was happy to help, but it made him dog sick. *Death* made him sick. And death was all around. "You shouldn't have killed him if you weren't going to eat him," he said, running his hand through his hair, stringy and grainy. When finished, his hand landed like a stone in his lap. The death visions took a lot out of him.

Scratch sat down, her tail curled tight around her body, hiding her front paws. Her yellow eyes seemed cold, and Berlin wondered what she was thinking. Probably that she could do whatever she wanted with the mouse. Kill it. Torture it. She would purr that she was a cat, after all. She was like that on her feeds, just saying what she felt. No edit. No padding for the public.

The cat stood, then walked up to the mouse. Sniffing it, she locked eyes with Berlin, then she took the mouse in her mouth and began crunching on it. Berlin watched, his lips fell open in a mixture of shock and disgust. He hadn't actually intended for her to eat the mouse, because she was really a human, wasn't she? Maybe this wasn't Scratch, but how else had she understood him? Here she was munching with purpose, chewing the rodent apart bit by bit until all that remained was the tail.

"Eww, I had some jerky if you wanted food." Berlin looked away. "But, that's better than killing for sport, I guess."

Sitting on her haunches, the cat began cleaning herself, and Berlin pushed himself up to his own feet. A few other inhabitants of the Firehouse grunted at him as he wove through the maze to his own spot. Mostly, everyone kept to themselves. In the southwest corner of the building, just behind the old elevator shaft, sat Berlin's corner. He used to share it with a lady named Tilly, but she'd disappeared one day and never came back. That was six months ago, and since then Berlin had been alone. He'd defended her things for a month, and then decided her things were better purposed to helping the others who might need them, so he parsed out her clothing and her treasures. The torn, stuffed rabbit doll went to a family with a little boy. Tilly's set of calligraphy pens went to the Governor, who wrote out rules and posted them in the hallways. Sometimes people followed the rules for a few weeks before everyone fell back to their familiar habits. Then he'd come up with a new set.

Berlin's corner behind the elevator shaft had a sleeping bag laid out on a bedroll from one of those outdoor stores, the kind that campers use. He even had an inflatable pillow. It had a tiny hole in it, so it was flat every morning, but when he went to sleep, it was perfect. A small ice chest sat near a jumble of books: things he'd collected from Goodwill and the salesmen sitting outside of Powell's when he tried to sell copies of Street Roots, the homeless paper.

His collection included a Bible and a Qur'an. He also had a slim book titled *The Worst Poetry Ever* and a science fiction book about a planet with dragons. That one blended the science of space travel and the fantasy of dragons. He'd always loved dragons; they were deadly, yet beautiful, and noble. He had a thing for nobility. Also in the pile were *Paradise Lost*, *Twilight*, *Birds of Asia*, and *Pride and Prejudice*. He'd read each one multiple times. The Paradise Flycatcher was his favorite bird.

There was also a nicely organized assortment of clothing that had been worn repeatedly and none of it clean. But the best thing about his nest was it had a window that he kept clear with water and rags and three walls. Sure, it was a kind of box canyon, but he liked the privacy.

The cat stood at the entrance to his abode and looked at him.

"This is my home." With open arms, he gestured to the niche behind the elevator shaft. "Isn't it good?" For some reason, he wanted Scratch to like his place, even though it had to be far below her normal standards. She was a hero, after all.

With a little chirrup, Scratch seemed to approve, and Berlin grinned. "Do you want something other than mouse to eat?" That got her attention, as she ran up to him and butted his leg with her head.

He laughed and scratched the kitty along her neck, then dug through a plastic grocery bag for some of the jerky. "I can ask Gregory to see if he has any canned meat." He broke a bit of jerky in two and gave her a piece and ate the other. "Sherry used to get bags of cookies and chips from this co-op her cousin worked for, but she's been gone. Liam and George are gone too."

Scratch tilted her head with a chirp.

Berlin nodded at her. "Lots of people are gone." He leaned forward and whispered. "And I don't think they went clean. I think someone is taking them." That's what he saw in the eyes of a dead man, anyway. The dead's eyes often revealed his or her last moments. For this corpse, a man had tried to drag him into a black van, and then his chest ached, a roaring wave of heaviness, and then he ended. The movie clip ran out of reel.

Then the kitty did a fantastically odd thing. She shook herself a little, the skin along her body rippling as she transformed from a four-legged animal-cat into a two footed woman-cat clad in Abyssinian-colored fur.

She grinned at him, showing some fang. He laughed. It was Scratch!

"People are being taken?" she asked. "Tell me more."

CHAPTER 14

Thomas

Thomas flipped through a *Forbes*, distracting his mind from a new project he'd been invited into. He approved of the Minidoka Project, though adopting such a name showed poor taste with its history of unfounded incarceration. Still, it was in the general location of the original Japanese internment camp and whoever had named it thought it insightful or on point or maybe was just having an indelicate laugh. It could suggest, for outside investors, distasteful captivity, which, in a way, it was. He'd even received some anonymous text message that warned him off of the project, which had caused him no end of nerves. He'd changed his number after that.

"Mr. Hallaman."

He looked up from the *Forbes*, eyes soaking up Lydia Holmsworth, Ed Blacklamp's secretary. He offered the woman a smile, and her return greeting registered on the more than professional scale.

"Thank you for waiting. Mr. Blacklamp will see you."

"Thank you, Lydia," he said. Lydia wasn't a young willow, ready to bend under a challenge, though she harbored an eager, wanting-to-please attitude that Thomas appreciated in staff. On the plus side—though he would never dip into the office pool—he wouldn't discount her appearance either: sharp, short hairstyle, brilliant smile, and a body both genes and physical dedication kept in prime shape.

And, above all, she was an exemplary assistant.

She could do so much better than Blacklamp, but to be honest, Thomas' own relationship with the development mogul was too important for him to raid an employee.

"Ah, Mr. Hallman, it's a pleasure." Ed Blacklamp was small, certainly smaller than Thomas, but his grip was solid when they shook, and he never let his eyes drop in any kind of submission. "How's business?"

"Always booming, Ed. Good to see you." He sat across from Blacklamp and pushed over a contract. Blacklamp picked it up as Thomas continued. "The Portland waterfront and the Old Town district are ripe for redevelopment. Specifically, along the rail lines paralleling Glisan Street. I've gone over the plans we've discussed and have Richards and Elliot in on the investment."

Blacklamp hmmed and nodded as he skimmed the paperwork. "Good to hear. I'll have Lee develop a campaign for redevelopment and post development use."

Thomas and Blacklamp volleyed terms. Lydia tapped on the door and entered to leave a tray with coffee, cream, and sugar, then slipped away, leaving them undisturbed in their conference.

"I like the new mock-up. Though, I believe you're shy on your percentage of return. Portland is booming." Blacklamp sipped his coffee. When he set down his cup, he wore a frown. "There is one problem with that location."

Thomas kept his face blank, meeting Blacklamp's eyes.

"My on-the-ground surveyors reported it's some hideout for the homeless; it's even got a name. The Hagia Sophia." The man kept his voice even.

"That's why this area is prime for redevelopment. The city council wants the area cleaned out, the old, crumbling buildings removed to reduce the places the unfortunate can squat, forcing them to turn to city resources instead of staying on the streets and living in such unsafe and unhealthy circumstances. Those buildings are a hazard. Of course, we'll go through the proper channels and have the site evacuated by demolition time. It won't delay the timeline."

Blacklamp smiled. "Well, good then. What do you say to golf next Wednesday?"

CHAPTER 15

The Myroi

It communicated with them today, the single one now called the Chief. With the light box communicator the Myroi had given it, the two parties were able to pass on basic needs, expectations, and questions without all of that noise. The Myroi were not comfortable with the sound the praenletta made. It scratched at their bodies, which were less substantial here in Jikon.

The praenletta had asked them to give it a name. And they had chosen the Chief, per its definition of the term.

According to this praenletta, the Chief, every singularity required a name. The people from Jikon named each other. They named their vehicles. They named the items they ate. To name something that was only used for food was preposterous.

The Myroi would endure such...oddness if the Chief fulfilled its agreement. It would gather the enriched praenletta and collect the needed praena for them.

They would do anything for the praena. Even give something a name.

CHAPTER 16

Nekoka

The morning had charged up like a swarm of locusts eating away at the night by the time Nekoka finally stood outside her hotel room. Jenni had to be pissed, a raging tornado of worry, and Nekoka was hesitant to go inside.

Nekoka leaned her forehead against the door—a flimsy barrier between them—and pressed the flat of her palm to the cool wooden veneer.

Jenni?

She waited, mind open like the sea, ready for any communication from her best friend: a gentle probing; a petulant huff; an anchor of retribution; anything.

Instead, she received nothing. A stone wall. Unforgiving. Aloof. Cold.

The previous day, with a certainty that Nekoka was typically victim of, she'd *known* that Jenni was disgusted by her attitude, despised her actions. Wanted her gone. But when she'd woken up curled around the hand of the albino guy who passed out at the sight of dead mice, that certainty was replaced with something completely different.

A solid What the Fuck.

Jenni would never turn on her.

Jenni. I'm sorry.

"Scratch?" came Berlin's tentative question. "Shouldn't you knock?"

"Not yet. I'm groveling," she whispered to her newest friend. Because he'd welcomed her into his house. Fed her. Didn't think she was a freak. He smiled and laughed and *adored* her. He could be nothing but a friend.

You didn't come back, Jenni finally said into Nekoka's thoughts.

Well, I was feeling fairly crapolla. Was that Pablo? Would he do that to her?

A tinge of regret. Due to their closeness, emotions slipped through their telepathic bond. Minnie had told Nekoka she'd never felt that from Jenni, simply the words and images that bound up communication from mind to mind. Nekoka had preened a little at that, but then, when she considered the open access Grace must have to Jenni's emotions, she gave up that ridiculous strutting.

Yes. Pablo pulled something on you.

Nekoka frowned, then updated her database—Emotional Whammy as evil weapon—for Pablo Castile. Currently, he was off her shag list.

Well, I felt very bad, and now you're not making me feel better.

You should have come home sooner. Anger. Annoyance.

It took me a while to realize you didn't hate me. Nekoka grudgingly admitted that. It seemed a failing on her part to even question Jenni.

"Or, I could just, you know, knock for you if you'd like," Berlin offered, white hand raised at the ready in a loose fist.

Nekoka shrugged. "Jenni, I have a guest. He's got something interesting you should hear." *One reason I'm late.*

Sepia gone, then you stayed away. A shiver of pain, of distress.

Nekoka's nerves jumped. Her mind reached out as she popped the electronic lock just as Berlin rapped against the wooden door. Jenni stood three strides away, and then Nekoka was in her arms. "*Tadaima,*" she whispered while hugging Jenni tight, sending her *I'm sorry I'm sorry I'm sorry* for making her worry, for making her think someone had taken Nekoka, for being selfish and not strong enough to fight Pablo's Emotional Whammy.

"I'm sorry."

Jenni buried her face in Nekoka's shoulder, her body rigid, her steel grip vicious in its tenacity. Nekoka took it, didn't harden herself at all, just took it until Jenni finally relaxed and released Nekoka. Her body sagged with relief.

Dark hair in a snaggle of disarray. Eyes red and puffy, though dry. Same clothing as yesterday. Another blade of guilt stabbed her chest when she realized how much she'd made Jenni worry.

Then Jenni's eyes shifted focus towards the door, and Nekoka remembered Berlin.

"Hi," Berlin said, shy, yet Nekoka could hear the smile in that simple greeting. "You must be Fiann."

"Call me Jenni. Please, come in. I—I'll make us some, ah, cocoa. Yeah. Sound good?" Jenni nodded and focused on the complementary coffee pot, shoulders still tight, but Nekoka knew Jenni just needed a second to let her relief sink in.

"Yes. Yes, it does," Berlin said, his eyes locked on Jenni as he pulled his hat off and set it on the bedside table. He tucked his gloves in the pockets of his light jacket that smelled like a box of Tide and an hour-long soak would struggle to cure it of its malady. Then his glasses came off, and Nekoka was struck by the solid white orbs without a dash of color. White, like nothing was there, the body an empty vessel.

Well, that was a tad unnerving. He must be Seeded. Nekoka updated her database once again and set SPYme on him now that she could see his complete face. Berlin Fisher, 17, albino. Used to go to Jefferson High School. His parents were dead, some accident at their house. He was subscribed to a few feeds, including Nekoka's, but hadn't been active since soon after his parent's deaths. She added: Seeded, homeless, white eyes, passes out at dead things, eternal optimist, good kid, needs a bath. She wondered what he could do.

Jenni set some water from the bathroom sink to heat in the room's coffee maker. Nekoka should have stopped and gotten some milk, but hadn't thought about that delicious nectar from a cow's teat all morning. She stiffened. Well, that wasn't like her. Through Whisker, she ordered cream from room service.

"So," Nekoka began, just to fill up the space between them with noise, creating a distraction from the pain in her heart that still slunk around like an unwanted dog. "Any news on Sepia?"

Jenni shook her head. "John is going to gather surveillance camera footage. But we didn't get far—with you gone."

Nekoka hmmed. "I wandered the waterfront, made a new friend." She gestured toward Berlin, who stood near the door, shifting from one foot to the other. "He lives in a building by the train station. He fed me."

Jenni offered the white-eyed albino a nod of thanks. "Well Berlin, thank you for taking care of this wayward cat."

Berlin brightened. "She *was* a cat too, when I found her. But I knew she was Scratch." His white eyebrows, camouflaged against his skin color, danced up his forehead in all intense earnestness. "But she was a bit scared, so I had to talk to her kindly."

Nekoka scratched at her nose, not meeting Jenni's eyes. "He's a bleeding heart, just like you. You'll probably get along."

The cream arrived with a quick rap at the door, and Nekoka took the metal container in shaking hands and gave it a good, long sniff. Ah, the creamy, frothy scent of milk fat. Usually better room temp or warmer, but this would do. She took a sip. Delight blossomed on her tongue. Tension eased from her body.

Until she opened her eyes and saw that Jenni's face had lost its welcome. She frowned at Nekoka. "You didn't have sex with him, did you?" she asked, sounding suddenly tired. Usually Jenni didn't care; she must be exhausted to babble about such inconsequential things.

Nekoka huffed. "No, I was a cat." And he wasn't too clean. She performed an eye roll for added effect. Maybe Jenni was worried for Berlin's innocence. Nekoka gave him a sideways glance; he could be a virgin. Were there any virgins over the age of fourteen anymore? "But he did have something interesting to tell me."

"Oh?" Jenni took the cream and began the technically difficult process of making a perfect hot cocoa with the rudimentary offerings of a hotel convenience tray.

"Yeah, he's one of the winos on the street and has lots of inside intel."

Jenni tore her eyes away from the frothy cream and glared at her. It amused Nekoka how Jenni tried to be so PC. Honestly, the show of displeasure lacked oomph and had no bite to it. Nekoka wondered if Jenni had slept at all.

"I'm underage. I don't drink," Berlin argued from where he continued to stand by the door. "Wine or anything. Well, water, and sometimes pop or something if I can get it. Coffee at the mission if it's available."

"Oh, you poor thing." Jenni handed Berlin the first cup of cocoa with a smile, exhaustion etching lines on Jenni's face that hadn't been there before last night. "Nekoka would implode if she didn't get a milk product on a daily basis. Please, sit down." She pulled out the one chair at the tiny desk that held the coffee machine, desk phone, and tourist pamphlets.

Berlin performed a half bow, half nod as he took the cocoa and perched on the edge of the chair, as if ready to jump to his feet at its inevitable collapse. His whiteness reflected the overhead incandescent lighting.

"Agreed, not a wino," Nekoka said with warmth in her voice. "What would you call yourself?"

Berlin's gaze shifted from one woman to the other, and under the attention, he shrunk into himself. That wouldn't do. Nekoka went to his side and patted him on the back. "It's all good. Whatever, you don't have to say anything."

Jenni was staring at her, and for a moment she couldn't quite read that expression, then Nekoka realized it was shock. "What?" she asked and took the cup Jenni offered with an eruption of purrs. Chocolate and cream. This must be the heaven Gregory talked about.

"Nothing." Jenni waved her hands through the air. "Just, nothing. So, Berlin, what did you tell Nekoka?"

"Well, some of the street people have been going missing. For a while now. More than before." He peered into the brown swirls of his cocoa, then lifted the cup to his white lips. "Since the developers came. This is really good. Thank you."

"No prob. So, the developers?" Jenni asked as she began crafting the next cup.

He turned to Jenni again, pulling at his colorless fringe to cover some of his face. "About three months ago, people began surveying the area around the Mission, important people with clipboards and business suits and an air of...well, they could just say something and expect everyone to do what they say. You know the type?"

Jenni nodded. "Like Nekoka?"

Nekoka laughed. She wished!

Berlin looked between the two women and let a smile tickle his lips. "No, they were bossy."

"And?" Jenni said, voice all teasing.

Berlin giggled, but continued. "These men, they'd just come on up and roust some buildings, kick all the people staying there out, telling them it was condemned and unsafe and that they had to go away. They never did that to the Firehouse, though.

"They told us they were going to put high rises up that would block out the sun. They just want to make sure there's nowhere for us to go." He tugged on his hair again. "Nowhere warm or safe because the normal people don't want to look at us."

Nekoka shrugged. "Well, your little tent cities and garbage piles are an eyesore."

Berlin frowned. "If we had a building, we wouldn't need a tent city."

Gracie's church often did food drives and clothing drives for the needy in New Orleans. Nekoka would donate cans of condensed milk, because the soothing coolness of milk in the mouth was a need. She understood needs.

"So," Jenni drew them back to the topic of the moment, "they tried to get you to leave the buildings, because of development."

"Well, yeah. But they haven't torn anything down yet. Just plastered the doors with yellow "Unsafe Building – No Entry" signs. Some of 'em would talk to the homeless. Ask them about how many of us there were, where we got our food. Some offered food vouchers for that restaurant that treats us like people. But I didn't ever get one."

Nekoka pulled her ears back. "Why not?"

"I avoided them. They gave me the shivers. The walk over your grave shivers."

Nekoka studied him, her creepy but sweet pet. For some reason, she trusted his instincts on this. "So, they gave people vouchers," she urged.

"And asked a lot of questions. Especially the paled-eyed people. Like what they could do."

"Not all pale eyes mean someone's Seeded or even has powers. There are tests to determine if someone truly has the Seed. MRIs are the easiest," Jenni explained as she stirred the hot milk and chocolate together. "So, there would be..." Jenni looked up to the ceiling as she thought, then grunted in annoyance. "Nekoka, how many Seeded in the Portland area?"

Nekoka shrugged. "An estimated 25,025.3, based on the most recent census and general percentage of expected Seeded."

"Do you know the homeless census?"

Nekoka checked the data streams. “Officially, about 9,321 homeless in the greater Portland area. And while approximately three percent of the world population is born Seeded, I wouldn’t attribute three percent of those 9,321 homeless to be Seeded.”

Jenni pondered that and nodded. She sipped at her drink, and a smile ghosted on her lips. She took another sip.

“Why not?” Berlin asked, licking his upper lip of hot chocolate residue.

Nekoka purred deep in her chest. “Seeded tend to be more successful. Especially if they show any sign of something supernatural. Even if their power is something useless, like absorbing tattoo ink into your skin or having breath that smells like roadkill, they tend to have more confidence. People often treat them with more respect, unsure if they can fly through the air and throw lightning at them. It’s like the whole ‘armed society is a polite society’ and nobody knows just what guns someone’s toting if she’s got pale eyes. But only about ten percent of Seeded show a noteworthy power, and I guess once someone’s homeless, her evol creds plummet.”

“Perhaps they were trying to determine if any of you were dangerous,” Jenni mused, though Nekoka knew she considered it was as plausible as Nekoka did.

Berlin thought about that, then shook his head. “Balloon Boy had a power. He blew hot air, made balloon animals at the Saturday market that would float for a little while until they got too cold.” He thought a little longer. “Martha suggested she could tear someone apart with her mind, but I never heard that she did anything of the sort. And Ursula painted with her blood that changed colors. I think the colors depended on her mood when she cut herself. Mood blood. Scars covered her all over.” Berlin shivered. “And me. I can see the last thoughts of the dead. And ghosts. That’s it. Nothing dangerous. None of us are dangerous.”

“Oh! That’s what you do.” Nekoka updated the database. “Ghosts?” Holy shit, lingering spirits actually existed?

Berlin nodded. “Yeah, they’re everywhere. And that’s how I knew about the black van and men taking that one guy. I didn’t see it myself. I *saw* it, through his dead eyes.”

Nekoka's mind stalled out. The world suddenly had to be re-ordered. There was life, of some sort, after death. She drank more of her chocolate milk.

"There used to be seventeen Seeded homeless that I knew of, well people with really light eyes, anyway. I didn't know them personally or anything, but word gets around. You know, we gather a lot of homeless here because of the mild weather. Some guys told me about how they had some buddies who'd froze to death during winter before." He frowned and bit his lip. "Oh, and Michael. He could hold things and change their color. He had to keep holding it, but he could turn it blue or yellow. It made things really pretty."

Nekoka almost laughed, if she didn't feel horrified about people freezing to death.

"I'm not sure how many pale eyes are still on the streets."

Nekoka swallowed a big mouthful of her cocoa, letting the mix of milky sweetness coat her tongue. Damn, that tasted good. "The cattle car, the homeless, Sepia...could they be related?" she asked.

Jenni held her cup in both hands, leaning her butt against the edge of the wimpy little table. "And is the missing homeless problem happening anywhere else?"

"Should I contact Zack or Eugene?" Nekoka thought back to her friends in New Orleans and suddenly missed them. Change was hard. Change was inevitable. She hated it, like wet fur. She, maybe—if she admitted it only to herself—missed them more than she hated the change.

"Yes, and I'll call Sedona."

Nekoka raised her eyebrows, impressed. "The leader of the Guardian Alliance? I didn't know you two were pals."

"Well, we aren't," Jenni said in mild exasperation. "I did call him Sedona after all. But there might be something going on in other parts of the States as well. We should give them a heads up."

Nekoka sought out the phone number for Sedona, the Leader of the worldwide Seeded organization, Guardian Alliance, and pushed it to Jenni's phone. "Fine by me. Keep Berlin entertained!"

Berlin sputtered. "No, I'll be okay," but Nekoka didn't hear the rest as she dove her brain into her computer.

Direct brain contact with her computer always sped up any connection to other systems out there. Anything connected to the wireless system could be breached as easily as slicing open a letter with a letter opener...however, Nekoka hated leaving traces. With a full brain connection, she left no ripped edges. Through the Wi-Fi, she sent packets of her thoughts, a breeze of electronic data, until she could peek into a computer in New Orleans. A computer so friendly to her, it virtually purred at her intrusion. True fact. She had programmed the sweet little thing herself, of course it adored her.

While Zack's computer was on, whether or not he was there was a different story.

Zack. The word appeared on his screen, blinking in a green box like an old DOS cursor. She liked to add these little effects to get people's attention. Zack. We are Borg. You will be Assimilated. The words slipped across the screen, perfectly paced.

She waited. Then, a reply appeared, jerky with bad spelling. Neko.... was in midle of scirmish.

She wasn't surprised. If he wasn't flying around like a bullet, he would have been signed onto *Heroes' Rise: Second Seed.* I can put you back in there if you'd like. After we're done talking.

Why don't u phone like normal ppl?

She returned the next line empty, no words written. She knew Zack was smarter than that.

Okay, yes, ur not normal. Fine. Anything wrong? How is Portland? How are you?

Portland is fine. Jenni and I are fine. Someone over here is kidnapping Seeded. Homeless specifically. Any newsthoughtsideas? She forgot to separate the words in her stream of thought question. The words disappeared from the screen, and she thought them into existence again. news, thoughts, or ideas?

Another pause and Nekoka waited, flipping through the files on Zack's computer for something interesting. Pictures of him and his girlfriend, pictures of unknown naked women, ripped movies, video games and.... This was what she was looking for. This was what she'd dreaded.

The files for the official certification of S-Force, a group of four vowing to protect New Orleans from crime by working with the local police force.

You did it. You went official. No more trial. I see Minnie stayed with you. A chill bloomed in her chest and spread throughout her body. She rattled off: You little weasel. You silver-plated weasel! You said it would be a trial. Guess it all worked out for you.

It took some time for the response. You did leave so we could make our own decision without you hissing and spitting about it. The complete sentence was unnerving. You and Jenni will be welcome if you did want to join us, of course.

I don't. You know that, but you couldn't be bothered to look beyond your own magnified ego.

She knew this was going to happen. Knew it. It had practically already happened, but the truth of it, the heavy, solid truth, hurt worse than she expected.

Ego! U want to talk ego!!!!

Zack went off with his terrible shorthand and Nekoka felt like she was floating, alone and adrift and hollow, like a special portion of her had gone missing. Her friends in New Orleans...gone. They were beyond her now.

RU still there?

...Yes.

Homeless S kidnapped?

...Yes.

No news here. Ill look into it. Get back to u. Gracie say hi to Jenni.

The words startled Nekoka. They haven't talked? How could they not have talked?

Another pause, the cursor blinking in quiet contemplation, then: U didn't no? They broke it off. Well, Gracie broke it off.

Oh my. Oh hell. Jenni had been hurting and hadn't even told Nekoka. A hundred things flared inside her, charring the more sensitive emotions, leaving behind only guilt. Nekoka hadn't even noticed!

What happened?

No idea. Not my business.

Ah, damned Zack. Though he was a perfect public face for the group, always smiling for the camera, he failed at gossip. You'd think a millionaire who hung with A-listers would be better at collecting dirt.

Hey, Nekoka.

What.

Keep me informed on what u find out. A pause. Yes?

Professional curiosity?

That, and I worry about u 2. Do come back.

For a moment, Nekoka didn't know what to say. So, she settled for Okay, then signed off, unplugging her connection to Zack's computer, separated by miles of empty space and sinking back into her own body. With a few blinks, she could hear Jenni still on the phone. The smell of hot chocolate tickled her nose. Tired heaviness settled under her skin, as always happened in a full dive.

A battery of feelings swarmed within her like gnats. She hated feelings. That expanse of hollow betrayal ate at her heart. They'd gone Certified. They'd left her behind. Then her mind skipped to the other bit of info, potently more important. Jenni was without her Gracie.

Climbing over the bed to her feet, Nekoka walked into the bathroom and ran some cool water, splashing her face just a little. Her heart hurt. Not only had Jenni been so angry with Nekoka that this cold wall had been erected between them, but this tremendous thing had happened to Jenni, and Jenni hadn't told her.

Nekoka told Jenni everything. That was what best friends did.

Maybe...Maybe Jenni didn't consider Nekoka as good of a friend as Nekoka considered her. Maybe Nekoka had some weird concept of how important she was to Jenni. Maybe Nekoka really had nobody. It was possible that she really was alone in this world. It wasn't an altogether radical concept. You let people down, and sometimes they never took you back. Sometimes, you weren't worth taking back.

And Nekoka had let a pile of people down.

She stared at herself in the mirror, Jenni's soft voice bobbing up and down as she discussed the missing Seeded with the leader of the Guardian Alliance.

But, if Nekoka didn't mean that much to Jenni, why had she come to Portland with her? Jenni hadn't been against the solidifying of a hero group like Nekoka had been. She left New Orleans right when she was having problems with her girlfriend, or around the time they'd parted ways... to make sure Nekoka wasn't alone.

Her face was all scrunched up, her fur matted where she'd watered it down. A horrid look for her, really. She flicked an ear.

She was being stupid.

"Yes, thank you. I'd like that. You have a good day, as well." Nekoka heard the faint beep of the end call.

Silence settled on the hotel room—Nekoka in the unlit bathroom, Jenni sitting on the bed. Separated and without words, like strangers.

"Jenni," Nekoka finally spoke, at exactly the same time she heard her own name come from the bedroom. The women laughed, a strained kind of laughter that had never existed between them before. Nekoka turned from the mirror, sick of that needy look in her eyes, and went into the main room. Berlin watched her, a worried frown on his lips.

She stood there, her arms sagging by her sides, unsure what to do with them. If she put them on her hips, she would look demanding, and if she crossed them, she would look aloof, like she was hiding behind a shield of forearms. Her tail drooped, touching the floor in dejection.

Jenni perched on the edge of the bed, her body twisted so her knees aimed towards the wall, away from Nekoka. Her back was rigid and her expression soft, though Nekoka did notice a few worry lines around her friend's eyes. It was unnerving to see them there.

"Berlin, do you want a shower?" Jenni asked.

"That would be...really nice, thank you." He stood and passed Nekoka as she left the bathroom. He patted her on the shoulder, and she wanted to hug him tight, for his perception and his support. Though the experience she'd shared with him was tiny, she felt like he was in her corner as much as Jenni was. He closed the door behind him and soon the shower started.

"Jenni, what's going on?"

"Listen," Jenni began, her eyes dancing between Nekoka's face and the tangle of hands in her lap. Nekoka let her shoulders relax. "I'm sorry about...earlier. I was just really worried, and you know how when I get worried, I sometimes get a little...."

"Yeah." Nekoka took a few steps closer to the bed. "I know."

"It's not that...." Jenni looked up, her eyes shining in the brilliant lighting of the room's lamp. Nekoka waited. "...I'm not really mad at you. It's just—" Jenni took in a deep breath and let it out, "—a lot of things."

Nekoka sat on the edge of the bed, pulling her tail around behind her so it wouldn't kink. "You do know that you can talk to me. I'm not just baggage here." She cringed at the annoyed tone to her words, but she was happy she got them all out.

Jenni fixed her gaze on her. "I know you're not baggage. If you remember, I did leave New Orleans because you needed a friend by your side. That's not something you do for baggage."

Nekoka looked away. Jenni had left her friends and her girlfriend. She'd even wanted the Certification herself. Jenni had dropped everything. Nekoka was such an idiot.

"I didn't really want to be there, either," Jenni finished in a small voice.

Finally, as if pulled by invisible ropes tied to her soul, Nekoka scooted her way across the bed and nestled next to Jenni's side, a low rumble bubbling from her chest. Jenni was hurting, and finally, she was letting Nekoka see it, letting Nekoka feel it through their link. Finally, Nekoka knew how torn up and bloody Jenni's heart was.

"Why didn't you tell me?" Nekoka asked, unfurling Jenni's fingers and taking one hand into her own, holding onto it tight.

"About Grace?" Jenni asked. Nekoka nodded. "I didn't want to talk about it. She..." Jenni pulled her hand away and barricaded the emotional seepage that Nekoka was picking up. Pain, frustration, guilt. It almost had a taste when they were touching, a brew of sour soup. "She wondered about our...ah, long-term relationship...about.... She'd always been a bit...."

"Conservative?" Nekoka offered. Gracie was wonderful, loving, and supportive. But she'd been raised prim and proper, and it had been an injection of amazement to everyone that she'd even admitted to favoring women. The real shocker hit when she and Jenni began officially dating.

"Yeah. And driven. I knew she wanted to make it in her company and be involved with her church. Her image is important to her...." Jenni trailed off, that strain slipping in again.

"And she didn't want to be seen in public with a woman?"

Jenni shrugged. "Something like that. And, I get it. I do. Not like I'm a big exhibitionist myself. But...you know, the whole dirty secret thing. Not my fave."

Nekoka didn't really get the whole sex being a dirty secret thing. Some concepts were too alien. Sex was natural, fun, and something Nekoka enjoyed regularly. The idea of not getting some nookie on the steady sent her imagination into horrific depths rivaling those in Bosch's depiction of hell in the frothing fanaticism of the Protestant Reformation. The threat of being cut off from Nekoka's cherished pastime almost delivered her into her own frothing terror.

And anyone who thought Jenni was a dirty secret.... Nekoka's hackles rose at the implication. Gracie deserved a sternly worded text, but dipping her nose between a lovers' argument sounded suicidal.

She pressed into Jenni's side. "I'm sorry. So sorry. I know you loved her. And I'm sorry that.... I was too...well, stuck on myself to notice. I'm, sometimes, well, a sucky friend." Nekoka sniffed, rubbed at her nose. Jenni was quiet, only mumbled an "it's okay," that wasn't the complete truth, but Nekoka appreciated her attempt to smooth things over.

"By the way," Nekoka said, wondering if she should wait, let their emotions have time to settle, but she'd never been good with self-control. "They did it. S-Force. Officially Certified. Even Minnie stayed."

Jenni looked up, her eyes flat in the lighting. "I'm really not surprised." Then, like the bones in her body all went to jelly, she fell back onto the bed, bouncing a little against the sensitive springs. "Not surprised at all. It's a good thing, Nekoka."

They remained silent for a while. Nekoka wanted to reach out and caress her friend telepathically, mentally nudge her to let her know she wasn't alone. But all she could do was remain open for Jenni to dip in and see how much Nekoka loved her. Even if she disagreed.

Jenni rolled over onto her side and said, "I'm so tired."

Nekoka glanced at the clock. Ten-thirteen in the morning.

"Sleep then. I know I'm knackered." Her time with Berlin hadn't amounted to restful. And she'd done a brain dive to talk to Zack. Nekoka crawled to her side of the bed and slipped under the covers. She loved that she didn't ever have to change clothing.

Jenni crawled in next to her, still in her clothes. Nekoka wrapped her in a hug.

The door to the bathroom opened, letting out a cloud of steam. "Is everything okay?"

Nekoka rolled her head to glance at the kid over her shoulder, white skin next to a whiter towel wrapped around his waist. "Yeah, come to bed. We'll put our thinky thoughts together in a few hours."

"Umm..."

Nekoka closed her eyes, and in a few moments, the bed dipped, and Berlin joined them. He was warm from the shower, and Jenni was warm under the covers and Nekoka did what her body wanted to do: fell asleep.

Inset 4
Mission Statement

Sapian True Mission Statement

I see a future. I see a future where people all glory in God. We have God-vision, and we see each other as children of God and that we are all loved, one and the same, by God and therefore, we should love each other just the same.

We, as God's children, will drop away our insecurities and selfish goals. We, as God's children, will abandon the need to find faults in other's words and deeds. We, as God's children, will dismiss the ideas that any of us shall lord over another, for God is our Lord above all.

We, who are made in the image of God, shall gather and treat and do good by each other and beware those not of God, for they are among us, and they speak with the tongue of lies. It is by their deeds we shall know them, and it is our duty to be ever vigilant to watch for these wolves among the flock.

I see a future of joined hearts and joined hands. For all children of God to band together in this great time of threat. Join me in my future and stand together in love and service, raise each other up, for there are those around us who will only tear us down.

Eliza Silva

Sapian True

CHAPTER 17

Nekoka

Nekoka seemed to store sleep like a camel stored water. She gathered a mad amount of it most of the time, and then pulled crazy all-nighters when she found some interesting electronic trail to follow, some enticing secret or theory that kept her rolling, burning hours up like fireworks until Jenni had to scoop up her ashen, lifeless body as if she'd contacted some alien wasting disease, and put her to bed.

And though her battery wasn't charged full to the brim with lovely dreams of chasing rats through electronic freeways of data with someone petting her ears, she still had enough stores to drag her ass to wakefulness barely four hours after she'd gone down for her mid-morning nap. She shimmied out from between her two bedmates and was out the door, a note scrawled on the hotel notepaper that she would be back in an hour.

She understood that Pablo had punished her because of her attitude, and though Pablo was a manipulative asshole—she'd updated her database—he did have a tiny point. But in Nekoka's defense, it wasn't like she backed the idea of some clandestine dark agency out there stealing evols from a Hub city.

So, she would take the high road—it was in her power—and do her best to find Sepia and the other kidnapped Seeded. In time, however. First, before she found Sepia and saved the day, she had to care for Berlin.

Near Powell's City of Books, she'd noticed a second-hand store earlier in their stay. With a monumental show of inner strength, she passed by the bookstore full of books and geeks, and slipped into the clothing store. Fancy and scanty clothing draped a few mannequins in the window, but Nekoka dove deeper into the store where racks of regular clothes lined up, doused in that unique smell only second-hand stores cultivated. While browsing the jeans and long-sleeved shirts, grabbing a bag of new socks and underwear, she was texting with John Geier, planning to meet at the police station at one that afternoon.

The idea of being surrounded by so many police threatened a case of hives, but needs must.

Hanging from a wire frame in a place of honor was a T-shirt that said "The Bullet Pierced My Heart" with a red heart shape leaking blood from a hole in the center. Nekoka laughed; Zack would love it. On a whim, she bought it. It was Jenni's size.

At a Fred Meyer's a few blocks away, she bought some milk, a few candy bars, and some Dr. Pepper for Jenni. A toothbrush for Berlin and a new hat, because that other one rated a solid line-up of tens among the grannies. He was already an albino freak; he didn't need to sport the old man look, too. This one had the option of a wide brim, but you could snap up the sides, Australian style. At a Burgerville, she grabbed lunch.

People watched her, whispered behind her back; she ignored them. No time to let the fans fawn over her. She had important things to do.

When she returned, Jenni was still sleeping, though Berlin was sitting up in bed, the blanket pulled up to his chin, the skin over his face a flush of vibrant pink. Was that a blush?

"Berlin, I got you some clothes. See if they fit." She handed him a bag and the toothbrush.

"You didn't have—"

Nekoka scoffed, shushing him with a wave of her hand. "I know. I wanted to. You're my friend, right?"

Berlin nodded, eyes full of adoration, lips readied for a smile but still unsure. Nekoka felt herself purring.

"If it makes you feel better, you earned it. You gave us important information, so, have some clothes. Toothpaste is in the bathroom."

He scuttled into the bathroom, the door clicking closed. Jenni opened an eye. Nekoka smiled and crawled over the bed to prop her chin on Jenni's arm.

"You like him," Jenni said.

Her purr strengthened. "Yeah. He's my pet."

Jenni snorted, then yawned. "You planning on keeping him?"

Nekoka sat up, an unfamiliar sense of uncertainty nosing around in her gut like a truffle pig. She grabbed her tail and played with the tip. It twitched and flicked in her fingers. "Well, he had nowhere else to go."

"Just ask. Give him a choice."

Nekoka nodded. Of course. "You okay with that? Keeping him?"

"He's a good kid. I don't mind him. But *ask*," she urged.

Nekoka landed on her friend and burrowed her face into the blankets near Jenni's neck. Jenni squealed, trying to push Nekoka off, but Nekoka could be quite the limpet if she wanted to.

"Get off. I can't breathe!" Jenni whined. "You menace."

Nekoka stopped clinging to Jenni and Jenni unburied herself from under the mat of blankets. "Time?"

"Just after noon. We need to be at the police station around one."

"Damn, that's soon." Jenni threw the covers off, huffing about having no time, but Nekoka knew Jenni wasn't really mad, because her eyes were narrowed, the edges crinkled, and only a sliver of absinthe green peeked through. "When did you get to be the ringleader? Setting up one meeting after another."

Nekoka scrunched up her nose. She wasn't a ringleader, or a leader of any type. Gah! The responsibility! "Well, we want to find Sepia and all the others, don't we?"

Jenni yanked the dresser drawer open and fished out some clean clothes. "Yes, we do. Thanks for letting me sleep; I didn't sleep well last night."

"Didn't sleep at all," Nekoka accused.

Jenni rubbed at her eyes, but didn't deny anything, so Nekoka threw the new T-shirt at her head. Jenni snatched it from the air and held it up. Blank incomprehension was quickly overcome by bright amusement. She whipped her shirt off, snapped on a bra, and drew on the new Bullet shirt right as Berlin opened the bathroom door, clad in clean jeans and fresh shirt. Nekoka had kept the shirts in the lighter color zone, so as not to make him look overexposed like a bad photograph. The one he picked was a cotton pullover of parchment beige.

Nekoka clapped. Jenni whistled. Berlin blushed some more.

"Thank you for the clothing."

"Really," Nekoka said, adding some purr to her voice. "I did myself a favor; you look so pettable in that shirt."

He blushed even more, and Jenni elbowed Nekoka in the ribs before she gathered up the rest of her clothing and passed by Berlin to complete her dressing in the bathroom. Nekoka laughed. "It's okay, you're safe from me with Jenni on guard."

Berlin's brows bunched; his mouth pursed in a confused pout that almost had Nekoka laughing harder. Instead, she swallowed down the response and said, "Lunch," and pointed at the Burgerville bag on the table. In seconds, Jenni popped out from the bathroom in fresh jeans and snatched up the bag, passing out a burger and bag of fries to everyone.

"Pop in the fridge," Nekoka said as she unwrapped her burger. Jenni sighed in contentment as she cracked the top of the Dr. Pepper can.

Once they'd finished, Nekoka offered Berlin her unnecessary room key. "Take this so you can come and go. We have to go talk to the police, but we'll be back for dinner."

Berlin gaped at them like a fish. "You don't have to."

Nekoka reached out and grabbed him. He was taller than her, most people were, but she could just nuzzle her throat around his if she pushed up on the balls of her feet: a horsey hug is what a kid at college used to call it—some rancher thing. "I want to."

Nekoka, Jenni thought, the scolding tone somehow holding more weight in her telepathic communication.

"Berlin, would you please stay with us? But you don't *have* to." Nekoka gave him a big, toothy grin. "You took me in and now I'd like to take you in. Deal?"

Berlin went pink again, fiddled with the hem of his new shirt, and slowly nodded. "Deal."

THE CITY OF PORTLAND Police Bureau building was comprised of a geometric concrete block of sharp lines and angles, with little windows giving it the air of a futuristic military bunker. Just the look of it gave Nekoka a limp tail. She almost wished Berlin was still with them, so he could pet her, but he'd gone off to talk to some of his friends and do whatever it was ex-homeless people did. She scratched the back of her neck, tangling her fingers up in her hair.

John was waiting for her and Jenni outside of the double glass doors, pretending to be casual, but his crossed arms were stiff, his shoulders an iron bar against the concrete bricks. The sunlight glinted off his specs. "Hey, thanks for coming." He didn't quite meet her eyes with his own cold gray-blue.

Nekoka didn't feel like empty platitudes—she had been judged unworthy, so the members of O.G.R.E. were not on her friendly list—so she made some non-committal noise and shrugged her shoulders. Jenni, however, reached out to shake John's hand.

"No problem. Sorry we didn't act sooner." Jenni's jaw flexed. "Nekoka said you'd gathered citywide surveillance..."

"Yeah, follow me and I'll take you to the records review room. Trior is already there."

Jenni flicked her gaze at Nekoka, but didn't linger. The inside of the police station was well lit and busy as an ant nest after an anteater had ripped through the ranks. Nekoka wondered if something was going on. She glanced from face to face, curious if any of these people were the informant who clued her in to MacRoe's arrest of Dana Schultz. Which of these men or women was a crack hacker as good as she was herself? Or was it someone outside of the department? The mystery made Nekoka's eyeteeth ache. She liked sussing out secrets.

They left behind the hive of workers to head into less populated corridors. Nekoka sought out anything telepathic from Jenni, but nothing came through. She was strangely cut off.

"Any news about the autodrive hack in that collision?" Jenni murmured.

John shook his head. "The feds are taking the case. Xenofontos is still the primary suspect, though they didn't claim it as their own."

Nekoka sighed. Everyone always wanted to blame the extremists. "Not really their style. Just because Silva was in the mash up, they think the separatists are involved? Maybe it was a religious attack. Or a simple attack on America. And what about all those people?"

"They've been taken to shelters or returned to their homes if they have one. Same story from most. Someone they knew from the streets attacked them, though some were too incapacitated by narcotics to have clear memory of their abduction." John kept walking, his broad shoulders taking up almost as much room as Nekoka and Jenni did side by side. "I agree that this doesn't look like anything Xenofontas would do. But I'm not in charge. I'm just worried it's the opening gambit to a bigger threat. Most terrorist activities with no demands aren't one-offs."

They rounded a corner, the halls nearly empty.

"Is Pablo going to be there?" Jenni asked.

John shook his head and huffed a sigh. "He had other business, but you know," he glanced over his shoulder at Nekoka, "he's pretty sorry about what he did. He was an ass, and he knows it."

Jenni mumbled, "Nekoka knows she was an ass, too."

Nekoka's ears went back, but she said nothing. She'd take her beatings and live with it.

They walked by a few officers in blue, who paid extra attention to their small group. They passed through more institutional tan hallways with cameras spying on them at the end of the corridors and keycode locks on all the doors. Using *kokogyo*, Nekoka reached out as she neared each electronic 'mind'; making friends with computers was easy.

John flipped through the code at their door. The door clicked open, and they entered a room packed with computer stations. The air was cold and Nekoka instinctively thickened her fur. Berlin would probably have a name for her new style. Burmese Mountain Cheetah or something.

Trior, without his hat or specs, sat at one station watching a slide show of images. Nekoka tilted her head and watched the endless shots of the world flip by. He waved at them all, his eyes a bloodshot shade of drunkenness, or worry.

"Good day to you, Nekoka, Jenni." He tipped an invisible hat.

"Hi, Trior. Any glimpse of Sepia yet?" Nekoka asked as she settled in a chair next to his, staring at the grainy image. What was this from? Some 1970s CCTV footage from a peephole camera in a dark elevator shaft?

"No. And it's hard going." He grimaced. "The quality of the footage leaves too much to the imagination." On the screen, what appeared to be a person was walking through a cosmic bowling scene, on low light.

"How is your facial recognition software?" she asked John.

"Top of the line..." he trailed off as he studied Nekoka. "The easy stuff is already being filtered through that, but some of these rougher recordings," he gestured at another monitor, the footage here apparently swimming under sea, "doesn't register well with the program."

Nekoka hmmed. "Well, let me just see about that. All the footage here?"

John nodded.

"Got pics of Sepia I can feed my program?"

Trior's interest ratcheted up to a solar blaze. "Sure. My specs." He pulled them out of an inner jacket pocket, and Nekoka took them in her fingers, accessing the photo gallery.

"What exactly is she doing?" John asked Jenni in a low voice.

"Her thing," Jenni said.

"Okay, let's see what I can do." Nekoka tugged at her form, letting the solid shape release as she shifted into a small cat, fuzzy to keep herself from going hypothermic, and cuddled around Trior's specs, wrapping her tail tight to her body. The shift took less than half a minute, and a wash of tiredness settled, then dissipated. Changing from catgirl to house cat didn't drain her that much, and really, being a cat was about as relaxing as one could get.

Jenni scratched between her ears. "Nekoka will be busy for a while. Anything we can do? She's got the vids covered. Trust me."

Nekoka purred at the praise and then synced the computers.

Her recognition program could already ID a single individual from a set of identical triplets in a mass as large as the Seeded Games attendance. It was the same engine she'd used for SPYme.

Trior's specs were a trove of Sepia pics, and Nekoka grabbed a variety that covered various hairstyles, colors, poses, amounts of metal in her face, as well as half- and partial-faced pictures. Trior must have a Sepia fetish, because there was an entire gallery of the woman. Pictures of them together, one arm thrown around each other like they were old friends. Nothing of them smooching or intimate, nothing like they were lovers, but best friends. Like her and Jenni, she supposed.

Then she wound up her program and set it free, a little mouse on wheels peeking at each image, categorizing how closely it related to Sepia's face, and shifting them from a definite no, to a maybe. The maybes then went through a more rigorous study by the program and so forth until it boiled down to definite yeses of Sepia caught on traffic cams, storefront recorders, public property safety CCTV, drone images uploaded to the cloud, home front door cams, and more.

The program would effortlessly run through all the storage the police department had collected. But Nekoka knew there had to be more. Though law enforcement had access to every person's smart device data, access didn't mean availability on the department's computers. Though front door and automobile dash cams were all uploaded to the department servers, other things like smart speakers, spec and phone storage, vacuum cleaners, webcams, laptops, etc., all took video or audio that the police could ask the bigger companies and suppliers for. Most people didn't realize there was no such thing as privacy, and many probably didn't care. Nekoka, of course, had only internally connected devices and scrubbed the electronic universe of her passing if she ever did something she wanted on the sly. She cared.

So, giggling to herself, she went to the invisispec network server and tweaked with the auto upgrade that synced with every set of VR-glasses out there at 2:00 am. Finessing a little bundle of code, she inserted it into the upgrade code so it would be uploaded to everyone's specs on the next upgrade. After download and install, it would search through their photos from the night Sepia went missing and if it found anything, upload that information back to Whisker.

She then forced the upgrade to occur several hours too early for Portland residents and waited.

It would take time. And wasn't by any means legal. But legality was always a subjective concept in Nekoka's mind.

Setting an alarm so it would ring when it found Sepia, she tucked her nose under her tail and settled in for a little nap.

THERE WERE FISHIES floating in the air before her, and Nekoka bounded from cloud to cloud, a little bell around her neck tinging each time she landed with a gentle fluff in the floating mist.

Ting. Ting.

One fishy, a bright, orange-striped clown, turned to her, swishing its fishy tail, and said, "Nekoka. Nekoka."

Nekoka leaped through the air in slow motion grace, her paws reaching for the tasty fishy.

"Nekoka."

"I'm coming. I'm coming to eat you," she said. Something gripped her body, and she shook, teetering on the edge of a cloud. The little bell rang again.

"Nekoka, wake up!"

With a yarl of shock, Nekoka jumped from her chair, elevating several feet, allowing herself to change skins into something large, ready to battle, a humanoid tiger, muscles boosted, claws out, teeth bared to tear and rend, to attack whatever dastardly fiend was trying to steal her dinner.

The chair tumbled away, rattling against the ancient linoleum floor. Her barrel chest heaved with breaths, her bulk nearly filling up the aisle between computer stations.

Jenni stared at her. "Nekoka, that damned chime's been going off for ten minutes. Do something about it."

Nekoka glared at Jenni until what she'd said sank in. Trior had backed away, keeping a chair between them. John had his hands up, palms out, in a calming gesture. Nekoka growled and huffed out a great tiger breath. With fluid finesse, she shifted down into catgirl form, opting for black fur, picked the chair back up, and sat with forced dignity to dip her brain back into her computer.

The city's open surveillance circuits found several references of Sepia's face, including shots from door cams. Even more through various personal invisispecs. She almost let loose one of those wacked-out witch cackles. Only those systems that were hardwired with no connections to outside systems were safe from her program. She had the *power*!

Like a hound dog after a bitch, sniffing the tail of every dog, cat, parakeet, and dinosaur it came across, it found Sepia. Well, Nekoka thought, Sepia probably did have a unique scent.

"Hey, I've found—"

Trior and John erupted into excited cheers laced with relief, assuming the entirety of Nekoka's words. Only Jenni hadn't interrupted her. "What did you find?" she asked. By now, the others had gotten a clue that something wasn't exactly as they had initially guessed.

"I found her passage. I don't know where she is now. Yet." The room grew silent.

"Well, what did you find?" asked Trior, his voice shaky, the drawl thickening like gravy.

"A series of images and a few videos." She sent her finds to the computer station in front of her. The screen blipped to life, causing Trior to jerk back.

Nekoka organized the images chronologically from the timestamp attached to each recording. The first one was of Sepia walking down Alberta past a computer store that recorded everyone walking by. Why anyone would waste the time and bandwidth to not only record, but upload pedestrians passage was beyond Nekoka. Sepia was dressed in baggy jeans, a tight knit shirt that barely contained her bust, and had her hair in pigtails like a six-year-old, only the hair of each tail was split into three and braided.

A backpack swung off one shoulder, and she seemed casual and at ease. That was at 5:32 pm.

A few front door cameras caught her passing down a residential street. Same pose, same manner.

Next, about forty-five minutes later, Sepia purchased a bag of groceries from the yuppie food store on 33rd. "That's the New Seasons near her house," Trior said. Nekoka guessed she'd probably got something organic or animal friendly or picked by poor, elderly old ladies at exorbitant prices to be 'fair'.

She must have leaked that, because Jenni scoffed. *You only eat dolphin-safe tuna.*

Nekoka did not respond.

After that, there were flashes from traffic cameras, security drones, street or door cams, and some random catches by dash cams, people's specs and GoPros, an image of her passing a secure parking lot, and finally, a single snapshot of her grappling with a man in a park.

"Is he familiar to anyone?" John pondered, pointing at the final image.

The assailant's back was to the camera. He wore a dark-colored jacket, which the drizzle could have called for, and he had about six inches and thirty pounds on Sepia.

Frozen on the screen, Sepia was pulling back to punch him, a feral, bulldog look on her face as she gritted her teeth in fury. The man had a hold of her other wrist and was reaching for Sepia's head with his other hand, his fingers splayed wide to encompass her entire face.

That image, captured forever, gave Nekoka the heebies. Someone facing down Sepia with a look like that. Sepia had the power to make powerful men wet themselves. Her bully Seeded power. Her hatred and fury could jump from her face, take form and eviscerate the man's will, but he didn't seem phased.

"What park is that?" Jenni asked the locals. "Nekoka, could you clean up this picture?

"It's cleaned," she responded, almost insulted that Jenni hadn't expected Nekoka to do that already. "It's through a dirty lens, and it's night, not the best photo circumstances."

Sepia stood on a bare patch of dirt, the lawn having been poorly cared for. A building stood behind her with horizontal paneling and a boarded-up window that looked like it once held a concessionaire stand. Evergreens and some other trees of the leafy variety were scattered around Sepia and her attacker.

It could be any park in North Portland, where Sepia lived.

"The last image was stamped 10:26 pm," Nekoka pointed out. "Any idea why she would be out there that late?"

John shrugged. "I don't claim to mark the comings and goings of that one," he said with an actual smile. "She helps the communities in the poorer areas of Portland quite a bit, benefit concerts and stuff. I think she did Meals on Wheels one year, until an old man threw food at her, and she stopped." He tried to smother his growing grin.

Trior huffed a single laugh. "It wasn't the old guy's fault; he had some jerking thing," he shrugged to show he had no idea of the ailments of the old, "and it was an accident."

Nekoka snorted. She didn't blame Sepia. Nobody likes food thrown at her, but the image implanted in her brain attached itself tight as a bur, and Nekoka shouldn't dislodge it even with a thorough combing.

"Damn." No amusement carried in Trior's voice anymore. "That bastard had better not hurt her."

Nekoka blinked. "You two close?"

Trior sighed as he sat back from squinting at the screen. "I know you don't like her."

"She's obnoxious," Nekoka said, never one to mince words.

"Everything that irritates us about others can lead us to an understanding of ourselves," John said quietly at a cadence that labeled it as a quote.

Jenni snorted. Nekoka pulled her ears back. SPYme alerted her it was a quote. Carl Jung.

Trior chuckled, warm and oaky, comforting as a glass of spiced rum, or hot cocoa made of cream straight from the cow's udder. "She certainly is," he said with pride. "I have taught her manners, I shall confess. She could enjoy high tea with the queen if the opportunity arose." Then he stiffened, his eyes widening. "Wait, see that, in the background. Some playground equipment."

Nekoka tilted her head. Jenni reached out and traced her finger over the screen. "Here? That's a jungle gym or something, yeah?"

Trior nodded. "Yes, and if it is, I know this place. Woodlawn Park on 13th. She used to play basketball there with some of the kids." His voice went wistful. "But that was years ago."

Nekoka wasn't about to ask. Oh fine, she would. "Are you two lovers?"

Trior closed his eyes, a small smile flittering across his lips. "No. Sepia isn't like that. She is my best friend, though. I found her on the streets years ago after she'd left her home in Chicago. Helped her clean herself up. She cares, and she cares deeply, but not in that way. She'd always just said she had a low sex drive."

Nekoka shivered in horror. Low sex drive?

"But that's probably one reason we are such good friends," he finished with a shrug. "So, it's almost six. John, shall we head to Woodlawn?"

Nekoka was still dazed at the shocking, alien news of someone not interested in the pleasures of the body, so Jenni had to walk her out the door. Her mind still wasn't quite righted to notice MacRoe glaring at the Seeded as they left the station.

CHAPTER 18

Nekoka

The sun, sliding towards the horizon, still put a valiant effort into roasting everyone in the park. Nekoka and the others stood around a patch of ground bare except for some struggling dandelions, near a newish building with horizontal siding painted dark brown. It wasn't boarded up, as Nekoka had first thought from the image, but a blank board hid the concessions window when not open. No elephant ears and pop late at night, kiddies. Tall trees surrounded them, dwarfed by high rises on one side. Surrounding the rest of the park were modest single-story cottages, most with lawns as golden as the dawn. Road traffic oozed along at slug speeds down Dekum with a few traffic and security drones buzzing by like dragonflies on the hunt. From Nekoka's vantage she spotted the basketball court and jungle gym, and just over her head was the streetlamp with surveillance camera. She smiled and waved, then immediately touched the light post to erase the records that she had even been there with a pulse of effort.

It was a reflexive habit for her. In all reality, nobody could find her the way she'd trailed Sepia.

The stalwart members of O.G.R.E.—minus the obvious missing member and Billie who had to watch Rain—were ringed by a squadron of gawkers from the neighborhood that had come to see the group of evols. Nekoka refused to even grant Pablo notice.

Chandler moved, drawing attention to himself. Nekoka cocked her head; he cocked his back, aiming his crown toward Pablo. Nekoka sniffed, sticking her nose up in the air.

"Do you think Berlin found something to eat?" Nekoka asked Jenni, a little put out that he didn't have specs or even a simple phone she could message him on. He was hers now, and she had to watch out for him.

"He's been on his own for a while, and you left him the last of my money. I'm sure he'll survive."

Well, she didn't want him to simply survive. Nekoka huffed. Guess she understood Trior's nerves better now.

"So, John," Trior said, pulling out the name with his slow speech, "have you had your forensics team come through here yet?"

The natural coldness from John's pale eyes seeped into his expression, though it wasn't directed at any of them. He took a deep breath, his nostrils flaring. "Even with the photo, they wouldn't assign the forensics team. Say it could have just been a domestic argument. There are too many other immediate issues pulling the department thin." John tried to keep his voice steady, but the dropped tone of it belied his irritation. "I was considering siccing Pablo on them," he added, forcing a cheerful smile that totally missed cheerful and hit manic instead.

Pablo, with a twist of discomfort, said, "I could if you really thought it would work, but..."

John shook his head. "No, Pablo. No. Don't worry about it; I won't ask you to do anything like that. It's just.... It can be frustrating." Nekoka lifted her brows, asking him to continue. John sucked air through his teeth and bottom lip. "Some people in the department don't think the Seeded deserve the same rights as normal humans."

Not much of a shock, but it still sent Nekoka's fur all on end. "Is MacRoe in the Seeded are cockroaches camp?"

John caught her eye and performed a long, steady series of nods. "And some of his friends."

Jenni crossed her arms. "What rights do they think we deserve? Obviously not police protection."

"The separatists could agree with Sargent MacRoe. He thinks since we're no longer 'human'—" he gave the word air quotes, "—that we should police ourselves. But he only thinks that way when we need protection. If one of the Seeded performs criminal events, he wants a special force of normals only to take Seeded criminals down. Doesn't trust our objectivity about our own population. It's not pretty in my precinct," he added, brushing his palm against his untamed hair, the gesture unconscious.

Though John Geier was a goody-goody, Nekoka found herself liking him. His good heart sometimes reminded her of Jenni. She hated seeing those she liked pushed to the edge. To appease her angst, she shot a glare at Pablo, who huffed, rolled his eyes, and looked about to say something.

"Well, screw 'em," Chandler interrupted, pacing behind Trior and Pablo, watching his sneakered feet as he walked. "We can do our own investigation. What do we know, and what don't we know?"

"We know Sepia was here at this park Thursday night just around ten thirty, being dragged away by a man..." Nekoka began.

Trior jumped on Nekoka's pause for breath, "Which means the man was one of us."

"Why do you say that?" Jenni asked, her stance casual as she eyed the growing crowd, her hands stuffed in her jeans pockets.

"No normal person could face down my girl," was all Trior said on the subject. "Plus, she's a fair scrapper, and unless he was an exceptional fighter, she would have gotten away in time."

Pablo nodded in agreement. "I've seen her take on three high and violent guys at once, down on the waterfront after the Blues Festival last year. She's no rollover."

"Someone could have drugged her," John said.

Chandler lifted one finger, his wheat-colored eyes looking up into the tree canopy. "Or she could have been mentally controlled or her powers were subdued."

Nekoka's ears swiveled forward. She'd done the model coding for a study on that exact potential with Dr. Carlson years ago. "I think it would be a rare discipline," Nekoka said. "Unless all the right triggers were in place, the power would shut itself off as well."

Chandler pursed his lips. "Well, sure it would be rare, but it is not beyond the realm of possibility. And if Sepia was targeted, they wouldn't send a loafer after her, but someone able to stand up to the full force of her fury. I saw that picture of her, she was in full on 'back the hell off.' Mortal men, normal Seeded, we'd all be dropping her arm, running away screaming while we wet ourselves. She was targeted."

Nekoka's stomach sank, a pit of something distasteful filling in the remaining space. "And homeless Seeded are targeted, too." She squatted down on the ground, drawing an extended claw through the hard-packed dirt. Just scratches, nothing meaningful, but her mind watched the patterns anyway, seeking concrete guidance from the chaos.

"We've, unfortunately, no motivation," Trior said. "Vengeance, hatred, maybe some sick sort of fascination with her. She is a public figure, a star of the west coast. She was planning on some east coast tours this fall. It could be anything. But not sure if this is connected to the homeless situation at all."

"Okay." Pablo lifted his hands, drawing everyone's attention from Trior's morbid summation. "We know someone with the proper powers took her. Trior, any idea why she would be at this park this late at night?"

Trior tapped his shiny leather shoe against the ground, his chin cupped by his fingers. "Any number of reasons." He glanced at John and then sighed. "She'd done some deals here in the past. She'd also play ball with the kids, though that wasn't typically a late-night function."

"Deals?" Jenni asked. "Drugs?"

Trior turned to Jenni, and for an instant Nekoka sensed the depths of the man's loyalty. "Yes. Which are all legal now. This was all years ago when she was much younger and wild. She used some of the local parks at night." He dropped his confrontational gaze from Jenni, whistled an off-tune series of descending notes as if all was right in the world.

"She's not a bad person because of a little pot," Pablo argued.

Trior mumbled something about it wasn't all just pot.

Nekoka burst out laughing, her mouth opened wide, almost biting herself with her own fang. "Oh no, none of us do anything outside the law." Trior glanced at Nekoka. Nekoka sobered and dropped her tone. "Human laws are not necessarily our laws."

Nekoka, Jenni warned.

Nekoka grinned evilly. It seemed she was never bound to be friends with the members of O.G.R.E.

John glared at Nekoka, well, most of them stared at Nekoka, but John's reaction was almost violent. Betrayal, then disgust, raced across his face, contorting it into something alien, visceral. "That sounds a lot like one of those Xenofontos, Nekoka."

Don't do it. Jenni stepped closer to Nekoka's side, the two women banding together as if surrounded by feral wolves.

Nekoka didn't listen. She was sick of it. "I should think so. *Homo superious.* We have elevated innate value. And then you have people like old MacRoe and Eliza Silva, who are practically pushing us out of their little world. They *want* us to be separate from them. Anyone can see the reason in Xenofontos' words."

"They're killers...Terrorists!"

"And like no norm is? Stopping throwing the buzz words around like you know what they mean." Nekoka hissed at John, startling everyone into taking a step away. John looked sickened; Pablo strained. Trior and Chandler frozen like porcelain dolls for the emotion they betrayed. Nekoka didn't care—didn't care what they thought, what anyone thought. They were all deluded with their everyone is equal bullshit.

She turned her back on them and was startled at the mass of people flooding the sidewalks along the edge of the park. People, swarming, all surrounding the spectacle she was performing.

Everything was their fault. Not intrinsically, but by nature of them being the basis of the argument, it was all their fault. She growled low.

"Nekoka." The word came abruptly, like a slap.

Jenni stepped close; a grip of restraint grabbed Nekoka through their telepathic link. It latched onto the heat in her head; the nameless fury was cowed.

Nekoka threw her hands up in the air. "Fine. You guys play at life like everything is fair and everyone is equal. Nothing is fair. You want to know what's on the list of what the universe owes you?

"Zilch. You get nothing. You are *owed* nothing," she yelled out to the crowd. One guy whooped in agreement. "You don't owe anyone anything either, unless you wish to give it. Life isn't equal and life isn't fair. It's the biggest damn lie we try to convince ourselves. Someone bigger, smarter, better will always come in and take, and you better be prepared. Someone came and took Sepia because he was bigger and better. You wanna get her back, then I'm in. I'm not doing it because I owe you anything. I'm not doing it because I have this well of goodness in my heart. I'm not doing this out of some duty that just because I can, I must. I'm doing it because I choose to, for my own reasons. So, get over whatever issue you have with me and let me know when you're ready to do something else about Sepia's abduction."

She could keep rattling on. They were all staring at her like she'd lost her ears and tail.

Nekoka turned to Jenni and thought out loud. *I'm going away now. I'm not disappearing, just going for a walk.*

She turned her back on the frowning O.G.R.E. members, heading for the crowd, the herd of people splitting down the middle as if letting the dangerous carnivore through.

Something hard and anxious inside her dissolved when she realized Jenni followed.

BERLIN HAD NOT BEEN in the room when she returned, so she asked Jenni to go for a walk with her, her voice meek and tired.

"You bring this on yourself," Jenni said. And Nekoka knew it was true, but she also wasn't going to smile and nod and toe a line she didn't believe in just to have false friends. True friends were hard to come by, and right now, Nekoka felt bereft of them. False gold was still false.

A few blocks from their hotel, across from the courthouse, was a large public square paved in red bricks with amphitheater type seating. Being a weekend on a non-rainy June evening, the tiered decks were covered in a fair number of people, some dressing up a bronze statue of a man with a sun hat and outdated specs, others just hanging around talking. Drones patrolled the area, so it lacked the human detritus found on the waterfront. In the center of the square, aimed towards one corner, was an echo chamber. Nekoka positioned Jenni to sit on the opposite side of the chamber as she stood in the center of the courtyard.

"I don't see why they can't see the truth of it," she said, facing Jenni. Nekoka glared at a stray dog that came too close to her. It slunk up some steps towards the coffee shop, searching for scraps of food. "It is proven that we are superior."

Jenni's words came to her in focused, reverberating tones. "We've had this conversation over and over, Nekoka. You can't tell the good people things like that. They feel guilty about their specialness or their class or their power or their wealth or their intelligence. It's socially programmed." Jenni leaned forward, her forearms resting on her knees as she spoke with Nekoka, twenty yards away.

People passed in between Nekoka and Jenni, so she waited to speak. With her arms crossed over her chest, Nekoka agreed, "Even those that aren't Seeded still are not created equal. It's so stupid. As if we're all supposed to yoke ourselves to be equal to the lowest common denominator." Her tail flipped about behind her. "The human race, all subsets of it, needs to accept that some people are smarter, more attractive, more athletic...just better, and be happy they aren't some poor, average loser."

Four teenagers rushed over to her.

"Are you Scratch? From S-Force?" asked a guy—Joey Milke, eighteen, student, a bit of a bastard who picked on some kid named Nick Doce repeatedly on his twitter feed—face full of enough piercings Sepia would have been proud.

"Sure thing." Nekoka pointed over at Jenni. "Guess who that is?"

One of the girls—Heather Smith, seventeen, student, subscribed to Fiann's rarely updated feed and had no recent pile-on participation—gasped. "Fiann," she said in reverent awe. Nekoka's face broke into a huge grin. Jenni had the devoted fans.

Heather ditched Nekoka and straight-lined it to Jenni. The group asked Nekoka for her autograph, which she happily granted, and left little secret birthday welcomes on each of their specs to pop up when their birthdays arrived.

After a few minutes of chatting with the young fanatics, Nekoka noticed Jenni give Heather a warm hug. The girl walked away in a daze and her pack pulled her to their center, everyone asking her about Fiann all at once. Nekoka grinned widely at her friend.

"I think," Jenni began, then snapped her jaw shut as a patrolman stopped ten feet away from Jenni and stared at her. His stance was official, his large cop specs covering his eyes. Thirty pounds overweight, there was no way he could take on Jenni. Few could. If his specs were working, he would know that already.

Jenni continued, ignoring the block of flesh trying to be intimidating, "That they don't understand that you think cats are far better than monkeys, but you also don't think that cats should rule the monkeys."

Nekoka's ears jerked erect. "Why would they think such a silly thing? I know I wouldn't want a pet monkey running around my feet all the time. They just get in the way. The monkeys really need to live and let live. That's what most of the cats want, anyway." She pointedly stared at the cop, his buttons barely containing his belly.

The cop's general displeasure had created a miasma around Jenni, and people began to give the women a wide swath, which amused Nekoka considering their current conversation.

Nekoka decided she didn't want their admirers to leave them alone and began doing a series of yoga poses that put any yogi to shame. She bent over in the wheel pose, then shifted her weight into a handstand, and while holding herself upside down by her hands, did the splits. She should join the Seeded Circus with her friend, Flip.

"But I don't think they understand that is what you want, Nekoka." Jenni stood and turned to the patrolman, who dropped his arms to the side, his posture switching to aggressive without any provocation. She stood there staring the man down, her weight settled on her back leg. "I think," she continued, "they are confused by lack of information. They don't bother to talk to you about your true beliefs and end up just making assumptions. And you never explain yourself."

The patrolman babbled something that Nekoka couldn't hear from this distance because he wasn't in the echo chamber acoustic path.

A drone arrived, hovering above the officer. Then another, filming the altercation. A scan of the crowd showed dozens of other people were also filming the scene.

"No, officer. I'm just hanging out, as you can see. Is it illegal to visit the public square?" Nekoka was bent backwards in camel pose, her back bowed like a fishing rod landing the one that wouldn't get away, her head a hand span from her heels. "I do not intend to move on," Jenni said. "There is no Act for Portland."

The crowd grew thicker, arcing around Jenni and the officer at a distance, like the spectators to a brawl. Whispers raced through the gathering like wildfire, and Nekoka could hear everyone asking what was going on. Nekoka unwound herself, stood and walked to the edge of the gathering. "That pig has issues with my friend sitting in a public place, minding her own business." The spectators began sending on the message, and like a game of telephone, by the time it reached the opposite side by Jenni, they all knew that the cop had threatened Jenni, had anti-Seeded sentiment, and they needed to save the woman from police brutality.

So, like a rising tide, the mob of old, young, men and women—some dressed like corporate drones, others just stray kids, tourists, too—all stepped forward, surrounding Jenni from the big, bad cop. Nekoka stood on the sidelines, her grin showing all her teeth, the fangs flashing in the lamplight.

"Hey, back off," one punk swathed in leather and chains said to the cop. He apparently had experience back-talking authority. "She's minding her own business, like you should do." He stood between Jenni and the cop, like he was defending his fair maiden from the ravenous dragon. Jenni glanced over at Nekoka.

Is this your doing?

Nekoka watched on and shrugged, then sent, *I just suggested that you were being unfairly harassed.*

A drone overhead began squawking: "You shall disperse. You shall disperse," in an aggressive robotic voice. At this point, the officer went for his club as a businesswoman shook her finger in his face, scolding him, and most likely bruising his ego as people laughed.

"Alright everyone," Jenni's voice rose over the whir of the crowd and the drone's alarm. "I don't want to cause any disturbance." Her tone was light and friendly, almost casually dissident, but Nekoka knew that Jenni didn't want any mad mob mentality to settle in. Nekoka thought it would inject some excitement to their day, but agreed with Jenni that they didn't want anyone to get hurt.

She stepped away from the cop, exuding friendly smiles and good-natured ease. The people's attention followed her like a dog followed the hand with a treat. "We've gotta be moving on. Thank you, everyone, for rescuing me." The crowd laughed, suddenly appeased, and the cop took his hand away from the club, glowering at every excited and relieved face.

Like a ship's prow parting the waters, Jenni waded through the crowd of people that opened up to leave her a path, people reaching out to shake her hand, or just touch her, like a messiah come to deliver them. It was amazing the camaraderie the woman could instill in people. She could rule the world if she wanted to, just with a smile and a word.

"Where to now?" Nekoka said once Jenni reached her. Jenni brushed her brown hair off her shoulders, letting it lie down her back. She began walking around the milling crowd towards the train line.

"Well, we have homeless being kidnapped, someone orchestrating freeway collisions, and Sepia taken, too. All very disturbing. Maybe if we find one group, we find another. Let's see if Berlin has any more info. Maybe he knows that park. Didn't he mention someone in a dark van taking one of the homeless?"

"Yes. Let's stop by a vendor, first, and get him a phone. I can't do this no-communication thing."

CHAPTER 19

The Myroi

The Myroi stood on the edge of the platform, it and two others of its moiety. They watched as the enriched praenletta were lined up, asked questions, handled physically by others of their kind, some even unenriched. The Myroi were told by one of the unenriched that most were gathered from the northwestern portion of one of the major separate spaces of Jikon, a place called the United States of America. Everything named. Everything separate. The Myroi possessed separate moieties, but the amount of partitioning among these praenletta didn't parse out for the Myroi. They did not understand how so many ideologies and creeds split up these praenletta and their unenriched brethren. Such scattered minds sickened them. The people of this place were alien. The Myroi would be happy when their assignment in Jikon ended, and they could return to the familiar.

The moiety turned away from their vantage point and began their patrol of the grounds. From the receiving lines, the praenletta were taken to holding areas and divided into groups based on their praena strength - those with strong praena and those with weak praena.

They passed through the holding zone, where most of the praenletta were corralled in either group compounds or singular enclosures if they proved difficult. One praenletta had caused much trouble and had been separated. It splashed colors of raw crimson and vitriolic purple. The praenletta squatted in the center of its square, its heavy form damaged from the exchange. With a feral look in its eyes, the violent praenletta watched as some guards passed it by, but it appeared to be properly cowed and didn't exude a stream of endless noise like it had earlier.

The other praenletta who had seen this one struggle and lose continued to observe it. The moiety slipped between their enclosures, silent in their passing. A call summoned the moiety; they were needed elsewhere for the whole. The praena they had collected needed to be sent home to aid their defense. They flickered out of one place and to another, leaving behind those disturbing faces full of emotion.

CHAPTER 20

Martha

Martha kept herself small in the middle of a circus cage, hoping to draw no attention to herself. It was a skill she'd used often to avoid Greg and Sven and others who wanted to use the freesteaders, who pushed Matoro and meth and sometimes hope, and that was the raunchiest business of them all.

Four other captives shared her cage; not the same ones who came with her in that van from Portland. Her cage was one of hundreds, set out in a grid on a cement floor, the ceilings crisscrossed with pipes and huge lamps that never turned off. Sometimes, when the guards were far away, the other captives would talk to each other, but Martha didn't bother. They were not her friends.

One of her cage mates was also from Portland, hung out near the south waterfront where the drones were thick, but she'd managed to get by. She sang like a blue jay and told the others everything about her life. The guards would bang the edges of the cage with a steel rod and squawk at them to shut up. Martha just kept her head down.

She didn't want to be taken. She'd seen others taken, complacent noobs who just did what they were told.

Well, most people. There was that one lady, not a freesteader, but Martha had seen her around Portland with those who made themselves feel better by helping those scrimping and scrambling to survive. She would come with that officer. She fought like a wolverine, clawing and spitting, and men would turn and run. Then they dunked her in something, and they beat the living shit out of her. Martha'd seen pimps and pushers, drugged out wack jobs lay into someone, and this woman...well, the guards had put her *down*.

In plain view for all to see.

Every so often, sprinklers overhead spritzed them with a metallic scented fluid. It was cold. Though they'd never wet them enough to soak them through, Martha's bones turned into shards of ice.

Footsteps. Martha curled in smaller.

A clicking noise and a voice. "Your turn."

Hands grabbed her.

Martha looked. A man, big, eyes pale, nose broken several times. On reflexive instinct, she lashed out, aiming for those fucking pale eyes, but he caught her hand and squeezed, a wicked grin breaking his face into something demonic.

"Wanna fight?" He jerked his eyebrows up once. "I'll take you, bag lady."

Martha ducked her head. She didn't want to be beat, and that was all these people wanted to dish out.

"Should we drug her?" asked another man Martha hadn't noticed. Her muscles tensed, waiting for the blow.

"They don't like their product when we do. This one's a nul anyway. We'll be fine."

He clamped his arm around her, and she crumbled like week old bread. Useless nul. Worthless. She wanted to stab herself in the gut. She never bent to street thugs, never played the lamb. But now, shackled and crushed, the fight drained from her like blood from an open wound.

The man smelled like coffee and whatever he used as deodorant. His arms radiated heat. She almost felt warm.

Don't take this!

Don't take this from this bastard!

But she'd seen them destroy that other woman, the fighter, the one who stood up for herself. She'd seen it, and they'd do the same to her.

Martha didn't want to be beaten. She'd worked hard to stay safe on the streets, and she could stay safe here, too. She just had to pay attention and be quick. That's all. Just pay attention.

They marched her out of the coliseum-sized room. She walked on, dazed, her palms slick and clammy. Her gaze kept slipping to her feet, watching them slide forward, tiny steps propelled by the men pushing her along. Attached to the end of the hall was a room, white, and in the center of the room was a solitary medical chair.

Martha twisted. The chair sent shivers over her body, sent her breath into hyper gasps. The man's grip tightened and tightened. Martha whimpered, certain her bones would snap.

"Now now. Stop fussing. We're just going to give you a little examination."

"Fuck you. Let me go. I didn't do nothing!" She shifted her body, aiming an elbow, but she'd always been better at avoiding the fights than winning them, and the two men grabbed her and stuffed her in the chair. Metal cuffs around her wrists. Straps around her ankles. Her chest.

"Why are you doing this to me?"

Her head was cupped against a pad, a strap against her forehead and one under her chin, holding her in place and keeping her immobile.

"What are you doing to me?" she whined through her closed jaw.

They didn't answer before they left the white room.

The door closed. Martha blinked against the blazing light, tears streaming down her cheeks like a river.

A whirring noise behind her.

Oh my God. Oh my God. Oh my God.

She tried to worm her hand around, see if she could undo the buckle, but she knew hope was deadly. She couldn't escape. She couldn't get out of this trap.

A nail jammed into her skull, punched through the skin and bone and flesh of her head, slipping into her brain, and she realized, even through a jaw strapped shut, she could still release a scream.

CHAPTER 21

Thomas

Thomas Hallaman stepped down the metal portable stairs from the Cessna jet, surveying the airstrip planted in the middle of an empty field—the only crop growing up from the scrub and dry grass. Thomas pondered the severity of the dryness in these fields, preventing agribusiness from transforming it into arable land. A dusty sedan that might have once been black purred to life as he and his new personal assistant approached it.

The assistant was a leggy blond, with small-rimmed glasses and severely buttoned up hair. Not a strand slid loose from the tight bun on the back of her head. A dark blue Prada suit framed her toned figure. She had introduced herself as Tricia, no last name, and she eyed him with a certain ferocity that Thomas found arousing.

He enjoyed women with a spine. In college, after Kathy's murder, things had changed for him. Admittedly, he wasn't at his full capacity, but he wouldn't use that as an excuse. He couldn't blame 'randy youth,' either. Setting blame was easy, but he was the kind of man to own his mistakes and in those few years he had made many.

He'd hurt dozens of women in those years. Broken their spirits. It hadn't been intentional.

Sourness tickled his tongue. And he pushed that bit of his past back into the dark along with Kathy's dead body laid out on a morgue's steel table.

His assistant's strong stride and heel-enhanced calves drew Thomas' attention back to her as she led him to the car. If it wasn't business, he'd make a point of seducing this confident woman the old-fashioned way, but he never blended his job with his personal life.

"Mr. Hallaman," Tricia said, eyes towards the car, not even looking at him, "after we get settled into the guest housing, you have a meeting with Director Jeon. He's eager to meet with you."

She had been assigned to him for this trip, his second visit to Minidoka, a camp of rehabilitation for the homeless displaced by his recent development interests, all at great expense for a group of private investors. The unemployed street people were lucky to have such an opportunity.

The name Minidoka was a remnant from World War II, distilled down to a whispered rumor for this generation who had libraries of information at their eyeswipe. The government had gathered thousands of Japanese, either immigrants or American born, and placed them in internment camps. These were not deadbeats, but hard-working men and women. People who pulled their weight. The camp had spread over 200 acres of empty high desert in southern Idaho. Now there remained no sign of that chapter to America's dark history, no memorial, no reminder of the country's deeds. How easily the inconvenient parts of history could be buried under ignorance.

The driver settled their luggage in the trunk and held the door open for Thomas. Soon they were cruising down a two-lane highway. Flat plains, endless and brown, passed by. The arid landscape swayed with genetically altered dryland crops, wheat mainly, though Thomas knew corn fields also edged along Minidoka's property. Every speck of land was under production to feed the billions of people of the United States and the world beyond. Unless the landscape was too dry, then even the GMO crops couldn't eke out a meager living.

Brown birds flushed from the road to dive back into the patches of wheat. No sign of human habitation this far away from any municipality.

Such isolation was necessary, since the project wasn't exactly open to public scrutiny. Some things the public just didn't need to know.

Director Jeon had congratulated Thomas over a secure message, telling him that he was responsible for about twenty percent of the participants, most of them previously homeless. But some of Thomas' teams also gathered individuals bordering on criminal lifestyles. Thieves, pimps, and hustlers. He'd gained a sense of responsibility for the West Coast. Each time a report on the reduction of homelessness and crime reached his specs, a greater sense of accomplishment fueled his actions.

Yes, he was making the world a better place.

A safer place.

A near silent hour passed by at their sedate, yet practical, speed. The driver hit the turn signal and Thomas searched for the road, but only found a dirt path barely wide enough for their automobile. More minutes on a slow, washboard road, and they entered a gap in a large chain-link fence that marked the demarcation line between no-man's-land and the private facility of Minidoka. More rocking, enough to agitate Thomas' nerves to want to get out and walk. A one-story squat warehouse, which had probably taken a week to erect, materialized out of the heat shimmer on the horizon. This main warehouse held classrooms and medical facilities. He considered sitting in on some of the lessons today if he had the time. Give the instructors a sense of evaluation so they didn't slide into lazy habits. Last time he'd actually learned something about diagnosing an automobile engine's failings.

A few new additions had nearly doubled the facility in size. The building process was so fast, Thomas guessed at shoddy construction. He'd have to assure they didn't use uncured plywood or other potentially harmful manufacturing materials. The Minidoka Project had reported that they'd added a gym and expanded the mess hall, as well as included more housing and counseling rooms. Good. He always had more of the destitute to send here.

Though, for all intents and purposes, some of them should be released soon. Now addiction free and offered proper mental health support. Basic job skills. Instilled with a sense of community. Of duty. They should be ready to rejoin society.

The driver opened his door and a wash of dry desert air closed in, sucking out his moisture, practically mummifying him. He knew he would have a nosebleed if he stayed here for very long.

A score of other cars were parked in a large gravel parking lot, all covered in a patina of dust. The only feature marring the sprawling wall of the warehouse was a single unimpressive aluminum door. A video camera was mounted above the door, the sole distinguishing characteristic.

The taciturn driver removed their luggage, and Thomas grabbed his own so the man could carry Tricia's. They fell into step behind the driver, waiting while he rapped on the door. It opened automatically, and they walked down a narrow plain hallway pumped full of cool air, the clacks of their footsteps loud compared to an incessant background hum. A small reception area with a man dressed in a military-styled uniform waited for them.

"ID please."

Thomas handed over his ID and his pass that showed he'd already gone through the background checks to appease the upper management of the compound. Tricia handed over her own credentials.

The guard smiled at her. "Welcome back, Tricia."

A tiny twitch of her lips alluded to a hint of a smile. She nodded. "Thank you, Jim."

Thomas almost snorted, but this was not the time nor the people around which he should let his guard down. Instead, he raised an eyebrow when Tricia caught his eye. Her face remained impassive. Well, he'd have fun cracking this nut. If he had any free time from this latest visit.

After checking in, he and Tricia were led down another hallway by a different staff member: a nondescript woman in a pants suit with long straight hair and a short, clipped stride that caused Thomas to go exceptionally slow so as not to overtake her.

The staff wing of the facility was no posher than the rehabilitation wing. The woman left Tricia at one room and escorted him to the next. Room 105. Why they didn't just call it room 5, he wasn't sure. There certainly were not a hundred rooms, nor was there an additional floor on this wing to keep track of.

"We've an orientation in a half hour, Mr. Hallaman."

"Fine. Thank you." He closed the door behind her and frowned at the spartan room. Last visit, he'd been assigned to room 107, and he would swear on his sister's grave it was furnished exactly the same. He found it dreary: white walls with no art—department store art or anything of style—and no windows to the outside. He did have an on suite bathroom, and for that, he was thankful.

He checked his private phone, the burner he'd purchased just before coming. He had another one of those texts. Anonymous and cryptic.

You had been warned. This is not the opportunity you blindly wish it to be.

Fuck off. He powered down the phone. Warnings without supportive data were useless.

After draping his suit jacket over the back of a desk chair, he unpacked his toiletries, setting his contact lens solution aside. He hated how his eyes always itched in this dry heat. He'd even taken his allergy medicine, but the sagebrush pollen seemed to seek him out like starving rats to a bloated corpse.

He blinked. A slipped contact revealed the blue of his right eye, icy, akin to the faint hue of an inner glacier. He pressed the contact into place, blinking again, his gaze now his typical dark blue.

Once his half hour ran dry, he grabbed his jacket, pulled it on, smoothing out the lines along his shoulders, and was gathered by Tricia, who took him to meet Director Jeon.

DIRECTOR JEON, A MAN in his fit upper fifties, came around his desk to shake Thomas' hand. "Mr. Hallaman, thank you for visiting again on such short notice." Though his English was perfect, he still held on to his Korean accent, advertised by softened words and the evident difficulty with Rs and Vs. The Director wore black cloth gloves and a shirt with a high mandarin collar, showing very little skin at all.

Thomas shook the Director's hand. Though Director Jeon was over a foot shorter than Thomas, the man's grip was firm, and he held Thomas' eyes with his dark brown, nearly black ones, like every glance was a challenge. Thomas was never a man to back down from a challenge.

Director Jeon offered a closed-lip smile.

"It's my pleasure, Director," Thomas said. "Though I am curious why you called me out here this time. Last visit, I thought we smoothed out the managerial issues of start-up."

Director Jeon returned to his chair behind his simple desk. "Mr. Hallaman, please have a seat."

Thomas sat in the narrow chair before the Director's desk, scanning the small office and judging it deficient. No art, no windows, much like his room. The desk was plain, the chair something honed out on an assembly line. Thomas' waiting room back at Arnold and Hallaman Development was better furnished than this. Hell, his broom closet had more class.

The Director folded his hands on the top of a manila envelope resting on the desk. "When you agreed to join us on this endeavor to better America, you knew it was your dedication to the cause that got you a place among us, not to mention your excellent business savvy. The Founders plan to open new branches of the project throughout the country. To do this with as few roadblocks as possible, we wanted you to learn more about our recent expansion and help us write up a business model for the new compounds, focus on what's working and cut out what's not. I'm sure you've excellent ideas that we could all benefit from."

With a skill sharpened through many boardroom clashes, Thomas kept his body relaxed, his posture casual but attentive, though his instincts crashed within him like a stampede of buffalo. Jeon was up to something. This decision to draw him to the boondocks lacked sense, plus his consultation fee would carve a chunk of their operational funds.

With all of his confident charm, Thomas offered the Director a smug grin. "Of course, sir. You can count on me. But I want to remind you that my original contract assures I would not have to relocate." God, he would hate to be stuck here in this asshole of the world for long, no matter the pay or benefits. "My company is of prime importance to me, and it's not something I could operate remotely."

The Director's brows bunched in thought, then he slowly nodded. "Yes, that is correct. We did make that agreement. Still, as you know, the next growth stage of any project can be delicate."

Thomas nodded, blocking all expression from his face.

The Director continued, "And it appears there is a problem with some of the subjects of the experiment."

"Experiment?" Thomas asked, his stomach souring. That word wouldn't pass his PR team; it held bad connotations. Plus, he did not like surprises, and Jeon was dumping a great steaming heap of a surprise on his lap.

"Of a sort. The Founders call it the experiment. A way to create something of value—" the Director mused, and Thomas guessed there had been more there, more words brewing in the man's brain, but that he had chosen to cut himself off. Thomas could read that the man found his choice of word amusing, though his lips hadn't even twitched. It was something in the set of his tone, in the extension of the word, like he tasted it against his tongue.

"What is it you think I can do?" Thomas allowed his eyes to narrow, playing up his incomprehension.

The Director opened up the file folder that had been resting on his side of the desk. On the top of a pile of documents was a photo of Thomas surrounded by a group of people, mostly women, at a party. From the angle, it wasn't apparent where the picture had been taken, but he knew the general time frame. College. Two decades old. His face smoother, before the tension of the real world carved faint lines in his skin, a trimmed beard as college kids tended to cultivate because it gave them a sense of adulthood.

"The Chief knows more about you than you have alluded to, Mr. Hallaman." He reached out and flipped over the photo. On the next paper, stamped across the page of typeface, was a large red CONFIDENTIAL.

Thomas couldn't read the small font from his chair without leaning forward, but he knew. Knew what it must mean. The heat of panic flushed through his face. They were aware of his secret, the one he'd worked so hard to keep hidden. How would these people have found out? And now the Director was playing a game with him. He refused to be baited. Thomas crossed his arms and relaxed into the chair, letting slip a bit of annoyance.

"Well, do you want to continue this long, drawn out game or would you rather get on with it?" Thomas asked.

Director Jeon's eyes widened. Just a tad. But enough. Thomas had caught him off guard.

"I see you're a man who likes to play it straight," said the Director.

"This should not come as a surprise."

Then, the Director closed the folder. "The Chief has been studying you for quite some time and has come to the conclusion you have a certain special skill that could help with some of the more unruly subjects."

Thomas swallowed once. "You have no idea about any *special skills* I might have. And I don't appreciate the threat..."

"Oh, come now, Mr. Hallaman. We both know if the city of Chicago discovers your secret, that everything you hold dear will crumble at your feet. A tower of accomplishments dashed to ruin by one rash decision. We offer significant compensation for every individual you help,"—he said help in such a dead, dry tone, that if Thomas wasn't smack in the middle of being blackmailed, his mind might have wandered—"and you will be fulfilling your goal to assure safer streets of America."

Chicago's Municipal Autonomy Act would seize his company from him if it came out. If they knew he was Seeded.

With fists clenched where they rested on his thighs, Thomas asked, "What exactly do you want me to do?"

THE ROOM COULD HAVE been like any other medical examination room: white-fronted cupboards, chrome sink, computer monitor that swiveled on an arm, medical bed with paper sheet, a rolling stool for the doctor to sit on, except for the man handcuffed with plastic coated manacles to a plastic chair.

When Thomas and Jeon entered the exam room, two doctors and three armed guards joined them. The precaution twisted Thomas' already taut nerves.

The overhead lighting buzzed in his ears. With his shoulders pulled back and chin up, he towered over most of the people in this room. The man in the chair, shackled hands resting in his lap, wouldn't look at any of them.

"This is Maximilian Scott," Director Jeon explained. "One of our recruits from the Midwest. He doesn't wish to reform."

Maximilian looked up, face bruised on one side, scowl masking the obvious fear in his eyes. He spat towards Jeon. The Director didn't even react, not a flinch, not frown, not a sigh.

Thomas did not want to do this.

"He electrocutes things," Jeon explained, "and before being brought into the facility, he electrocuted three security guards to death while he was breaking into a convenience store. He stole three hundred and forty-seven dollars, a carton of Marlboros, and a pack of Juicy Fruit gum. The local police could not contain him, and so we took him off their hands for rehabilitation."

Thomas stared into Maximilian's eyes, searching for something...remorse, maybe. That sentient spark that people had in them that revealed their sense of morality, of the desire to do good by their fellow man.

Maximilian just looked scared. And right he should be.

"What can I do about it?" Thomas asked. "You've already incarcerated him. He's chained up in non-conductive restraints. If—"

Jeon leveled a bland stare at Thomas. "I think you can help him achieve a different mindset about his rehabilitation."

The criminal's sea-green eyes, like watercolor splashed on white paper, gazed up at him.

"Fine. Leave me."

"But—" one of the doctors began, but Jeon ushered them out of the exam room. Thomas hit the intercom and demanded surveillance be cut off from the room.

"Sir," the security sergeant said, "that is highly inadvisable."

"I can take care of myself. Do it. Now."

"Yes, sir."

Thomas was alone with Maximilian.

"What can you do to me, you dark eye?"

Thomas stepped forward, as if threatening the man. This time he spat at Thomas. The spittle splattered his tie.

"You think there isn't anything I can do to you? You are an idiot," Thomas began. He had to make this play convincing because he was under no assumption that he still wasn't being watched by Jeon. "You're Seeded.

You have power and what do you do? Kill a man for some cigarettes and gum? Instead of working to provide for yourself, you steal from people's bowed backs. It's filth like you," and Thomas got into the man's space, using his bulk to bend the man backwards, "who cause problems for those who abide by the laws."

Maximilian flinched and cowered as Thomas spread spittle over his face in his vehemence. It was only fair play. And with how his day was unfolding, it wasn't hard for Thomas to let go, unleash his anger on this criminal. He ensured some of his saliva landed in the man's mouth, in his eyes, mingling with Maximilian's own bodily fluids. Now, he just needed to do one more thing, and every civilized cell in his body cringed at what it must be.

He spun away from the man, putting on the show of exasperation, of barely bridled anger. Clenching his fists, he pounded against his chest, his tie, rubbing the criminal's spit onto his hand. Swiftly, he licked it up, letting the other man's DNA mix with his own.

Thomas nearly gagged.

Unclean.

He turned back, glowering over the man who was cringing in his plastic chair, and a fission of power coursed through Thomas at seeing this societal leach cower.

"Now," he said slowly, capturing the man's gaze with his own, letting his power flow from him into Maximilian. Once they'd shared DNA, his target was captured. Thomas' thrall. He hated his power on every level, but his balls were in a vice, and until he could figure out Jeon's true game, he would play along. "Now," he repeated, "you will do as the doctors and guards say and work to be a worthwhile person, to help your fellow man and work hard."

Maximilian shuddered. The smell of urine saturated the air.

"Do you comply, Maximilian?"

"Y—yes, sir."

Thomas stood, grabbed a napkin from above the sink and wiped off his tie. He needed to return to his room and brush his teeth. The filth of the other man's spittle ground around in Thomas' mouth like grit.

"Good."

Thomas banged on the door and the guard opened it. "He should behave now." Thomas strode down the hall without looking back.

CHAPTER 22

Berlin

Together with Nekoka and Jenni, Berlin walked along, not paying attention to his feet, as he inexpertly typed into his new phone with his thumbs. Nekoka had offered him specs, but his eyes couldn't read the augmented reality well, so she picked a phone instead. All his old passwords had faded from his memory, so he went about setting up new accounts for everything. Email, the old gaming chat group, the feeds for Scratch and Fiann, and now S-force, O.G.R.E., and Guardian Alliance. Nekoka had already installed her and Jenni's info so he could contact them if needed.

His new jeans were a little snug in the crotch, but Nekoka had nodded with approval, so he hadn't swapped them out. The hat kept his face shaded from the sun. He'd been touched she'd remembered that he needed a hat. The shoes fit perfectly, and his T-shirt has a big S on the front. Nekoka suggested he wear the ashy gray S shirt. He could tell, though she hadn't said anything, that Jenni thought the S shirt was dumb. Nekoka also got him a shirt with a leafy motif. That one was his favorite. It reminded him of trees he'd climbed as a kid.

He hadn't looked up his parents' old feeds or searched his address to see if anything new had been built on the ruins.

Nekoka and Jenni were chatting about some guys back from where they were from. It sounded fun, to be a part of a group. He tucked his phone away when the front of the hotel towered above them. He felt vaguely guilty for even being in this hotel, meant for fancy people, people better than he was, but Jenni held the door open for him, so he slipped in, hoping not to block the way for anyone else entering.

"Those jeans look great on you," Nekoka said from behind him. Berlin's face heated, and he could only smile at her through the reflection in the elevator doors. Jenni snorted.

Nekoka glanced over at Jenni and the two seemed to be sharing some inside joke. Berlin looked down. He hoped they weren't teasing him. Just being nice now, and then later leaving him, mocking him on their feeds for everyone to read. He swallowed and clenched his hands together before him, wishing his jeans were loose enough to stuff them in the pockets.

"I'm sorry, Berlin," Nekoka said out of the blue, draping her arms over his shoulders. "I didn't mean to make you feel awkward—" she paused, flicked her eyes to Jenni, then amended, "uncomfortable."

"I'm not uncomfortable," he said, because he wanted to make Nekoka feel better.

"It's okay if you are," Jenni said. "You just met us. We're giving you things. You must wonder what we want."

"No! No, you aren't like that. I know that..." Jenni and Nekoka were good people.

"Don't trust everything you read, kid. But we do mean you well. Especially Nekoka. She's kind of claimed you as her own, and once Nekoka claims you, there is no escape."

Nekoka bristled. "Hey! You make that sound like that's a bad thing."

Jenni dropped her chin, leveling a 'do you see' look at Berlin, who could only laugh at them. He wished he'd had a friendship like Jenni's and Nekoka's. He wished he had friends.

"We'll be your friends. We are your friends," Jenni said, startling Berlin. She smiled at him, and in that smile was a kind of sorrow that reminded him of himself. Jenni understood, somehow, just how Berlin felt.

"Was there any doubt?" Nekoka asked.

Berlin relaxed, just let the worry vanish and the joy rise; the two women grinned back.

IN THE ROOM, NEKOKA slipped down into cat form. Berlin stared in queasy fascination. Her body shrank, going all soft and then reshaping itself. At least it didn't appear painful. In only seconds, all that remained was a yellow-brown striped tabby, which hopped up on the bed, circled on a pillow and settled down.

"What's she doing?" he asked Jenni.

"Something computery," Jenni said, flopping in a stiff backed but nicely upholstered chair with some formal looking pattern. She picked up the remote and clicked on the TV. "Wanna see what's on?"

Berlin sat his butt on the edge of the bed, facing the TV, feet cemented to the ground. Jenni flipped from a reality show, to a game show, to a sitcom she stalled on for about two minutes, then flipped again.

"See anything you like?" she asked.

He blinked, squished his eyes shut and shifted his attention to Jenni. He shrugged. "It's all interesting." Something flashed on the screen, and his eyes jumped back to it.

"Why don't we get comfy? Nekoka won't mind sharing the bed with us. But first, room service! Hungry?"

Jenni picked up a laminated menu brochure that folded into thirds. "Hmm, salmon rolls." She flipped a panel. "Let's get some of those for when Nekoka pops out of it. Anything you'd like? A burger, steak? They have kinda upscale food here. Calamari...actually, that sounds gross. Aren't squids as intelligent as cats?" Her eyes flicked to Nekoka with an amused glint. "I'm going to get some pasta."

"Whatever you're having."

Jenni glanced up from the menu, her soft green eyes going softer. "Well, I'm going to try a lot of different things. How often do you get to stay at a snazzy place like this?" She scooped up her phone and began tapping out her order.

"I've never stayed at a place like this," Berlin admitted.

"Me neither," Jenni said, shaking her head but not taking her attention away from her order.

Not too much time passed before the order came. Piles of food that set Berlin's eyes and stomach in a kind of desperate shock. Where to start first? Jenni just grabbed a plate and dug in, scooping up pasta, some chicken, and piles of this gross looking asparagus dish. There were vegetables in various stages of being cooked, and Berlin dutifully put some carrots on his plate.

They had some glaze on them, and he hoped it wasn't icky, but generally he liked carrots.

Jenni scooped up Nekoka's pillow, with Nekoka on it, and settled her at the foot of the bed, then climbed up to the headboard, patting the space next to her for Berlin.

"You're eating in bed?" Berlin's mother never would have allowed that. Jenni was such a rebel.

"Sure. Come on. Let's find something good."

Berlin leaned against the headboard, his socked feet stretched out before him, almost tucked under Nekoka's pillow. Every so often her paw would twitch or an ear would flick, but she was motionless as a snoozing cat.

A reality show where they put one normal person in with a house of Seeded and they all bickered caught Jenni's attention for about two seconds. "Hate that shit," she explained as she flipped to the next channel. She paused there, mainly to bite into her chicken leg, and the fast-paced announcer rattled off: "Bad credit, no problem. No credit, just fine. You deserve that big house. You want your coworkers to wish that they were *you* with *your* new car? Credit Today can—" She flipped away with a frown. Berlin quietly watched, trying to eat slowly and cleanly, but he kept getting grease on his fingers and face, and he didn't want to bother anyone by getting up.

"Oh no," Jenni said in quiet awe.

Berlin forgot his filthy hands and paid attention to the television.

On the screen was a woman, not very pretty. Her jaw was square, cheeks a little doughy, hair an untidy mane of brown curls, but the woman still held the eye. Her magnetism wasn't from her general appearance.

She was talking and Berlin's brain hadn't caught up yet. The area was windy, an ocean churned in the background, and the woman kept putting her hair behind her ear.

Jenni turned the volume up, sitting forward.

"—our bonds and make the path our own. Time and time again, the humans blame us for every evil, for every disaster or accident, and when we do help—as many of my sisters and brothers do—they are often questioned if they couldn't have done more, been better." She narrowed her pale gray eyes, so varied, the color shifted like smoke.

"And the hijacking of autopilots on cars in Portland, Oregon?" the interviewer behind the camera asked.

"The authorities need to question what the real purpose was? An act of terrorism or something deeper? Why would we send cars into a massive collision? It isn't our goal to eradicate humans. Humans just have to realize Seeded are not bound by their laws."

"But Eliza Silva of Sapian True—"

The woman shook her head, cutting the interviewer off. "Means nothing."

"Who is that?" Berlin whispered.

"Samantha Fontos," Jenni said, as if that should mean something to Berlin. He took a sip of his water as the woman continued.

"So, we, Xenofontos—" Oh, Berlin understood now, "—declare ourselves a sovereign entity. We remove ourselves from under the control of human governments that do not hold our safety and best possible well-being in high regard. We will govern ourselves and police ourselves. Our constitution will be sent to every nation's government. Any member of the Seeded community can petition for membership."

She faced the camera, stoic and severe. "We've suffered your injustices for too long. This is our declaration. It is time we took a stand and though we seek a peaceful separation, make no mistake—we possess the strength to protect our freedom. If you dare to intervene, we'll perceive it as an act of aggression."

THE SHOWER WAS HOT, and the bathroom filled with steam. Jenni had gone silent after the announcement, and Nekoka was still doing whatever it was she was doing on the pillow. Napping, it seemed to Berlin, but everyone needed a nap now and then. Berlin had nothing else to do.

He'd scrubbed himself pink and now wiped the condensation off the mirror, his fingers pruney and face washed out.

When he started seeing ghosts, his eyes had gone white. All white. He examined his eyes searching for the ring that separated his iris from his pupil, much like Tony in his gym class in tenth grade, who'd tried to count his own freckles. Tony was a redhead and liked to talk about his father and fishing and sneered at Berlin whenever he was caught listening. He lived three houses down and was one of the ones who hadn't survived that night.

He squished his eyes together, willing himself not to cry.

That was two years ago and not his fault. Not his fault.

Not his fault.

He wiped his skin down with the fluffy hotel towel and frowned at the pile of his dirty clothing. Well, not dirty, not like he was used to. All his new clean clothes were still in the hotel room. Feeling self-conscious, very self-conscious, he wrapped the towel around his waist and opened the door to slip out, grab his new clothes, and sneak back into the bathroom before anyone noticed.

Well, Nekoka noticed. She was back in human form, apparently done with her cat nap, and her eyes locked on him, narrowed, and a slightly scary smile slipped onto her lips.

That slightly scary smile did awkward things to his body.

"I forgot clean clothes."

"Oh, clothing is optional." Nekoka rolled to her hands and knees on the bed, tail high, canine's showing.

Berlin shifted his weight from one foot to the other, unsure what to do. What she meant. If he should run or—

"Nekoka," Jenni said from her spot on the foot of the bed, her back to Nekoka. She flipped the channel from some pop star reality TV show to a sit-com with canned laughter. He hadn't even realized the TV was on. "Stop eyeing the poor boy like you're going to eat him."

Berlin stilled.

Nekoka flicked an ear and stared at Jenni's back. "How do you know I'm even looking at him?"

"I know you. Naked boy in room equals Nekoka's second favorite pastime. Berlin, just ignore her."

Berlin's body, cooling in the bedroom after the shower, went blazing hot.

Nekoka chuckled, her smile turning softer.

He took a step towards where he'd stowed his clothing. "I won't be naked long. I just need to get my clothes."

"Oh Berlin, I don't mind. I don't mind at all." Nekoka laid back down on the bed, stretching her body out long atop the comforter.

Jenni flipped off the television and looked at Nekoka over her shoulder. Nekoka frowned.

Jenni tilted her head, eyebrows raised. "Nekoka, I think you should be less a letch with Berlin."

Nekoka's ears perked forward, her attention back on Berlin, studying him. "Are you a virgin, Berlin?"

Berlin's jaw fell slack. His skin heated to surface-of-the-sun degrees, and he wished he could be invisible instead of see ghosts, that he could simply disappear and avoid all of this humiliation.

"Leave him alone," Jenni said with exasperation. "You don't need to jump some poor innocent kid."

"I'm not a kid," Berlin said. "I'm almost 18!" He steeled himself. Nekoka was his hero. He adored her. He inhaled, filling his chest, making himself look more manly, and smiled at Nekoka. Nekoka smiled back.

"See, he's underage," Jenni said.

Berlin's smile faltered.

Nekoka pulled her ears back and glowered at Jenni. "I'm being good."

He had to gain control. "Really, I don't mind," Berlin said, pushing happiness into his voice. "Anything to help."

Jenni burst out laughing. "Berlin, you've no idea what you would be getting into. Trust me on this—wait until you've been with a nice, sweet girl before you tackle Nekoka."

Nekoka scowled at Jenni's back. "Don't listen to her, Berlin. I can be sweet *and* innocent."

"Only through years of practice could you play innocent, Nekoka."

Nekoka's body went still, her lips pressed together tight enough to crush grapes. Then her face smoothed. "Okay." She nodded at Jenni, then put on a smile. "Well, I'll be back later. You two have fun."

Jenni scowled in annoyance. Berlin released a sad whine, then gulped it down.

"Here's my computer." Nekoka dug her fingers into her stomach. They sank in, as if she was made of mud. Berlin leaned away. Her hand came out with a very little computer. Had she kept that in her gut? "I've got some useful information there. I'm taking your phone, Jenni. Have fun, Berlin." With a swish of her tail, she left the hotel room.

Berlin watched his dream woman leave, right after she'd hinted at sex. He felt like crying.

"I'm sorry," Jenni said, genuine compassion on her face.

"Why?" he asked. How could she be sorry when the current situation was something of her own creation?

"Well, I know you like Nekoka. But you don't really know her."

"She was a lovely cat," he said. He didn't know what else to say. Anything else would make him sound demanding or whiny or too young. In the end, the cat got his tongue. He groaned at his own joke.

Jenni snorted. "Corny."

Berlin's shoulders stiffened. Then he thought hard, sending out his thoughts like arrows, piercing the walls, the furniture, all the way through the door and windows. *Are you in my mind?*

Ow! Quiet down there, Berlin, Jenni's words evolved in his mind as she held a hand to her temple, a small smile dancing across her lips.

"You can read minds," he said aloud.

"Yes. Though, not everyone. I've had direct skin and eye contact with you, and during that time, touched your mind. Others, I can't read well, unless they scream at me. Sometimes I can pick up really strong senders even if I haven't touched them or met their eyes."

She climbed out of the chair and snatched up one of the bags of clothing they'd got and tossed it at him. Unprepared, he almost dropped it, barely holding the towel up with his other hand.

She blushed and turned away. "Sorry. I'm not trying to get you naked like Nekoka would."

This was the most positive attention Berlin had ever had from women, even better than his few dates with Desere in seventh grade where they'd shared dry and closed-mouth kisses, and he was somewhat disheartened Jenni didn't want to flirt with him as well. "That's okay, I understand." At least she was nice to him.

Jenni laughed. "Oh, don't sound so disappointed. It's not you. You're pretty cute." Berlin almost dropped the clothing. "I just like women. Men are," she shrugged, "meh."

So, she was a lesbian. Fiann's online dossier hadn't even hinted about that. "Oh," was all he said. Not sure what to do with the gift of knowledge.

"Go dress," Jenni said, and Berlin turned with a hop and trotted back into the bathroom.

He pulled on a pair of light brown khakis and the leafy T-shirt, some of the greens the same shade as Jenni's eyes. He dressed like one of the homed kids. With his fingers, he combed through his white hair. Popping from the bathroom, he held out his arms. "How do I look?"

"Splendid! Now, let's see what Nekoka got for us?"

Berlin settled next to Jenni on the bed, their legs touching, as she plugged a laptop into Nekoka's tiny computer and pulled up some program. His skin felt warm at their contact. Jenni flipped through files. Berlin was immediately lost. Jenni cursed.

"Damn Nekoka. I can't figure out what's what." Most of the files had numbers as their extensions and when she attempted to open one, it asked for which program to use. Write was not the correct choice.

Jenni huffed, then closed out those files and switched to another folder. "Sorry I chased Nekoka away. I thought it was best. She has two minds like a man, you know, but her little brain is her clitoris."

Berlin, unsure exactly what Jenni was trying to say—was she saying he, a man, only thought with his penis, or that Nekoka would sleep with everyone, or that, like the Ladder Theory, there was no way they could be friends, not that they weren't friends already, right?—tried to nonchalantly shrug. "It's not a big deal."

Jenni found Nekoka's photo files and an array of faces—smiling, laughing, scowling—scrolled by. "Are these your friends?" Berlin asked.

"Yep, that's Minnie." Jenni pointed to a black woman with washed-out brown eyes. "She goes by Arbortia because she has power over plants. She can talk to plants like Nekoka can talk to cats." Minnie's smile was wide, full of unfettered happiness. Berlin thought she looked nice.

"She came to us last." Jenni sounded thoughtful as she stared at the picture. "Zack met her when he was hunting for a new landscaper. She told him half his trees had some weird fungal disease and offered to cure them. Nekoka immediately adopted her.

"It was only after we brought her into the group that she confessed she was a healer. For a while she'd worn herself out trying to save everyone. She still goes to hospitals and secretly heals terminally ill people. I don't know how she does it."

Berlin could only imagine the strain of such a power. Of everyone needing you, wanting you to save them, and only being able to save a few, and the guilt that you couldn't save everyone.

Then she pointed to a blond guy, his eyes a near-match to the shade of his hair. "Eugene. Our resident thief. Though don't tell him I told you that. I brought him in, after suspecting he was involved in an armored car robbery. He's since cleaned up his ways." Eugene was looking up from a pile of books spread out over a large wooden table. An expression of put out distraction at first made Berlin wonder if he was a jerk, but the next few pics had him in the middle of the group, laughing with everyone else, playing board games or darts.

"I'm sure you know Zack?" Jenni asked when they stopped on a prominent photo of a dark blond man with a huge closed-lipped smile, dimples digging into his cheeks.

Berlin nodded. The Bullet. Everyone knew him. He could fly and turn his body into hard silver. He was fast, and he was pretty and rich, and everyone liked him. "You live with him?" Berlin asked.

"Oh yeah, we totally mooch off him. He doesn't care." Jenni shrugged and moved through another array of photos.

"And this is Grace Bravo, no hero name." Jenni's tone had gone soft, gentle in a way he'd only ever noticed when she talked about Nekoka, and only when Nekoka wasn't annoying her. Grace was Hispanic, darker skin, thick dark hair. She wore a high-collared shirt with a golden cross around her neck. In the photo, the group was outside at one of those iron tables with curly metal shapes making it look gothic and fancy. Grace was setting a big pot of something on the table before Zack, who was flailing a serving spoon around. Grace was concentrating on the food.

"She's a booster, can affect all of us if she focuses," Jenni said, "and a bit of a pacifist."

"Not like you and Nekoka?" Berlin said, couching it as a question, though he knew the answer.

Jenni shook her head. "No. Not like us."

Then Jenni flipped through more photos, so fast Berlin couldn't follow until a new picture showed up. Not one of the friends, but of someone else. A woman with a fancy hairstyle with spikes all over it singing into a mic. "And this is Sepia, the O.G.R.E. member who went missing. The woman we are looking for."

Jenni and Nekoka had all these friends. All these people important to them. Everyone that was important to Berlin had died two years ago. So, now, for these new friends, for Jenni and Nekoka, he would be strong and do anything he could to help.

CHAPTER 23

Thomas

Not a man to be idle, Thomas knew the necessity of building his own case of dirt on Minidoka—not only to protect himself, but to put Jeon and his *Founders* in their place. He'd been backed into a corner, and for a moment he was admittedly at a loss, but then anger and boldness struck him like a high-speed truck. He would not sit by and let others dictate to him, force his hand.

Oh no.

The first thing Thomas did was collect data on the Minidoka Project. Oh, he had done his due diligence before he'd signed on, aware of certain legalities and illegalities that were in bed with the project, but there was more. There must be more.

Thomas was a man with connections. Using his burner phone he'd brought along *just in case,* he'd made a few phone calls and sent some allies on the hunt. That completed, Thomas sat at the computer they'd provided for him in his sad little office, digging around through every avenue the server allowed him to snoop. He was able to discover blueprints for the facility that showed plans for an expansion deep below the complex. But more telling than some future plans were the references to files that didn't exist, to products that were undefined, to redacted or vague phrasing in emails or surveillance that was conveniently cut off.

Pay no attention to the man behind the curtain. Well, Thomas was going to toss that curtain aside.

That morning, he prepared himself. He'd ensured his full access to the facility from the security sergeant and let him know he would be surveying the complex to find any areas needing restructuring. The sergeant had nodded, knowingly.

He probably thought Thomas was on a firing spree. He certainly had no idea Thomas was after dirt on his employers. A lesson long ago learned: act like you belong and you have power; most were only willing to buy the song and dance. Confidence and competence won authority. Dressed in his beige suit, tie a dark blue, his shoes shined to sparkle, Thomas began his morning inspection. With a clipboard in hand, he spoke briefly with each person, jotting nonsense on the paper before silently moving on. Keeping his workforce cowed kept them on the defensive, preventing them from probing into Thomas's true intentions.

"Mr. Hallaman, good morning," a guard greeted.

With so many staff at the compound, Thomas couldn't remember everyone's names, but that didn't mean he couldn't offer respect. He nodded in greeting. "Good morning." Being personal ingratiated people to you, and Thomas knew how to work people. Forcing them to cow using his supernatural power had never been satisfying. All of those women he'd unintentionally coerced when his power had first developed in college had turned to putty, without will and tractable. Thomas preferred the personal touch. He preferred to win people over by example, that they acknowledge his ability and authority.

A door marked "Authorized Personnel" that he'd never passed through caught his attention. He swiped his card over the sensor and punched in his code. The door unlocked. This would undoubtedly create a record of his passing, but today was the day. He could not stop now.

The door opened to stairs leading down.

The stairs led to another hall, with branches extending off, an unmarked door at regular intervals on either side. Thomas tried a few doors, but they were all locked with conventional key locks.

Thomas brought up a copy of the blueprints on his phone and realized these were not future expansions, but existing portions of the Minidoka compound he had never toured. The dark underbelly of the beast.

The air held an odd smell to it as he descended another flight. The hairs on the back of his neck rose and a small weak speck within himself wanted to turn around and continue in ignorance. Thomas took photos with a pocket camera, not putting anything on his phone. A phone was the first place the guards would look if they confronted him. Down here, everything had been scrubbed of detail. The light seemed washed out, gray.

Thomas strode down a hall to a single door at the end. He did not look down at his feet; he did not look away from the door, plain steel, chrome handle. It stood out as unique. Announcing something of interest was hiding behind. He had to force himself to continue forward, because something wasn't right. Something was very, very wrong. Cowering wasn't in his blood, but right now his frayed nerves screamed at him, commanding: *run, Thomas, do not go forward.*

At the door, he turned the handle. It opened.

He stepped onto a catwalk-landing fifteen feet above the floor. Thomas stared below him. Anyone who looked up and spotted the businessman on the catwalk would not be aware of the depth of his amazement, he was so locked up. Nothing seeped through.

He knew about the housing complex, the dorms, the cafeteria for the rehabilitated participants. There were medical clinics and classrooms. It was, truly, a benevolent project.

But he had no idea what went on underneath the surface.

Below him, in a sprawling underground complex, were cages. Barred cages. Instead of lions or rhinoceroses, each cage contained between one to five *people*. Though industrial fans pumped fresh air from above, they struggled against the oppressive mix of a metallic chemical, unwashed bodies, and the pervasive scent of panic. Fear permeated everything.

Who were they?

A vast collection of men and women trapped under a sea of dirt and stone, wrapped within metal. His gut cried out. Told him things of which he had no proof. These were all Seeded. Powered people. Thomas finally understood why he'd been brought in. About those specific Seeded he'd been directed to subdue. How had the Director controlled the truly powerful individuals before he'd asked Thomas for his help?

Perhaps they simply hadn't lasted long.

With his camera, he snapped a few shots, then settled it back into his pocket. To the right of the landing, down amid the huge warehouse of cages, led a wide hallway, white lights washing out all color from the walls.

Above the entrance to this hallway, a second landing and door were linked to the one Thomas occupied via an extensive steel-grated catwalk.

With sure strides, clipboard tucked under one arm, Thomas crossed the catwalk to the other landing, not looking around, acting like he belonged.

Hell, he was the acting manager of the Minidoka Project, of course he belonged.

A question blared in Thomas' mind. How could people, five to a cage, be rehabilitated? These individuals were not here to receive job training or drug treatment. They were captives. Treated like food animals. Or those rats and rabbits scientists tested new medicines on.

The Director had swayed him with lies and progressive ideas, and Thomas had fallen for the promise of reform.

He reached the other landing and the next door. He opened it and entered back into the sweet scent of recycled air. Thomas strode down the hallway, brightly lit, until he came upon a door recessed into the pristine blank walls. Another keypad and sensor. Thomas worried it wouldn't work, but he flashed his card over the square next to the door, punched in his key and the lock clicked.

Thomas pushed the door open and was met with screams.

Inset 5
Monster Town Chat Room

::Welcome Yolo321 to Monster Town::

::Hurly:: No, I don't think that MAAD cities should jail Seeded for no reason, but registering them, knowing who can do what, who might be dangerous, makes sense. People have to register gun ownership. For God's sake. Quit blowing this up to some great civil liberties farce. Hey Yolo.

::Yolo321:: Yo boys.

::Dickwhistle:: Hey. My cousin can't get a job anywhere with kids because his MRI came back as 'yes' to the Seed and his eyes are a tad pale. He has no fucking power. He's a complete spunk. Nothing. Do you know how many service jobs put you near kids? He can't even dishwasher at McDonald's in a MAAD city.

::Hurly:: and I think that's too far. I'm saying that's not right...

::Dickwhistle:: The whole concept of a city being able to restrict specific citizens' lives is unconstitutional.

::Hurly:: Then I guess your option is a hub city.

::Yolo321:: Okay boys, time to take a blue. No point in screaming at each other.

::Hurley:: We can't scream. It's typing. We're only typing. And it's anonymous and digital and we'll never know each other in real life, so screw you and your blues.

::Yolo321:: You *think* it's anonymous...

::Dickwhistle:: I hear they dispense Prozac by the bucket loads. Should have invested in pharmaceuticals years ago.

::RevKillJoy:: Throw off the yoke of the stabilizing drugs. Flush the blues down the toilet. Moods are the opiates of the masses.

::Dickwhistle:: Literally. Duh.

::Yolo321:: No, that's religion.

::Duckwhistle:: So, I hear Guardian Alliance saved a cruise ship from tipping over in a hurricane. Cool footage on ESPN...

CHAPTER 24

Nekoka

Nekoka returned later that evening, stealthily slipping into the room. After leaving the hotel, she'd made a quick stop at a local Dispensary to get her pill and let the drug soothe her over-torqued headspace, then had flipped through her contacts to find some likely evening's entertainment. Between the drug and the sex, she was much more relaxed.

In the sliver of light leaking through the open door, she spotted two lumps marring the smooth surface of the bed, each strategically resting on opposite sides. She felt great, enjoying a bit of fun with Cyrus from the restaurant—he was fast becoming her go-to-guy. The door snicked shut, and she let her eyes acclimate to the room's gentle darkness. All was quiet. Peaceful. After a quick shower and a nibble on some leftover food from no less than seven plates, she crawled in between the two lumps that, within seconds, gravitated towards her. She purred in pleasure. She loved being in the middle.

SHE WOKE WITH A NOSE pressed into her neck, an arm around her belly and a thigh resting against her own. A soft purr buzzed through her chest; she never wanted to get up. Unfortunately, her personal computer was emitting a silent alarm in her head. The soundless electrical waves annoyed her mind, making it itch, pulling her from her contented slumber. She'd rather remain encased within a yin-yang symbol of black and white, male and female. Night and day? Yeah, she decided, that fit, too, and she continued to put each one of her friends—old and new—into opposite sides of a spectrum. Remaining warm and nestled between the two was a far cry better than fiddling with her computer. The data could wait.

She rolled her face away from Jenni's dark hair. Jenni looked peaceful, that eternal line between her eyes smoothed out. Nekoka reached out and brushed some hair off her friend's cheek. Jenni's eyelashes fluttered and a slip of light green emerged.

"Morning," Nekoka said softly. She had an urge to lick Jenni's nose, but refrained. It had been a hard choice not to. Sometimes Nekoka had control issues.

"Ugnn," Jenni said. She closed her eyes again, swallowed and asked, "Good night?"

"'Tsokay," she said. Jenni didn't like details. "You?"

From behind her, the arm that had wrapped around her middle tightened in a squeeze. "It was a good night," the man behind her said. "We ate and watched late night TV with people making raunchy jokes, and Jenni showed me pictures, and we talked all night."

Nekoka's purr roared now that both of her bedmates were awake. She secretly hoped one of them would start petting her.

"So needy." Jenni reached up and petted Nekoka's head.

Nekoka closed her eyes in delight. "Am not."

"I bet you can get Berlin to give you a good scritching if you do something with that data you'd gathered yesterday."

Nekoka's eyes popped open. She was faced with Jenni's amusement.

Berlin sat up behind her. "I would!" Her side felt cool where his arm had been.

Nekoka frowned. "Okay, if that's what you want." She'd been perfectly content cuddling.

Popping out of bed and seeing that the computers were hooked up correctly, Nekoka took a few minutes to set up the data she'd collected in a readable format for mere mortals, wondering what Sparks from Guardian Alliance would think of Whisker. Or if Guardian Alliance's computer guru had powers similar to what Nekoka had. Maybe Sparks was the elusive informant who sent untraceable communications.

"Just sit back and wait for the magic." She pulled the laptop onto her legs, scooted between her yin and yang, and leaned against the headboard. She was curious what her little rooting mouses had found as well.

She opened the first report: data collected from compiling police and private security reports from available databases, which, in this modern era, were many. Also data from various homeless support agencies. Sometimes she worried that if she'd been born in an earlier era, she'd be utterly useless. But then, if she'd been born more than thirty years ago, she'd be disturbingly normal. She shivered. From the data she'd hacked, she filtered the information three ways—missing persons reports, Seeded individuals, and the homeless census. Two reports were generated: the missing Seeded and the missing homeless Seeded.

The results were statistically valid. A large percentage of the reported missing Seeded within the last six months were homeless. About 40 percent, nothing to sneeze at. Those that were not homeless often had police records.

The next report she thought up was a map of the missing. Nekoka designed the map to show dots of red representing the missing people, the circumference of the circle broadening in ratio to the number of missing. Three sections of the United States were heavily red, meaning they had more missing Seeded. The West Coast, the Northeast, and Midwest. The larger cities were nearly all red splotches; the higher the population center, the more homeless. She wasn't sure why the Southwest and South were less affected.

The third report she'd snagged from Sparks. The report comprised a large database of known Seeded. To Nekoka's burning jealous rage, Sparks' list was more expansive than her own. She even had a power rating system based on colors: Gray for the highest, then Purple, Green, Brown, and Black for the lowest, those Seeded who had the Seed, or at least pale eyes, but showed no strange or superhuman abilities. It felt strangely dystopian. Sparks, to Nekoka's further fury, was not in her own database.

"What are we?" Berlin asked, leaning against Nekoka's shoulder. "See if we're in there."

Nekoka typed a few commands and Berlin Fischer popped up.

Berlin Fischer - Brown

Portland, OR, currently no known address. Parents deceased, died in the Glass House incident. 17 years of age.

Potential vision power, undefined

Notes: Physical deviant – Albino

"Brown. Isn't that low? Am I really so low?"

Nekoka was stunned. The Glass House incident.... How had SPYme not delivered this info? *Jenni, do we bring it up?*

Jenni kept her eyes on the screen. *Only if he does. But, wow. Ares and Blowback killed, what, 70 or so people in that?*

Entire neighborhood. An eight-block area got flattened in a full-on battle between two high powered Seeded. Later, when America-based Guardian Alliance members caught him, before there was an official Guardian Alliance, Blowback had said, "It wouldn't have been so bad if all them losers didn't live in glass houses." Ares was still on the loose.

But Berlin survived, Jenni thought at Nekoka, lips pressed together. At the edge of her thoughts, Nekoka could sense the whirlwind turmoil.

That's our Berlin.

Nekoka patted Berlin on the arm. "Pah! They don't know what you can do, don't forget that. Sparks is clueless about your amazingness. Let's find Jenni."

Jennifer McGuire, AKA Fiann - Purple

Vacherie, LA, residing at 222 Louisiana 18, owned by Zackary Silversmith. Parents, Michael and Kathy McGuire, both residing in Chicago, IL. 25 years old.

Enhanced Speed, Enhanced Strength, Enhanced Endurance. Unconfirmed telepathic abilities.

Notes: Background member of S-Force?

Nekoka pointed at the screen. "See Berlin, she doesn't have everything Jenni can do listed, and she's famous." Nekoka couldn't wait to check out everyone's files, update her own, and internally crow at Sparks, because she would have the better data.

"Now you," Berlin urged, bouncing on the bed.

Michiko Yoshida, AKA Nekoka, AKA Scratch – Purple/Gray

Vacherie, LA, residing at 222 Louisiana 18, owned by Zackary Silversmith. Parents, Mokoto and Kaede Yoshida, residing in Akita, Japan. 30 years old.

Shapeshifting [extensive power with unknown limits. Can extend claws to use in fighting], Communicating with felines [unsure if other animals included]. Also, skilled with computer programming and hacking, unknown if this is a special ability or simple skill.

Notes: Physical deviant – Anthropomorphic cat appearance. Background member of S-Force?

Berlin grinned. "Well, they don't have you completely pegged, either. But an almost gray? You're amazing, Scratch!"

Nekoka initially wanted to purr at the attention, but being so transparent to the other Seeded frayed her need to be obscure. *She* was supposed to know all the secrets, not Sparks. "She's got a lot of guesses that are close to correct."

For the next half hour, the three flipped through files on people they had always wondered about. Unfortunately, none of the dossiers on the Guardian Alliance members were listed. Pablo had been categorized as a Green, with his powers listed as emotional manipulation and enhanced perception, though Sepia was a Brown/Green fence sitter. John was also listed as a Green.

There were only thirty listed Grays. Samantha Fontos, the leader of the Seeded superiorists group Xenofontos, was listed, as well as a list of names that Nekoka recognized from news reports. A few she had met. Zackary Silversmith was on the list. Nekoka knew that Jenni could take him in a hand-to-hand fight, but he did have quite a few flashy powers.

By far the largest group was the Blacks. How this passel of people had been ensured of having a Seed, Nekoka didn't know. Perhaps Sparks was going purely off pale eyes. The only accurate test to identify if someone was Seeded, other than seeing them bend reality of course, was an MRI to find the peanut-sized Seed that had grown in their heads. That tiny organ that had been implanted, maybe by the government, maybe by aliens, maybe by some secret scientific organization. Nobody knew.

When they returned to business, she queried this database on those that were currently missing. A list of hundreds appeared. A large number of those missing were rated Black or Brown, which made sense since most Seeded displayed no powers.

Berlin stared at the numbers. "How can all these people go missing and nobody's done anything about it? How can these people not be missed?"

"This is unbelievable," Jenni said. "I would never have thought...." The steel in her voice grated against her vocal cords. Jenni rarely let her emotions go unchecked, when her agitation became a tangible entity floating among them. Nekoka began to stress-purr. Jenni reached out and ran a hand across her furred back.

"We've got to do something," Berlin said, the conviction in his voice stoking Nekoka's current disposition into an indignant blaze.

"We will," she said, her words barely audible over her roaring purr.

AFTER MUCH DELIBERATION, the three decided to talk with the homeless first, get the personal news from ground zero. Nekoka gathered a few disapproving scowls as she followed Jenni and Berlin out of the hotel. She was on all fours, going as a marmalade house cat, so she didn't blame the hotel staff, but.... Screw them. While walking to the Mission to ask the residents if they had any information on where their friends and neighbors might have gotten dragged off to, Nekoka chatted with each cat they came across, which, sadly, wasn't many.

"It might be a good thing, Nekoka," Berlin said, all perky grins and unicorn rays. "It means there aren't that many cats without homes in the city."

Nekoka sauntered over to a filthy gray beast with orange eyes. He twitched his tail as Nekoka approached and meowed. Sparks was right, Nekoka could talk to cats only, but it was all types of felines. House cats, admittedly, were easiest for her to understand. The twitch of an ear, the casual glance away, the soft rumble within a cat's chest, Nekoka could listen and watch and interpret it all as human-style communication.

She flicked her tail and licked a paw. "Hello," she said. "You look like a fierce hunter." Half of cat talk was all about the compliments and brown nosing. Cats loved it.

The cat licked at the air; his lip caught on his gum where a tooth had gone missing. "I am. Rats fear me." Which in this city, with cat-sized rats, was quite the boast. The tom sniffed at her. "You look fierce as well." He stood and walked sideways towards her, an obvious sign of interest in the determined set of his paws. "You shall be mine."

Nekoka sat her butt down and hissed. "You must prove yourself." With cats, it was all about the gifts.

"Dead rat for you?" He walked closer and sniffed her nose. She allowed it.

"I want to know about missing humans." And in a long and arduous fashion, she explained to the gray tom what she wished.

"Yes. Many less to leave food now. Female human with brown fur on head used to feed me and others. Gone now."

"How long?" Nekoka asked through a flick of her skin and a blink.

The tom swished his tail towards a blue dumpster. "Food box emptied by humans more than, hmmm, five times."

Nekoka got up and rubbed her clean nose up against the tom's scarred one in thank you, and his tail lifted. She turned and ran off behind Jenni, who emptied a can of tuna on the curb.

The tom watched her walk off with the two humans. His disappointment set his tail to curl at the tip and his shoulders drooped, but he scarfed down the food in two bites.

In this manner, and from conversations with some of the people Berlin knew, they realized people had started going missing in significant numbers about two months ago. While waiting in a free food line put on by Love not War in a local neighborhood park, they learned that the organization ended up with a lot of extra food lately.

A tattooed butch with a shaved head and more metal than Sepia was chatting up Jenni as she scooped up cous cous onto paper plates for people as they passed down the line. The organization was weirdly Portland. They only served vegan food and most of the ladies volunteering were more beefy than penitentiary guards. Though Nekoka knew that Jenni wasn't into the butch type, she kept watch on the entire conversation from where she interviewed some of the younger crowd, all of them wanting to touch her fur. Normally she liked that, but not when Jenni might be in danger from another pierced freak.

"So," Nekoka asked a teenage girl with long, dirty blond hair. Annie Hildebrand from Vancouver, Washington, one time attendee of York

Elementary, but hadn't gone to school since she'd graduated from that illustrious institution. She had no presence on social media, no criminal record, not even a missing persons case. Just a few pictures on a local news website where she'd once shown sheep for the neighborhood 4-H club. "When did you notice fewer people came to these feeds?"

Annie laughed, delight in her eyes, though she had a nasty scar down the side of her face, still puffy and red. "Well honestly, I noticed when they told us we could come back for seconds. I mean, they never give us anything good, like chicken or eggs or anything from an animal, but it's better than garbage."

Well, wasn't that a grand endorsement?

"So, can you change into a cat for us?" asked Annie.

Another teen, in ripped jeans, her skin cursed with a bad case of acne, looked over at Annie with a superior nose in the air. "Annie, I doubt all the rumors you hear are true."

Nekoka promptly shrank down to a tabby, sat there and stared at zit girl—Jana Mell, fifteen, Jefferson High and had a Match account where she faked her age and, on record, lived with her single mother. Jana's nose quickly dropped as she stared in shock at Nekoka. "Wow, it's true!"

After that, Nekoka got no new information on the missing people, because everyone wanted to know about her. Normally, this was the preferred state of things, but right now, with the ugly woman laughing with Jenni, and Berlin stuffing his face with lettuce, and Sepia who knew where, she didn't feel she had the time.

Pulling her form back into the normal human-cat mix, she tried to steer the questions away from her. "Yes, I can change shape. It's magic. Now, do you have any idea why people left? Why there's fewer people eating Love not War compassion food?"

A ratty man who had been sitting on the edge of the teen circle snorted and then spat onto the green lawn. His mish-mashed clothing—new shoes, decent jeans, clashing with the tatty brown overcoat—held a desperate air of survival. Nekoka looked at him; he looked at her chest.

No way in hell.

She darted her eyes over to Jenni to make sure she hadn't sold her body for information and was relieved to see Jenni had taken a step away from the server.

"Gov'ments been snatchin' 'em," Miguel Birch said, once a member of United Steelworkers, now homeless, destitute, and jobless, probably due to his four DUIs and meth habit—who was now digging through his nose with a finger caked in...something brown. With a lecherous laugh, he asked, "If yer a shapeshifter, ya kin make 'em bigger, yeah?" He lifted his chin in Nekoka's general direction.

Nekoka's tail flicked. "It doesn't work that way." Though that was a total lie; Nekoka could use her tits as flotation devices if she was caught out at sea, but the drunk didn't need to know that. "What do you mean the government's been snatching them?" A dart of her gaze to Jenni showed that Jenni had stopped talking with the woman to listen to the man.

Annie leaned forward and shot out in a harsh whisper, "He's nasty, don't talk to him. Nobody talks to him."

"Ya'll talk to me when I got somethin' ya want." He cackled, and the fur along Nekoka's spine rose. She didn't like this man. Miguel was the type of man who would rape young women, hack up their bodies, and throw them in the hospital medical waste incinerator. She remained with the teenagers, staring him down, not that she could stare someone down who wouldn't meet her eyes.

To Nekoka's left, away from the group, Berlin put his plate down.

The air was still, heavy, just like the air gets before someone throws a punch, anticipation pulling everything tight. Nekoka didn't understand it. Other than his high creep rating, why did this man trigger as a threat? Looking at Miguel, right now he couldn't walk a straight line let alone hurt them, but still, there was a certain quality in the way he was so sure. He knew something. Maybe he couldn't hurt them physically...

Nekoka closed her eyes and sent out her electrical senses. The skeezy guy had a small transmitter on him that was sending out a signal.

She sauntered closer to him. Annie dramatically choked. Nekoka thought to Jenni, *Can you see what he's thinking about?* Nekoka needed to be closer to dig into that signal. Jenni couldn't get much off a stranger if he wasn't projecting.

The electromagnetic signal, within the 3.8 gigahertz range, was mid-level, and Nekoka surmised the receiver could be anywhere within the city. So, what could he be sending out?

He's gloating. I'm not getting complete thoughts, mostly some wicked witch "I'll get you, my pretty," mental mumbling.

He's sending out a signal—

Berlin stepped between Nekoka and Miguel. Nekoka wanted to grab Berlin and thrust him behind her. "It's been you..." Berlin said to the creeper, sounding lost and then angry. "You've been selling us out. Gregory said he saw you talking to some men, but I didn't think it was this.... I thought you were doing something with Matoro, not...."

Miguel cackled again, then wheezed, his laugh catching on a gasping hack. A splat of green glopped onto the ground. He grinned, revealing a scatted row of pocked teeth. "Won't make much diff'rence anyways. They gonna get us all in the end."

"They? Who are they?" Jenni demanded, striding towards the sell-out.

The small gathering of people who'd been chill, eating free lunch, and listening to the conversation, all began doing that herd-mulling-about-talking-among-themselves thing that drove Nekoka crazy.

"Don't stand there and talk about it," Nekoka roared. "Someone's coming. They will capture you and take you away! Scatter!" And with that order, quite a few of them did. Nekoka didn't think anyone was in any real danger, but not being in the area was probably the safest bet.

Miguel ran for it.

Berlin, all skin and bones, pounded after the dirty traitor and tackled him as the man tried to lope away on a bum leg. Nekoka's ire climbed up her throat. The kid should stay out of it.

"Ger'off me." The old guy wriggled like a boy scout trying to extricate himself from a too tight sleeping bag. Berlin clung to his legs, even as Miguel beat him around the head and shoulders. Nekoka and Jenni grabbed his arms.

The guy stopped struggling once Jenni's hands circled his wrists. Pain flinched across his face. Nekoka loomed over him, trying to discharge electrical snaps of hatred. He had to know there was no escape. Berlin loosened his hold, and the guy feebly tried to scramble away. Jenni jerked his wrists, subduing him. Perhaps he was stupid. Well, to play turncoat on your own guys, that was pretty stupid. Nekoka bared her fangs and hissed.

"Who are you working for?" Jenni asked, flipping him to his belly and twisting his arm behind his back, keeping him pinned to the ground.

"Hold him a second," Nekoka said as she began to search for the device he had in his pockets. She was aware of a few stragglers taking vid of them that Nekoka would have to erase later. Stupid gawkers. Jenni pressed harder, but as Nekoka reached forward, the letch tried to snatch at her. Jenni dropped to a knee, clasping the man's neck, pressing his face into the grass. "You do not touch. You do not struggle. You do not ask. You just sit there until I tell you otherwise." The coldness, the utter intimidation Jenni commanded, put pause to Nekoka's actions. Berlin took a step away, his jaw open in awe.

Miguel's skin had gone as white as Berlin's around the indentation Jenni's fingers were making in his neck and wrist. Nekoka began rummaging again and found the square transmitter. She took a step away, beyond arm's reach, and brushed her mind against the machine.

It was sending a simple signal, triggered when a button on the side was pushed. Nothing outstanding and would hide under all the other electrical chatter in the world.

Nekoka felt a shiver trail up her spine and shake out the end of her tail.

"I've got what I need from this guy." Jenni's face screwed up in disgust, and Nekoka knew that she'd joined her mind with the skanky traitor's. She couldn't imagine the pit that place must have been. The man looked out of it, his eyes rolled up into his head, and the rotten scent of his breath pooled around them like a cloud.

Berlin stood to the side, his hands gripped together at his sides. Surely, only the iron shackles of common sense kept him from getting between Jenni and her prey to pound him one in the chin. "Nekoka. Something's wrong," Berlin said, glancing around, up and at the sky and at nothing at all. Seeing something only he could see. "Nekoka! We gotta go. Now."

The squeal of tires pulled her attention away from Berlin's white, worried face. Three dark blue vans jumped the concrete curb, tearing ruts through the park's manicured lawn as they drove right for them.

CHAPTER 25

Berlin

Everything was so loud, moved so fast, Berlin didn't have a chance to take it all in.

A churning fog of ghosts closed in on him. It'd happened once before like this. When he'd thought the ghosts were trying to smother him, take his life away, but now he was sure they'd been trying to warn him of the Seeded who would kill his parents and his neighbors. The ghosts were here again, trying to warn him.

His heart fluttered like a bird, and then he rabbited, fleeing the vans as they charged right over the nice lawn toward the group. One of the men eating with the volunteers stood like a stone, unmoving, so Berlin had to grab him and yank him towards a tree, hoping the solid object would protect them from the renegade vehicle. The homeless guy, the one who had the device, Berlin was sure he saw him get run over, the van jumping over his body. Then, in some odd choreography, all the vans jerked to a halt and unloaded. People in SWAT-like armor poured out: soldiers to some hidden cause. Berlin tried to count, maybe four per van, maybe five, but bystanders scurrying about in the chaos swirled his brain. Then his attention was captured by Jenni, good, sweet-hearted Jenni, becoming someone else. Becoming Fiann, the Celtic Warrior. He understood that many Seeded picked a public name, and he had one given to him by some others of the Mission—the Ghost—but he didn't realize before that it truly signified a change in personality. Right before his eyes, Fiann emerged. Not the woman who laughed at his jokes and talked him out of having sex for the first time with Nekoka. Not the woman who ordered massive room service with him. This woman burned with anger, a kind of animalistic thunder charging under her skin as she thrashed on the attacking soldiers.

He'd lost sight of Nekoka, and he frantically searched around for her through the ghosts, but then she was by his side, grabbing his shoulder and running across the park towards a large pond. "Come on, they can't touch her, but you and I are more breakable."

Berlin turned his back on Fiann and raced alongside Nekoka, struggling to keep up. As a kid, he'd never spent a lot of time doing things like sports and running out in the harsh sun. Soon he was panting, his feet inexpertly slapping against the pavement of the trail, glancing over his head to see if Fiann was okay. He hated leaving her. He hated that Nekoka left her, because he knew the truth. Nekoka was helping him get away, abandoning her friend because *he* was breakable, not Nekoka.

Because he was too helpless.

He glanced over his shoulder again and stumbled to a slow jog. Three of the people dressed in that black body armor closed the distance with Jenni. She dropped to the ground, swiped one of the attacker's legs out from under him, then swung her fist around to smack another in the gut, and in the next blink of his eye, she stepped to the final one standing and brought her knee up into his jaw. With a sharp snap, the man's head jerked backwards, and Berlin wondered if his neck had been snapped.

Her movements were smooth, like a dancer, and he was caught off guard, so mesmerized, that when Nekoka grabbed his forearm to keep him going, he tripped and fell to the ground.

"Get up, damn it," Nekoka demanded, nearly jerking his arm from its socket to right him on his feet. His blood pounded in his ears, his breath huffed from the exercise, or from the fear, he wasn't sure. The hazy gray tempest brewed above the fight, above the vans, all around, swirling with a kind of fevered passion.

Coughing, he tried to catch his breath. They rounded the end of one pond, scattering a flock of ducks. A large man blocked their way. Behind him, Berlin caught sight of more vans. Nekoka pushed him behind her, arching her spine, and though she still walked on two legs, she seemed more cat than person. Bigger, arms bulkier, she'd morphed into the warrior cat-woman he'd read about but never seen.

Back here, the park was deserted, as if all the people had been vaporized and turned into the coalescing gray mist thickening into a London fog.

He'd never experienced the like of it, these fevered ghosts. Maybe these organized men had gassed the place. Maybe they'd already killed everyone, turned them into the dead, and would kill Nekoka and him next.

The man was enormous, a professional wrestler type, and he wore the same black SWAT head-to-toe armor as those who had attacked Fiann. His arms hung from his body like extra attachments and a thin material covered his face, making his features hard to distinguish.

"Just come with me, and you won't get hurt."

Nekoka hissed. The gray mist swirled over the man's head. Nekoka sprang.

The man was ready for her and reached out, plucking her from the air. She lashed out, scraping long claws across his front, slicing open some of the fabric; a metallic scream ripped through the air, and Berlin could see a shiny layer glint in the muted light.

Nekoka squirmed, getting behind him, and planted talons into the ground. Now armed with finger length claws, she dug them into his neck. The man didn't even react. Those claws hadn't dug into his flesh, but only released that same metallic scream.

It wasn't metal in the black armor, but metal instead of skin.

"Damn it. Get off me." The man reached back and grabbed Nekoka around the waist as she tried to rip out his throat. Then came the most horrific sound, like someone was gutting a baby right before him, and then the man's neck began to drip red.

Trapped in some fatal deadlock, the man continued to crush Nekoka's middle as she pushed her claws deeper through the thick armor of his neck. Her muscles bulged, huge like a bodybuilder, rippling under a layer of tiger-striped fur. Berlin watched, frightened, and as the air filled with cries of their frustration and pain, the ghosts swam around the two struggling Seeded.

Within the mass of gray, rising over Nekoka's hisses, Berlin could hear the calls of lost souls, the howl of frustration, the screams of blood. The spirits had risen, and as they swarmed the man, he tore Nekoka's claws from his body and threw her to the ground.

Berlin gasped. Nekoka! The spirits faltered. Like a contained storm, they writhed through the air, seeking an outlet. Berlin fell to his knees, thrusting out some part of him—his own soul, his Seed?—and the gray of the mass darkened, the definition of individuals disappeared as they once again descended on Nekoka's attacker.

"Save us!" he begged the ghosts. "He'll kill Nekoka!"

Wind tore at his hat. Berlin crawled over the sloping lawn to Nekoka. He didn't see the death halo around her, knew she was injured but not on the borderlands.

Standing in a squat, he grabbed her under her armpits and dragged her to a line of broad-leafed bushes. Scentless red blooms covered the plants. A few petals fell over Nekoka's limp form as he pulled her underneath. A dull lethargy filled his arms and legs.

"Come on, Nekoka. Snap out of it. Come on." He patted the side of her face; her head flopped to the side, eyes closed. She looked dead. His heart trembled, some missed beat that hurt. "Nekoka!" He slapped her hard, tossing her face to aim the other direction. "Wake up!"

"Over here."

Oh crap. People were jogging towards them. Berlin's hands were shaking. He knew what he had to do. He shook his hands out and jumped from the bushes, paused just a moment, and ran.

This was not an act of cowardice. Physically, he had no means to defend her. She had gotten hurt because he was the weak one. She'd gotten hurt because she was trying to protect *him*. His only power was in diversion: get them to chase him and leave her alone.

The swirling mass of gray was gone, and the large man who'd hurt Nekoka lay motionless on the ground, another of the black dressed attackers leaning over him.

Two of the SWAT team chased him like hounds.

He put all of his heart and soul into pumping his arms and legs, racing across the park to the packed street on the eastern side. He waved his arms, hoping someone would pop out of their car. Drones zipped overhead.

"Call the police!" he yelled

Somewhere in the background, a man screamed.

Sharp, hot pain bit into his back, through the new shirt that Nekoka had gotten him. His body slammed into the ground. Strength left his body. Feeling left his body. Sinking into the earth, eyes still open, he saw two sets of black boots come up to him. His ears latched onto noise, a muddled sound with the cadence of talking, but he couldn't separate one sound from another. Behind them, he could make out men in black carrying a body away, a body with a long tail.

He blinked once. Twice. He couldn't open his eyes a third time.

CHAPTER 26

Thomas

A new shipment from Portland rolled in, and Thomas had massive damage control eating up his precious time. The Director, after having unfolded his complete line of blackmail, demanded he handle several of the more violent and unruly intakes. Thomas played along. He would not be leaving Minidoka soon. But when he did leave, he would have the insurance to keep the Director and his superiors off his back.

Now, embracing the role his managerial position required, he became fed up with the lax discipline, the lack of foresight and accountability, and the complete buffoonery displayed by some of the staff.

Apparently, not only had the collection squad performed a snatch and grab in full public, but they also took a fairly well-known Seeded with backing and allies.

So much for the project remaining secret.

Even when he'd thought Minidoka was strictly a homeless rehabilitation center, he'd known some bleeding-hearts would condemn the stark efficiency of the project, declaring it inhumane. Now, when even *Thomas* saw the inhumanity, it was doomed to crash and burn. He'd thrown the resources of the Founders at the local sheriff who'd been sniffing around and a few curious reporters, but without direct contact with people, there wasn't much else he could do, and the Director was not letting him leave.

Almost as if he was afraid Thomas would bolt.

After Thomas' impromptu tour, he'd demanded Jeon level with him. "Who are those people in those cages?"

"The dangerous. The ones who cannot be rehabilitated. Those, Mr. Hallaman, are the Seeded dregs of society. The ones who put regular civilians in danger. They are criminals. And, while we try to assure their safety, some refuse to comply." The Director's dead eyes bored into him. "You are here to help with those."

So, that was who he was controlling. That rage flared within him.

"What is really going on here? What are you doing to those people? In that chair?" His mind constantly echoed with that scream.

"It's a simple procedure to improve their worth to society," Jeon said, and that, that simple accounting had put fire under Thomas' feet. Torture, even he could not condone torture. He needed out, sooner better than later, setting miles between himself and this camp of misery.

But not without his insurance.

Now, Jeon had given him almost the entire run of the facility. He only needed to find out more about that room and the apparatus and what was happening to those individuals. Were they being lobotomized? No, maybe something close to that, but not exactly. He'd heard the doctors call the process "letting", the very word bringing to mind the archaic act of draining someone of blood. Of what exactly were they draining these people? What happened to them once the process was complete?

Too many questions. He needed answers.

Thomas had searched, but all he'd discovered so far was that after a few procedures, those being letted were stricken from the records. Gone. Disappeared to who knew where out here in this corner of uninhabited America.

Standing on the observation platform, Thomas forced himself to look upon the acres of cages and their doomed inhabitants. He'd spent yesterday reading reports of the numbers of people who had been "processed", astounded at the utter atrocity. Astounded. An unwanted shiver rattled his shoulders. He hated looking down at them, the smell of the place, the sticky mist of toxic Nutrix that hung in the air that he'd learned not only dampened Seeded powers but also caused nausea, headaches, body-aches, and other ill effects.

The newest arrivals were going through processing right now.

Though it only happened rarely, when the popular or well-known ones got brought through, it made everyone edgy. The detainees seemed to think that the wrestling stars or the self-proclaimed heroes would save them. They couldn't save them. Nothing could save them. At this point,

Thomas couldn't even save them. He'd make a point of upping the sedative in everyone's fluid for the afternoon meal; he didn't need any injuries.

"Mr. Hallaman." Thomas turned away from the sea of hopelessness and looked impassively at Tricia. "There seems to be a problem in receiving line seven, sir. They've asked for your assistance."

Thomas nodded. That would be their new retrievals. Couldn't these...these incompetents do anything without his guidance and supervision? He passed Tricia as he headed for the stairs. What did she think of all of this? She was an icy wall, no hint of a crack in her facade. He'd respect that under normal circumstances.

Thomas knew that Seeded cat-woman captured in Portland would unload a world of problems for them. She'd been in the news far too much, saving people, doing stupid stunts to garner attention. She was a liability. Sometimes there were losses; this might just be one of those times.

Flashing his ID over the sensor, he pushed open the heavy door at the bottom of the stairs that led to the receiving area. He passed by a few employees preparing to hand out the dinners and was assured of the extra sedative. "Got it all set up, Mr. Hallaman," one eager young man said, nodding at him. Seeking approval while the brutality he was a part of didn't even phase him. Did any of these people have a spine? Thomas nodded back and kept walking until he reached a room with a large sign over the door: Receiving Room #7.

He flashed his card and pushed through, entering into chaos.

"Grab her, quick. There she goes."

"Anymore Nutrix? Damn it! Spray her, she keeps shifting."

"Go Scratch! Rip their eyes out."

Mayhem overwhelmed the room like a case of leprosy, eating away at the beautiful efficiency of the system. Thomas felt almost sickened by the lack of focus the guards and scientists were displaying as five of the new intakes shifted around, blocking their actions and thwarting their every goal.

Amateurs.

Three high-level armored guards, one with a tranq pistol, surrounded a small cat, a tiny Russian blue, while a white-coated scientist by the name of Rich Yontz, was lunging at the target with a syringe. Three other low-level uniformed guards—he never learned their names, there were so many of them—were trying to corral the remaining Seeded intakes, but they were lunging and throwing things, pushing barriers they shouldn't have even thought to push. The cat arched its back, hissing and slicing its claws in defense, not allowing anyone close.

Before Thomas called out a warning, the guard with the tranq aimed and shot. The cat flipped through the air, rebounded off Yontz' chest and landed on a guard's shoulder. It leapt again, and when it landed, it darted behind a desk. The tranquilizer that the cat so deftly avoided had buried into Yontz' thigh, and the man melted to the ground in a pile of limp limbs. The syringe fell to the linoleum and rolled away in an arc.

"Where did she go?" a guard asked. The chaos continued to breed.

"You're all dumb!" shouted an albino intake. "You'll never catch Scratch."

"Be quiet," Thomas said, eyes touching on the gaze of each of the intakes. The room fell to a tense static moment, carved out of time. "Keep the doors closed, make sure she can't get out. Who is the subject and what are the known talents?" It was Scratch, he knew, but going through the data would calm everyone down.

The guard who'd shot the tranquilizer fiddled with the pistol. Another guard, one who seemed to have some initiative, straightened his shoulders like a soldier addressing his superiors and stared ahead as he spoke. "Mr. Hallaman, the subject is known as Scratch. Affiliated with the newly Certified group S-Force from New Orleans. She is capable of feline influenced shapeshifting," he glanced at Thomas' eyes and quickly dropped his gaze, scanning the crowded room. A desk, a few chairs, a glass-fronted refrigeration cabinet, a table with medical equipment on it. No cat. "And, um, apparently she can go invisible."

"I take it that is new information?" Thomas asked as he searched around people's legs and the furniture for a small gray cat. Yontz sprawled across the floor.

"Yes, sir," the man said, shifting his weight.

Few things ground against Thomas' nerves more than working with incompetents, but he did acknowledge that keeping track of all the possible talents one of the subjects could utilize was not an easy task.

"You've sprayed the area down with Nutrix?" Thomas asked, noticing the metallic scent. He'd have to have the room cleared out and vented before he allowed anyone to use it again.

"With the amount we had on hand, sir."

"Meaning? Will someone prop Yontz against a wall?"

The guard that had tranquilized the scientist grabbed Yontz under the arms and dragged him near a glass cabinet out of danger of being trod upon.

"We used the amount on hand..." repeated the guard.

"These other Seeded got in the way," explained a female guard. "They're all doused."

Thomas looked at the five remaining men and women pushed into the corner. The albino, a scrawny blond man, a black man, and two white women, one a redhead. Hatred burned in their eyes, but that kind of hatred dewed off Thomas' fine suit. These were probably all leaches on society's hard-working members.

Then something unpleasant bloomed in his gut as he thought about the cages and the letting room.

"Well..." Thomas pulled out a metal chair behind a desk scattered with paper and sat. "Unless she can turn into invisible mist, she's still in this room. We will wait her out."

For the next thirty minutes, the guards and intakes lingered in the room, not talking. Yontz lifted an arm to wipe the drool from his face, but didn't get up; is legs probably still numb from the potent tranquilizers. The intakes huddled together on the far side. Despite likely being nulls, he worried the Nutrix effect might dissipate before the guards finished processing and moved them into cells. This was all a waste of his time. Though, to maintain composure, he framed it as a challenge. He could out-stubborn even a cat.

He pulled out his phone to find it dead. Another tick mark to make this day extra trying. Things should work, should go smoothly if you planned well enough. Where had the short circuit happened?

And then the door opened—"Mr. Hallaman?"–and he realized, above all, he hated it when people did incredibly thoughtless things.

Jumping to his feet, he demanded, “Close that God-damned door,” even as the soft part of himself felt a fractional sliver of hope.

Marcus Mahoney, a junior manager with a sadistic streak and too many bright ideas, untested and thoroughly unwanted by Thomas, scurried into the room and slammed the door shut, pressing his back to it.

“What’s going on? We’ve been looking all over for you.” After a slow perusal of the state of the room, he added, “Sir.” The two men’s gazes battled, and with reluctance, Mahoney submitted.

“You’ve probably just let loose a dangerous subject.” Thomas wanted to punish the upstart. One of the new intakes snickered. “Set about a System Red.”

“A System Red?” The man dropped one shoulder; the left side of his mouth shifted down.

“You’ve an amazing ability to repeat exactly what I say. I doubt it will do much for your career advancement, however.” Thomas stood and walked directly towards Marcus where he was pressed against the door. At the final moment, Marcus popped out of the way, mouth in full frown now.

“See that you follow orders.” Thomas punched in his code and flashed his ID over the sensor. “No point in wasting more time.” He pulled on the door, only to have it remain securely locked.

CHAPTER 27

Nekoka

As the door clanged shut behind her, Nekoka jammed the lock, overriding it until someone with the skills and tools to rewire the damned thing arrived to release the trapped, mad scientists. Slinking down the hallway outside of that room, in a shape tinier than any cat in nature, she clung to the corner between wall trim and tile, blending in with the colors as well as any chameleon.

It was hard work, something that was as natural to her as ignoring a secret. As she scurried along, she worried that the baseboard seam delineating the wall and floor wasn't aligned perfectly as it sliced down her body. However, she was about the size of a pet rat, so that significantly aided in her concealment. Unfortunately, the bulge of her computer at this size was terribly unbalancing.

Exhausted, overwhelmed by the fear and anger that permeated everything, she found a metal trolley waiting outside another room and crawled underneath it so she would have time to think.

What she would give for her pill. Ugh. They probably had a crate of them somewhere. A crate full of sexy jars brimming with diazepam, little blue pills of chill. All she needed was one little pill, and some contact with Jenni, and life would be as peachy as a Georgian orchard.

That was all that was needed to make the world a little less shitty.

When she'd first arrived, she'd been groggy and out of sorts, her thoughts equating everything to a drunk tank: a large, enclosed room with about twenty other people. She had to have been drunk, though she couldn't quite remember how she'd got there, or even the fun act of drinking. Usually drinking was followed by some other form of athletic fun, and there had been no fun. Still, it was her prominent theory until she saw the shower heads hanging from the walls. Berlin was there, but she hadn't recognized anyone else. Nekoka kept him by her side, watching as some of the captives used the showers to minor efficiency, washing faces and hands and drinking. Nekoka, though thirsty herself, didn't trust it.

It made some sick, dark-world kind of sense. It was inevitable the governments and the anti-Seeded movement would create some sort of hidden collection and incarceration program for them. The proverbial Men in Black had descended upon them in the park, had battled them with tech and their own Seeded militia.

The world had suddenly changed.

Unsure of what to do next—she'd never been much of a fighter, which was always Jenni's forte—she decided to keep still, stay low, and amount to no consequence. She had tried to speed up her metabolism to process the drug in her body, but it hadn't quite worked how she'd hoped. By the time some men had come to pull out the first six people from the shower room, Nekoka still wasn't at her best.

"Are you Scratch?" a redhead prisoner asked after the first six were removed. Her pale face telegraphed the pain her limply hanging wrist was putting her through. "Can you help us? Please, I've got kids at home."

"She'll take care of us," Berlin had said, once the silent pause had gone on uncomfortably long. Nekoka hated being relied upon...and what was she going to do? Take on the entire anti-Seeded mafioso? She was just going to let these people, and especially Berlin, down.

"Please. I know you're strong. You can save us all," the mother pleaded. Then another noticed her and another, and soon the amazing knowledge that Scratch was among them had dispersed throughout the small congregation of Seeded, all worshiping the one hope they saw on offer.

"You gotta be quiet," Berlin urged. "Don't let the guards know who she is."

"But she can save us," one prisoner said, almost begged, as if hoping for that assurance.

In that instant, though fuzzy still and a little panicked without Jenni by her side, Nekoka felt like a hero, like Obi-Wan when Leia sought help. A little buoyed, a little hopeful. Guards in heavy-duty body armor broke the moment of high spirits when they came into the room to separate the next group. They couldn't tear her desperate grip from Berlin, though Nekoka's fingers were numb with whatever drug they had given her. So, they took the two with four others and sent them through a processing line, categorizing them like victims of war camps. Name, birth date, place of origin, skills, family history, medical history, and, of course, Seeded ability. Nekoka, at the back of the line, listened impassively, updating her database and exploring the cameras, door locks, and special coms the guards and doctor held.

When the drug finally burned through her system, a clarity settled into her brain like the initial sunrise of human illumination. All the electronics planted through the walls, on people's persons and on desktops reached out to her, sang to her, whispered all the knowledge they contained. Gave up their secrets. The clouds parted, and she saw her chance. Slipping down into a cat, she'd made her move.

With a fury she'd admired in Jenni, Nekoka hissed and clawed at the guards and doctors, imagining the moves Jenni would make. Jenni would own the match. She'd wade into the flurry of fists and do some combo strikes from judo and boxing; she would break ribs with the barest brush of her fingertips. Jenni had tried to train Nekoka in martial arts, but Nekoka insisted she was a lover, not a fighter. Now, with a kind of sickening acceptance, she knew that if she didn't do something, she'd be a dead lover, and there wasn't much love in that.

The other five prisoners cheered and generally got in the way, helping to create enough chaos that when the door opened, Nekoka pulled her body tight, squeezed the empty spaces within her, and shrank her size as tightly as possible.

Her head screamed at the change. Her spine sizzled like an electrical jolt shot through her. But she did it. For how long, she didn't know.

Her minicomputer was tucked right under her skin, her body no longer large enough to house it within, a bulky protuberance poking out of her side in a mimicry of a tumor. She wished her computer shrank with her. She wished Jenni was with her. She wished she'd never been taken.

Crap.

That was probably a wish in high demand today.

Now, hiding in the hallway under the trolley, jacked into the complex's computers and cameras, her mind and senses overwhelmed by the mass of data streaming in, she wasn't sure what to do. Few people walked down the hall, and none seemed to notice her. The cameras were close enough that if Nekoka kept contact with the wall, she could erase her passage with the flick of thought, but keeping control of that and her abnormally small shape, plus the camouflage, was sending her already frizzling energy on the freeway to nappyville. Unfortunately, that land of sleep came with a ticket for a class A migraine.

This place, this horrible place, trapped thousands of people. She knew many were homeless, and many more were criminals having been officially shipped here, but even accounting for those numbers, someone had to have noticed. This many people simply did not disappear without notice. Was there some secret war in America? Against the Seeded? Some hidden government mandate to collect the Seeded and trap them away and start with the easy ones first?

Something huge was happening here. Something larger and more insidious than she could imagine. She wished she could tell Jenni or Zack or even Pablo.

Then a face solidified out of the camera feed of the lines and lines of cells she'd been slipping her mind through. Sepia.

Through the murky view of the camera, it was apparent that Sepia wasn't quite herself. She was curled in a corner of a small cage all on her own, not moving, lifeless.

There were hundreds of cages, lined up for acres. Acres! How could something like this exist? She blinked. And blinked again. It was incomprehensible to her. Some cages were empty. And others held multiple people, she guessed maybe the Browns and Blacks of Sparks' classification system. The poor, powerless nuls.

With adrenaline setting her nerves to jittery, she waited by the door that led into the room of cages. Her skin prickled with the exertion of staying small, staying camouflaged against the wall, but after twenty-seven minutes, someone came and opened the door. She slipped in.

The smell. Cats were not known for their sense of smell, but the room held the foul mixture of chemicals and human waste.

Most of the people were quiet, others were whispering to themselves or whimpering in total misery. Nekoka's tail twitched, flicked around though she tried to subdue it. It wouldn't be tamed as she passed through the cells of the damned.

It took her some time to triangulate via various cameras where Sepia was kept, but she padded carefully down the ten-foot aisle between cages until she got to the one that housed her frenemy.

Sepia was soaking wet. That chemical scent strong all around her.

Nekoka slunk close to the ground, feeling exposed. A shaky sense overtook her. She couldn't hold her size for long. Her skin began to shiver, like a herd of fleas crawling over her flesh. Her fur sank into her skin, disappearing. The control on her size slipped. She grew a few inches. Kitten-sized. Her grasp on her size was weakening.

When she got out of this alive, she'd have to experiment even more with her Alter Shape. Stop taking life for granted and build up her strength, because war was on the horizon.

"Meow."

She's been so complacent before with just changing her cat coat. How simple, she thought with a shake of her head. Simple and short-sighted.

Her heart felt empty, suddenly swamped with loneliness, missing Jenni.

"Mrow," she cried again. Then added a hiss and a swipe at the air for effect.

Sepia shifted, rolled to her side an inch to look towards Nekoka's voice. "I'm hallucinating now."

Nekoka pawed a few steps back. This wasn't Sepia. There was no spark in the woman. That vibrancy in her eyes had turned hard, into something more rigid than hate.

"Meow?" Nekoka let her camouflage fade enough until Sepia's eyes widened in surprise.

"Nekoka?" she whispered.

Well, who else? Nekoka nodded.

Sepia squinted as Nekoka faded again, but not completely. "Get me out of here," Sepia whispered, her voice ragged. Then her face hardened. "Nekoka, get me the hell out of here, right now." She licked her lips and swallowed; Nekoka heard the dry click of the woman's throat.

Nekoka cursed her lack of Jenni. If Jenni was there, she'd talk to Sepia telepathically, telling the other woman everything. Instead, Nekoka released a questioning meow.

"Fine." She spat the word. "What can you do? You're just a fucking loser of a cat. You're not a battle bitch like your galpal." She tore her gaze away from Nekoka's. "There's nowhere I could go. Too many guards, too many eyes." Her voice broke, and Nekoka had to suppress the urge to comfort purr. "And I can't seem to do anything. They've got me drugged to the gills and not the good kind of drugs." She barked out a soft, self-depreciating laugh. "My mind's all fucked. I can only focus when I'm pissed. And lately, I'm too tired to be pissed anymore." She swallowed again, suddenly crazed, churning with panic. "Nekoka, they're doing things to us. They're taking something away." Sepia pressed her forehead against the metal bar. "They're jamming needles in our brains—taking something away."

Nekoka mreowed, a loud despairing noise that caused heads to turn her way.

"Get out of here," Sepia whispered. "Help us if you can. If you can't save me, at least save the others." She blinked once, hard. "The stuff from the sprinklers. It's not water. Nekoka...don't let it get on you. It stops Seeded abilities. Be careful of it. Got it?"

Nekoka gazed into Sepia's lidded eyes. Obviously, the other woman was struggling to stay awake, to stay aware. Nekoka nodded once, lifted a paw in a wave and turned tail to zip out of that factory of pain.

Wandering between the cells, she couldn't shift her camouflage anymore. She struggled to hold onto gray, the color of the floor. Her mind burned. Her body barely held onto her size. She wanted to sleep, crawl into a corner and pass out. With squinted eyes, she tried to ward off the headache, but it beat up on her. She was all turned around, not exactly sure where she'd come from, which way was north. Which way was out? Her control on her size failed. A groan of relief alerted anyone paying attention she was near, as Whisker shifted under her skin to settle in a more comfortable position. Luckily, most of the captives were drugged into a stupor, so nobody called out, pointed, or drew attention to her. Soon enough, she was next to the far wall, staring at a door that would take her away. Away from the draining energy, away from the scent of piss and defeat. Away from the nagging sense of panic that chewed at Nekoka's gut.

She must find out more. The enhanced storage space on her computer was close to full with all of the information she'd gleaned off this compound and from previous searches. She could dump a good number of gigs of data. She growled; she'd probably need to. All that information, gone. The door opened and someone entered the megaroom. Nekoka dropped her size once more and slipped to the white hallway, scurrying along the wall. It was amazing how filthy corners were, filled with dirt, and hair and other detritus. It collected on her whiskers.

She scratched at her face.

If only Jenni was there. Nekoka hated being alone. She sniffed along the floor, blocking the cameras from noticing her. Bonding with the computers and video streams became easier once she left the cavernous room.

Her paws took her farther down the hallway. She would stop before each door and send out her electrical whiskers. Electrical systems peeped back at her, but she was too far away to take control of anything. Outside one room, she connected to an internal system, though it didn't reach the outside world. Without spending much time data-digging, she did discover one corner of the system so tightly locked down, the codes and engineering so alien to her knowledge of modern computers, that she couldn't sneak a look. But she kept coming across a term, one she'd never heard of before. That term was Praena, and the meaning was a secret she couldn't discover.

CHAPTER 28

Berlin

Being homeless, Berlin was used to huddled masses of unwashed bodies. Also, the quiet mumblings to oneself, the splash of crazy in everyone's face, those were not unknown to him either. However, the shell-shocked expressions, the sweaty scent of fear, the completely forlorn, thoughtless going-through-the-motions actions of everyone, *that* gave him the creeps.

His cell had four other people, and since he was last in, he got stuck in the middle. Each of the others, three women and another man, had staked claim to a corner on which to lean their backs. Berlin was trapped in a perpetual hunch, because he had nothing to rest on. A bucket was their only ornamentation.

They'd taken his phone, which he had expected, but also his hat and glasses in their 'processing'. A man in a white coat asked him a series of questions in a deadpan voice. What was his name? Where did he come from? What 'talents' did he have? He'd told them he had a talent for hating the bright light and could he have his sunglasses back please, and they'd injected him with something that made his head swim and after that he'd just answered their questions like he wasn't in control anymore.

And the worst thing about that was he hadn't really cared, either.

They'd taken blood, spit, cut off some of his hair. It was all so clinical, like he'd imagine joining the army would be.

Nekoka had gotten away. Thank God, Nekoka had gotten away.

Now the drug had worn off, yet a hammer throbbed in his chest whenever he caught sight of a man or woman in a lab coat, and he instinctively tried to make himself small. Maybe they wouldn't notice him. He was just some homeless person, nobody of note. Maybe they would realize how uninteresting he was and keep walking. Just keep walking.

The lab coat passed, and Berlin sighed in relief. Another bullet dodged.

Time slunk along at an agonizing rate. The lights always burned his eyes. His back hurt, so he lay on his side against the cement floor, just trying to not touch anyone, but it was hard, and soon all of them lay about, feet, head, arms touching. The concrete bit into his hip, so he had to turn over every few minutes, never getting comfortable. He eventually sat back up.

"Umm," he finally said. His cellmates roused. "Are you all from Portland?" His voice cracked, and he stared at his hand pressed to the gray floor as he asked.

"I'm from Salem," said the man. One woman said she was from Gresham. The others didn't say a thing.

"How?" he started, leaning towards the man, lowering his voice even more, "How did they get you?"

The man shrugged. "I was walking the dog, and someone shot me in the shoulder with a dart of some sort. I went down. Chester ran off." He looked down at his hands. "That's all I remember." Berlin learned his name was Devon.

Another of the women sat up. She was Rachael. "I was coming home from work, I work graveyard, and there was a roadblock, so I stopped. I was the only car, and they just came up to my window, and because I'm a trusting fool, I rolled it down to talk and they sprayed some crap in my face. I woke up later in a van."

One by one, the people in his cell, and those adjacent who could hear the conversation, each told their story. Few of these were homeless nobodies like himself. Most were taken quietly, quickly immobilized by a drug. Some had a chance to fight back. "I'd clawed one guy across the face," a woman with silver-dyed hair said with pride, flashing inch long fingernails at everyone for their inspection.

"Hey, quiet down over there. No talking!" A man in a guard's uniform strolled up, a metal stun stick in his hand. The captives spun away, hunched over, and slipped into their previous torpor. Berlin lay back down on his side in the middle.

Fed twice a day, bucket changed once a day, he understood what a zoo animal felt like. Their area was left alone, but sometimes, farther towards the front, he could hear screams. He wondered what the lab coats and guards were doing to them. What terrible things made people beg and cry out like that?

On the third day, they came for him.

First, they grabbed Devon. He tried to struggle, but the uniformed guards with stiff expressions covered his cellmate's face with a cloth, and Devon lost his strength for it. Berlin didn't want to be drugged; he had to keep his wits about him, so he didn't struggle.

He was led through the walkway between the cells. He peered at everyone. Most cells had five, some even six, but a few had only two or three people, and the closer he got to the door in the wall, more often there was only one person per cell, each looking a sigh away from death. He tried to identify them through his crappy vision, to see if there was anyone he knew, anyone he would recognize. But he didn't see any of his friends, any of the homeless from Portland, and he didn't see Nekoka.

As he passed near a cell with a woman whose face was bruised and swollen, their eyes met. Finally, someone he recognized. A dark shadow shimmered around her, a death halo, like many of the captives here. Death was near. He knew that bitter face, that mouth of vitriol; now, this face was different: sunken, hollowed out.

Her eyes widened in recognition and something in his heart quivered for the first time since he'd been captured by those men. She mouthed something at him, and as he was dragged off, he kept staring at her, trying to read her lips, but he was jerked away, and she was soon out of sight.

He was certain, *certain* that the woman was Martha from Portland, one of the ones on the street with Berlin, and he was certain she was telling him to fight.

CHAPTER 29

Nekoka

She'd wasted nearly two days getting out of the lowest level of the prison. She'd thief away food when she could find it. Someone's unattended granola bar or cup of coffee. A banana or apple. She hadn't been picky. It never amounted to enough to sustain her constant need for calories while using both her powers on overdrive. She couldn't sleep, never letting her guard down. Muscles shook; mind zoned out. Her limit was cresting fast to its peak. Her salvation had been delivered with an elevator ding. Small and camouflaged and utterly exhausted, she snuck onto the elevator and was born to the floor above. There, she found rows of offices, group housing like you'd find in a kid's summer camp or the military, kitchens, showers. That must have been where the hired help stayed. Broom closets and supply closets and finally she found the server room.

Jackpot.

By then she was tapped out. Her control was already slipping: a moment of visibility, or a paw would go large until she struggled to bring it back into line with the rest of her body. She'd never lost control of her powers before. It felt a little like wetting herself in public. She'd tell no one, of course. When her tail went full size, she finally relaxed her Alter Shape and returned to her normal catgirl form and used those amazing hands to slip into a broom closet, her last ounce of strength dribbling out of her. With a mind fried to a cinder, she crawled onto the upper shelf in the closet and hid behind some brown rolls of recycled paper towels.

They tortured and killed people, but by damn, they supported the recycling system.

Twelve hours and forty-seven minutes later—thirteen lost hours—she woke, stiff and sore and senses on high alert. Whisker had two percent battery left and someone was in the closet. The overhead light cast the small space in deep shadow. Shifting boxes, rummaging, a muttered, "Where are they?" and more rummaging and the door opened, the light flipped off and the door closed.

As if on cue from her relaxed muscles, her stomach rumbled. She was not a person of sacrifice and going too long without food made for a grumpy kitty. And as a Seeded constantly using her powers, she was even more ravenous. If she didn't eat soon, her body would start eating itself, cutting her off from her Alter Shape and *kokogyo* and everything else that made her special.

Soon, she soothed her belly. We will eat soon. It was a hard lie.

The benefit of her broom closet and her high shelf was that it was around the corner from the server room. Though the server room's door was heavily guarded, the closet was not. The problem was she needed to touch one of the computers to send her mind into the system for full access.

She easily reached the acoustic tiles above, slipped one to the side, and crawled up. She couldn't see a thing. But all she really needed was to follow the electrical signal. She replaced the tile and, though her body protested, dropped into a cat to carefully walk over wires and pipes until she knew she was directly above the server.

The world laughed at her, somewhere, somehow. The entire universe thought this was funny. Due to her need to lift the tile, she needed hands again. She had to be prepared for people inside to see her. With her computer senses, she searched for specs or a phone that she could talk to, but the devices were too far away, the employees were forced to remove such devices when inside the server room, or she was just too damned tired.

Taking a huge swallow, she tried to dispel her anxiety. What if she was caught? Well, she'd just get away again. The information she gathered here could be what helped them save everyone. Helped them shut this shit down. She wasn't a hero, but she wasn't a fucking loser, either.

Finding a ceiling tile not blocked by a water pipe or bundle of cables, she lifted it an inch. Bright light beamed in through the crack. Below, protective gray metal racks housed banks of servers. The whir of the electronics was soothing and almost put her into a relaxed state until she noticed a shadow. She lowered the tile, leaned in toward the crack, and peeked through with one eye. A woman was down there, in a suit—what computer techs were forced to wear suits?—walking across the room.

There was no way she was actual IT; she must be some suit monkey there to yell, or direct, or generally get in the way. Nekoka waited. A conversation happened. Nothing important...the suit was scolding about something. Nekoka's focus swam in and out. Wait...a mention of an escape. A dangerous criminal. "Watch out," the woman said. "We believe the criminal has gotten out of the secure zone." The suit left.

Nekoka nudged the tile more and dropped to the top of a cabinet, landing as a soft-pawed Russian blue. The tile didn't quite close. Nekoka clawed at it, but couldn't move it with her paw, so gave up. The important thing, she was right on a server rack. Now...she had to touch the server; this exhausted and starved, proximity was crucial.

She inhaled, thought of Jenni. Of how hard she worked all the time. Of her love for every damned person on this earth.

When Nekoka was young, her parents had worked her hard, as the Japanese did. She'd been a focused child, studied constantly, excelled, was top in her class to make them proud. That focus. She once had awesome focus.

She dropped to the ground, making no noise. Her senses noted two cameras nearby. One on the door and one on the far end. She went to the wall and slipped from case to case, skulking, until she spotted the server guru. He was mid-thirties, a bit chunky with a military style haircut. And, on the desk next to him was a spread-out napkin with a wrapped sandwich gloriously presented on it.

Oh, the sweet aroma of the ham and cheese glued together with mayo made her stomach rumble again. The man stopped and looked around. Nekoka slunk away. This was no time to think with her stomach. The IT guy turned back to his dual screens. Nekoka noted a camera on him housed in the upper corner of the room, but there was no way it was actually recording with that food right there in the server room.

She sent her senses out to it. It was on, but it wasn't recording. The system was probably playing some prerecorded footage. Way to go, rebel, Nekoka internally cheered.

Making a desperate, possibly hunger-driven decision, she ran towards him. She leapt. In midair, she reverted to her typical shape, boosting her hands to give them strength as she wrapped them around his throat. He didn't put up much of a fight, mainly gurgled a bit before he went limp. Nekoka released her hold; she didn't want to kill him.

But she did want his lunch.

She ate his sandwich. Damn, it was good. Her stomach grumbled in thanks, then decided it wanted more. Well, snap to you, stomach.

After wiping her hands off on her fur, she sucked down his energy drink. Ah calories. She felt better. Ready to jump into the servers. She sat down with her back to a server case and got comfortable. Not that she had long to rip the server's secrets from it. Nekoka detached her mind, unhappy and nervous with the untended aspect of her body. Anyone could come, find her, kill her, and she'd be poof, gone.

Her mind disassociated and sank into the electronic data stream. Flying through the server, information streamed around her, urgent and focused. She let it flow by, got a sense of where it came from, where it was going and what it carried. It was too much. She couldn't nail it down with her mental claw. She found the security code and petted it, letting it know she meant no harm. It bit her. Nekoka had to pounce a nodule of information the security code released and rip it apart before it sent a warning to something...an anti-virus? An anti-*kokogyo*?

She growled and paced around the security, watched it, until she found the way in, piggybacking on a log in from an outside source. She hopped on and the doors opened wide, and inside she went.

Seconds were ticking by. Not that Whisker counted them for her anymore. Her poor computer had silently ceased operation. Quiet, no comforting buzz of companionship.

Luckily, she didn't need the battery to get info on the solid-state drive. Not with *kokogyo*.

Okay, what were the most important aspects she needed to know? What was this compound? Who was behind it? What was praena? She sent out little squirrels to collect the information, squirrels with bushy tails to wipe away their tracks. Nekoka sat in the center and watched and kept all eyes open for more security, more hunters looking for any intrusion that could find her and cut her.

She manually filed the information onto Whisker's hard drive.

The compound was built on three levels. Nekoka sucked in the blueprints. She was on Floor 1, one floor below the ground. There were rooms upon rooms that had no label, but she recognized the cavernous storehouse of cages. No idea where she was in the greater world, though. Was she still in Oregon? Still in America?

Nothing on the organization in control other than cryptic titles of hierarchy. The Founders. The Chief. The Director. The actors at the tippy top were called Myroi. They were here to collect praena.

Without a body, Nekoka didn't have such urges of fear and anxiety or anything that had to do with juices produced by the adrenal gland, but the cold, clear consciousness of a mind separated from the endocrine system could still feel horror.

She learned about the harvest, the letting, and what happened when they drained a praenletta—a Seeded—dry.

Something in her mind shifted, shuddered, didn't want to see this as real, couldn't face the utter nastiness of the entire endeavor. Nekoka wasn't a cloistered innocent who thought that the world was full of happy, nice people who only wanted to do good. She'd been raised on manga by horror giants like Naoki Urasawa and Hiroaki Samura. Sometimes, when others watched it, she caught the daily news.

But this.... It was an internment camp on a different level.

Even though she had cracked into their mainframe, Nekoka was still in the dark about so many things. She didn't quite know who the Myroi were, nor what they were doing with this praena stuff.

Praena, the substance they drained from the Seed. They called the draining 'letting', like giving it a different name didn't make it insane.

In that instant of discovery, she'd wanted to get violent. She wanted to go crazy and carve out their computers, send a virus to infect everything, then lock the doors, the air system. Poison them all with their own exhalations. But she couldn't do that. There were the prisoners. Sepia and Berlin. She wasn't inclined to add mass murder—even if it might be a mercy—to her list of crimes, which traditionally only held those of the hedonistic variety.

She had to get help.

Whisker's hard drive had reached maximum capacity. She dumped some vids of her friends, data collected through SPYme on strangers she passed by, and other superficial information to stuff more data in the cracks. No more room, no more time. With Whisker's battery dead, she couldn't reach an outside network. But from what she found on the facility's schematics, it had been built to be a giant Faraday cage, so it was a moot point, anyway.

Slipping out of the server room was easy, though she was still so hungry she could eat kale. She did manage to get small and followed a man in uniform, a guard probably, in the elevator up to the ground floor. There she waited and waited until someone left, and she slipped out, rustled across a gravel parking lot and dashed through a fence.

Surrounding the compound was open, flat, scraggy desert, too dry here to turn the landscape into farms. Ravenous and tired to the roots of her fur, she knew she had to get far, far away.

Free of the compound, Nekoka ate three grasshoppers, then shifted into the fastest form she could and moved.

Cheetahs held the land speed records for large animals. They could accelerate from zero to sixty miles per hour in under three seconds: faster than most gas-powered cars. Nekoka was no cheetah. She was better. Muscles hardened, tendons strengthened. Body modified to overcome stress weaknesses. When Nekoka wanted to move, she moved, and nothing could stop her.

Legs bunching under her, muscles contracting into knots under her skin of black splotched, yellowish tan, she barreled across the desert landscape of cheatgrass, fescue, and sagebrush, launching herself helter-skelter over the soft-soiled ground, the pebbles and volcanic rocks planted within barely registering under her calloused pads. She charged forward like a Sherman tank, nothing slowing her, nothing impeding her, as she sought out any electronic signal in this deserted wasteland that represented someone's invisispecs or car or tablet, anything, so she could call out to Jenni: *Jenni come stop these monsters, come save the captives, save*

Berlin! and destroy this prison because you are the hero, not me, and *Jenni, Jenni I cannot do this without you.*

In cat form she couldn't cry. It was one of the many benefits.

Small hillocks rose from the flat high desert. Her tongue felt tacky, dry. Her throat raw as she panted in her race. No signs of drones, of houses even. She needed a working device, or a charging pad.

She guessed that days had passed since she'd been taken. Nekoka harbored a deep discontent because she didn't know the precise count of hours and minutes. Without Whisker, well, Nekoka wasn't quite herself. Days, though. She knew it had been days. Seconds ticking by. Every moment another instant when Berlin, or Sepia, or any number of other people would be reduced to bone and skin and some unresponsive meat.

So, now she ran. Just being able to move, to stretch, to shed the fear of discovery, was a relief. If she could cry, she would be releasing an entire river from her eyes, a string of sparkling desperation. But she couldn't, and so she ran, panting, her chest heaving as her pace consumed the open ground as her stomach wanted to consume the stones, the fragrant sage, the dry soil.

Distance running had always been something she excelled at, and she'd been running awhile before the harsh fallow land was converted to crops of wheat and barley, and before long the scent of cows turned her nose towards human habitation.

Food. Food. Food, rampaged through her brain. Her tongue was swollen dry.

She released her Alter Shape and reduced down into her human felinoid form. The rush of relief made her stagger. Her sight grew dim, and she had to squat a moment through a bout of dizziness like she'd been tossed in the spin cycle. Her sour stomach spasmed. She was going to set upon the first edible thing she saw. Once her mind quit swirling, she stood and walked towards the distinct scent of cow paddies and irrigated farms. The ground rounded in a hill and at first she saw the top of a black locust tree, then more of the tree and finally a rickety single-story ranch home huddling under the meager shade the tree provided. Two cars, a beige compact and a rusty red pickup, parked by the final death throes of a lawn that was now bare dirt with the corpses of grass tufts. Offset from the house was a weathered barn that might be large enough to hold farming equipment and a hayloft. One of the double doors was open.

Beyond the farmhouse were miles and miles of cultivated fields. Wheat or barley, she didn't have a clue without Whisker to tell her. Part of the drive to feed the U.S. population; if you could get water to it and there was arable soil, it made food.

Normally, Nekoka would just barge into the house and ask for food. However, she didn't have Jenni there to do the socializing for her, so she had to invent her own brand of caution. A cow lowed from the paddock, then another. To Nekoka's shock, the rancher didn't appear to have dogs.

Out here, far from modern civilization of the cities, she still didn't catch a trace of Wi-Fi. How could anyone survive being so cut off? The house's off-white paint had long gone to a dull brown, the paint peeling up along the edges. The single-paned windows were covered with curtains shredded by age.

She stepped up to the door and knocked. And waited. She knocked again. The lock on the door was completely key driven. She hated being useless in an archaic world. She could sneak out of a maximum-security torture ward, but breaking into a house with no security except for a simple doorknob lock...Of course not!

If she had some picks...

"Hello?"

She walked around the house to see if someone might be enjoying some lemonade in the back and would want to share. A jumble of rusted heaps defacing the grassy field behind the barn and a trough of algae-coated water was all she found. She licked her lips at the water, but decided she had too much dignity to stick her face in that larvae laden muck.

A cow lifted its head and sniffed at her. She mumbled, "Don't worry, I have no intentions of hunting you down and eating you," even though her stomach railed against that decision.

Checking the weathered barn, she found a pile of equipment pushed under a mezzanine and covered with thick canvas sheets: a four by four, a backhoe, and a Komatsu front-end loader.

A bump. A knock.

Deeper inside, something moved.

CHAPTER 30

Nekoka

Freezing her body, Nekoka's ears scanned the surrounding area, swiveling upon the top of her head where they poked through her unkempt black hair. Amazingly accurate, she quickly pinpointed where the sound emerged when it came again. Up above her, on the mezzanine.

Walking with care, one foot down, secure, then the next, silent in her passing, she crossed the hard-packed dirt floor of the barn. A wooden ladder nailed to the side of the building reached the upper level. Wrapping her hand around the rung, she pulled herself up. The ladder creaked. Rung by rung, she climbed, going with cautious timidity until she was able to peek over the edge of the hayloft.

More stuff. Boxes filled with who knew what, a spinning wheel in one corner, a pile of old musty hay long diffused of the rich scent of growth and replaced by the smell of dust and mold. A mouse scurried from one hay pile to another, and Nekoka immediately thought: lunch.

But the mouse hadn't made that noise.

Keeping low to the floor, she crawled over the lip and waited, poised for the sound again. It took another ten minutes of holding her position, but she was a cat, and cats were good at waiting when they were on the hunt. Behind a wall of boxes came the creak. It could have been the settling of the old building, but it could have been a footstep.

Step by precisely placed step, Nekoka crawled over to the boxes, then jumped over them to land on...

A woman.

A woman in a torn, black linen dress with short hair, a tomboyish cut. Nekoka felt so, so cut off without Whisker to host SPYme and give her all the information she needed to interact with people. The woman crab-walked deeper in the shadows, an awkward move, but nonetheless it did deliver distance between them. Nekoka sat up, not completely at ease, but a ratty looking runaway was the last thing she'd expected to find in the barn's loft in the middle of the ass-end of nowhere.

"Who are you?" she asked the woman, who huddled like an abused dog in the dark connection between slanted roof and wood-paneled floor.

Unsurprisingly, the woman didn't make a peep, just huddled, and really, Nekoka did not have time for this. She peered closer at the woman, but other than the fact that she looked scared and young, she didn't get any other details.

"Listen. Is that house yours?" Nekoka flicked her ear in annoyance.

The woman shook her head, then cautiously sat forward, peering at Nekoka. Nekoka straightened and held her chin up. "Are you...?" the woman began, then went quiet, seemingly startled to silence by hearing her own voice.

Nekoka cocked her head. "Yes?"

"Are you one of the super people?"

"*Homo superious*?" Nekoka asked, cocking her brows.

The woman dipped her chin to her chest, bangs nearly hiding her eyes, taking on the look of generally confused.

"Seeded?" Nekoka said again with a groan. "Evol?" The woman's posture shifted, and she nodded. Nekoka wished she could see the woman's face, but the shadows hid all but the most gross of her expressions. "Yeah." As if it wasn't obvious.

"Oh."

What? That was it? Nekoka swallowed a growl. "So, you didn't come from the house. Where did you come from?"

With a tilt to her head, the woman looked up, then she whistled through her teeth. "Boise." Her voice was soft, an almost whisper, though it carried well in the small cave behind the pile of boxes.

"Why are you here?" Annoyance rattled within Nekoka at the game of twenty questions. She just wanted an uplink to the World Out There and to eat something. She wasn't made for podunkville.

The woman leaned forward, and her face came into the half-light. "Because I didn't want to be in *there*." Her eyes were a soft, light peach.

"You're Seeded!" Nekoka said, shocked. "Were you kidnapped, too? Were you in that place?"

The woman blinked, then slid away from Nekoka again, going shy. Time was wasting, but this waif might know something. Obviously, she'd gotten out, too. So, she did the only thing she thought would help. She purred.

With slow, delicate movements, she crawled towards the woman. If she still wore a black dress, presumably her own clothing, then she must have escaped before she was processed, like Nekoka had. Maybe she, too, was a shapeshifter.

"Why are you coming at me?" The woman's eyes grew huge, and suddenly, she was gone. A sharp pain pressed into Nekoka's throat. "Stop."

Nekoka dropped herself into cat form to escape the blade at her vulnerable bits. She spun on the woman, back arched, all seven pounds of Abyssinian in full pissy mood.

"Oh," the woman said, relaxing the arm that held the knife to dangle at her side, though Nekoka noted she didn't drop the weapon. "Kitty." Nekoka blinked. Now that the woman was in the full light, Nekoka could tell she was early twenties, and a spark of something glittered in her eyes, like a kind of delight that didn't quite fit. Her hair, the short pixie style, was a dark blond and her skin was the cultivated pale of an Elizabethan noble girl.

Nekoka pulled into her human form once again. "Please stop trying to slit my throat," she said. "I just need to ask some questions. I won't hurt you."

"You were going to take me," she said, her voice still soft.

"I just want to talk. I was trying to calm you down." Nekoka hissed in annoyance. Jenni was so much better at this. "Fine, don't be calm. I just need to know what you know about that place."

The woman laughed, a Tinkerbell kind of giggle, and Nekoka squinted her eyes, studying the woman. "You were trying to calm me down? Well, that was nice of you. Are you a nice person?"

What kind of a question was that? "Of course not. I need you to tell me how you got out, or any other information you have, so I can go back, kick some ass, and get my friends out."

Then the pixie girl's face smoothed of all emotion, not a line marring that silken complexion. "You're going back?"

Nekoka sighed. Now the escapee would probably be too scared to tell her anything. "Yes. They have two of my friends." Well, not that Sepia was really a friend....

"I need to go back, too."

Nekoka blinked. This wisp of a thing wanted to go back? Well, she was quick; Nekoka would give her that much rope to hang herself with.

"I want to go back in there, too. Now that I've got this." The woman lifted the blade that she'd held to Nekoka's neck. It looked like an old hunting knife, but the blade shone with thoughtful care and deadly beauty.

Nekoka studied her. Assuming she couldn't get Jenni, she did need help. And why not the crazy blade-wielding speedster?

"Okay. But I need two things. First, I need a phone, or specs, or charging pad, or some way to contact the outside world." The woman only shook her head, lifting her arms to show she had nothing but the harbinger of death in her hands. "Then, food. Lots of food. And some water." She needed a nap, too, but time was not on her side. "I should jack a car," she said to herself, thinking of the distance back to the compound. "While I work on the car, you can tell me what you know, how you got out?"

The woman shook her head in disagreement, not appearing to be in any hurry. "I'll get you some food."

Nekoka perked up at that. "Really?"

"Yeah." She smiled, and her entire face lit up. "I know where some is."

THE TWO CARS WERE PERFECTLY operational, but the truck needed a new tire. The Hyundai Excel was in the best condition. Good battery and had been manufactured in the early electric start years, so with gentle coaxing using *kokogyo*, the car should rev to life. She wanted to check other systems first, though. Back in New Orleans, where Jenni tried to teach her to fight, and Minnie tried to teach her first aid, Eugene covered all the tracks of breaking and entering, stealing, and hotwiring cars. It was good to have friends.

A deep wash of loneliness set Nekoka momentarily adrift.

They were her first. Friends, that was. Growing up, she hadn't had time. Friends were deemed a distraction.

The smell of roasting meat pulled her out of her fugue, sending Nekoka's salivary glands into overdrive. She was elbow deep in the car, checking hoses, fluids and the like, when she caught the mouthwatering smells over the less savory scents of oil and gasoline. She scrubbed her hands off with a rag and followed her nose.

Near a backyard fire pit, now roaring with wood and various other forms of garbage, was the large carcass of a Hereford, throat slit and a bloody hunk carved out of it. The woman was squatting next to the fire with a wire mesh over the flames and two slabs of meat roasting away. There were plates and forks and paper napkins kept in place on the ground with a round rock.

Well, cows were where steak came from, Nekoka guessed. But still...talk about overkill.

Nekoka approached, and the woman looked up and smiled, manic and full of teeth.

"Thanks for lunch." Nekoka squatted next to her. "I'm Nekoka."

"Sally. Sally Greenly. I'm from Boise, or I was, before they put me away."

Nekoka nodded, watching the steaks slowly cook. She ate raw mice and grasshoppers; somewhat raw steak shouldn't be too bad. She reached out for it, and Sally smacked her hand. "It's not ready. You'll have to wait." She pushed a bucket of water to Nekoka with her dainty foot. "Drink something."

Nekoka grimaced at first, but then picked the bucket up, and not finding any larvae writhing around in it, drank her fill. "Car should be ready soon enough. Gotta check the gas and make sure it's not soured. Other fluids are good."

Sally tilted her head. "I didn't know that could happen."

Nekoka nodded, eyes still on the steak. "In the old oil versions, it could happen if a car sits too long." The meat was inching from pink to brown at the speed of a glacial ice age.

"You know a lot about cars?"

Nekoka shrugged. "Easier to understand than people."

That high tittering laughter again. She really was a pixie.

"So, how did you get out? I mean, I had to get tiny and ride the elevator without anyone seeing me." Nekoka's fingers twitched. She could probably snatch the meat from the wire frame before Sally could do a thing, though she was quite quick. Nekoka needed to remember to update her dossier later.

"When they took me from Wolf Walker, I just waited until the drug they gave me wore off, and then I killed them all." Sally poked the meat with a long BBQ fork.

Nekoka nodded, feeling the saliva pool in her mouth, then stopped nodding and stared at Sally. Killed them all?

"Killed them all?"

Sally nodded, apparently happy Nekoka understood her grand achievement. "The driver and the guards."

"Wait. Wolf Walker Institute? You're one of the escapees?"

The scent of blood from the dead cow suddenly dominated all other scents. She remembered the news feeds discussing the escape from Wolf Walker, the Seeded mental hospital for the criminal psychos who would normally land on death row if not for their insanity. So, Sally was a wack job. Nekoka felt that happy delight within her shrivel at the edges.

"Oh no, well yes. I am from Wolf Walker, but I didn't escape from that place. That place is impossible to escape from. Some people tried and were shocked into vegetable matter. I was being transferred to some other place. A place they told us would *cure* us." She laughed, amused to no end. "Cure us! Like, any of us needed cured."

"Can the criminally insane be fixed?" Nekoka asked.

And in the next blink, the fork prongs were pressing into Nekoka's temple. "I don't like that word," Sally said. "I don't think it's right. I'm not broken."

Nekoka jerked her head away and hissed at the woman. Nekoka had been told for ages she wasn't quite normal. This girl...well, Sally was so far from normal that Nekoka exemplified Jane Doe Average American. "Fine. Fine. So, the point being," —not that you killed them all— "you didn't break out of the same compound I did. The place where they're killing other Seeded?"

"Oh, well, I don't know that place." She put the fork to poking at the meat again. Fat sizzled as it fell on the flames, releasing a relishing odor. Despite the current predicament, Nekoka's stomach ached. "I got away from the truck and have been hiding out here for days. I would love to go back to the Institute. People there hurt me. I want to hurt them back."

As sick as it all sounded, Nekoka could totally understand that sentiment.

"Your steak is done." Sally forked it up and placed it on one of the plates, giving Nekoka a knife and fork and one of the napkins.

Nekoka ignored the utensils. With oily, smelly hands, Nekoka grabbed up the steak and bit into it, letting her canines elongate in response to the near bloody flesh. So good. So sweet. Nekoka's stomach clenched as she swallowed the first bite. Sally watched her for a while, nodding in approval, then followed Nekoka's lead and picked up and bit into her own steak.

Jenni would be so disgusted.

The meat was raw in the center, and something about it brought her animal side out. It was nice, sometimes, to go a bit feral and eat with her hands, ripping apart the meat with the tools nature had given her, or whoever had inserted the Seed, anyway.

"So, they told you they were taking you to the compound?" Nekoka bit again, tearing off a hunk, then did a perfunctory chew before she swallowed it down.

"They'd come to the hospital—"

Nekoka held her snort when Sally said hospital. For criminally insane. Criminal. That's a prison, no matter what shiny titles you gave it.

"—and taken some of us away. I thought it was a field trip to the bird museum, but Brian said that they were taking us way up north to Silverwood. Then they told us they were going to *fix* us." She'd taken to using a fork and knife after constantly cleaning her chin of grease. Now she stared down at her meat, only a quarter of it gone. "They never let us out to do anything."

"Why were you in the hospital?" She wanted to hear why Sally thought she was trapped in that institution.

Slowly, Sally sliced a small bite from the center of her steak, red and almost dripping with the raw juices. Contemplating the meat, she hmmed for a moment, then flashed Nekoka a winning smile and gobbled the bit of steak from the end of her fork.

"The group of us? Ah, I think it's because we killed people with our powers."

Nekoka feigned blasé as the woman stared up into the bright sky, the blue a pale, weak thing, the sun blazing with no clouds to filter its fierceness. Time. She was still losing time.

"Have you killed anyone?" Sally asked, looking up into the same sky.

"No. Never. Jenni would never talk to me again." And the idea was more than a little abhorrent. Sure, she was superior to everyone else, but that didn't mean they should die for being lesser. People still had rights, and living was one of those inalienable ones.

"It's so nice to be out," Sally said. "To be alive again. They stripped us of life in that place."

Though she thought better of it, Nekoka cocked her head and chirruped in question.

Sally blinked her clear, peach eyes and dropped her chin, making those eyes look even larger as she studied Nekoka. She was completely elfin, cute and dainty, and part of Nekoka both loved and hated her for the false packaging. "They kept our brains boiling in a soup. None of us could think. Fed only mush—" she made a face, "—and carted around in a wheeled chair. Our lives had been stolen from us and we were placed in cocoons." She flashed that daring smile again, possessed of so much self-assurance Nekoka suddenly longed for Jenni. "Now, I've taken flight and recaptured life."

Man, this woman was a herd of cows short of a herd. Nekoka nodded, to appease her, and vowed to get the hell on the road as soon as possible so she could contact Jenni.

Nekoka swallowed down a quarter of the water from the bucket, then washed her hands in the rest. "Well, thanks for the munch, but I gotta get back to the cars." Nekoka stood and spun around on her heel, her tail whipping through the air. Gas. She still needed gas.

The psychotic Seeded woman was standing next to the passenger side door.

"I want to come with you," she said.

Nekoka looked back the way she'd come, towards the fire, then studied Sally again, standing next to the car. Teleportation? Superspeed?

With a solid certainty, Nekoka knew she couldn't contend with that. She unscrewed the gas cap and sniffed. Smelled normal. She checked the fuel filter. Dirty, but should be operable.

"I'm coming with you," Sally said again.

Nekoka slammed down the hood and yanked the driver's side door open with a metallic squeal. "No."

"Why not?" Sally opened the passenger door.

"Because, I've got things to do, people to break out. An army to raise."

"Then you'll need me. I can help you break them all out."

Nekoka paused for a moment before slipping into the front seat of the little hatchback. The seat was cloth and stained by a mosaic of substances that made it look ready for the NOMA. An Elmo on a chain dangled from the rearview mirror, bleached to a pink as pale as the hero, Battle Axe's, eyes. Nekoka stared at the steering column and tickled the computer start system. The engine chugged, then died. Nekoka cursed, then tried again. This time the engine agreed to continue running, though with every sputter and cough, it put up its own protest.

Nekoka surreptitiously hardened the skin around her vital organs into a thick armor in case slicey girl decided to go rabid during the car ride. Preparation, Jenni echoed in her mind. Plan for the obvious, at least.

Nekoka squeezed the steering wheel. "Fine. But there are some rules."

Sally slipped into the passenger seat and made one of those pouty, put-upon faces. "I hate rules."

Nekoka sighed; she hated rules, too. "You don't attack any of my friends."

"Oh, okay. I can follow that rule."

"And I would prefer it if you didn't attack any of the prisoners in that place once we get back in."

Sally nodded. "Got it. I'll just introduce the men in white coats and their friends to my little buddy here." She lifted the knife, now clean of cow blood. The woman giggled. Nekoka sighed.

"Alright then, let's blaze." Nekoka shifted into first, spun the car around, and hit the small two-lane highway going west.

CHAPTER 31

The Myroi

Thirty praenletta had been letted that morning. Through much experimentation, they'd developed a swifter method of letting the praena from them without extinguishing them outright. A gulf full of charred bones marked their progress.

The praenletta were a complex species in a solid world where light and shadow only affected the sight. Even with these deficiencies, they proved useful to the Myroi. The way the properly prepared praenletta produced so much praena had impressed the Myroi. Truly a marvel. This praena would save them all.

Though often the praenletta would not die from one or two lettings, a third usually used it up. Some moiety had argued that they only let each individual once, then set it free, but that plan hadn't seemed prudent. Even the unenriched praenletta who had agreed to help confirmed that freeing the praenletta once it had been letted would be a mistake.

That was the thing it didn't understand about this species at all. That they would turn on their own moiety. Perhaps their value on the reason of life was sickened. All minds should work together towards the common goal: existence.

The Myroi found they could not abide the noises the praenletta exuded when they went to the letting chamber. Their fear tainted the air with sallow yellows and vivid pinks. Almost blinding. They leaked from their outer coating and seemed to lose their sanity when pushed into the room, secured into the chair, and then inserted with the letting needle. That sanity, perhaps more fragile than their bodies.

Interesting species indeed.

The moiety sent to Jikon watched some of the lettings to ensure the praenletta doing the Myroi's business did not make some vital mistake. But they did. They always made mistakes. Some of the unenriched pressed their physical forms into that of a praenletta, who then made the noises and tried to press its physical form at them in return. Or the praenletta had been thrust into the chair and the needle inserted incorrectly. The precious praena had been lost, the praenletta dead.

The moiety watched it all from the corner of the room. They would converse with the others, address the Chief, which they learned had yet another designation: Enrique Silva. The moiety could not separate all of the individual identities. That one would need to stop this waste. Now, though, all ignored them, all but the next praenletta they were ready to let. It was unique from its species, having completely colorless features. Even its eyes—which seemed to be more varied than rainbow flies—had no color. But those eyes saw, and the moiety knew that it was looking at them as few of the beings from Jikon could unless the Myroi wished it.

This set the singularity's being to want to fade. None of the praenletta had ever stared at it before, instead swamping the room with sickly colors. This one still seeped out its fear, but it also didn't lose itself to that fear.

The moiety watched for the ever-shifting muscular twitches over the face of the praenletta as the letting tube was inserted. They had grown skilled at noticing specific facial reactions. As the tube was inserted, the praenletta's eyes grew round and its mouth fell open. It didn't struggle, but remained still in the chair.

The eyes began leaking, and it opened its mouth, looking at the moiety, and said one word. "Why?"

CHAPTER 32

Nekoka

They passed three cars in the span of forever. The blacktop whizzed under their bald tires in a sibilant chorus. Sally hadn't said a word, just sat there, her hands tucked under her thighs as she watched the passing wheat fields. Once in a while she'd make some whistling noise through her teeth, but that was about it.

Without Whisker, Nekoka had no idea how late it was, only that twilight was upon them and a dash of stormy blue flirted along the horizon behind her, reflected in the review mirror. Sleep pounded on her mental door, whispering, coaxing: Nekoka, time for a little nap. Only a little one. Little one.

Her tail hurt, cramped against the car seat. She hated traveling in conventional equipment without the ability to wiggle. Usually, Jenni drove.

In the distance, stationary lights grew brighter as they charged down the road as fast as the old hatchback would take them. She'd almost plowed over five coyotes, seven birds, and too many rabbits to count, but they had all been quick with a healthy dose of fear.

The lights turned into a small two-story farmhouse with a huge shop stationed behind it like some angry bodyguard. Nekoka wondered if it was required that each rural house have a shop bigger than the actual house. She slipped up the long driveway, so pitted it sent the car rocking and rolling. A motion detecting light went on and a dog began barking, and by the sound of the bark, it was a big mother.

Nekoka involuntarily hissed. Sally giggled.

"I could take care of the doggy for you," she said with bright eyes and a quick nod.

Nekoka almost felt tempted, but shook her head. "Let's try this the normal way first, Jenni would insist."

"Jenni?"

Nekoka stiffened, then relaxed. For some reason, she hadn't explained Jenni. Now that she spoke the name loud enough, she couldn't pull the words back into her mouth. She might as well give the full explanation of the essence that was Jenni. "*My friend*. She's the one I'm trying to call."

The tires crackled through the dirt and thin gravel as she parked behind another vehicle. Nekoka pushed the car door open and swung her hips around, releasing her tail with a sigh of pleasure. She closed her eyes and sent out her thoughts, seeking any kind of local connection that allowed her to tap into the global communication system hovering far above, mocking her by its inaccessibility.

Yes. There was Wi-Fi! Now, she just needed to charge her device. She looked off into the vast distance. The small two-lane road unfolded forever until the night swallowed it up. The land outside of the cities was almost all farmed now. Nearly emptied of humans except for a few brave, and stupid, neo-pioneers. The scent of cows told her they'd found another rancher, the bovine's subsisting on scrub. She was surprised this place hadn't been sucked in by some agribusiness growing low-water need GMO corn or soybeans or kale. Everyone raved about kale. Nekoka shivered, but then her horror was disturbed by the sound of a loud knocking. Sally was at the front door, one hand held before the door, the other tucked behind her back, the fingers neatly closed around the knife handle.

Cursing, Nekoka ran up to Sally, grabbing for her arm. "You can't kill these people," she said.

Sally looked over her shoulder, a serene smile making her beautiful. "You better go hide," she said. "If they see you, they might not let us use the phone. I look normal; they'll let me use the phone."

"You don't even know the number I need to call," Nekoka said, the tone as flat as the road she'd just driven.

Sally's mouth slowly turned into an 'o' of wonder. "I guess you're right."

But by then Nekoka could hear someone walking towards the door, so she rattled off Jenni's number, then slipped down into a tabby. While she was becoming smaller and furrier, she hissed at Sally, "Don't hurt these people."

The door opened a crack. An older man, balding with quite the bow-legged stance, gazed down at Sally. "Car troubles?" he asked. He didn't look like they'd woken him up; the smell of liquor settled onto him like a cloak of heavy wool.

Sally nodded. "Yes, sir. And my phone's dead." She shrugged. "No charger. Can I use yours?"

The man leaned back a little, getting a good look at Sally. "Sure thing." He stood back, leaving the door opened wide, and Sally walked in, artfully shifting her knife around so the man couldn't see it. Nekoka slipped in while he watched Sally, and hid in the many darkened corners of the cluttered house. Weeks of mail and other papers piled up on the dining room table. It smelled of disuse and illness, the tang of the old. Knitted afghans rested over the backs of chairs and the couch.

He led Sally into a well-lit kitchen where a green phone with a mile-long cord was mounted to the wall. An honest to god landline. He gestured to it and stepped away, resting his butt against the edge of the kitchen counter. Nekoka, hiding under an antique roll top desk, watched.

Sally picked up the phone and dialed. She smiled over at the man. "I really appreciate it."

He shrugged, staring at Sally's thin, boyish body. "Whatever. Just glad to help a traveler."

"Hello?" Nekoka heard on the other side of the phone. It was Jenni, and she almost burst from her hiding place to more clearly hear her voice, to say "Jenni, I'm here. I'm here. Come get me." But she stayed in place and put her faith, though stretched fairly thin, in Sally.

"Hello, is this Jenni?" Sally asked, twirling the long, spiraled phone cord around one finger, the knife having been secreted away somewhere within the straight-lined skirt of the dress.

As if the sound came from the end of a long tube, Nekoka heard Jenni reply. "Yes." A pause. "Who is this?"

Very few people had Jenni's number.

"Oh, this is Sally. Sally Greenly. I'm a friend of Nekoka's and..."

"What! Nekoka?" The frantic fear and excitement in Jenni's voice almost set Nekoka to purring. "Is she there? Is she safe? Where are you?"

Sally laughed, soft and sweet. "She's safe. We're..." She put the phone to her chest. "Sir, can you tell me where we are?"

The man had let his gaze shift away from her body, finally locking onto her eyes. "You one of them freaks, little girl?" His entire posture changed. He stood stall, almost leaning towards her, and his face twisted into something mean. Deadly. "You one of them bastards that screwed with my herds?" He took a step towards her, and Sally simply stood her ground, appearing totally unconcerned.

"I think we're in Idaho, is that right?" she asked again, the phone still pressed to her chest.

Nekoka bunched up her hind end, ready to pounce.

"Get the hell outta my house." He raised his arm as if to strike, but Sally was much, much quicker. She brought forth her knife and between one blink and the next, she had the edge of the blade against the man's throat, an expression of horror on his face and one of sublime joy on hers.

"Shall I cut the location out of you, or are you going to tell me?" She pressed her body up against his, the knife bit deeper, and Nekoka could see a red bead of blood dribble along the stubble of the man's neck.

"You're just outside of Kimaquia. Now, get out."

Sally pressed closer, plastered to the guy, and Nekoka wondered if he had sufficient liquid courage to seize her or if his sense of self-preservation was strong enough that he wouldn't move.

He reached up to grab Sally's arm, right as she leaned in to catch the drop of blood on the tip of her tongue. Nekoka leapt through the air, and everything slowed, her perception sharp as Sally brought the blade up and around the man's throat, not deep enough to sever his jugular, but he dropped his grip on Sally and clutched at the opening gash in his skin, shocked, a look of wonder and 'why' written across the deepening lines of his face.

Times like these, Nekoka wished her transformation was instantaneous, but instead her body grew, fleshed out as she grabbed for Sally, pulling her away. Sally turned a reproachful gaze at Nekoka. "He didn't like us," she said, as if that explained everything and shouldn't

Nekoka totally support her? "I didn't kill him," she added with a tone of disappointment.

"Yeah." Nekoka looked at the man, crying and writhing on the floor, trying to contain his precious bodily fluids. Nekoka grabbed a grimy dishtowel and thrust it at the man, but he only tried to crawl further away. Nekoka turned to Sally and said, "Give me the phone." There wasn't anything she could do for the filthy farmer, anyway.

Sally handed Nekoka the phone, then proceeded to turn her blade this way and that, catching the blood in the different flavors of light coming from the kitchen and the living room.

Nekoka turned her back on Sally, hardening her skin like she had in the car in case a stray knife thrust tried to pierce her.

"Jenni?"

"Nekoka!"

It was so good to hear the voice of her best friend. All that taut tension gave a little.

"Jenni. I'm in Idaho. You wouldn't believe, there's this huge compound, with thousands of Seeded, both Sepia and Berlin are—Holy crap. Sally, stop!" She cut off mid-babble. Sally was carving something into the bald spot on the man's head. His scream ricocheting sharply off the walls churned Nekoka's stomach.

Sally stopped. "Why?" Her captive's noises cut off; his body went limp but his chest still rose and fell with breath. Sally neatly twisted her wrist and the finished Z, or was it an S, came to bloody life in the man's skin. "It's pretty, isn't it?"

"Nekoka? Nekoka?" Jenni's voice echoed from the phone in Nekoka's hand. "What's going on?"

Nekoka lifted the phone to her mouth, watching as Sally ran her finger over the cut. "Jenni?" All emotion had dried up from Nekoka's voice. "I'm in Idaho. In a town called Kimaquia. Nearby is a compound where they are holding and torturing, and eventually killing Seeded. It's heavily guarded and heavily fortified. Who can you bring and how soon can you get here?"

"Kimaquia? Just a second." Then Jenni continued, obviously talking to somebody else. "Can we charter to Kimaquia?" A pause. "Kimaquia,

Idaho." Then, "Nekoka, I'm coming. I'll bring everyone. We'll be there soon. There is a small airfield near there. Can you get there?"

She gave Nekoka directions, and Nekoka nodded to herself, mesmerized by Sally wiping the blood off her knife, how it caught in the yellowed kitchen lighting, flashing and brilliant. Then, she said, "Yeah. I can get there. I'll be waiting."

"Nekoka, are you okay?" Nekoka blinked, and Jenni continued. "What's going on?"

Nekoka swallowed past the log jam in her throat. "Nothing you can help with far away, Jenni," she said, trying to sound as normal as she usually sounded. "Just get here soon, could you? Please? And bring food. A lot. Cream, please, and anything with calories. And a charging pad and batteries. Whisker is dead."

There was a long silence, and Nekoka wondered if Jenni had hung up. Then she said, "I'll get there as soon as humanly possible. As possible for any Seeded with good connections. 'kay?"

"Yeah. I'll be waiting."

"Okay. Be safe, Nekoka. Okay?"

"Yeah. I better get going. You be safe, too."

She hung up, stunned by the butcher before her. Retreating a step, Nekoka wondered if insanity was contagious.

"Are we going somewhere else?" Sally asked. "I wish he'd had hair," she said. "I would have liked some." The bloody S was marred now, so much blood seeping out of the wound. Sally's hands, and her weapon, were behind her back. "I'm ready."

Nekoka blinked, then nodded. "Yeah, but make sure he won't bleed to death."

Sally glanced down at the prone man and casually waved her knife wielding hand at him. "Oh, he won't bleed to death; I didn't cut him that badly."

Nekoka wiped down the phone, then Alter Shaped her fingers...bye-bye fingerprints. After a quick call to 911, "No, I don't know the address, somewhere near Kimaquia, just trace this damned call," she rummaged through drawers and found some paper towels and duct tape and wrapped up the cut on his throat as well as the head carving. The blood pooling around his head caused Nekoka's nostrils to flare. In a way, it smelled good. She liked the smell of blood: rich, metallic, and nourishing, but the fact that it was human blood, and she thought it smelled good, churned her stomach.

As she doctored the man, Sally rummaged through more cupboards and began snagging one thing after another and stuffing them in a thin paper grocery sack. Nekoka had only the first aid skill Minnie taught her, very minor, but she figured if she could at least stop the blood flow, it would probably save his life. Afterwards, she scrubbed her hands with soap and hot water.

"Alright Sally." Nekoka left the man and his misfortune for the car. Sally followed in that puppy quality of someone who had no other guidance, her pilfered items swinging in their sack. "You didn't have to do that. *Baka. I* don't want to lecture you on what is right and wrong. Don't make me do it again."

Sally nodded, her head down in a semblance of shame that Nekoka figured was all show. Then the pixie slasher rummaged through her sack and pulled out a granola bar. "Food?" she asked, showing the bar to Nekoka. The steak had been hours in her past, and she was still trying to add more fuel to her stomach to combat her exhaustion and keep her awake. Nekoka snatched it up, tore off the wrapper, and stuffed it in her mouth. It was stale and dry, but she ate it anyway as she sparked the car to life and headed for the airport.

Inset 6
Blog Post

Seth Michaels Road Trip Blog

Day 110:

It's not big, but all my world is contained in this car. An old gas Suzuki because out in rural America, chargers are as rare as the buffalo. I've got my clothes, my laptop, and even a new drone which I use to capture these images. I've got food, a stove, and tent and sleeping gear. I have a tablet with books and a constant uplink to the world. Everything.

It's not big, but the world certainly is.

It's beautiful out here, quiet and almost wild, and in my isolation, I feel like I've found a peace that I can't find in the mega cities like Chicago and DC and New York and every other place I've driven through on this Great American Finding Myself Road Trip. As I head into the west, I find fewer and fewer cities, mainly mid-sized towns populated by farmers and the support industries for food and energy production. In the late 00s, it was the first time in man's history that the populations were higher in the cities than outside them, and now, decades later, it's an even starker statement. Nobody lives out here. You'll find just wind farms and cultivated fields. The smallest towns have been eaten up by the great food production machine. Acres of wheat and corn and soy, the energy rich foods, climbing right up to the edge of this crumbling two-lane highway. And in the distance, upon the sloping hills, the vertical-veined wind turbines constantly gyrating in the wind.

I read an article that speculated that the population rate will finally decrease in the US, even with current immigration, due to the free availability of birth control in the Betterment Stations, but these lands have already been plowed under. The wild grasslands Lewis and Clark traveled through, a thing of history, long dead, like the passenger pigeon and the black-footed ferret. It's a changed landscape few witness through their own eyes, a mystery maybe, or worse, a tired old lecture you flick aside with a twist of your fingers to jump to the better news about the greatest superheroes or pop stars or who will win on the Bachelorette.

The good thing about driving along vast stretches of these megafarms is that the roads are straight, and I can just think. The bad thing about this drive is...I can just think. And sometimes, I don't think we've engineered a better place.

CHAPTER 33

Berlin

Berlin curled up in a tight ball on the floor of his cell. They'd stuck his head with a needle and sucked something out of him. He could feel that it had left him, feel the hollow place inside where it had once been. He couldn't describe it. It was a nightmare completely unlike anything he'd ever experienced, a pain that was tallied on its own scoreboard. He'd cried. It hadn't helped, though, so he decided not to cry anymore.

Two of his original inmates remained in the cell. Heather and Rachael. Other than where they came from, that's all he knew. They weren't allowed to talk. None of them knew where the other two had been taken to. Devon had been taken away, like Berlin, and never returned. Berlin, losing his parents, being homeless and hungry and cold, seeing the last minutes of life from dead eyes, held a certain foreknowledge about death, and it didn't frighten him. The two that were gone were dead. The three in the cell were dead. They were all dead and just didn't know it.

The ghosts were gathering.

He remembered seeing the odd ghost in the place where they'd hurt him. So different from the morass of ghosts haunting this circus of horror. It watched. It stood in the corner, a dark smear on the wall, and watched as they pierced him and extracted his soul. The ghost had watched and with a moment of clear thought, Berlin realized it wasn't a ghost at all, but something other.

A shadow.

He wondered how Martha was. He wondered where Nekoka had gone and hoped that she'd gotten free. Only a small portion of him resented that she hadn't taken him with her, only because he knew it wasn't possible. He was insignificant. If she could get help to save more people, then he was a worthy sacrifice. He would make that sacrifice, be a casualty, because the many was worth more than just him, just one freakish albino homeless kid.

The ghosts swarmed around him, getting closer and closer. "You'll join us soon," they said.

His limbs lay heavy with exhaustion. His heart lay heavy with worry. He lay there, waiting for the hours to pass, dreading when they came for him again to finish the job.

CHAPTER 34

Nekoka

"Damned lousy, slacking, lazy bastards."

Nekoka stalked the airfield after a tiny but life-sustaining nap during the dark of night. Now, she marched up and down the strip on her fifth pass, her tail flicking left, right, left, slicing through the air like it aimed to split atoms. It was full on day; birds were singing, and she had a strong desire to go hunting and fill more of that gaping hole in her belly. Sally sat cross-legged on the crumbling, dry soil on the edge of the airfield, her black dress pooled in her lap to expose her legs, basking in the sun.

The staff of the small county airfield hadn't been pleased when Nekoka informed them of an incoming bird, but Nekoka didn't stick around for them to tell her no again. There was no 'no', only, 'be prepared'.

They had bottles of water and snack bars stolen from that redneck Sally had tagged to build up her reserves, but it tasted too close to sawdust and abandonment. If Nekoka squinted every time she swallowed, she could almost forget the cruelty of the woman happily facing the sun each time she took a swig from the bottle. But the bloody S was as neatly carved into Nekoka's memory as it was in that man's scalp.

"Well," Sally said, attempting, again, to placate Nekoka without any of Nekoka's consent. "You didn't ask how long they would take to get here."

"They should be here by now." Nekoka's tail continued to cut through the air. She was super annoyed that the crazy bitch with control issues was the calm one.

"Perhaps." Then Sally shaded her eyes and fixed her gaze on Nekoka. "But I think you secretly are happy they're not here yet."

Nekoka gave her a glare that said, "Hot damn, woman, you really are a twisted fuck."

"I think you're secretly happy because it gives you a reason to use all the bad language you've been using."

"Screw you."

"See!"

Nekoka grumbled again. She hated waiting. Though many aspects of her feline persona shone through true, since becoming Nekoka, patience wasn't one of her natural attributes. She'd already fixed up and stolen another car: this one an old 1990s panel van, windowless in the back. She had no idea how many people Jenni was bringing, nor from where.

Weeds had punched through the edges of the airfield pavement, and mingled with the jagged cracks were a passel of snakes with yellow stripes baking themselves in the sun. Nekoka kept toeing them, getting them to hide in the grasses, but they continued their eternal pilgrimage back to the warmth. Sally and snakes: sun worshipers. "Go on," she ordered the garter snake. It lazily slithered back into the cheatgrass. By the time her sensitive ears caught the hint of roaring engines, Nekoka was halfway back to the cars. "They're coming!"

"How do you know?" Sally asked, slitting leaves of dried grass with the edge of her blade.

"The engines. I can hear them."

Sally nodded and looked up for a moment into the sky, shading her eyes with her hand, then continued slicing grass. She took a still green one from a large clump and wiggled it out of its sheath and began sucking on the pale green stem. In this guise, as sweet country lass, she looked harmless. Nekoka snorted. She was as harmless as one of those tiny frogs in the Amazon, brilliant and beautiful with colors of the rainbow that killed you with a touch.

Nekoka squinted her eyes in the direction she'd pinpointed the sound. Her ears swiveled. Slowly, from bug to bird to man sized, the plane grew nearer. By the time she could see the full size of the machine, way too big for this little runway, she noticed a smaller escort to the oddly shaped plane. A flash of brilliance. Starburst.

Starburst from the Guardian Alliance.

The airplane, something painted olive drab, certainly military, had a Cro-Magnon brow with stubby wings that gave it the appearance of a bug rather than a bird. The wings teeter tottered. Nekoka leapt in the air, waving back. Sally had gained her feet and leaned her butt against the door to the Hyundai, hands pressed into the side of the car as she watched the plane.

The plane circled once, then banked low and came back around, aligned with the runway. Nekoka really didn't want to watch; Jenni was in there. Starburst zipped before the plane's nose. The plane practically kissed her feet as it flew, tight to her toes as a pair of dancing shoes. Before the runway even started, it rode inches from the ground. The ground crew were running around waving glowing wands about in some frantic need for order. Unfortunately for them, chaos reigned, and Nekoka would have enjoyed it more if her heart wasn't lodged in her temples and her hands clutched together like a little old lady worried about missing an episode of *The Price is Right.*

When the plane tickled the ground, it bounced once, then settled, the bitter scent of charred rubber and metal spreading through the air as the rear of the stubby plane fishtailed. The brakes screeched out, high and painful. The speed slowed, but still the machine barreled down the pavement. Luckily, beyond the runway's end, there were no trees or hills, only a long stretch of dirt and brush.

The plane reached about a third of the way from the end of the concrete runway when Starburst spun in midair and braced her hands against its nose. Her fire flared; the plane lurched, the tail end swinging around to the left, but the speed slowed incrementally every hundred feet, and before it tumbled off the end of the runway, it rested to a complete stop.

"Did you just see that, Janice?"

Nekoka glanced at the two airfield attendants.

"Did I just see a flying woman, who's on fire by the way, stop a Sherpa from overtaking the airfield on our strip, you mean? Yeah. I just saw that." Janice nodded slowly, her red wands resting uselessly against her thighs.

Nekoka waited as the plane was swung around through the brute force of Starburst's strength and its own mechanical aptitude and taxied up to her. Before it came to a full stop, Nekoka was already sprinting over to the rear door. With a pop, it opened, and as she watched it lower, someone pushed through the opening crack and leapt down to the ground.

"Jenni!" Nekoka called out. Jenni's face was a hurricane of relief and worry, excitement, and anger, and when they were within five feet of each other, Nekoka threw herself forward, arms wide, and Jenni snatched her up, wrapped her arms around her and twirled. Nekoka's legs flew behind her as she hugged Jenni back. Tight, so tight. "Jenni, you're here. I'm so glad you're here."

"You charged into the unknown again, Nekoka. Without me. What were you thinking? We're on this rum run together."

Jenni squeezed her around the middle, each woman's head buried in the other's neck their heights were so aligned. All through Nekoka's mind she heard, *You're alive. You're alive. You're alive*, in a mantra of relief.

Yes, Jenni. I'm alive.

I'm here. I'm here.

As the women hugged, going through the actions of reunion, assuring that each was unharmed, the rest of the rescue team descended the stairs. Eventually a man called out, "You two done yet? Need a room?"

Nekoka glared out over Jenni's shoulder. Zack was flashing his media smile. Nekoka gave in to her urge to grin. Jenni boosted Nekoka as she threw herself at him next.

Zack caught her and twirled her around. "You crazy cat. Going on such a *heroic* adventure without us." Zack smirked.

Nekoka scratched at her nose after he set her down, then leaned into him. "I know. It *is* crazy. It's downright stupid!" She laughed, then turned to squish Eugene with a hug, who kept his hands stuffed in his pockets and looked entirely too amused.

Minnie smiled brilliantly, her own relief making Nekoka's guilt bloom into a thorny rose. Her shirt had a big, stylized S on the front, for S-Force, though she wore her usual casual jeans. Even Minnie was embracing the team.

"Minnie, Whisker died," she whined into her friend's shoulder.

Minnie patted her. "Oh well, dear. You'll just have to bury poor Whisker in this dry dirt and hope for some resurrection. Or, perhaps you can just recharge it."

Nekoka pulled her face off of Minnie's shoulder, scanning the clear blue overhead sky. "I'm so...yeah, sorry. For leaving."

Minnie shook her head and pushed Nekoka off her, holding her at arm's length. "Well, all that self-pity amounts to a hill of beans."

"Magical beans?" Nekoka asked.

"No, normal beans," Minnie said simply. "Magical beans would actually be worth something." Then, with the flourish of a magician, Minnie brought out a cooler with cream and sandwiches. Nekoka squealed and dove for the cream.

More eyes were on her—her friends from New Orleans, members of O.G.R.E., and others from the international group Guardian Alliance. About fifteen people in all. Everyone wore some semblance of the organization they were with. Badges, uniforms, insignia. Everyone but Jenni.

And there was Grace, full-hipped Gracie with kind eyes almost as light as Berlin's but with hints of Easter yellow in them. Gracie, whose pinched face softened when Nekoka turned to her.

Nekoka wrapped her in her arms, sinking into Gracie's warmth. "I watched over her for you," she said, then remembered, Gracie and Jenni weren't together anymore. Nekoka wanted to know, needed to know why, but felt too shy, too uncertain to ask in front of that large crowd.

"I'm glad you did," Gracie said, pulling away, her crucifix catching the afternoon light. "I counted on it."

Nekoka nodded at her. Grace could count on Nekoka.

Nekoka began charging Whisker with a set of batteries and a charging pad that Jenni had brought, another wad of anxiety loosening. She'd been blind, deaf, and dumb without her portable computer. No way to communicate, no SPYme, no clock, for God's sake.

Then she finally settled and faced everyone. "You all came!"

"'Course we came," said Eugene. "Though, running off like that." An uncharacteristic wash of emotion crossed his face. "I don't see how Jenni puts up with you."

"There was a workshop. She earned a certificate," Nekoka said.

Eugene grinned wearily. "I'm not surprised. Care and feeding of crazy catgirls."

Nekoka ducked her head.

"And know this," he poked her in the chest, "you're still one of us. The Usual Suspects, you idiot. Think we'd leave you to fend for yourself against an army of evil doers?" He winked, and Nekoka huffed out a laugh, so happy to see them all.

"I don't know about an army, but I got some information on the compound on Whisker's hard drive, but Whisker is silent. Needs to charge. They're doing some really sick shit." Nekoka's hide twitched.

"Let's talk about it on the way there." Zack turned towards the cars and noticed the airport attendants. "Ah, damn. The authorities. Let me handle this."

Zack walked towards the two wand holders and a uniformed officer, who was cautiously approaching them. Pablo trotted up next to Zack. "Why don't you let me help?" The two men put on matching, winning smiles and cut the three onlookers off from reaching the rest of the group.

While they waited and Nekoka continued to munch on ham and cheese, Jenni began introducing her to the Guardian Alliance members, though she knew who each and every one was. She got to meet Starburst, who was a very down-to-earth woman, and her husband, Mozart, who was a medic but whose powers mainly involved scents. Also, a TK-powered Seeded from Portland, named Cherry who was the local Guardian Alliance member. There was also Battle Axe, the big shy man almost didn't meet Nekoka's eyes, and Devana, a tall woman with a thick head of golden-brown hair on the edge of blond who was the Second of the Guardian Alliance and sent people to nap nap land with a touch. And last but not least of the Guardian Alliance members was Sparks.

"Sparks, it is my deepest pleasure to meet you," Nekoka said with an awkward bow, her Japanese upbringing suddenly coming to the forefront of her mind. At least she hadn't added *-san* to the woman's name.

A line of deep dimples popped out as Sparks' oval face. "I tried to get my sister to come, too, but Trixie's on another assignment." She brushed her thin hair back as the gentle wind picked it up and swirled it around her face. It seemed to spark with static cling.

All in all, Nekoka had to shuttle seventeen people to the compound out in the tulies. The Excel held five, the van could fit ten. Well, maybe fifteen if they had no personal space. Either way, it would just have to work.

"Nekoka, you forgot me," Sally said. She had her hands behind her back and was looking sweet and innocent. How did she do that? Nekoka thought she'd had sweet and innocent down, but she was a neophyte compared to this champ.

"Crap, sorry. Everyone, this is Sally. Sally," Nekoka waved her hand over the assembly, "everyone."

She's an escapee, sort of, from Wolf Walker. Unstable. Violent. Teleports, I think. Maybe superspeed. I would love her on this mission.

Jenni's color faded.

"You're Jenni?" Sally said with a certain thoughtful tone. "The one Nekoka said I must not kill."

Almost everyone else there had VR-glasses on, and each had to have at least the less-robust version of ISpy churning data at them. It was Chandler who pointed out the dead pony in the pie first. "Aren't you the Darkener? A federally wanted criminal?"

Nekoka went cold.

The Darkener?

Sally nodded, a bit of pride in the sharp snap of the motion. "Yes. I've killed so many people they wanted to hang me."

Everyone turned their attention to Nekoka. Battle Axe shifted, taking a step forward.

Nekoka's fur puffed up. "What? I found her in a barn. I didn't know!" At the time, she amended mentally. In retrospect, watching the things she had done to that drunk, Nekoka shouldn't at all be surprised she should be on death row. "And she promised to help break out Sepia and Berlin, along with the other hundreds of Seeded they've got caged in there. I figured we need all the help we can get." Nekoka found she couldn't meet anyone's gaze. "You haven't been in that place." The chill caused her to shiver, the motion shifted all of her fur to settle again. "You don't understand what it's like. Berlin's been in there for days, longer for Sepia. We need to hit them, hit them hard, and hit them fast to save our friends."

Jenni touched her arm briefly, and Nekoka offered up a meek smile of thanks.

Sally stood in the center of the crowd, their hostility mounting like a Midwestern whirlwind. "What? Do you worry I might kill you?" With a quick glance over at Nekoka, she asked, "I assume these are on the no kill list, too?"

"Yes...no kill." Nekoka slashed her hands through the air. "These are allies. Don't kill them."

Sally shrugged. "Okay." She began walking towards the little red hatchback.

Nekoka watched her go, then called out. "Sally, we need a plan."

Casting a glance over her shoulder and dropping her chin to peer through her parted bangs, Sally said as she continued walking, "We drive to the compound; we shut the place down. Is there anything else we need to know?"

Nekoka looked at Jenni, then at Starburst. With a quick lift to her eyebrows, and a crooked smile, Starburst said, "That sounds about right."

Jenni's gaze shifted over Nekoka's face. "Nekoka, why don't you drive the Hyundai. I'll take the van and we can plan as we go. You're right. We need to move." Jenni brushed Nekoka's cheek. "You okay?"

Nekoka's heart sank at being separated from Jenni again, but she nodded. "Of course, though.... I am tired, hungry...exhausted, really. But I can do this."

I want to ride with you, curl up on your lap. The words seeped through, though Nekoka hadn't meant to project them.

I know. I feel the same, Jenni thought.

The small crowd climbed into the two vehicles, and as Nekoka watched man after woman climb into the van, it reminded her of one of those clown cars, filling up some indomitable internal space with chaos. Pablo came up to Nekoka's car. "Mind if I ride with you?"

Nekoka pouted a little, eyeing Pablo like he might attack at any moment.

"I'm sorry," Pablo said.

Then someone patted her on the back. Chandler. Just out of the blue, there, by her side. "He is sorry. Sometimes he's an ass who gets emotionally caught up in his own woes and anger. But generally, he's a good guy." He leaned closer and whispered, "Don't sic the Darkener on him."

Pablo shouted, "Hey!" at his friend.

Nekoka released a slow exhale, her tail flicking, but she dropped her shoulders and nodded, holding out her hand. "Okay. I'm sorry too. I can be a bit...blunt sometimes."

Pablo smiled, and for a moment Nekoka's heart melted at his beauty, at his sexy charm, but it grew solid again. He would probably be an excellent lay, but there would always be sour emotion between them. Sex and emotion were never a good cocktail. "Get in," she ordered.

So, Pablo, Chandler, and Trior got into the back seat; Sally sat next to Nekoka as she had on the way over. Nekoka liked it better that way; she could keep a close eye on the woman.

Whisker sat on the shifter console between them, happily recharging and giving Nekoka back her sixth sense. Satellites up in the sky, she thought, tell me where I'd been and where I need to go. Her mind zipped through satellite images pulled through Whisker, blocks of data going farther and farther out from the house she'd found Sally at.

There. A cluster of buildings surrounding a large above-ground warehouse. She knew, from the blueprints she'd nabbed earlier, that this was where the offices were, the server room, and some housing. This wasn't where they wanted to go. She kept searching and a mile or so away, she found the receiving building where the prisoners were brought in.

"Found it. Let's roll."

The airport personnel waved, and Nekoka wondered what Zack and Pablo had told them. Probably just glad-handed them. Ah, the adoration of fans. They popped out onto an old highway and cruised northeast. Flat fields of mixed dry farms and brown grass with hills in the faded distance. Wheat heads dipped in the breeze, not yet ripe with grain. Flat and endless and brown. More brown. Then the carcass of a dead cow. Must be getting close. Sally hummed to herself, rocking her head back and forth to an internal song.

During their drive, Nekoka sent over gigs of the data she'd siphoned off the servers to Sparks, who had her own computer on hand. Not as awesome or small as Whisker, but it wasn't a roll-over puppy dog, either.

Another fifteen minutes of driving down the empty road and Nekoka pulled over; the van rumbled onto the gravel shoulder behind her. She popped the door open and walked to the passenger side of the van. Jenni leaned out the window. "What's up?"

"Well, I came cross country from here. Satellite imagery has this being the most direct route. The road does go around to the compound, but that will be watched. Also, there appears to be a gate." She shrugged. "So, cross country, or let them know two unknown vehicles are coming."

"Let's charge in, blazing, give 'em little time to respond," Zack said from the driver's seat. Zack's usual tactic was to charge in, blazing. A few of the van members agreed, including Starburst. Nekoka had always been more of a stealth agent.

Jenni surveyed the crowd of people squished together in the back. Battle Axe shifted uncomfortably, visibly contrite that he took up so much room. John watched her, stuck between two members of Guardian Alliance. She turned back to Zack. "Well, we've only got four heavy hitters."

Nekoka counted quickly in her head who Jenni might be suggesting: Zack, Starburst, Battle Axe, and Jenni. Nekoka shook her head. "Five, at least. You've gotta count Sally. Maybe not a 'heavy' hitter, but she can do a lot of damage."

"Don't worry about who's a heavy hitter or not," Sparks said. "We've each got some helpful talent that will help take people out of the fight without bonking them over the head."

Nekoka nodded in agreement.

Trior, Pablo, and Chandler walked up to Zack's side of the van. "We having a bit of a council?" Trior asked. "Time's a wasting, ya know."

"We're planning," John whispered at Trior.

"And," Sparks added, "when we free some of the other Seeded, they'll probably join the fight."

Nekoka began to nod, but stalled her agreement. "Maybe," she said. "When I was in there, there was some...chemical that they were spraying on everyone. It stopped my Alter Shape from working."

"Is this how they stopped them from fighting during the testing?" Minnie asked. Apparently, Sparks had been sharing the information. Good.

Nekoka shifted her gaze to Minnie and shook her head. "It's not testing...it's harvesting. They are taking something they call praena from us Seeded. And it kills us."

Sparks looked up from her screen. "Is that in here somewhere?"

"Yeah, I couldn't get everything, and I didn't have time to organize it. I'm sure some links of data are missing. Sorry." Her gaze shifted to Jenni, to seek out strength and comfort. "It's like," she ground her teeth, "their life force is being drained. Like that old movie, with the gelflings, and they would drain them in that machine."

"The Dark Crystal?" John asked.

"Yes! So, many might not be able to fight...or just won't."

"So, we've got a chemical that can render our powers useless, armed guards, some of them Seeded, a high security compound, and a lot of injured people," Cherry summarized. "And who is doing this?"

Nekoka shook her head. "Myroi.... I don't know who they are."

Zack pounded his fists into the steering wheel. "Is there any planning we can do? Nekoka and Sparks get the electronic security, most of us take out the goons, Gracie, Minnie, Mozart, and Cherry do the best with the injured. Pablo and Devana put others out of commission by making them cry or sleep. The rest of us, kick ass or do what we can. Any more thoughts?"

"No," Trior said, already returning to the little car. "Sepia is hurting. Let's go."

"Storming the castle, then?" Jenni asked, her eyes scanning the crowd of faces, all eager and worried, ready to do something good and right. Nekoka actually, for once, knew how they felt.

Before she even heard an answer, Nekoka turned and hopped back into the driver's seat of her car, then continued down the road. During the drive, she educated those in the car about the layout, the security—electronic versions she could deal with, and the human versions they would deal with. She told them about the pit of hell underground.

Nekoka turned onto the access road and stopped.

Gotta get the gate, she told Jenni, and then told everyone in her car to stay put.

She dropped into her cat form, a brown cast to her fur to blend in nicely. Slinking up to the gate, she sent out her feelers to any electronic equipment watching them drive up. Video camera on the gate. Nekoka drew close behind its blind spot, purred at it, copied some feed onto Whisker, then looped that back around and fed it to the camera. She shifted back as she returned to the car.

Eugene. Get the gate ahead, please? Padlock. Looks simple. Nothing else electronic.

Simple? then you can do it, he texted back.

She saw Eugene already climbing out of the van, but she still texted: You're faster.

He high fived her as he passed. Eugene took some tools out of a bag, and in seconds, he had the lock open, the chain unwound, and the gate swinging wide.

She thumbs-upped him, hopped in the car, and continued the drive.

She crept forward, halfway hanging out of the car, trying to catch the cameras before the little spies caught them. At her first sense of an electronic signal, Nekoka nearly swerved the car into the ditch. Sally gingerly grabbed the wheel to keep them on the road. It was already too late, though. The camera's range was excellent and the camera beyond that had already recorded them as well.

She'd tripped the trap. The Myroi knew they were coming.

Without another thought, she slammed down the gas and kicked up a cloud of dirt as she raced to the compound.

CHAPTER 35

Martha

Damn spooks and demons were running this show. Martha knew it. The demons came, usually three times for a gal or guy, and then that person never came back. Some never came back after two.

Martha released a held breath with a gush.

Damn spooks. In their suits and their grins. That's what the rulers of this world were doing. The hidden masterminds with their fingers on all the strings. Taking people like Martha, the throwaways, taking them and doing this evil, twisted thing to them.

She wiped away her tears. They kept coming. She'd never fallen to crying as a way of livin', but she had nothing else to fall back on anymore.

Folks from Portland were here, from her streets. She'd seen the Ghost. They'd bagged *the Ghost*. The spooks came in with their drugs and their notices and scooped 'em all up and dumped them here, in this slaughterhouse.

Martha sucked in a deep breath and held it again. Susan, who had a tent on Everett, told her that was how you made your power show. She read it in the paper. You had to put your life at risk and the power would show up—the bigger the risk, the bigger the power. Martha had been in that room two times, only one more time now and she was a goner, and still her power hadn't shown. Hadn't saved her. Maybe holding her breath would do it.

She gasped, her lungs filling. Wasn't nobody in her cage with her to tell her she was stupid, so she did it again. And again. All she got was light-headed. Wouldn't that just be the cheese if her power was light-headedness?

"Oh God," she pleaded. It was something she said every time she thought about going back to that room. But if God was listening, he sure didn't do nothing about it.

She touched the back of her head, at the hole there. It didn't bleed, not really, just a little around the edges. The hole went inside her head. Sore to the touch, it throbbed, like a banged-up thumb would. Worse, her brain felt deflated. Like the pressure inside that kept it pushed out to the edges of her skull had leaked out, and that her brain would deflate to an empty skin like a whoopee cushion that had a hole.

She sniffed snot back up her nose and wiped it with a dry patch of her shirt. Hopefully, they wouldn't spray them again anytime soon. She hated being damp, and that stuff they rained down on them made her skin itch. She liked to think about these other things, like the bucket full of her piss and shit, or the chemical spray, or if she could see anyone else from Portland she knew. She liked to think of these things instead of...

Her door opened. "Come on. Up."

Two men in armored uniforms stood at the door to her cage, smaller guys with batons and walkie-talkies and bindings for her hands. Two of the monkeys who fed on pain.

"No."

One sighed and gestured to the other. "You get her."

"I don't wanna touch her."

"Get out here."

This was her third time.

"No!" Her scream was one they'd all heard before, but still jarring, pulling her neighbors out of their stupor to turn their empty, flat eyes on her. "You can't just kill us like this!"

"We aren't killing you, lady," one said.

The other apparently didn't want to do the lie-game they'd memorized and recited like fourth graders, and he just walked in and smacked her in the head.

"Not the head, dude! Shit. You wanna get your pay docked?" the other guard said, pushing his way into her cell and elbowing the other man away.

"Fucking bullshit. Just grab her."

"Hold your dick."

Martha's vision had gone blurry, and she wanted to vomit. The man grabbed her under her arms and hoisted her up like they did those losers on Matoro who passed out on the streets and the paramedics had to come and collect from under the bridges. She had never done that stuff. Had stayed clean! Her legs gave out. They dragged her from the cell.

"Get off me!" she said, half-loud, not loud enough. She took in a deep breath and yelled it again. "Get off me!"

"Yeah, yeah," said the one who hadn't hit her.

Eyes followed her, hollow cavernous gazes that watched as the guards carried her off, and Martha wanted to spit at them all, spit a big old wad in those eyes. She wanted to say to them, "You just wait your turn. Sitting there, pretty in your cages. You just wait. Your. Turn." But she didn't. She screamed and screamed for the axmen to let her go instead.

And in her next breath, she realized she was already in the room.

"No. No. Please, God, no." It was about time for that power to kick in. She had the pale eyes. She had the Seed. Why didn't she have a power?

Her eyes and nose leaked as the men dropped her into the chair. The white chair. The white walls. The windows above where people could look down and watch as they drained the last bit of her life.

Vampires. They were vampires. Bottling up her years so they could drink them up and live forever.

Metal cuffs on her wrists. Straps on her legs. She thrashed, but they were grass-fed fat cats with everything, everything, and Martha had nothing but her life and they were going to take it from her, too.

Then the strap around her forehead. The velcro held tight no matter how hard she pulled and yanked. Her mouth muttered pleas and promises, and she hated it for that, for being so weak in the face of these Haves, and now they would have it all.

Have it all.

The needle slid in.

She screamed as it dug deep, and deep, and even deeper.

She screamed and she screamed and she screamed...until the last of her life drained away.

CHAPTER 36

Thomas

Thomas paced through wide aisles between the cages, regarding the poor wretches, secretly wishing he could teleport them out of this place with his mind. He still hadn't found out what exactly happened to them after they had completed their letting, but had a solid belief the end of that process only delivered death.

He'd seen the needle in their heads.... Could only imagine that piercing pain. Wished he didn't have to imagine it. But wishing was a feeble attempt to rewrite a history he had no power to rewrite. He could only move forward.

It had occurred to him to transfer some of these out of the cages and back into the rehabilitation center. They already had a memory re-writer on staff, someone who had the Seeded power to modify another's memories. It would be a simple thing, to make them forget their time here, just like all the others would forget their time at Minidoka in general.

He passed by a cage with the albino he'd taken in. The kid was curled around himself, arms wrapped around his legs, face pressed into his knees. Thomas swallowed. He'd helped do that to this man. No matter who he'd been before. No matter his worth, this...this was too much.

He continued on, then rounded a cage. He had to stop doing this to himself, pacing these acres of horror. Unless he could figure a way around Jeon and Tricia and all the others, he couldn't help these people. They were beyond him.

A woman stood in a cage, clutching the bars. He stopped, momentarily, then continued walking, steady, smooth, unruffled.

He recognized the woman in that cage. She hissed at him. "Thomas. Is that you? What the fuck!"

He continued past the cell. He remembered her. His sister Kathy had tutored that kid before that meth-head had knifed her. A teenage hellion who couldn't grasp math, now grown up.

He knew her.

Sylvia Montgomery.

THE FIELDS AROUND THE compound stretched out as far as the eye could see. Out here, beyond the cities, few could live. Either transformed to farmland or the conditions were too harsh. Services were limited. Isolated. Here, even the dryland-boosted wheat didn't do well. Using his burner phone, Thomas had sent off the photos he'd taken with his camera, then hidden the SD card in his shoe. In a business shorthand, he'd written up reports and sent those off. He still hadn't quite found out what the individuals were being letted for, but he'd spotted a white van leaving every morning at 5 a.m. Thomas had a gut feeling about the cargo.

He continued to participate in the legitimate reason Minidoka existed and was always pleased to see people appreciative of their experience here. The memory manipulator on staff cleansed the location and general details of Minidoka from those they released, so nobody could trace their disappearance and rehabilitation to Idaho and the compound in the middle of the grassy desert. But those released left with new skills, with prospects for jobs, eager to see family and friends again. Eager for this second chance.

Every evening, every morning, every hour of his day, he waited for the mind-wiper to show up, smile, and take it all away. He'd prepared himself for either a battle or to give in. It all depended on circumstances. He prepared his notes and secreted them away. He did his job, spent time in his office, watched the letting to remind himself, to make it all clear and fresh, just what was happening here. How the spiral to damnation pulled him along.

He didn't sleep well. Screams punched through his dreams every night.

As with most staff, he wasn't allowed the use of a vehicle, and he couldn't leave on foot. It was at least two-hundred miles to Boise. He couldn't walk through this desert, not without being caught, not without dying of thirst. He was no outdoorsman.

So, he would collect information and bide his time and strike when he could ensure his freedom.

He took a deep breath of the dry air. The smell of grasses, dirt, and sagebrush. A dust devil spun up along the gravel parking lot to caper down the dirt drive. His eyes scratched. He squeezed them once, then went back inside Minidoka.

THE INTERNAL PHONE rang, distracting Thomas from the report he'd been reading on staffing costs, boarding their internees and teachers, and the amount of money coming from their benefactors: the Founders. He'd been placed in charge of this portion of the process, a lower rung on the hierarchy than he was used to, but no higher than he wanted with this business anymore, and people were constantly annoying him to solve their piddly problems.

"Hallaman," he greeted.

"Mr. Hallaman, would you please come to the main office? There is a problem."

Hallaman didn't bother bottling up his sigh. They blackmailed him to make sure the compound functioned smoothly, not to babysit every little decision. "What now?"

After a brief conversation, Thomas hung up. Couldn't these people solve anything on their own? The two unauthorized vehicles were probably just more rednecks looking for some wild animal to kill or a place to ditch their trash without paying for the tipping fees nearer the municipal centers.

The halls were busier than usual. More guards, a few of the office staff walking with short, fast strides, implying some important duty. He entered the control center and the flurry of motion within was worse than a prairie dog town. Tricia thrust a clipboard out to him with a terse, "Sir."

He flipped through the pages, mainly grainy prints from their external surveillance of the two vehicles, a beat up old foreign hatchback and what his college buddies would have called a drug van. The smaller car's registration had expired years ago. The van didn't have plates.

"They are arriving at the back receiving area," Tricia said. That area was removed from the main buildings of Minidoka. Thomas had recently learned about it. That entrance was where the violent ones came through. The ones marked for the experiment.

A picture, a poor zoom, showed the car was full, a woman with boyish hair in the passenger seat, though the driver couldn't be distinguished from the angle.

"Any idea who this is?" Thomas asked.

The woman was turned towards the camera, the window down, her face pointed into the wind with her eyes half-closed. It was a clear shot of her face, triangular and at peace. She didn't look like the typical inbred inhabitants of rural western America who held disdain for the civilizing agency of the metropolises.

"Sir. Keep reading."

He looked up and caught Tricia's eyes. Her expression remained impassive, like a wax statue. With another flip, he came upon one of the compound's placement files, a printout covering one of the inmates the compound was to receive from the Wolf Walker Institute a few weeks ago.

Apparently, Minidoka took the incurably violent off the hospital's hands to do their experiment on.

"Sally Greenly." Oh. Her. He remembered her. How could he not? If she had been sane, she would have been on death row. No remorse. The woman's psych eval read, "nonredeemable." Wolf Walker had sent her and a few of the most dangerous criminals they held to Minidoka, though they never arrived. The hospital had claimed it was a breakout. It wasn't difficult to surmise that most of the staff of Wolf Walker had no idea their inmates were being sent to a different version of death row.

Sally Greenly. The Darkener. Body count: 42. She was one of the many reasons he did his job so diligently. Normal people were just not safe. Someone needed to control these untethered psychopaths.

They needed to be leashed, subdued to make it safe for everyone.

But the experiment...the letting. That, in Thomas' reoccurring nightmare, was torture.

Sally Greenly—criminally insane, a murderer, and very powerful—plus two other Wolf Walker inmates had escaped from the transport vehicle on the way to Minidoka. Killed the guards, rolled the van, set a field on fire. Death row was too good for this kind, and now she was driving up with some of her crazy buddies to do who knew what.

"Lockdown," Thomas ordered. Tricia acknowledged him with a nod. "Wait." His assistant stopped and turned to him, face neutral. "Prepare for lock down, but let them in. Have the militia ready to welcome them. We can't let her escape again. These are dangerous people. Call Director Jeon and Sergeant Lusha. We need to meet."

And perhaps these dangerous people would solve part of his little problem for him.

CHAPTER 37

Nekoka

No guards waited for them at the receiving entrance. No rockets, or missiles, or bombs from a military plane came plummeting down to bathe them in a shower of purifying flame. Not even a drone cut through the air to survey them. Nekoka growled. This wasn't right. It was a trap. She smelled a trap.

It's a trap, she thought at Jenni.

Ready for anything, she braked hard at the single shack about half the size of a mini mart. Weathered wood with peeling paint, a corrugated tin roof, it had the dressing of forgotten history. The place was filthy with stationary surveillance, though none of it was visible. Deep tire tracks had spun out in the thick gravel, but no vehicles were here.

She looked in her rearview mirror at the van behind her, caught sight of Jenni and thought at her, *Well, no welcoming committee. I'm a little insulted.*

We all figured they're going to let us in, but not out.

Like a lobster?

Jenni paused. *Like a roach.*

Nekoka popped out of the car and raced up to the shack, shutting the cameras and motion sensors off within her *kokogyo* reach once she touched the building. It was as close to holding up a bullhorn and shouting: "Hi there boys, we'll be right down," as she could get.

Nekoka returned to the car, leaning against the passenger side door, sticking her head in the window. She wasn't really looking forward to this, unlike Sally, who was wiggling in her seat like a five-year-old ready for her first pony ride.

Pablo muttered about wishing they had a plan. Trior, squished between the other two men, said, "We go in, free everyone, and leave. Two teams go down in groups of six. One group of four protects our getaway here. One computer expert per group."

"There are only two computer experts," Nekoka said for the third time. Trior seemed to take comfort in repeating their thin plan over and over.

"Yes, and those two are going in. We concentrate on getting to the underground caging facility, freeing everyone, and getting out. That is our goal."

"We'll find Sepia," Pablo said, patting the man's arm.

"Pablo, you are a dear friend," Trior said through gritted teeth, "but if you continue to attempt to calm me down, I might have to break your fingers." Pablo pulled his hand away. "Nekoka said that there are two elevators, the one in the main building over that rise and this one. Gaining control of those is very important."

He continued going over their plan, the contingencies, the what ifs they'd all discussed over phones, laptops, and through telepathy on the drive up to the receiving building. Nekoka felt disjointed. She stood and stared up into the darkening sky. Everything was quiet, not like the city, not like inhabited places. Out here things could settle, be still, sink into a kind of catatonic stasis. The others talked around her as they exited the vehicles. Still tired from the last few days, she struggled holding all the conversations straight. There were too many people to coordinate. To worry about. Luckily, Pablo and Zack took care of most of that.

Nekoka's group would be Pablo, John, Battle Axe from the Guardian Alliance, Grace, and because nobody else wanted her on their team, Sally—the Darkener. Nekoka got two of the combative powered on her team. She wanted Jenni on her team, but everyone agreed that it was best to split them up because of their telepathic connection. Which, she argued, wouldn't work if they were too far apart. She was tired of being separated from Jenni. She wanted to also point out that Grace had a telepathic connection with Jenni, too, along with all of the S-Force, so the two could switch. But Grace's biggest asset was her power to affect multiple people. Their hopes were for her to boost the weakened captives, while Minnie, on the other team, would heal the most injured. Battle Axe was supposed to protect Grace first and foremost, but if he found himself with the opportunity to kick other people's asses as they came along, then he should let loose. Pablo would be the face man if they needed to talk anyone to death and he could make a few cry and run home to be hugged by momma, like he'd done to Nekoka. John had a knack for finding people and certainly wasn't a wet noodle in a fight. He was also geared up with some nifty tech of his own.

Jenni would go in team two, going through the main building about a half mile away, taking Minnie along the other path to reach their intended targets. Team three would protect this shack, their escape route. Zack was with that last group, one of the strongest Seeded on earth and they were leaving him to guard the back door. Nekoka wasn't sure of the wisdom of that, but she'd never been a tactician. Apparently, that was Trior's forte. Who knew that about the Southern gentleman?

The only thing Nekoka was certain about was the first casualty to any plan was the plan itself.

It didn't help between the three teams, few knew everyone else's skills or abilities. Seeded tended to keep a trick or two tucked away. She guessed the O.G.R.E. people had a good idea about each other, as well as the Guardian Alliance, and of course she knew about all the aces up the sleeves of her friends, but on a whole, they were not a cohesive group. Some shit was going to hit the fan, scatter all over them, and truly muck up the workings of this breakout.

This rescue mission.

The sun had cut itself and was beginning to bleed across the desert. In the darkening east, the sky was washed in the blue gray of distant clouds. It might rain, she thought, and wondered if there would be lightning storms tonight and wouldn't that just be poetic.

The teams split. The van drove off.

With a glance at John, their appointed team leader, he nodded, and Nekoka tried the door.

Locked.

The lock was mechanically bolted as well as electronically powered. She cut the electrical circuit with a thought, tried the handle again and still couldn't open it. She began jerking on the lever in frustration. "I could try to pick it. Damn, wish Eugene was on our team."

"Here, woncha let me. I got it." Right behind her stood Battle Axe, his voice gruff, his manner modest. Nekoka looked up and up and simply stepped aside. Battle Axe leaned his double-headed ax against the wall—one that could be bought at a market in a Final Fantasy game—gripped the handle of the metal door and slowly pulled. The door screeched in pain.

"Are you, ah, just going to tear the door out of the frame?" John asked. "Impressive," he said under his breath.

Nekoka couldn't help but agree. The muscles on Battle Axe's forearms completely captured her attention. The corded ropes, the bulging strength. He gritted his teeth. The scream of metal continued. Battle Axe grunted with the effort.

The door buckled around the lock, tearing away part of the frame. Battle Axe grasped the torn metal and peeled the door open like a steel orange rind. A ragged gash of metal hung from the building walls. Under the flimsy rotting wood, a solid building hid. One that could withstand a tank bombing, but obviously not Battle Axe's tug.

Nekoka imagined what beauty she would see if the man's shirt suddenly fell from his body, like John's often did. Then she closed her eyes. This was not the time to ogle the big man. He wouldn't be interested in a high-tension, hallway quickie. Move on, libido, move on.

Pablo clapped. "Nicely done."

Battle Axe lifted one broad shoulder that shifted his entire mass and smiled. "Nay. Weren't nothing, mate," he said in his Irish lilt as he shyly ran his fingers through his pile of red hair.

He hoisted his ax, the edge, though thick, probably as sharp as Sally's dagger. John had a Ruger Mini 14 rifle at the ready, the specs of the gun rolling through Nekoka's SPYme, though she didn't bother looking up what it all meant. A Glock pistol was in a hip holster, extra magazines, a knife was strapped to his calf, and he wore a flak jacket and tactical helmet. He'd strapped Grace and Pablo each into their own jackets—how many did he have?—but neither of them agreed to carry a pistol he offered.

"No idea how to use it," Grace had said with a shake of her head. Nekoka remembered when Jenni had tried to teach Gracie some fighting techniques, but all Gracie learned was how to disarm, saying she didn't want to hurt people. She would lead by example, like Jesus, or something like that. Turning the other cheek. Some had the thirst for blood, the tendency to violence—that was not Gracie.

They'd all laughed at that back then. Now, Nekoka wondered how long it'd been that the two women had been on the rocks, and why Nekoka hadn't noticed. Jenni had run off with her without even a chat beforehand with her girlfriend. Nekoka hadn't thought that through at the time; she had only been focused on herself. They'd all been friends, carefree in a world where nothing could stop them, and the future was laid at their feet. They'd been together for years, mooching off Zack, living their own lives, but still having a relationship like an extended family.

She loved these people more than her own birth parents, who had retreated back to Japan when they'd found out their teenager could hack into police records and turn into a cat. She'd tried so hard, back then, to make them proud. To fulfill the plans they'd had for her. It had been a constant struggle.

Then, one day, like freak angels, she'd met Jenni and Zack.

"Hey! You're one of those abominations," Zack had said, this attractive man with a smile that turned heads from miles away. "That is so awesome."

Nobody had thought her awesome before. And from then on, he had her complete loyalty.

The others stood outside, eyeing the inside of the shack. Nekoka glanced at Grace, who had a pensive expression, then spotted Nekoka and offered a weak smile. Nekoka wondered about a gazillion things, but the heaviest on her brain was how could Gracie have given up on Jenni.

"You going to be okay?" Nekoka asked.

Gracie shrugged and tugged at the armored jacket tight around her body, then shook her head to dismiss Nekoka's concern. "I'm good. Just.... The things you reported, the..." She shivered. "I'm usually not on the ground when Jenni and Zack go in like an action hero squad. Plus, this place gives me the creeps." Gracie's face scrunched up. "What are we going to find inside?"

Nekoka rubbed Gracie's arm. "Just stick by me and Battle Axe, got it?"

Gracie nodded.

John approached, bouncing two hefty helmets in his hands. "Hey, got two more riot helmets." John held one out to Gracie, who wrinkled her nose but took it.

"Hey, Sally, you look, ah, squishy. Did you want a helmet?" John asked, holding one out.

Sally studied the offered helmet, not taking it. "What do I do with it? Throw it at them?"

"Ah, yeah, no." He turned away from her and handed it to Pablo. "You should take this."

"I will, and thank you."

Everyone as prepared as they were going to be, Nekoka entered the shack.

The room was about fifteen by thirty feet and an elevator waited for them on the far side. The doors were of some black burnished material with one slot for a card but no buttons, no jaunty light on top telling you what floor the elevator was now on. No curved label stating "Purgatory," "Hell," and "Run, You Sorry Bastard, Run" for each level of the compound.

She brushed the edges of her callused fingertips along the metal walls. They were cold. Sending out her thoughts, she tickled the card lock, letting it know everything was fine and she was supposed to get in that elevator.

The doors slid open.

The elevator was huge, larger than anything she'd come across except for those freight elevators that carried entire pallets of bathroom tissue or cans of beans to a hotel kitchen. A tangy scent clung to the air. Pablo shivered; his tension rose off him like heat waves.

"What's wrong?" she asked, flicking her ear.

"The place smells like blood and urine, and that nasty industrial cleaner they use in hospitals. And something metallic, not blood, but close. Don't you guys smell that?" Pablo pressed the back of his arm against his nose. Nekoka could smell the chemicals, but her nose wasn't that fine-tuned.

More updates to Pablo's file. Good sense of smell.

The rest stepped into the elevator, easily standing apart so none of them were crowded. Battle Axe kept closest to the doors, his big body shielding Pablo and Grace. This was where these people brought down their captives; frightened cattle ready for the slaughter. Sally, still wearing her simple dress, chuckled low, fingering the sharp edge of her blade. Battle Axe shifted from foot to foot, his namesake clutched in his two large hands.

Nekoka told the elevator to take them down. It obliged happily, zipping down at a steady speed, and in seconds they stopped.

"Guess this is it," John said, his rifle in both hands, pointed towards the ground. All of his law enforcement training came through in his posture and ready attention. "There's a group of people on the other side of that door." Nekoka wondered how his power presented itself, how his *life sense* worked for him. Was it just a sixth sense, a kind of tingle in his nerves, a heat that washed over his skin, or just a knowledge of which he was immediately made aware?

"What?" Pablo nearly jumped out of his shoes. "What else can you tell?"

"Just people. About," he closed his eyes, "six in a narrow line in front of us, more off to the sides, I assume behind walls. Some of the farther ones are Seeded."

"You can tell that?" Gracie asked, impressed. John nodded.

Nekoka consulted the map. "This door opens to a hallway that has a sharp turn to the right and yes, there are other rooms off of it to the left. Also, to the left of the hall is the containment room where they are keeping everyone. It's farther away, though."

Nekoka pushed out her computer senses once more and slipped through the walls into the wires twining within and into the cameras that lined the hallway on the other side of the elevator doors. "He's right. Just outside the door I can see six men, armed and armored, poised to fire guns. Beyond them, around the corner, are more. All in armor gear. Full face helmets."

"I'll be aiming for extremities." John was down on one knee, rifle braced against his shoulder as he took aim at the closed doors.

Sally laughed. "Can I go first?" Everyone looked at her. Battle Axe grunted. Then, with all innocence, she said, "Well, I don't want to miss the fun. What if you guys take them all out before I get my chance?"

Pablo opened his mouth, as if to deny her, but Nekoka interrupted. "Okay, Sally. But just remember. You can't kill the prisoners or anyone running away or begging you to stop. Got it?"

Sally pouted, then nodded, her short hair bouncing, as eager as her bloodthirsty grin. Gripped like a bundle of bridesmaid flowers, she held her knife pointed up to the sky in both hands, then with a flick of her wrist, she sent it spinning through the air. Sharp as a bat homing in on a bug, she snatched it up. "Got it."

"Everyone else ready?"

Jenni, we're going in. Got some unfriendlies.

It took a while for the reply, the thoughts a weak flicker. *Be safe.*

You too.

Battle Axe nodded, hefting his ax. Grace and Pablo took a step back, letting the combat-trained lead the pack. Nekoka inhaled deep, and let her body shift, a complete metamorphosis rippling through her body. She grew in height, muscles bulging, claws lengthening, as deadly as Sally's blade. Battle cat. Her fighting form that drained her of all spit and vinegar if she held it too long. It gave her more power, more speed, and built in weapons that couldn't be disarmed.

"Holy shit," John said. "And you're not a heavy?"

With a wink and flick of her tail, she stepped behind Sally, Battle Axe, and John. "Not like these others. Here it goes." The door opened with her thought.

In the span of a breath, Sally popped from her place by Battle Axe to the last man of the six. With a delicate pull, she drew a red line across the man's exposed throat, and before he even hit the ground, she was moving on to the next. In that same instance, Battle Axe charged into the flood of bullets like a pissed off bull.

John took his shots with steady precision, the pop announcing each bullet as it raced through the air. Battle Axe swung his heavy weapon, slamming into a man's midsection, picking him off the ground and sending him flying into another behind him. It was quick, and it seemed that only seconds passed before the six men lay bleeding on the ground: the three Sally sliced open, motionless, the other three whining like kicked and battered dogs.

Nekoka hadn't done a thing.

Heavy silence thickened the air.

Sally sauntered up to one of the shot men, blade out. In another second, the man was dead, blood pooling around this throat. Sally made a pleased little sound, then strode over to the next injured guard.

"Darkener, no!" John called.

Sally glanced over her shoulder at the officer. "But they're bad guys." She shifted her attention to Nekoka. "Right?"

"Ah," Nekoka said, eyes caught by the blade as she closed in on the man. "Don't kill him, Sally. They're, um, already down. Their deaths are beneath you."

"But, Nekoka," Sally scolded. "They are *bad guys.*" She tilted her wrist, bringing the blade closer to the man's throat.

The man cried out, "No, please!"

"Okay, remember the rules!" Nekoka barked. "No killing my friends, the prisoners, or people who can't fight you. Who are running away or begging."

Sally pouted. "You added one."

The man cried out, "Please, don't kill me. I surrender. I surrender."

Sally released her grip on the guard's armored vest and threw her hands up in the air. "Ah, fine."

A shot rang down through the hallway and Sally disappeared, suddenly standing next to Nekoka. Another pinked into Battle Axe's shoulder, causing the man to step back with a grunt. The infiltration team retreated back into the elevator. The doors closed; Nekoka hoped the thick metal of the elevator doors had some bullet stopping power.

Grace pulled back Battle Axe's linen pullover, stretching the neck of the shirt, and found a bud of blood beginning to bloom through his undershirt. She made eye contact with Battle Axe and began to chant, weaving her magic like some hermetic order of Wiccan priestesses. As she pressed her palm to the skin under the bloodied shirt, the look on Battle Axe's face went from pinched to relieved as she took away his pain. She couldn't heal a wound like Minnie could, but she could deaden the nerves.

"You should save yer energy, Miss," he said. "I've had worse."

Grace looked up at him with her compassionate eyes and patted him on his shoulder. "I can only do so much, Battle Axe. Please take it easy. You've still got a bullet in there."

The huge man blushed, and said, "Ah, thank you, Miss. Please, just Murph."

A bang pounded into the elevator door, punching a fist sized indent into the metal. Nekoka jumped, and Sally started laughing.

"You squeaked!" Sally said, pointing at Nekoka, one hand over her mouth and nose. "Like a little mouse."

Nekoka bristled. "I did not!" A loud argument on the other side of the door cut her off, but she couldn't make out the words. Sally hiccupped and started laughing again.

"Nekoka," Pablo said, grabbing Nekoka and positioning her so they could look into each other's eyes. "Who can you see down there? Focus." He let Nekoka go and asked, "John, can you get a sense of numbers?"

"Eight," Nekoka said, when John said, "Eleven." Nekoka flicked an ear. John shrugged.

"Perhaps some are Seeded? Invisible Seeded?" Battle Axe asked. "Why they'd work for these lowlifes..." He shook his head, saddened.

"Why wouldn't Seeded work for them?" Pablo said. "Lots of bad people of any group." His blue eyes briefly graced Sally, who was examining the blood pattern on her dagger's blade. "And money speaks wonders to mercenaries."

"All are Seeded." John closed his eyes. "Various levels of power. Nobody too scary."

Life sense? Power sense? What else did his power do?

"These have better gear," Nekoka said, peeking through the cameras watching the hallway. "SWAT gear. Body armor. Tactical helmets, exo legs, looks like guns with some sighting aids...and some other non-projectile weapons. Wait." Nekoka focused on one image from the camera. "One has something, a flame thrower or something. Not sure. Got a tank on his back and a nozzle in his hands."

"We need to keep moving," John said. "Everyone ready? Sally, you take out the flame thrower man first, Battle Axe, keep to the left, Nekoka and I will keep to the right. Grace and Pablo will do what they can in the rear. Pablo, see if you can pacify any." He looked at Gracie.

"I can certainly do something. I just need a little time." She clapped her hands and began rubbing them together in slow circles.

Everyone nodded. Nekoka, body hulking, opened the door to their enemy one more time.

Sally was gone and appeared behind the individual with the pack and nozzle. Nekoka waffled, then camouflaged her body; cool white—the color of the walls—shivered over her fur, giving her a snowball coat that would have been cute if she wasn't walking into a bloodbath.

"Nekoka!" John called out. "In front of you. About twenty yards!"

Sally cut someone; red splattered the wall. A scream of pain. Nekoka had no idea who she was supposed to attack. There were plenty of targets. Men and women in riot gear, their helmets singing out an electronic chorus. She forwent the camouflage, too many people, too many shades and colors to keep focused on. Another scream, this time Battle Axe. His body jerked as bullets pounded into him from empty mid-air. Following the trajectory, Nekoka launched herself forward, bracing for an impact.

Instincts told her to expect to keep sailing until she hit the ground; she hit something invisible instead. Landing hard on the floor, she spun around, raking her claws through the air. Blood speckled her fur. Someone was there. Full on invisibility, the person's gear and everything.

Sending her senses out in bursts, she found all eleven sets of helmets. She wrapped her brain around the data signal in the visually blank spot in front of her. Bunching her legs, she readied a pounce as a bullet ripped into her calf. A roar tore through her throat. Pain flared throughout her leg, and she bit down on another scream. With a quick manipulation of her body, she tightened her arteries in the area of the wound.

Nekoka! Jenni's yell tore Nekoka's attention from her fight.

I'm okay. Still fighting!

Nekoka bared her teeth and leapt for the chatter of electronics before her. She sliced out, quick, sharp like a tiger, and cut through something hard. Nekoka rolled again, popped up on her feet, gingerly keeping most of her weight off her injured leg, and sliced again at her hidden foe. Dagger-sharp claws flashed out. Another swipe caught armor. Another fabric. Something hammered into her side. She oofed, but wasn't too hurt through her own armored flesh. Then she dropped into near splits and brought her claws up. They dug into fabric and they dug into flesh and finally her foe screamed.

She hopped six feet into the air and came directly down again, digging her claws into flesh, fisting her hands and then tearing away. The blood, when it came free from the body, appeared out of blank air, red and brilliant as it painted her coat and the institutional white wall.

Another shot ripped through the air and another. A flurry of action spun all around her, but she kept her focus on the bundle of electronics before her. She never stayed still, making herself as hard a target as possible. Spin left, hop in the air, leap to the right.

Another shot screamed from her target, but Nekoka was already diving, her chest heaving with every breath. She rolled and launched herself, tackling the invisible person. Together, they slammed against the floor. Nekoka's teeth came together with jaw cracking force. Her opponent popped into visibility; the armored head lolled to the side. Nekoka didn't have time to think, to worry.... Was her enemy dead? Did she kill this person? Around her, all was quiet.

Pablo was holding onto his arm, fixated on an armored assailant. Everyone else was staring at the carnage of their fallen enemy. So far, her group had prevailed.

"This is fun!" Sally laughed.

John shouted, "More coming!"

CHAPTER 38

Thomas

From the main control room, Thomas watched his frontal militia gather in the staging area. He'd handpicked these men and women from the masses that had been brought in, many recruited to work for the Founders rather than being treated like cows to be milked and then shipped away in a nondescript van in the early morning. He'd urged them to join up, the volunteers fast and strong and keen to follow directions. All happy to be of use, to be a part of something. One unfortunate fact was that many were picked because of their weakness of mind and were given to Thomas to...persuade. Thomas' gut hadn't stood up to such demands; the demand for him to intake the DNA of random people enough to keep him hovering over a toilet whenever the thought surfaced. Thankfully, some he hadn't even had to influence. They willingly pledged to the Founder's cause for a nice paycheck and good benefits. Men of every creed could be bought, if you had the right currency.

There were thirty-seven in all.

Seeded who could teleport, move at great speeds, people who could take one look at you and set your blood to boil. Shape-changers and even a man with invulnerable, metallic skin. All of them had special talents to allow them to defeat other Seeded. He wondered how this militia would handle the intrusion into Minidoka, if the greatest heroes could stop them.

If they couldn't, there wasn't much he could do.

"Ratchet," he said into the mic. On screen, one of the militia looked up. "Send half to the receiving area, the other half of you address those on the main floor. I've sent you dossiers on the intruders."

"Yes, Mr. Hallaman. I've received the package and have organized the two teams. Will the defense team remain inside the containment area?"

"Yes, though I hope they will not be needed," Thomas responded.

"Of course, sir. We'll stop them, no worries."

Thomas watched as Ratchet, a Seeded with excellent strength, a sharpshooter, and an ability to increase his body's density, sent off one team and led his own down the tunnel to the receiving area.

Thomas returned his attention to some footage recorded a few minutes ago. Sally Greenly. He watched as his regular human-grade troops in the battle stilled, stuck in impossible positions, and she ran to one area and then time caught again. The convicted murderer somehow froze reality in her vicinity. Fortunately, it didn't appear that she could maintain the freeze indefinitely. And he wasn't clear how far her Seeded influence reached, but he watched her do it again, and again. Freezing everyone around her, her allies included, only to position herself in the best location to slit a throat. His men had no chance. They had to take her on from a distance.

The others might be heroes, but that one, that one was a danger to everyone.

"Sir." Tricia looked him straight in the eyes, her jaw muscle flexing just the slightest. "We believe both groups have some method to see beyond basic vision. Either they are hacking our computer system, using our surveillance against us, or have some other clairvoyant ability. Perhaps they have invisible members spying ahead. It's unclear."

He nodded. Just another possibility when dealing with people who could perform magic. "When the teams go in, cut the lights. See if that slows them down. They can't all see in the dark." His men, on the other hand.... These sewer rats couldn't have the technology he had available.

"And, sir." Tricia's tone remained level. "There has been a call for a cull."

Thomas stiffened. "A what?" A cull? Was that even a logical conclusion for a sane mind? "Who called it?"

"A cull, sir." Tricia glanced down, sharp and quick, then she cleared her throat, a light delicate noise. "The order came from above the Director."

The Founders. These elusive, mysterious Founders had made such a call? "Tricia. I need a confirmation on a cull. I'm making no decisions until I hear it from Jeon, so just contact him."

Thomas couldn't let that happen. All those people, dead and buried and burned away. Their ashes tossed on the wind to blend with the dry, thirsty ground. His imagination went wild for a moment, before he stomped it down with the here and now. He understood what the Founders were up to. This entire compound was compromised; the evidence must be destroyed. But he needed that evidence, something, anything, to remain.

Tricia got on her phone, face stiff.

An explosion roared overhead. Everything on the tables rattled; a desk worker jumped from her chair and pushed her back against the wall.

"Any news on the force that came through the main entrance?" Thomas asked her.

"Currently, they are still blocked by the reinforced doors, sir," the assistant said, running back to her computer and hitting some buttons on a keyboard to bring up the sharp feed on Starburst and her group of heroes. Certified Hero groups were on their doorstep. "The one called Starburst is sending her firestorm against it. It's going to give any minute now." She glanced at him.

Thomas nodded. Well, there was the hard way, and there was the easy way. The Founders had given a brilliant scientist, a Dr. Demopoulos, guidance to create something immensely invaluable against the talents of the Seeded. He was the scientist who poisoned the streets with Matoro, but his true work of art was Nutrix.

Nutrix, the chemical that neutralized the powers of the Seeded.

The only problem was that unless it was in its most stable liquid form, it degraded quickly. As an aerosol, it faded and lost potency, having little effect after a few moments depending on atmospheric conditions.

They drenched the detainees with it regularly. Due to its toxicity, he kept his staff out of the containment chamber whenever they were ready to spray.

"Sir." Tricia held out the phone.

He took it. "Jeon?" Thomas asked.

"No, this is the Chief," said a deep voice with a slight Hispanic accent.

"I've never met any Chief; therefore, you have no power over this decision," Thomas said, more anger than he wanted slipping into his words.

"You are Thomas Hallaman, a Seeded with mind-control powers, though you have been very secretive on how you actually perform this perversion."

Thomas stood straighter. "Perversion?"

"God would not allow such deceits, Mr. Hallaman. You are a partner in a lucrative business in Chicago," he continued, "that would be taken from you if your mutation was discovered. What would you do if your company were taken from you?"

"Who are you?"

"The Chief. The Founders gave me that name. They knew nothing about human titles, about individual identities. My daughter thought it funny, to call me a Chief. It stuck." He chuckled. "Now, you will complete the cull and evacuate staff. Minidoka is sinking. Do you intend to go down with the sinking ship?"

On the screen Ratchet announced, "Ready, sir," rifle in hand.

"Human titles? What? Are you suggesting...?" What exactly had Thomas gotten mixed up in?

"Call the cull, Mr. Hallaman," the Chief commanded. "Do as directed and in two hours, the files we have on you will be in the deposit box you and Director Jeon had agreed upon. The electronic versions destroyed. I hope you continue to have a fruitful life, mutant." The man hung up.

Thomas gritted his teeth and ordered, "Cut the lights to the halls."

He wasn't calling any fucking cull.

UPSTAIRS, THE HEROES were breaking down the compound. His militia could hold them off for an extended duration, but Thomas hoped their aggressors would prevail. Who else could put an end to this place?

These Founders. Were they even human?

He stood in the letting chamber: that room with the white walls and scary chair. Almost camouflaged, it resembled some sort of high-tech scanning device or dentist's chair, but to Thomas' intense disquiet, it was more like something from a Star Trek episode. One of the next generation ones. Where people had been abducted and probed by evil aliens. Straps were attached to the arms, back, and leg braces to hold a person down if he struggled. As well as the head, that was perhaps the creepiest. Head restraints. A long needle rested on a cradle behind the chair. A tube slipped away into a hole in the floor. Is that where they took the blood? Why blood, though? It couldn't be blood.

What exactly were they stealing from the Seeded?

"So, you haven't figured it out?"

Thomas jumped and cursed. He turned, smoothing down his tie, to see Director Jeon.

Thomas had so many questions, needed so many answers. But the one that barely held him together demanded attention more than the others. "What happens to the people when you're done with them?" Were they dead, or let go?

Jeon studied Thomas, face cold, and in a way, that expression of nothing was far scarier than the sadistic smile of Sally Greenly as she cut down his men.

Then the Director shook his head. "You didn't call the cull, so I did."

Thomas growled, gaze settled behind Jeon, back into the detention chamber.

"I'm curious to see Dr. Demopoulos' latest creation work upon these Seeded. Even the tough ones can't all be immune to poison."

Thomas felt sick.

Jeon sighed. "I knew you would be a mistake. Useful, but still a mistake. You were never fully brought in, and without the full knowledge of what—" He pressed his lips together, that almost smile, but this time there was more animation, a hint of emotion. "Of the true purpose of Minidoka. I appreciated how you handled the cover installation above. Quite efficient. But, this—" He looked at the chair. "This, this is thievery, something I don't expect you would approve of."

Thomas had to leave, to get out there and somehow stop the murder of all those people. He made to push by Jeon, but Jeon shot a hand out and grabbed his arm. Not a terribly strong grip, but sturdy enough. Thomas could tear away easily, but the look in Jeon's eyes stopped him.

"They are too powerful to fight, Mr. Hallaman." Jeon blinked once, almost thoughtful, then he continued. "I suggest you don't wait. Leave now. This place is finished, and there will be no quarter for the likes of us. There is nothing you can do. We are not the enemy, Mr. Hallaman." Jeon lifted his eyes and scanned the viewing windows above them. Thomas followed his gaze and saw no one. "They are out there, invisible, and they are after something only the Seeded have. We were just middlemen." He let go.

"Who? Who are they? The Founders? Who is this Chief?"

Director Jeon huffed out a flat laugh. "The Chief. He is safe. His famous daughter, with her thousands of followers, holds less power than he with his connections to the Founders. They appeared to him, for some reason. They, they are not from our world. Aliens, I suppose. Ghosts, maybe. I don't really know." He turned and walked towards the back door, the one they must take people through once they were finished in the chair. "You should go."

"How can I? You've blocked all my exits."

"Not all of them." Jeon opened the door and left.

Thomas made to follow, but then he looked back into the sub-chamber. He could stop this, he thought.

He returned to his office.

Inset 7
Fast Talk Interview

Heather Ritter – Welcome to Fast Talk—all the *SCOOP* in under ten minutes. I'm Heather Ritter and today our guest star is Lily Cleveland, Oregon State Seeded and Guardian Alliance member more well known by the identity Cherry. So, should I call you Lily or Cherry?

Lily Cleveland – (LAUGHTER) Well, I don't mind either way. I'm here as myself, though, and not a hero, so Lily works.

HR - How did you get Cherry, by the way? You've light peach eyes, I would have assumed you'd go by that fruit.

LC – (MORE LAUGHTER) It's more a childhood name than due to my eyes. We had a cherry tree at my house, and I would live in that thing when the fruit was ripe and gorge myself. I constantly had red lips and fingers. It stuck.

HR – This was before your Seed awakened?

LC – Oh yeah, I was just a kid.

HR – What was the impetus, for you, that caused your powers to awaken?

LC – Oh, I evolved when I got in a car accident. I was older, seventeen. My mother was driving. We'd just had a spa day, a mani-pedi kind of thing, and this truck barrels through the intersection, his brakes were bad, or something, and it smacks right into us. My mother was bleeding, I was screaming, and then I knew I had to get out, you know, and so I climbed out of the car, I'd cut up my leg, and hobbled to my mom's side and checked on her, made sure she was okay. It wasn't like a bright light, or there wasn't any explosion or anything crazy like that, but just the stress of that event and...well, I tore open the car door with telekinesis and here I am now.

HR – You are one of the rare individuals with more than one power. Does this make you a dual Seed?

LC – (CRINGES) Dual Seed? Oh no, that literally means having two Seeds, and I think that's all smoke. An urban legend. But, (GRINS) I do have two powers, two of the regulars—powers that show up frequently. Telekinesis and Psychometry. I see you brought me something?

HR – (HOLDS UP AN OLD STUFFED ANIMAL)

(THE STUFFED ANIMAL FLOATS FROM HEATHER'S HAND TO LILY'S)

LC – Oh. (CHUCKLES) This has a long history. This item is full of your love. Your grandfather gave it to you when you were...seven?

CHAPTER 39

Nekoka

The lights went out. Nekoka blinked, then she flinched as a high-powered LED beam flashed off John's shoulder, illuminating the hallway before them and splashing the far wall in faded white light. Grace pulled Pablo and Nekoka to the side. With a few pokes, she found Nekoka's injury, then Pablo's, and soon she began a quiet chant. Cool warmth spread over Nekoka's fur, overpowering the pinch of the bullet in her flesh; the purr came automatically.

John grunted, sounding frustrated more than anything. "Some are pretty powerful. Crap. I wish there was some scale..."

"Just compare them to one of us, then," Pablo suggested, the thickening of his Caribbean accent giving more clue to his injury than any amount of blood.

In the harsh light of John's flashlight, the shadows cut his attractive face into deep crevasses. He closed his eyes, licked his lower lip, then shook his head. "Not that I have a lot of time to explain how my sense works, but I would say Nekoka's got us all beat. Battle Axe and Sally are closest. They've got a few Battle Axes, and a lot of me and Pablos, who are the weakest in this group," he said with a snort. "Some Graces, too, who's a tad more...bright? than Pablo and me. No Nekokas, though. So, that's good."

Nekoka categorized them using Spark's color code: So, most were greens, multiple lows or one high-level power. That was going to be a challenge. Of course, they wouldn't send any browns out against them, wimpy guys, or the black duds. That meant a few purples...at least one high-level power plus additional low-level powers. But none like Nekoka. She had two high-level powers, plus a low-level if you considered cat talk a separate power or part of Alter Shape, and Sparks thought she might be a gray, equal to Zack, though she doubted that. Not that she was complaining.

With half her mind, she updated her database, the other half of her mind worried. Nekoka didn't feel confident in any of this if she was the most powerful of the group. If only Jenni were there.

The pain in her calf was dull and easy to ignore now. She gave Grace a squeeze. Grace patted Nekoka on the head.

"We're trapped in our own dead end," Pablo said, his voice strained. "We could escape, head back up, wait for more.... Shit." He paused. "I'm sorry. I know we can't leave." He sounded frustrated with himself. His anxiety was leaking off him, giving Nekoka the itches. "I'm shit in a fight. Damn. Damn!" He slammed his fist into himself, Nekoka guessed a thigh by the meaty thunk of it. Nekoka wished there were more rabbits up her hat. Shooting fireballs, turning into silver, teleporting around like a bouncing ball. Anything. They weren't going to make it.

Wait. That wasn't how she was feeling when they came down the elevator shaft. When she went toe to toe with an invisible armed militant.

"Pablo. Stop," Nekoka said. "You're making us all feel worthless." She almost wanted to hug him, offer him comfort because, due to his power, she knew exactly how helpless he currently felt, but they had little time for such compassion.

Pablo's dark skin made him nearly invisible in the poorly lit corridor. "Sorry. Yeah, sorry about that." He put on a smile. "I've got this thing.... Thanks, Nekoka."

Battle Axe shifted, grumbling under his breath. "Didn't like that much, mate."

Then a feeling of power, confidence, hope washed over Nekoka. "Better?" Pablo asked.

Nekoka grinned. "Oh yeah."

With the lights out, she had little use for the cameras that watched the hall. Reaching out with *kokogyo*, she sensed the electronics on the armed individuals coming their way around the corner and down the hall. With her Seeded senses, she tickled the headgear. It didn't react. Too far away. If she could touch them.

"They've stopped?" John whispered.

"I'm going out there," Nekoka said. "I can tell where they are because of their electronics. If I touch them, I can overload their coms and sensory gear. If I go fast and small, they won't see me." She was super. She was untouchable. She should just have everyone else hang out here and she'd deal with the danger. Then reality niggled at her. "Then, you come in and kick some butt."

"Nekoka, wait." It was Grace. She grabbed Nekoka and pulled her into a hug. Nekoka purred at the friendly contact, then remembered she was supposed to be saving everyone.

"Nekoka, I think you might be a little overconfident from Pablo's power. Why not send Sally?"

Sally bopped on the balls of her feet. "Can't see well. But I'll go!"

Nekoka inhaled. No, she just felt awesome. Because she was awesome. "Thanks Grace, but even if that's true, it's still the smart decision. Sally can get 'em when she sees 'em, and you should support me. It will help save more people!"

"Since when did you care about saving people?" Grace asked, a light tone to soothe her words.

Though her ears pulled back at the question, Nekoka carefully explained, "Since one of my friends is stuck in there, and another woman I know, and lots of other people who are being violated in the worst way." Duh, Grace, she wanted to add.

Grace patted her on the head, right between the ears. Nekoka pulled her ears down more. "You're a good person, Nekoka. I'm glad for that."

Nekoka's ears relaxed, and she purred at the praise. And to think, she thought they had no time for the touchy-feely stuff.

Quietly, so she almost couldn't hear it, John said, "About twenty feet away."

Grace let her go and began chanting a different song, a low blurring of tones that had more layers to it than sound.

The advancing group was near silent, the only sound was Grace's chanting, which increased in speed. Nekoka had seen her send out a massive wave of heat or coolness using this type of chant. She certainly hoped Grace wasn't planning to air-condition the interior, like she did for them in the humid south nearly every day in summer.

Nekoka dropped to all fours, shifting into a tiny kitty, worried that she'd drain herself too much with this new, not quite comfortable form. She boosted her small muscles and charged out down the corridor, zipping around the corner and leaping for a bundle of electronics.

Her senses strained and reached. When her paws hit the headset, she pulsed data through the wires. The wires held for a moment, then Nekoka pushed harder, and the system fried. Nekoka hissed to herself. The unit was protected against overloading. This would not be as quick as she had hoped.

"Update," the man said quietly as Nekoka bounded off his helmet onto the next. "I'm blind. Repeat. Blind." His calm reaction planted an itch of concern in Nekoka's whiskers.

Paws on another helmet. Nekoka sent her power into the electronics and had to *push* again. The woman she'd landed on brushed her arm over her head, trying to dislodge Nekoka, but Nekoka spring-boarded off to the next helmet.

"Something small is attacking us, landing on our helmets, shutting down the NVDs," the woman said.

Only two down. Only two. An elephant began stomping on her head. This wasn't good. If only she'd had some sleep, more food, a round of thorough petting.

The squad was babbling at each other, talking about the small, dark blob. Nekoka tried to pay attention, but then they were at the corner, and everything was flashes and bangs as her team met that of the guards.

Paws on another headset.

"Get off me!" No more need to be quiet, the woman yelled. A gloved hand almost grabbed Nekoka. She sprang off before she could shut the helmet down. Crap. Crap. Crap.

Off to another helmet, but they were moving fast now. Nekoka sent streams of data through Whisker to John's own headset, giving him pinpoint targets of the armored guards. Bullets barked through the enclosed space, and she hoped to the heavens that John was unleashing fury, not the merciless guards. Then she received a text from Grace.

Nekoka. Plug your ears.

Perplexed, Nekoka shifted her flesh to form a cover over her ear canals right as Grace shrieked, letting go of her spell that she'd spent the last few minutes weaving. Like a shock wave, it raced past Nekoka, brushing against the fur of her small body.

Screams intensified the chaos from the fight. Two individuals dropped to the ground, another staggered. Though Nekoka had taken precautions, the flap of flesh clogging her ears did little to dampen the wave of sonic power barreling down on her. A painful slash of sound, high range and piercing, still resonated into her ears, drilling needles of pain through her eardrums to the center of her brain.

Though the sound only lasted a few seconds, her Alter Shape failed as her misery tore apart all of her control. In full catgirl form, Nekoka scrambled to the edge of the corridor, away from her thrashing foes. Her ears felt like a burning poker had punctured them. Everything hurt, and everything was muted. Nekoka wanted to hiss and growl at Gracie. This was not a great plan, but a quick surveillance showed many of the guards were equally affected, confused, dazed, not acting like the organized group they had been before.

Fine, she could do this without hearing. She gave Pablo and his own heightened sensory abilities a split second of worry, then staggered to her feet. Under the onslaught of pain, she couldn't focus on her physical form, so she stayed in her everyday shape, still quick and generally small. She sought out her next target and jumped forward. Hands on headset, a push of her power—something wacked into her body, tearing her from the headset. As she rocketed through the air, she twisted, bunched her legs and rebounded off the wall. With a twist of her tail, she took control of her flight and sensed for her assailant. Nobody.

Sure, within the battle's frenzy, armored guards hemmed her in, her companions fought desperately for survival, yet from where the blow landed, there was no electronic presence. A teleporter like Sally? Regardless, she had to hold her ground amidst the swirling chaos. Reinforced boots thudded around her, the flashes from John's shoulder-mounted light offering only fleeting glimpses in the darkness. Her hearing was compromised. She hopped and pounced, struggling to navigate the melee, targeting headsets, but the rapid movements of everything left her vulnerable to unintended strikes.

Her hand landed on another helmet; she shut it down.

"It got me!"

A strike again, sending her smashing against the wall. Screw this! She took a breath, let it out, centered herself and focused. In the next breath, she released her tiger.

How the lion got the misnomer of King, she didn't know. The tiger was pure power in a lovely shade of orange. At two-hundred and fifty pounds, she packed a punch with each swipe of her frying pan-sized paw, each swing powerful enough to cave in the skull of a cow. Her fangs could dig into the leathery hides of water buffalo, the muscles around her jaw strong enough to snap metal rebar.

Normally, she would make herself stronger still, because she was Nekoka. Now though, just the effort of maintaining a normal feline shape bled off too much energy.

Muscles rippled as she bunched her hind end. Her tail flicked. The tiger's eyes allowed more light to filter in, giving more illumination to the dim setting. Electronics beeped before her; somehow, she'd gotten behind the main fighting forces. Poised, she waited, waited for the second invisible foe she had to fight, this one without electronics to aim for.

Something thick and heavy slithered over her paw. Nekoka jerked away. The appendage struck, encircling her foreleg, holding tight with the force of a gorilla to crush and crush.... Nekoka bit down, sinking teeth into the constricting flesh. Hot blood seeped into her mouth. It didn't force the bastard to let go; he pulled her forward. She locked her jaws and tore flesh from the appendage. The thing grunted. Nekoka roared. Both sounds were muffled by her damaged eardrums. Insidious and persistent, the strength of the tentacle bore down on her, crushing her leg. The bones shifted as the Seeded monster dragged her down the hall, away from the fighting, away from her friends and her team.

Oh no, he wouldn't. Nekoka was pretty good in a fight as a tiger, but she didn't have to play games by any measure of normal rules. In one moment, she was huge and menacing, the next, just a few breaths of passing time, and she was small, a house cat, and she slithered from his grip, dodging like a March hare, diving left and right, tail high like a flag, whiskers extra-long seeking out any shift in the air, electronics, scent, sound, anything that would alert her to the hentai beast before her.

The swish of air disturbed a whisker. Nekoka jumped. In the next span of seconds, she grew into a tiger again, barreling forward on full charge, near silent and aiming for full body contact.

Bam! She slammed into something hard, solid, and far larger than a normal human.

He must be a physical aberration or a shape-changer, just like Nekoka. Like old Davy Jones, an octopus man out of water or a vine man: half plant, half human.

Flipping onto her back, she raked all four claws against her foe. Hits pounded into her sides; her entire body took on a deep-rooted ache. Sharp, acidic pain sluiced through her brain. Back into a cat, the shift taking a few breaths longer, the shift more sluggish, demanding more effort. It registered in her hindbrain, but the focus on her opponent took up all of her concentration. Taking on the tiger's shape required double the time; she'd guessed almost ten seconds. Her body, in mid-shift, wasn't as agile, though she struggled to keep in constant movement to avoid repeated blows. But he did hit her, over and *over*.

He had to be able to see her in this low light.

Life was so unfair.

Well, time to switch hands; Nekoka didn't much like her current set of cards.

She bit into something firm and fleshy. The man shrieked a bestial roar, only half hollow to her busted ears. Well, she guessed it was a man, and not some cow beast tentacle hybrid. This *was* a mad scientists' laboratory, if you got right down to it. She tightened her tiger jaws, one-thousand pounds per square inch of force, and tore.

A tentacle ripped free, going limp in her mouth, boneless and floppy.

"You bitch."

Yes, her hearing was clearly returning, and with it the sharp and chaotic noises of her friends fighting the evil overlord's army farther away. The air smelled of gun smoke and blood.

She focused on where the words came from and batted out with her claws. Contact with her unseen foe. Tangy, hot blood sprayed over her face. Her combatant choked on his cry and was gone. Nekoka waited, used all of her senses but couldn't get any ping on him. John's flashlight beamed her direction, then was gone again. This darkness crap was really starting to annoy her.

Kokogyo let her know nobody else was down this far equipped with communication devices. Her map on Whisker showed the hallway ended in about one hundred yards, with electrically controlled doors on either side. The doors she could manipulate and did. As she passed each one, she overloaded the circuits, essentially welding them closed so no new evil SWAT soldiers could join in on the fray.

Far enough from the main fighting and beyond the faint light offered by John's lamp, darkness enveloped everything. Soft padding of something approached her...not shoes, not feet. Maybe paws?

She charged.

Something slapped her across the muzzle. "Back off," a man said. Another strike, this time to her head, but the brush was light, misaimed. She dropped her belly to the floor, rolled left. In the middle of her tumble, she smacked into something solid; she bit it. Another cry of pain, anguish, and fury. Her teeth hit bone. A leg, maybe, a calf most likely. Raising her paws up, she raked where she thought the hentai man's groin might be.

She hit something solid—a thigh?—and a tentacle wrapped around her hind leg and squeezed, crushing her as the man panted. She stuck again; this time she thought she hit the juncture between her opponent's legs. The tentacle's desperate grip loosened; the man let loose a breathless huff.

She definitely heard that. And so, finding her target, she reached back and batted again, putting full tiger force behind her strike, hitting something other than his most tender bits. Probably more tentacles, she couldn't tell. The beastman let her go. In an instant, she sprang, hoping to land on his back, but instead hitting nothing and only landing on the ground.

A step sounded behind her. She whirled around. Something massive slammed into her side, evacuating all the air she had in her lungs. Pain seized her chest and wouldn't release its terrible hold. Something had broken inside. Her breath came in a wheeze. A hot iron of agony pinpointed to one spot in her right chest, lower along her rib cage.

She wished she could see: see how bad her injury was; see the face of the beast that ended her.

Jenni, she screamed out in her mind. *Jenni!*

If she had to die, she wished it wouldn't be alone. She'd always hated being alone.

CHAPTER 40

Nekoka

Stop panicking. Stop panicking, Jenni would say.

That Jenni wasn't saying anything now, Nekoka had to ignore. With extreme effort, she tried to gain her feet, but the broken thing within her made it so she couldn't breathe and couldn't move and couldn't focus. *Think!* she commanded herself. Her rib had broken...not a big deal. Just a rib. No deal at all! It wasn't like you'd die from a broken rib. It wouldn't kill her.

But her foe would. Another blow. More branding pain in her chest. She wanted to run away, get beyond the reach of this demon hunting her in the dark. All those training exercises her team practiced, but she'd blown off. She thought she was strong enough, but reality was always a cruel teacher.

Of course, she'd never expected to be doing such dangerous, heroic things, either.

She lay on her side, panting, each breath a wash of agony. Hot from exertion, warm from his blood. She couldn't focus anymore.

Don't give up! Jenni would say. Use your strengths.

If she was small, he wouldn't be able to find her.

But she couldn't concentrate. She couldn't do anything but breathe. In one of those ego moments, her life zipped before her on fast forward. All of those years she spent learning and studying and being what everyone else wanted. Proving she was a rational being. She still was. Still could be. First order of business, survival. How did she attain that? Get away from this multi-armed demon. She crawled along the wall as silently as possible in her huge, battered form, sharp claws scraping against the cold tile, trying to gather her power, to pull her shape into a design she wanted.

Not tiger form, but one that was small and lithe, a fleet beast of four-legged perfection.

Small and hopefully hard to find in the dark.

The beastman growled. Frantic buzzing static short-circuited her hearing. She couldn't pinpoint his location, just that he was near, and he was growling.

Would he eat her? Take in her Seed? Evolve like some video game warrior?

She tried to shift, to change, but her power wasn't doing anything. The pain was body-numbing now. Eternal. Had been written into her DNA. A fission of horror shook her fur, and she tried again. Gritted her dagger teeth in her over-sized mouth and focused on her body changing, melting down, giving up the hold on one shape and taking on another.

Nothing.

A sob busted from her throat. She was trapped. Stuck.

Taking in one deep breath, she released her tension, didn't think about the waiting death stalking her. With intention, she thought about that broken bone, imagined what it looked like, the arc of a rib, the strength of the bone. Calmly, she thought about it being complete. A flash of pain; it moved, hurting and cutting and...No. No, she thought. No. I'm a shape-changer. Body manipulation is what I do.

Releasing all tension, she let go, let her body do what it knew how to do, no longer directing her big brain to orchestrate any of this desperate production. This was her *power*, her strength. The paws shrank, huge paw pads shorting into the smaller pads of a house cat. Her barrel chest slimmed down. Everything closed in around her as she transitioned from a large tiger to her small tabby. The rib inside shifted, pulled, aligned and in a remarkably fluid motion, fused together, dimming down all pain in her chest. As she settled into her feline form, it was like the heavens opened up and poured tuna juice all over her. The pain wasn't all gone. She guessed damage remained she hadn't healed, but this—this rib—she could do this.

She fluttered her eyelids, totally useless in the perfect darkness. Lifting one paw, then the other, using careful actions, she could move without discomfort.

A shift of air. He was close. This was it.

Shoring up her constitution, muscles ready for one final assault, she attacked. Four sets of claws out. She climbed over his leg, across his torso and found his face, only to shred it apart as his tentacles battered desperately against her weak kitty flanks. His warm blood matted her fur, thicker and thicker after each onslaught.

"My eyes. Fuck! You stupid bitch." Hands grabbed around her belly. She dug her claws into his fingers and squirmed out of his grasp, dashing around his shoulders to scratch at the back of his head. He grazed her a few times, with tentacles and fists, bruising her further around the hind end, but never enough to halt her attack, and as she batted at his body, her vicious claws slapping across his eyes again, he finally caught her with his hands and threw her away like a smelly gym shirt.

It had been a double barrel final assault. She meowed and crumbled to the ground as the man screamed in pain and fury.

Her sides heaved with huge breaths. The man still threatened her. She'd struggled and tried, and now she was completely drained of whatever reserves had allowed her one final morph. She needed rest and food and time to recuperate. With hot defiance, she lurched across the floor, returning towards the main fight, hoping her friends had survived, were chattering about their success, high-fiving and patting each other's backs.

The man growled. "Where you at, bitch?"

On cat paws, she limped down the hall, tail dragging behind, body way too battered, her energy too exhausted. Forward. Just go forward.

There was an oof and a curse. A high female giggle. A hand on her head. A body hitting the floor. She hissed, front claw flashing frantically, paws hitting something hard, then slipped off, connecting with soft skin.

"Nekoka," came the harsh whisper. "Damn it, stop. Nekoka."

She held her next strike. "Meow?" she questioned. It sounded like Pablo.

A light steadily bobbed her way

"Let's check you out. Just, stop attacking me," Pablo said softly.

The light showed Pablo. The helmet sending his eyes in shadow while he tenderly touched his cheek. She'd barely brushed against him, but the cut bled. To Pablo's left stood Battle Axe, the weapon's blade darker in the low light. "I've been looking for you," John said when he reached them.

Nekoka realized there was no more battle. She shifted her ears forward, rotated them around. Groaning and heavy breathing. The sounds of active fighting were gone.

"I think the guards are dispatched," John said, squatting down next to Nekoka and Pablo, his cold light flashing against the walls of the hallway. "I can sense a lot of life still, but none of them are moving about but us."

Sally stepped into the halo of light, coming from the direction of a large heaping form obscured by the darkness. The beastman. "Oh, they weren't all killed?" Sally whined.

"I disabled quite a few in my first chant," Grace said. "They were never in the fight."

"I sent one or two off with despair," Pablo said a little smugly.

Glimpses of ghostly faces in the light of John's flashlight let Nekoka know her friends were all around her, close and safe and alive.

"How is everybody? Anybody hurt?" Grace asked, pushing at her helmet so it sat more balanced on her head.

Nekoka murfed.

"I think I've got a twisted ankle, some bullet wounds, and lots of bruising."

"Head hurts like a real bugger."

"Took a few shots."

"I feel good," Sally said.

"Oh, for Christ's sake. Will you all just sit down for a moment?" Gracie began chanting.

Everyone was banged up to some extent, except speedster Sally. Pablo had it the worst; not only had he taken a wallop from Gracie's initial shriek attack, but he also had several injuries from a guard he couldn't whammy with his emotional bomb and the cut from Nekoka's razor-wire claws.

Nekoka's ears were down in contrition, though the light wasn't on her and nobody was paying her much attention. She'd marred his beautiful face. She'd *destroyed* perfection.

Gracie chanted in a low, soft voice, mainly in Spanish, of which Nekoka only knew a few words. It was steady, intoned like a prayer you'd hear in a grand cathedral. With his giant ax as a prop, Battle Axe sighed as a cooling wash settled over them all. "Oh, thank God," Pablo said. Nekoka took in a breath, letting her chest expand. Even though she'd healed her own rib, this wave of soothing relief was a blessing.

"Nekoka, how are you?" Gracie asked as she knelt next to her belly. Nekoka swiveled her ears forward. With gentle hands, Gracie brushed over her side, running fingers through her brown and gray fur. Nekoka licked at her friend, then rubbed her whiskers against Gracie's fingers. She couldn't access Alter Shape or even *kokogyo* right now to text her friends to let them know her status.

For the second time in a handful of hours, Nekoka had no way of communicating when she normally had so many options.

"Can you change?" John asked. "Text us?"

Nekoka shook her head and padded at him with a paw.

"You hurt?" Gracie asked.

Nekoka purred and shook her head again, quite proud of herself for being able to heal her own broken rib, even if it currently cut her off from using her other powers.

John cupped his hand before her and poured some water from a military issue canteen into it. Nekoka greedily lapped at the water, ignoring the polluted flavor of it from his dirty hand. She'd drunk worse. She licked him in thanks, and he rubbed her head. A purr rumbled from her narrow chest, so happy that everyone was okay. Nobody had died, though she knew she'd been close.

Jenni, she thought aloud. *I almost died.*

She decided this would be the only time she confessed this to her friend; that she was outside of their normal range was a detail she chose to file away as unimportant. *I almost died.*

But she hadn't.

Without that pain tugging at her mind, she tried Alter Shape again. John continued to scratch behind her ears, and she let the touch and kindness dash away her anxiety. It should be effortless, as it always was, but her body just clung onto this current one. It was okay. It was all okay. It would happen, she just had to relax.

Just relax.

If only she could have a quickie in the middle of the enemy compound, that would relax her. Or take a blue, but she didn't have any of the moods on her, only John stroking her head.

Her paws shifted into hands, fingers stretched out long against the floor. Her shoulders and hips retracted and bent in new ways. It wasn't smooth, and it wasn't easy. It felt like her bones ground against each other. The organs in her belly grew and shifted. The teeth sinking into her mouth ached. Her whole body felt *squeezed*, like that gross liquid cheese you pushed through a tube.

She lay on her side, panting, eyes pressed shut. The feel of her body let her know she'd succeeded her Alter Shape. John rubbed along her shoulder. His strong hand was gentle, gentler than she had expected. "That didn't look right. Are you okay?"

"No," she groaned. "I feel bulldozed over." She flicked her eyes up to him. Squinting at his light, she smiled her thanks. With contrition, she shifted her attention to Pablo, ears pulled back. "Pablo, I'm so very sorry for scratching you."

Pablo flashed her his bright smile, dimples and contentment, and Nekoka's adoration for him swelled all over again. Perhaps she had repaid him for the mood swing he'd given her a few days ago at Rain. They were even, and no more enmity needed to be carried. With his steady strength, he pulled her to her feet, only to lay his arm over her shoulders to squeeze her tight against his chest. "Ah Nekoka, I hold no grudge. I know you didn't know it was me. My eardrums are more messed up from Grace's chant," Pablo said, giving the woman a friendly pout.

Grace muttered something, not meeting anyone's eyes, then said, "Sorry Pablo, I thought I'd given you enough warning."

Nekoka hunched her shoulders. "Ah, well, Gracie, that did really hurt." She flicked an ear.

"I, personally, want to offer my thanks for taking out the small fry," said Sally earnestly, pressing a hand to her chest. "I'd hate to waste my time. You know?"

Nobody said anything else as they caught their breath, probably all agreeing with Sally but not wanting to voice their support. So, they sat in silence, waiting in the dark hallway, listening for any incoming menace.

"Oi there, Nekoka." It was Battle Axe, his deep voice hesitant. "If you can shapeshift, I was just wondering, can you turn into anything?"

Nekoka shrugged. "I tried to turn into a tree once." Minnie had bet her to do it. If she could change into a tree, Minnie would make her three-cheese lasagna for dinner that night. If Nekoka failed, Nekoka would modify Minnie's favorite game's avatar to look just like her, springy curls and everything, and have all the wimpy monsters have the face of the last boss she'd worked for. It wasn't much of a challenge to get her involved; Nekoka rarely backed down from a bet where she could show off. She'd stood under one of the live oaks lining the drive up to the manor for a good thirty minutes, thinking *tree tree tree* and not even a twitch. Then she Alter Shaped into a cat to chase the squirrels. "Didn't work. Why?"

"Well, I was wondering if you could turn glowy. Like those fish in the deep ocean. Or fireflies..." His voice trailed off. "More light than just John's torch would be nice." He shifted again, sticking close to John's side.

Ah, the big guy didn't like the dark. Nekoka wanted to help him, but she shook her head. "Nope, nada, ain't gonna happen." She wasn't even going to try, not after her previous struggles. "I'm stretched thin, Battle Axe. Sorry. My best bet would be if I could get the lights turned back on, but I...I can't even sense computers right now."

Grace gasped. Nekoka wouldn't meet her eyes.

"What do you need?" she asked, so warm and kind.

"Rest, I think. Food." She looked up, waggled her eyebrows at the men. "Sex."

"Umm," John said, while Battle Axe's pale face just looked bewildered. Well, he didn't know her very well.

"Okay," Pablo drew out. "Here, have a granola bar." Pablo held out a wrapped rectangle, and Nekoka tore off the wrapper and stuffed it in her face, munching. John held out his canteen patiently while Nekoka chewed.

It felt like wasted time. Sally's shadowed form, behind John at the edges of the light, flipped a knife through the air, catching it and tossing it up again. Gracie rubbed Nekoka's temples as she continued to eat the granola bar, and then a package of dry cookies that Sally had in the pocket of her dress, probably from that farmer's house. He wouldn't be needing them anymore. She guzzled down John's water, leaving him just a few mouthfuls, and finally she felt a bit more alive than Idaho roadkill. Her aches had been soothed by Gracie and her reserves fueled by food and water.

“Okay...I’m, ah...better?” Nekoka said, knowing she was nowhere near where she should be to continue forward through the compound. But there was no going back. People depended on them all, to save them, to break them free of this cave. Sepia and Berlin. She’d claimed him. Berlin was hers, and she was going to get him back. Plus, this time she had back-up. She wasn’t alone. “I think...”

From where he’d been squatting next to Nekoka, John jumped to his feet, facing deeper into the compound. “People coming for us. We’ve got to move.”

“Okay, through there,” Nekoka pointed up the hallway to a door, “is the cage room.”

John nodded. “Lots and lots of people on the other side. Some right at the door. The ones close are all Seeded, all about Sally level or just below. I say let Sally jump through first, then Axe, and if there’s light, me, if not, Nekoka. Pablo and Grace, you okay with being last?”

Nekoka trotted up to the door and leaned against it, carefully letting her cyber-senses spread through the electronics.

A faint connection clicked. It wasn’t steady or strong, but it was her power, and it was back. “There is light.” Nekoka scanned through the cameras with views of the doors and cages, flittering through the surveillance as far as her weakened power let her reach. “There are twelve armed men that I can see through this camera angle. Another aberration who looks a bit like a walking tree. Some more of those flame throwers...what was that anyway?”

“Don’t know. Sally took that one out,” Pablo said. “Didn’t smell like any combustible fuel that I’ve smelled before, though. Don’t trust it.”

“Don’t trust any o’ this,” Battle Axe mumbled.

A bullet pinged against the wall next to Pablo a split second before the pow of the gun. Pablo skipped to the left, away from the direction of the shot. They all shuffled after him. John faced down the corridor, on his knee, gun aimed steady and sure. He pulled off one shot. Then another.

“I’m cutting the light,” John said. Everything went dark.

Battle Axe grumbled.

"So, Nekoka...door?" John whispered. He fired another shot. The sparks from the muzzle flashed in the total absence of light. Nekoka flinched, feeling vulnerable without her armored-up flesh.

"On it," she said. With a soft touch, she ran her fingers over the door. The electronic lock mechanism released. The deadbolt still held. "Still has a mechanical lock. I can try to pick it.... Though, never mind. I've no picks. I'm not doing shit."

John popped off another series of shots.

"Here, why dontcha let me," Battle Axe said. His huge presence drew close to her, and then a gentle hand pushed her aside.

CHAPTER 41

Nekoka

Nekoka heard the rattle of the handle. Her ears swiveled, taking in everything she could. Through the camera, Nekoka saw one of the guards on the other side of the door flinch.

For a moment, silence curled around them. Down the hall, Nekoka thought she might have heard a boot step. John fired again. After a few seconds, a deep groaning discontentment squealed from the door. The strain on the metal reverberated through the hallway.

"The whole lock encasement is probably reinforced," Nekoka complained. She extended one claw and sliced through the wall's plaster next to the door; in no time, she met metal.

"I wish Starburst were here," Battle Axe said, stepping away from the door, his breath coming in heavy pants. "She'd be able to blast her way through that at the wag of a dog's tail."

"So, we've three people trying to take shots at us from down the hallway, but they apparently don't have night vision. Must not be the main guards we found earlier," John said. "I think I can keep them low by laying cover fire, but I'll run out of bullets if that's all we do here."

Pablo cursed. "So, they've efficiently barricaded themselves in there." The man paced in the dark, each footstep a tiny scratch Nekoka's ears picked up. "They know we're here, plus our other groups. If we don't succeed on our own, obviously we'll pull in more authority, more groups, more power. The higher ups have to have other ways in and out."

"The main compound?" Grace suggested.

"Jenni and the others are up there, maybe they'll get through and..."

John fired another shot.

"That wasn't the plan," Nekoka reminded them. "We were supposed to get down here and do our part. Come on, guys. Think." She was growing frustrated. Was the entire wall reinforced?

"Battle Axe, can you annihilate this wall?"

"They'll know we're coming from there," came Pablo's flat assessment.

"They know that anyway," Gracie argued.

"I'll need some light," Battle Axe said. Something was pressed into Nekoka's hands. She gripped the firm, smooth, plastic cylinder of a flashlight.

Groping about, she found Battle Axe's big hand, and with a gentle tug, she led the man down the hall, away from their snipers, and flicked on the flashlight. Battle Axe's shoulders relaxed, and with a nod, he hoisted his ax. With a heavy swing, he planted the steel blade into the wall, twisted, and tore away a chunk of plaster.

His first hit revealed the steel reinforcement. That couldn't encase the whole place. The costs and construction would be astounding.

"Guys, more people coming this way. Could be better equipped," John warned.

"Try lower," Nekoka told Battle Axe.

With short, quick strikes, he gouged apart the wall nearer the floor. Dust motes floated in the flashlight's dim light, tickling her whiskers. He kept going into the drywall long after he would have met metal farther up. Bingo. Battle Axe used his ax as a lever and tore apart the wall. At about two and a half feet from the ground, he met the reinforced banding. Two and a half feet. An array of shots came through the hole from the other side, then another from down the hallway.

They found themselves in a crossfire, not a very tight crossfire, but it still wasn't at all pleasant.

Sally approached them, a sensual swing to her arms, a sway to her hips. "If you give me the light, I can do something about those down the hall."

Nekoka didn't even argue. She handed over the light. In just a few seconds, the light was gone, then appeared down the hallway, then was gone again, and appeared a few feet to the right. Gasps and gurgles churned with a breathy laugh.

A bang and a high-pitched yelp of pain, then another cry as the light blinked out and moved again.

Sally returned, holding onto her arm, lips twisted into a pained pout. Dark splatters flecked her face and clothes. "One of them got me." She handed over the flashlight and a tactical helmet to John. "Maybe this will have a radio so we can snoop?"

Gracie took a few seconds to jump to Sally's aid, using the cupped light from the flashlight to examine her. Sally lolled her head to the side, smiling dreamily at Gracie, apparently pleased to get personal attention from their resident pain dampener.

Battle Axe pointed to the hole where the barrage of bullets had come from, shaking his head.

They would be sitting ducks crawling through there, and there was no way Battle Axe could shimmy through that tight opening at all, sitting duck or not. Nekoka could go first, wreak havoc and distract people, but that was no guarantee she'd pull all the guards away from the hole so the others could belly-crawl through. Maybe, if she was fully in control of her power again, she could become tiny and camouflaged and scamper in, find a way to open the door from the other side.

Pablo stuffed his hands in his pockets. "No way could Axe get through that."

Nekoka hissed. "Oh really, Captain Obvious?"

"Hey, hey, kitty," Pablo continued. "Don't take it out on me."

"I'm not." She crossed her arms over her chest. Her tail flicked in agitation. "I'm running out of ideas."

Battle Axe shifted his entire body in a shrug. "We can't sit here. 'Ts not helping anyone."

Gracie snuffed the light, sending them all in darkness again.

"They'll shoot us if we crawl through," Pablo said, and Nekoka stopped herself from saying, "Duh."

She felt like hissing again.

Maybe she could find out if any more guards were coming, find out just how much time she had to rest. She patted her hands over everyone, earning some "Heys" until she found John, and snatched the helmet Sally had confiscated from the dead guard. Using a tiny bit of her power and going by feel, she found the radio. At low volume, she filtered through several channels until she heard chatter on one.

Based on the conversation, she was sure it came from the guards on the other side of the door, in the warehouse where the cages of captives were held. They were waiting, expecting them to break through the wall or door with enough time. Many guards griped that the insurgents were up to something with the lights out. All of them sounded tense, on edge, trigger-happy. They all knew that other guards were fighting Starburst at the main compound and were unhappy at the blind wait down here.

"Damn, sounds like a better fight than this waiting bullshit," one of the guards said.

And just like that, a proverbial light bulb lit in Nekoka's mind.

She wished she had more time, but in reality, the guards gave her everything she needed. As quick as the guards spoke, Nekoka recorded the conversation on Whisker, and after two or three minutes she had what she needed. Quickly, using her base level of *kokogyo*, she pulled apart their words and phrases and reorganized them into the phrase she wanted. Then, just to be safe, created a few responses. She sent the phrases through a sound smoother on Whisker, so all the words sounded uniform. There.

The exercise was straightforward, but annoyingly enough, it left her feeling drained.

Through the radio comms, she sent to the guards positioned on the other side of the door a message: "Extra men needed to fight Starburst and other insurgents. Go engage."

She waited. Then from the other end, "Confirm again?" Nekoka had no idea what the protocol was. She'd decided to use one of the upper-level goons' names, not the main Director. "This is Thomas Hallaman, confirmed. Engage Starburst." She hoped it sounded official. That she used the right lingo. She didn't have time to sit back and observe much longer, Jenni and squad two might not be faring well.

"Yes, sir."

Nekoka spied their reaction through the video feed. To her annoyance, only about half left.

"Okay, I'm going in. I'll cause a bit of chaos, and those who can, get through the hole. I'll try to figure out how to open the door, but don't count on it being quick. Ready?" Nekoka's tail hung limp behind her. After all this, a nap. She'd definitely take a nap.

Confirmation all around. Nobody wanted to wait anymore. She hardened her body, considered taking a Kevlar jacket, but nixed the idea. She didn't want to deprive the others of theirs. Anyway, it would limit her flexibility and couldn't shift with her. She was mighty. She was fast. She could do this. *She could do this.*

Nekoka dropped to her hands and knees outside of the hole Battle Axe had carved into the wall, took a breath, and rolled through.

Hell was about to be split into tiny little pieces.

CHAPTER 42

Berlin

The compound had turned into a frenzied ant hill, reminding Berlin of nights when the police would come to the abandoned buildings to rout out the homeless. Only this time, the homeless were stationary, trapped. Something big was in the works. Many of the cells had been emptied, but some still held a few people, like his own. Sepia, that pierced woman Nekoka had been looking for, was in a cell all on her own. He hadn't seen Martha in some time.

Everyone was gray.

At the far end of the building, about seven rows of cells away, a blurry pack of guards dressed in dark uniforms held up weapons—very futuristic to his awful eyesight—aiming at the double doors everyone got brought in through. Berlin squinted at them, trying to make out details, but the lights were bright and his vision as sharp as a hot dog. Their helmets looked fully enclosed, like something a soldier from an alien invading army would wear. If he wasn't trapped and hurting, he might almost take an interest. Instead, he let his body rest against the metal bars. His back hurt after hours in that position, but he needed to keep his head elevated. The needle they jammed into his brain wasn't a tiny thing. The resulting head pain threatened to knock him down for the count.

One of the guards jumped, his weapon pointing at the doors. Berlin had no idea who the threat was. Certainly, nobody could make it through those doors. Berlin wished he could simply grab it with his mind and open it, like some of the Seeded could do. That way, whoever they were guarding against could come on in, and it would finally be all over. They'd probably be nicer than these brain piercers. Anyone would be nicer. But he couldn't do much in this cell, damp with that stuff they sprayed over everyone with timed regularity.

"They're coming through," one of the guards barked out, like it was an order.

Maybe it was more of those shadows, the ones who hung around watching him. He only saw them when he wasn't soaking with the smelly chemical spray. They received the same treatment as the vegetables in a grocery store. Always spritzed moist. Upon a fresh misting, all the ghosts and shadows faded away, but after he dried a bit, he could see them again. He'd talk to the shadows, but they never talked back. He knew everyone thought he was crazy, but that was nothing new. What they thought didn't matter. Not much did. He would be dead soon. That is what all the ghostly spirits—not the shadow, which was different—would whisper to him when the lights dimmed, and people pretended to sleep. They'd gather around him like lost children and whisper, "Not long now. You'll walk with us soon. You'll be welcome. No more pain."

If he were to be honest with himself, but only to his most inner self, he thought the concept of no pain sounded delightful. But it was out of his hands. Once you were taken away by the men in white coats three times, you didn't ever come back.

He looked away from the agitated guards toward Sepia's cell. Though he couldn't see her well now, he'd passed by her cell on the way to the torture chair and knew its exact location. He wanted to get her attention, because he had a feeling that she would be interested in the fact that 'they were coming through'. She seemed like an opportunist to him.

Well, no point in not trying.

He gripped the bars of his cage and, assuring none of the regular guards were watching him, called out quietly to an Asian man. He used to have neighbors in the cell between them, but that morning they'd been taken away. In the last few hours, a lot had been taken away.

"Hey."

The man rolled his head towards Berlin. The prisoners never talked to each other; the guards were quick to punish collaborative efforts.

"Hey, I need you to get her attention for me. The woman alone."

The man grunted, then licked his lips. "Why?"

"Well, because I asked you to. And," Berlin jerked his head to the doors where the guards were preparing for a great onslaught, "they're busy with something else right now."

The man looked over at the big doors, then towards Sepia. He crawled across his cell floor and whispered to the next cell, which housed two people. One of them waved. Berlin squinted; his eyes watered. It seemed the man finally got her attention. Berlin heard her annoyed, "What?" all the way to his cell.

He waved, hoping she was looking at him, and pointed to the commotion. Now, the guards were down on one knee, aiming their guns at the wall. A hail of gunshots pounded through the air. Berlin ducked, pressing his body to the cold floor. More people were shouting farther away. The hounds of hell seemed to have broken their leashes. Sepia stood up, trying to get a better look. Berlin cautiously got to his feet, but no matter how careful he was, the action caused a dizzying cyclone to shift his world. He gripped the cage bars to steady himself and prayed he wouldn't throw up.

A huge flurry of action, splashes of darks and lighter colors danced together. A frenzy of motion. Berlin pressed his face to the bars, squinting. More gun shots, each loud retort causing Berlin to cower, crouching low. A scream of agony.

Berlin couldn't tell what was happening. All that existed was noise and fear pounding in his ears.

"Oh yeah!" someone yelled.

Berlin swallowed and focused again, narrowing his eyes in the bright light. There were people fighting the guards. The pop pop of gunfire gave Berlin chills. Someone was twirling a rope.... No, a tail trailed behind her as she tore the helmet off a guard's head.

Berlin cheered. "Nekoka!" It had to be Nekoka! She'd come back, to save him, to save everyone. He couldn't help but cheering. "Go Scratch! Kick their asses!"

He watched with rapt attention as she bounced and pounced. She swatted the guards with her claws, then moved again, never staying in one place. Nekoka looked to be aiming for the guards with the bulky packs on their backs. Bullets zinged through the room. Berlin gasped when Nekoka's body went down, but she was up again, never really slowing.

A siren shrieked through the air. Berlin pressed his palms to his ears, but it did little to muffle the alarm.

A girl in a dark dress was in the room now. A cloud of gray surrounded her: ghosts. Nekoka was screaming and creating havoc, another person was by her side, shooting out at armored guards. The woman with the ghosts stood by the doors, hands on her hips, staring at it.

"Stop her!" a guard yelled over the alarm.

Then the woman laughed, a high childish noise that rose above the screams and raucous noise. The doors opened.

A huge man crashed through the opening doors. He wielded an ax—so large Berlin could tell it was an ax—high over his head. Delivering a challenging roar, he swiped the weapon through the guards, knocked several to the ground. Berlin worried about how such a large, stationary man like that could avoid the incessant gunfire. It was obvious, even to Berlin, who this was. Battle Axe. The biggest, strongest, toughest hero out there. He'd been on the cover of S! Magazine and was a member of Guardian Alliance. Guardian Alliance was here! Others came through after him. It was chaos; Berlin couldn't keep track of everything. He tried to spot others he would recognize. Was Starburst here?

Other prisoners climbed to their feet, some of them called out, others wept. A few stood silently, just watching their saviors—only six!—fight the guards. Battle Axe sliced his weapon in a wide arch and tossed three guards into the air. One of the saviors got drenched in a spray of liquid.

Oh no.

"Nekoka!" Sepia cried out. "Nekoka, get me the hell out of here! I'll fight, too. Let me out!"

More of the prisoners took up the mantra, crying out for freedom, crying out for retribution. Berlin closed his eyes and pulled forth the spirits, for the place was fertile with the dead. They stirred at his calling.

"Yes, we are here," the spirits said. "Come, be with us. Come, together we will be free. Soon."

"Not if we can help it," he said to them.

"Nekoka!" Berlin yelled at her. "Don't let that spray touch you! It turns off powers!"

Nekoka raced over to him. She pressed her hand against his cell's lock, and it popped open. The fur around her eyes and ears was damp, and her lip curled up, baring her fangs. He stumbled out, wrapped his arms around her body, wanting to ask so many questions: would they get out, what would happen now, who were these people who'd kidnapped them all, but the only words that formed were: "You came. You came."

"You're okay."

Wrapped in Nekoka's arms, it was all he could do to breathe, she hugged him so tight. With utter tenderness, she pressed her lips to the side of his head, and he worried that his hair was disgusting and greasy. She hadn't liked that he'd been dirty before. He wanted to pull away, not subject her to what must be a powerful stench, but she clung onto him a moment longer, then gently let him go.

"You're okay." Her eyes were glistening. He brushed her cheek, the layer of fuzz covering it soft. "*Yokatta.* I'm glad—" Her voice broke. She swallowed and said more softly, "you're alive."

A warm brilliance blossomed in his chest. The emotion so overwhelming he could do nothing but stand there and stare at her.

"I've got to let everyone else out, but you should hide." She scanned the huge room, her head barely swiveling left, then right, a kind of disconnected awe. "Or stay here. I'll be back. Just, lie low. Got it?"

He nodded, still unable to speak, unable to process what had just been born within him.

She smiled once, then with a near stumble to the floor, she bounded down the row between the cells, her tail swiping out as she slapped one lock, then the next, opening the doors in her wake like a catgirl Houdini.

Underneath obvious exhaustion, she was pissed. Her tail flicked; her teeth were bared. There was something about the determined planting of each foot that seemed to be a flimsy yoke to the fury that wanted to lash out. He found her anger profoundly comforting. He understood, in that moment balanced between fear and joy, that he loved her. It shocked him, because he'd never been in love before, and he wasn't sure what he was supposed to do next.

Well, for the time being, he had to wait as Nekoka opened all the cages. The prisoners rattled their bars trying to get her attention, get freed next, but Nekoka was on a deliberate path and would not be swayed. Above him, a gray mass of ghosts swirled, obscuring his view of the harsh light.

"Will you help?" he asked the ghosts, not expecting an answer. But he hoped, because he thought of them as a type of ally, without truly understanding their intentions. And if the ghosts didn't help against the shadows, how would they, the solid people, fight them?

There was something about the shadows, some sort of inhumanity to them. If they knew what it was like to be a human, if they understood humanness, Berlin hoped they might not want to hurt them anymore.

Squatting next to the outside of his cage, Berlin stayed out of the way as some of the prisoners charged for the guards. The swirling mass grew. It was sad really, these broken people, falling under gunfire, failing due to weakened bodies.

Others, like him, were hiding, trying to draw nobody's attention, appear small and inconsequential. To be nothing of concern.

Nekoka landed near him, hand reaching out.

"Let's get you someplace safe," she said. Berlin grabbed her hand, threading his fingers through hers, and let her lead him through the mass of people, lost and confused and needing some sort of guidance.

He wondered, should he kiss her, right here in front of everyone, to tell her of his new discovery, but thought better of it. It was only a moment before when he realized his feelings; he wasn't sure what he would do if she told him she didn't like him like that. And in the middle of a battle was never the time nor the place to pause and make such a confession, no matter what the movies suggested.

Guards filled the area. The cell guards as well as those more military-like guys. The prisoners had plenty of targets for their anger.

In the distance, he saw Sepia, pushing people from her path as she stalked towards them. Berlin waved, and Nekoka changed their direction to head towards her.

"Wow, they screwed you up!" Nekoka said. Berlin gave her a shushing look.

Sepia flipped Nekoka off. "I don't give a fuck if you like my new style or not. It's called, 'I'm Not Dead', and I like it." Sepia sneered, but there was no heat behind it. "I've got something to deal with. You need to see this."

Sepia pushed her way through the crowd, shoulders and hands driving people out of their way, leading them from the fighting. Bile tickled up Berlin's throat, burning. He recognized where they were going. To the chair. He slowed, squeezing Nekoka's hand.

She looked at him. "Okay?"

"I—I don't want to go there," he said, settling his pleading eyes on Nekoka. He shook his head and planted his feet. Nekoka looked from Sepia to Berlin, her facial features under the fine layer of fur playing through various emotions.

The siren continued to wail, and the dark mass of ghosts above was shifting, swirling like a storm ready to throw down thunder and lightning.

"Hey, where are you going?" one man asked Sepia. He had a sickly pallor to his face, tinged a little green.

"I'm going to go fuck up the chair room. Wanna come?" Sepia asked, a spark of life flashing in her eye.

The man's eyes darted towards the hall, shadowed, and fearful. He nodded, head shaky, but with a certain determination Berlin felt himself. He did *not* want to go back to that place as much as these two needed to.

Nekoka released his hand, and Berlin felt cold. She brushed his arm and shoulder, attempting to offer him support, he guessed, but it wasn't working. "You don't have to come."

Sepia stood nearby, glaring down at the floor, obviously wanting to keep moving, but not wanting to continue without Nekoka.

The smile Nekoka gave him was reassuring, sweet almost, if it wasn't for the visible flash of fang. "I'll be back. Stay out of the fighting. Look for an Hispanic woman, wearing an S-Force shirt. Thick dark hair, a little chunky, beautiful." She pointed to where she'd come from. "Her name is Grace. Tell her you're my friend, okay?"

Berlin nodded and watched as Nekoka, Sepia, and a few others went down the hallway toward that room of shadows.

CHAPTER 43

Thomas

But Director Jeon—" the doctor argued.

"Isn't here, is he?" Thomas wondered about meeting the Director in the minutes he had left, wasting them arguing with this Mengele wanna-be. But he had no other way out. He still needed Jeon. Thomas thrust his finger above them, where pounding and booms and gunshots of the conflict above could be heard. "There are people trying to come in and destroy *you*. Worry about that. I've told you that no, we will not gas these people. Just because they can't be used doesn't mean they should be thrown away."

A small sneer, pleased and smug, flickered across the doctor's face. "But, sir. It's too late—"

His phone rang. He turned his back on the doctor and answered.

"We captured three of them, sir," Ratchet informed him.

"Three." Thomas wasn't impressed. Thirty-seven highly trained, exceptionally equipped Seeded, and they had captured three. "Where are they now?"

"Uh, in one of the labs. Incapacitated."

It didn't matter, really. Not like they could keep them tied up forever. Thomas knew what those higher up than him would say: send them to the letting chamber. But that was all over now. Minidoka had fallen. The collapse of the compound was inevitable. He'd always known that.

His personal phone beeped. He exited the command center and wandered down the hall for privacy before he looked at the phone, hoping it was confirmation from his contacts. The firestorm blasted against the building. With dread, he read the text on his phone. You see it is as I said.

Thomas wanted to throw his phone against the wall, watch the tiny computer pieces splatter over the clean tile floor.

It beeped again.

My warning was unheeded. You collaborated with the Formless.

Thomas was sick of these enigmatic messages. He'd had the number traced, but it went nowhere. Didn't even bounce off of other providers.

He quickly texted back: What do you suggest?

The breach is coming. Prepare yourself.

More details would always be nice: he texted in reply.

Thomas Hallaman returned to the control room. Screw the Founders. Screw the Director. Screw this mysterious Chief. He punched on the microphone. "Evacuate. All personnel evacuate. Abandon Minidoka." Abandon ship and all hope, ye who enter. He tapped the button that would release all the locks. Let them out. The captives. The employees. Everyone. Let them free. The blackmail meant nothing if he wasn't alive. He was washing his hands of this failure.

CHAPTER 44

Nekoka

Tight on Sepia's heels, Nekoka and their gathered stragglers jogged down the nondescript hallway adjacent to the cage-filled chamber. The warning siren continued to cry out. Warning, insurgents, warning, defend the compound. Clinical Formica covered the floor; the walls were whitewashed to a level of hyperactive brilliance under the fluorescent lighting. A door stood at the end of the hallway, one of those shiny metallic jobs that took a big man with an ax to rip open or a cyberkinetic catgirl to unlock.

Nekoka sent her thoughts to the door, to tickle the lock open, but it was already unlatched. Sepia slowed her approach, one foot before the other, hesitant, almost, as her fingertips touched the shiny metal and pushed. The woman was gun shy, waiting for the punch, for the death blow. Nekoka stiffened, ready for a trap. The door swung open with ease, and Sepia lurched in, back hunched, head shifting left, then right, though there was no threat.

Sepia of the now was a sham. It wasn't just her physical state—the bruises, the cuts, the ruination of her once pierced appearance—but that fire that Nekoka despised, but grudgingly respected, had lessened. Something had been stripped from her, torn away by the roots. Nekoka had a guess at the name: praena. These people they were 'saving' would never be the same. They had been too late.

As Sepia passed into the room, almost timidly, the others followed. Nekoka hung back, letting them enter first, though her whiskers twitched to know what exactly was in there. She slipped in behind the last, a small woman with sunken eyes.

The ceiling was high. The room was square and blank except for windows at the top where sick people must have watched the letting she'd read about in the files she'd hacked. The alarm's blare was damped, not piped directly into this room of horrors. Nekoka's nose wrinkled at the sharp scent of cleaners. The entire room set her fur on end, and a low growl burred the back of her throat. It reminded her of a stage for one of those one-man slasher flicks. In the center of the room was a chair, like a dentist's chair or some sort of special brain surgical equipment. Attached to the sides were metal cuffs. A cushion was available where the head rested with straps to hold the head in place. At the base of the cushion, a hole awaited, roughly fist-sized. Positioned right behind the hole was a hefty syringe with a needle, long and shiny in the light, and a silicon tube slithering down through an opening in the floor.

The sight of that syringe sent spiders up Nekoka's back. The thing seemed to have eyes, to be looking right at her, hungry for her blood...or her praena.

Sepia glanced at the others, a sharp, jerking motion. One woman nodded at her. Another man bared his teeth. In a brutal fury, Sepia lifted her foot and pounded her heel into the contraption. The soft soles of the shoes she wore did little damage, but soon the other captives joined in on the attack. A man ripped the syringe off the stand and slammed it into the ground. An Arabic woman tugged at the metal cuffs screaming through a stream of tears. Another man, thin and emaciated, gripped the bottom of the seat and tried to tear the entire thing from the floor.

Nekoka watched.

Their yells echoed within the small chamber, an unnatural sound that felt full though it sounded hollow. It overflowed with pain and anger, harnessed by a desperate drive at vengeance, to reclaim their pride, take their dignity back. Nekoka felt surrounded by battered wives learning to rescue themselves, shrieking at the injustice of their fates.

"Where does this even go?" the woman with sunken eyes asked, staring down the hole in the floor the plastic tube had once trailed into. "What were they doing to us?"

"They were taking your praena," Nekoka offered, the sound of her statement sounding flat in her own head.

Everyone in the room looked at her. Sepia downright scowled. "What the hell's that?"

Nekoka shook her head. "Your soul, or life force.... I don't really know. It comes from the Seed."

In a sad choreography, over half the crowd reached up and touched the base of their skulls.

"Fuck that," Sepia said. "We want it back." The gathering rumbled in agreement, each one hissed and spat like a wet cat. Nekoka didn't blame them. She watched, realizing she could never understand what drove them to rip apart metal and beat at the walls. Nor did she ever want to.

Nekoka left, leaving them to their therapy and to watch for trouble that might come their way. Just outside of the hall's exit, she bumped into Berlin.

"I thought I told you to find Grace," Nekoka said over the alarm, pointing to where she could see Battle Axe looming over a mob of rescuees. Berlin didn't look as bad as Sepia—nobody had beaten him—but something vital was still missing. She wished she'd thought of bringing him a hat or sunglasses to protect his shiny white eyes. The place was piercingly bright, and he constantly squinted, hiding under the shielding of his unwashed hair.

"I wanted to help you," he said, barely audible over the blaring noise. She could track the movement of his white eyes, even if she wasn't quite sure where he was looking. They never stilled. She wrapped him up in her arms, again, unable to resist consoling him, touching him. Making sure he was really there and safe. Though he was larger than she was, she wanted to let him know she would always protect him.

But she hadn't. Nekoka had let the enemy, whoever they were, take him away after she had claimed him as her own.

She'd let him down.

"I'm sorry, Berlin." Her voice hitched. *I left you here, and they vivisected you, and I should have tried to get you out.* But he couldn't hear her thoughts, and she couldn't birth the words.

Berlin petted her. "You have nothing to be sorry for. You didn't do this to me."

"But..." She tried again. He *needed* to know. "I left you." *I failed you.*

He cooed at her. "You came back for me. You couldn't save me on your own, and so you got help and came back for me." She felt the press of his lips to the side of her head. "You didn't fail me."

Nekoka blinked. Had he heard her? Read her mind? Or had she actually spoken aloud, loud enough he could hear her over the incessant alarm? Berlin's kindness burned in her chest. She *had* failed him. But Nekoka wasn't one to dwell on the past. That was done and gone, swept under the rug. She could only face the future, and for that, she would fight. There might be more of these compounds around, and she would find them all and tear them to the ground. Brick by brick.

"Will you be okay?" she asked, offering a soothing purr.

Berlin smiled shyly, sweetly almost. She couldn't wait to get him home and wash him up again. Dress him in new clothes with a new hat.

"Yeah, I'm fine. Now." He glanced beyond Nekoka down the hall. An avalanche of curses tumbled around with the sound of screaming metal. "Your friend is killing that thing."

Nekoka tilted her head, studying him. "Don't you need any vengeance?"

Berlin turned away from the hallway to face the corner of the room. He shrugged. "I guess I'm not that vengeful, as long as I know it isn't going to happen anymore. I would like to ask *it*, though." He gestured to the empty corner.

"What?" Nekoka glanced between Berlin and the wall.

"The shadows. They're there, watching. I don't think they're happy."

"Wait?" Nekoka stared hard at Berlin, then back to the corner, swiveling her ears forward. "You telling me people are there? Are they invisible?" To her *kokogyo* senses, there were no personal electronics. Her eyes, ears, and whiskers caught nothing. She'd had it up to her chin with fighting enemies she couldn't sense.

Berlin's previously shy look vanished in a blink of his white eyes. "Yes, I think. I can see them, though. Nobody notices them but me."

"I'm going to get John over here." She hailed John via text, each minor use of *kokogyo* less of a strain as her body slowly recovered from her previous exertions. Last thing she wanted was an ambush, a swarm of these *shadows* to smother them all. "So, it's not a dead person, a soul?" Nekoka had no idea how Berlin's power worked, what exactly he could see.

Berlin shook his head. "No, they're not human. They've never been human."

That proverbial dawn broke.

The Founders.

"There's more going on here than a little kidnap and murder," Nekoka said. Berlin snorted.

"Nekoka?" Blood splattered John's arms and legs, and holes spotted the material on his armored vest.

"Wow." Her brows rose. "You took a beating."

John puffed out his chest, looking pleased and prideful. "Well, yeah, some of us had to fight those bastards while you were out socializing."

"Um, guys," Berlin said.

Nekoka tilted her ear towards Berlin, but continued to defend herself. She did have her pride. "I was letting the prisoners free!"

"So, up there..." Berlin continued.

"Yeah, about that...." John scowled. "The guards shot some. A few died."

Nekoka hissed, but then John held out his hands to placate her. "The rest are...ambulatory. Ready to get out of here. Why did you need me?"

"Over there—" Nekoka pointed, "—by that corner, is there anyone invisible?"

John popped into alertness and peered at the corner. His eyes narrowed. "No...but.... No. Wait. There's nobody there, but, ah, something odd. Well...that's new. Not a *life* like I'm used to seeing."

The siren cut out. In the void, Nekoka's ears rang.

Berlin grabbed Nekoka's shoulder and pointed up. "There's something coming through the vents!"

A thin mist-like cloud drifted from the horizontal slats of the ceiling-high vent.

The intercom blared a commanding male voice. "*Evacuate. All personnel evacuate. Abandon Minidoka.*" A resounding clank from the cages echoed through the air before the siren began to whoop again.

For a moment everyone stilled, caught by the order. Across the vast room, Pablo screamed for everyone not to panic and head towards the doors. Sepia's gang, watchful and defensive, jogged out of the hallway. Nekoka, Berlin, and John joined their wake as they headed towards where Battle Axe was waving them over.

Nekoka's brain scanned through the data on Whisker. Gas. Gas.

There. The final contingency.

"Get out! Everyone, get out," she screamed. "Get them out, Pablo!" She turned to John, grabbing his shirt. "It's a poison mist. Bad for everyone, even Seeded with boosted tolerance. We need to get out now."

"Can't you stop it?" John asked.

Nekoka zipped through the files on Whisker. "Yes, maybe. I need to get to the maintenance room one floor up. I think I can shut down the vents at least."

She turned to run, but Berlin grabbed her. "I'm coming too."

Nekoka shook her head. She would not put another one of hers in any more danger. Berlin had already suffered enough. "Please, go with John. I can get in and out better on my own." She flashed him a smile. "I can get quite little, remember." Not that she thought she'd be able to shift that much so soon.

Berlin looked almost ready to cry, but he nodded. He lunged for her, hugged her ferociously, then let go, and stepped away.

As she ran for the double doors, Berlin and John were calling out, getting people to snap out of their daze. The spicy scent of cinnamon tickled her nose, overpowering the persistent metallic scent. The gas was filling the room.

She sent out an all-team text, explaining about the deadly poison now flooding Minidoka.

Jenni? Jenni! Just get out! Okay. Just get out!

No response. Jenni was still too far away. And she got no response through Whisker.

She pushed through the mob, twisting her lithe body to press through, then she was running down the hall, heading for the stairs that would take her one level up to the maintenance room. Someone behind yelled out in shock. She tried to take shallow breaths, but she was moving fast and even though she was a shapeshifter and could modify herself in so many ways, she couldn't stop her need for air.

She tore through the door to the stairway, charged up the steps two at a time. The gas was growing thick; cinnamon and now a hint of sourness scented the air. She pressed her nostrils shut, then opened them for a deep breath, then shut them tight again. Her head was beginning to spin.

On the next floor up, one floor underground, more alarms were going off, and she could smell the hint of fire mixed in with cinnamon and sour.

Yabai. They must be hiding their tracks, purifying this level of hell in its own cleansing flames.

CHAPTER 45

Berlin

Now that she had come for him, he scoffed that Nekoka thought he would let her go off on her own. She was his as much as he was hers. Though she was fast, shifting her body in contortionist ways to get through the crowd, Berlin was determined. He was weak and tired and felt generally like a locomotive had rolled him over, but so did everyone else. He found an elbow and a polite "Excuse me" worked well enough amidst the mob.

When he got through, he saw the stairway door closing. She must have gone there. He trotted along the hallway, his arm covering his mouth, mind churning over various scenarios as to what the gas would do. It wasn't like the wet mist that made powers not work, it was more insidious, like a fog bank rising from the Willamette in winter.

The stairway had lights flashing red, a warning, an alarm to evacuate. Berlin was already losing his get-up-and-go. One step, another, and another. He would make it. The ghosts had followed him, swirling around, playing in the gas, calling to Berlin. "You can play with us soon."

Berlin growled. "I play with you, anyway."

"We'll play forever!"

Berlin ignored them. The encompassing cinnamon began to make his mouth water. When was the last time he'd had a cinnamon roll?

The next floor had an altogether different scent. Charred paper, burned plaster, and the delicious spice.

Nekoka yarled somewhere up front. Berlin ran down the hall past a series of doors. The smell of fire grew stronger. He followed another hiss and found Nekoka in a room with computers and banks of gray cabinets with lights and buttons.

"What can I do?" Berlin asked.

Nekoka twitched an ear at him. He hoped she wasn't mad. "Find out how to shut down the HVAC system." She sat at a computer, the screen flicking from one page to another, pictures and tabs that Berlin couldn't study long enough to understand. He went back to a wall of switches and buttons. None of them said HVAC.

The crackling of fire drew his attention; he peeked out the door towards an open area with desks and cubical walls. In a corner, a fire licked up the walls.

"Nekoka?"

"I know. I can't turn on the fire suppressant, and I can't shut the air units down."

She popped to her feet and ran for the door, grabbing Berlin's hands in her own. "If I had more time.... Bastards. They'll destroy all the physical evidence."

Berlin's lungs were burning now, as well as his nose and eyes. He didn't want to say anything, because Nekoka must be feeling it too. As they dashed up the next set of stairs, he fell, banging his knee, his cry of pain buried under the siren. Shock gave him pause. His legs just stopped working. Nekoka spun around, and grew big, right there, and hoisted him up like he was a princess. His head rested against her chest, her arms were tight around him, and surrounding them was the cloud of poison.

It took a minute for Berlin to notice, but Nekoka kept saying, "It'll be okay. We're almost out. It'll be okay."

Of course, it would be okay, he wanted to tell her. You've got me.

When they came out at the top of the next set of stairs, a flash flood of chaos washed away Berlin's sense of reality. Other people were here; guards and scientists from the compound and heroes he knew. Starburst was throwing guards around as everyone tried to make for the door. Dark tentacles of shadow—not the things watching him, but actual shadow—were pummeling others.

A man with a pack on his back sprayed something over the crowd. He swept it left and right, and Nekoka twisted around, hunching herself over Berlin, letting the liquid land on her back instead of hitting him. The scent was unmistakable.

It was the stuff they sprayed over them when he was in the cage. The stuff that killed powers.

The shadow arms disappeared; Starburst's fire sputtered into smoke.

Nekoka's grip failed, and she dropped him as she slumped to the ground. Her fur sloughed off like a layer of moss, her body mass dimmed to her normal size, the ears and tail gone. Nekoka lay there, naked and gasping, dark brown eyes blinking, looking lost and desperate and afraid.

All around, his comrades fell like dead trees in a windstorm. Soon, no one would be left standing.

"Run," Nekoka gasped. "The elevator...that way."

The gas kept coming, flaring pain throughout his body, and the guards ran by in their evacuation. Berlin could hear shots bark through the klaxon wails. A downed person flinched. Berlin sobbed out in fury. Who was that? Had a guard shot one of his saviors as the bastards fled the compound?

They would all die here. Nekoka and Jenni, his only friends other than a crazy homeless man who talked to God. Berlin didn't know anything about God, but he did know about ghosts. In this chamber of torment, the specters swirled around him, mournful wails shivering his belly. Ghosts of the recent dead and others which had hitchhiked with their saviors. The gray dead were everywhere. Cried for justice. Lying next to Nekoka's human body, Berlin screamed — a tuneless cry, more a sound than words. Primal. Desperate. In his mind he begged, pleading for the dead to help him. It was pure need, life and death and nothing more.

The poison in the air clouded his lungs. His body lost tension. It wouldn't work anymore. But his power still did. Nekoka had saved him from the spray. She was always saving him.

"Help me! Help us all. Stop the gas. Stop the guards." It became a mantra, a chant that entwined with his one long call, high and desperate and so, so needy. He needed their help or Nekoka would die, he would die, they all would die.

Berlin tightened his power, sending the ghosts to the air vents, letting them pull at the slats, affect the world, solidify enough to stall any more gas from flooding the compound.

The air thickened around the edges of the room as the spirits obeyed his desperation.

CHAPTER 46

The Myroi

The praenletta were revolting. From the dark recesses beyond its sight, the moiety watched as the enriched praenletta escaped the cages the traitorous praenletta had explained would hold them forever. Not that forever was required, only three lettings and the cage would be available for the next.

The dampening agent that Myroi had given the praenletta sprayed from the ceiling in liquid form. They called it Nutrix. Every singularity required a name.

Few things had enough value to require a name.

They were all praenletta. Each and every one.

The white enriched praenletta, the one with empty eyes that could see more than the others, was screaming. The moiety saw a reflection of the precious praena from the praenletta flare up in a singular blaze. Then, it became aware of something new. Other energies were amassing, filling the room and the cavern. To its vision, lacking in this solid world, it could barely read the colors, formless yet distinct. There were traces of praena in each energy, only tarnished. Impure. So unlike the pure essence letted from the praenletta.

The moiety was watching. The bright flashes of color shimmering over their forms conveyed the need to do something about these new, unwhole praenletta who seeped into the cavern.

One of the moiety flashed pink then blue as a crowd of the new unwhole praenletta descended upon it and the blue grew brighter and brighter. Chaos. Uncertainty. Emotion. The single Myroi was no more.

It watched. Stunned. Unable to act. A slow slip of force pulled it. A summoning by the white praenletta. It fought, seeking out its moiety. But they were gone. Vanished.

It was the single one left. A true singularity. It flashed through an array of colors. It struggled, pulsing and turning. Confused and unsure, drawn down to the white praenletta, it was carried to it on a gust of air.

No. This would not be. The single Myroi thrust itself towards the praenletta, phased through its solid body, and seeped *into* its bones.

And as it settled into the cells of the (human, man, Berlin Fischer, lonely, person) it knew (fear) and (panic) and (love) as it looked down at another praenletta (Nekoka, woman, friend, love) and felt sadness as the Nutrix battled with the implanted (Seed) within its body.

It understood want. It understood hope. It understood individuality in that brief instant when their beings merged and in that membrane between one second to the next, it knew that what the Myroi were doing to these humans, to save themselves, was wrong.

CHAPTER 47

Nekoka

Flashes of pain, like little bombs of napalm, exploded over her entire body. Her skin was on fire, scorching, growing roots of thorns into her flesh. Gas filled her lungs, and she knew...she knew she'd failed. Failed Berlin. And Jenni. And everyone else out there.

Her lungs spasmed, causing her to gasp, and the fire continued to burn. A gunshot rang out, and then there was only the siren. She'd nearly made it. Nearly gotten them out.

Nothing had ever hurt like this before.

She pried open her eyes and realized there was no real fire—that was downstairs. No red flames. Just Berlin, glowing with a shimmering aura. *Glowing.* His body lay slumped on the ground, motionless.

"No." She tried to reach out. Her arm wouldn't move. She spotted herself. Her hairless, naked self. Panic set her heart flittering in her chest, a weak and unsteady cadence.

She was human...normal...useless. No wonder she had failed. Somehow, they had killed the Seed inside of her. Burned out all that was special.

Her mind buzzed. A colony of bees had moved in between her eyes and were telling her stories of destruction. She blinked. Berlin still glowed. She was still normal. Someone said something, not far away, but Nekoka couldn't tease out real language from the sound. Bile bubbled up from her throat.

Normal and dying.

The bile turned to harsh acid. Her blood to ice. Everything within her raged. The swarm of bees morphed into a swarm of ants that crawled under her skin. Everything within her had turned toxic.

Nekoka squeezed her eyes shut and prayed that Jenni had gotten away. That Jenni was out of there with all the other people they'd freed and the other heroes, and they were all running across miles of empty fields.

Above her—maybe it was a trick of the light—the air was filling with a different kind of gas. A thicker soup that churned and swirled like a mesmerizing mixture of gray shades of paint.

Ghosts. It must be Berlin's ghosts. And they were everywhere. She could see them. Nekoka sighed, but it turned into a wracking cough. She guessed she sat on the cusp of death. As the pain spiked each nerve, she welcomed it.

"Nekoka!"

Nekoka sucked in air. Her body spasmed, sending her gut into a titan cramp. That was Jenni! Jenni was *here*. Still *inside*. No, Nekoka wanted to say. Run! Nekoka couldn't die now, because right here, somewhere near, Jenni was in danger.

Her tongue wouldn't work, not that Jenni could hear her through the whooping alarm.

"Nekoka!" Jenni's voice was going frantic. Nekoka tried to cry out, flick her tail that wasn't there or lift her hand, but nothing would move.

Something touched her bare skin, and it was agony. She swallowed her scream—she didn't have the energy anyway—and forced her eyes open. Jenni, a cut down her cheek, standing livid against her smooth flesh. Nekoka read the exhaustion in every line of her face, saw the desperation etch out its home in the edges of her eyes.

Nekoka bubbled up a groan, which was all she was able to do as Jenni lifted her up. Each connection of pressure on her skin felt like needles jammed into her bones. The pain scorched her mind into oblivion.

CHAPTER 48

Jenni

The siren blared on, so monotonous Jenni McGuire could ignore it, like the ticking of a clock setting the slow decay of time. They'd broken into the compound, fought guards, and found their way down into this vast prison. A SWAT team had captured a few of their numbers, knocking down their effectiveness until others had rescued them, just before she'd noticed the gas and received Nekoka's warning text. Jenni could not fathom how people could do that to each other. Nekoka's team had already gotten everyone out of their cages by the time Jenni's had arrived. Minnie had erupted into tears at the sight, working hard to heal those in the most immediate need, including several who had been recently shot.

She'd discovered Grace casting a wide spell over everyone. When she saw Jenni, she gestured her over, her attention lingering over the cut on her cheek.

"You need to get everyone out," Jenni told her ex. "We've got to save as many as we can."

"I know!" Grace's eyes blazed. "These people will be very susceptible to this gas due to their current physical status. I'm trying to, oh, I don't know, boost their immune systems. I don't even know if it will work," she added desperately.

Jenni cursed, looking over the tired, weak men and women. "The front elevator only takes so many people. Can you take them back the way you entered?"

Grace nodded. "Zack's got it covered."

Jenni called out for Chandler, who appeared from nowhere, his arm over his mouth. "We should get out of here," he mumbled, eyeing the gas seeping from the vents.

"Agreed." She thought about the size of the elevator in which they descended, a normal sized box that might hold ten. "Take about thirty of these people out the way we came in. Take them up in shifts and come back to get more when you're done. Got it?"

"Me?" Chandler asked. "If you say so—if they even notice me."

"Can't you turn that off?" Jenni demanded.

Chandler shook his head.

"Well, get Trior to join you. I don't know, just do it."

"Trior is looking for Sepia, but fine. Got it."

Jenni turned her back on him, forgetting he had even been there when she asked Grace, "Where is Nekoka?"

Jenni didn't want to get into it with Grace. They both recognized the need for a serious discussion, but now was not the time. Grace made her decision back in New Orleans, and in a way, Jenni was thankful to her for that. She loved Grace, beautiful and kind Gracie, but both of them knew it wasn't enough.

"She went down that hall." Grace pointed, not meeting Jenni's eyes. "She was going to stop the poisonous gas release, I think."

Jenni was already on the run. Some middle-aged guy fell to his knees, gasping. Time, ticking by with the whoop whoop of the alarm, was counting down for all of them. The gas continued to hiss into the room.

Her phone buzzed. As Jenni tore through the stairwell, banging the metal door against the wall, she checked the screen, hoping for something from Nekoka. It was from Trior: Ground Level, more bad guys.

Crap.

Hopping up the steps as fast as her legs would let her go, a gunshot ratcheted her worry. On the next level up, she spotted a mass of swirling gray mixing with acrid gas. Jenni wasn't sure what the hell that was, another gaseous weapon? A whiff of smoke caught her attention. Was the compound on fire?

Doors lined the long hall, and Jenni checked each one, calling out telepathically and with her aching lungs. The floor appeared empty.

"Nekoka!"

Upstairs, she must be upstairs.

Jenni raced up the next flight and banged through the stairway door and ran down a hall to another stairway. She hadn't been to this area yet, wasn't sure where she was. People were lying everywhere. Starburst! Some coughing, several struggling to their feet. That chemical smell of the power dampener one of the myriad of stinks tainting the air. Then her gaze snagged on something glowing. *Berlin?* He lay on the ground, his skin giving off a gray light.

She ran to his side. With a gentle touch to his throat, she discovered a pulse, weak but steady.

Poor kid. What was he doing up here? Following his hero, probably. Jenni scanned the room. Her eyes snapped to the prone form of Nekoka...furless, human, but still Nekoka. Nekoka's Japanese features were stronger as a human than as a felinoid human. It was odd, how Jenni's attention focused on that. Her hair was darker, her skin had warm yellowish undertones Jenni had never seen before, and her eyes lost their cat roundness and were a dark, chocolate brown, almost black. This was Nekoka before her awakening, before she became who she was meant to be. But it was still Nekoka.

"Nekoka!"

The mass of gray continued to churn like a chaotic storm, swirling against the walls near the ceilings, far enough from Jenni that she didn't give it much thought. Nekoka took up all of that.

"Nekoka." Oh God, was she breathing? "Nekoka. I'm here. Nekoka, don't be dead. Are you okay? *Please.*"

Jenni coughed. Her lungs burned like she'd snorted a pile of powdered ghost peppers. Searching for aid, she noticed the gas wasn't coming through the gray mass. There was no smoke. She scooped her arms around Nekoka's body, trying not to touch her damp skin with her own flesh. Nekoka whimpered and then screamed when Jenni lifted her up.

Jenni stilled, holding her breath, examining Nekoka's face. It was passive now, no more flinches, no more scrunched-up masks of agony. She hefted Nekoka easily, her friend's body a fluff of weight. She needed to get her to Minnie. Minnie would give Nekoka a clean slate of health, no more pain, no more poison. Nekoka groaned. Jenni almost dropped her, needing to touch her, to stop touching her. Nekoka couldn't die. Of everyone here, it was Nekoka Jenni wanted to save. Nekoka above all else.

Stupid cat. Getting herself into this situation. Didn't she think?

Jenni glanced back at Berlin, still glowing. How how was she going to get them out of here? And Trior and Starburst? Her eyes scanned the ten or so people gassed out splayed across the floor. Screw it. One step at a time. She grabbed Nekoka and tossed her over one shoulder. A cut Jenni had received on her arm gnawed at her with persistent glee, the blood seeping out sluggish, but steady. Nekoka weighed so little, she knew she could toss Berlin over her other shoulder. It wouldn't be the most eloquent of fireman holds, but she didn't have time to worry about the inconsequentials.

She turned around to grab Berlin when she stopped in mid-step. Standing next to Berlin were two men in half-face respirators: a barrel-chested white man dressed in a suit that screamed business executive flanked by a mousy Indian man in light blue scrubs. The doctor carried a steel case, something, to Jenni's untrained eye, which might contain biological samples.

"Sir, that's, ah, Jennifer McGuire and Michiko Yoshida," said the doctor, body turned away as if to continue down the hall in flight. If Nekoka were awake, she'd know who they were; Jenni, with no specs on, had no clue. "Two top tier Seeded. Jennifer, that's, ah, Fiann, is fast, strong, and telepathic." Jenni took a step away from the men, away from Berlin. "Michiko is a shape-changer. Scratch, or Nekoka...you've heard of her. She's the escapee. She, well, she normally doesn't appear human." The gas mask muffled his tentative speech.

Neither of the men had pale eyes. Did they have more of the spray to terminate Seeded abilities? While the white guy was built, Jenni was sure she could throw him down like a misbehaving ghetto junkie. However, being five foot five if stretched on a rack, if her enhanced strength failed her, she'd fall like a field of wheat in a storm. The hair on her arms prickled. Maybe she should run.

"Miss McGuire." The businessman pulled his shoulders back, enhancing his stature, if that was possible. "You and your companions," his gaze lingered over the fallen, "have destroyed this research compound." His eyes gleamed with coldness.

Nekoka coughed, her body jerking across Jenni's shoulder.

"Mr. Hallaman, I, ah, gotta go and deliver these..." The smaller man edged toward a door, feet slowly inching him away in tiny little shimmies.

"Go, I'll handle this." Mr. Hallaman shifted his weight as the other man bounded off like a deer escaping a forest inferno, metal case clasped to his chest. Jenni wanted to know what was in that case and what damage potential it held.

She glanced down at Nekoka. She had more important things to worry about. With one step back, she had a better view of Berlin. She took mere seconds to scan around her, but the edges of the room weren't visible through the gray storm and smoke. With this goon in her way, she worried she couldn't get to Berlin in time, couldn't save both him and Nekoka.

Minnie, can you hear me?

Nothing. Only her own desperate thoughts. Jenni hoped Minnie hadn't been doused in that liquid, prayed she was just beyond her normal telepathic range.

Berlin groaned. Again, Jenni's eyes darted to him. His glow had turned incandescent while his body arced, his back tightly bowed as if caught in a seizure. He thrashed and twisted. Jenni returned her attention to the man. "Stop whatever it is you're doing to him."

"Why don't you put her down?" said Mr. Hallaman.

"Why don't you back away, let me pass, and I won't hand you your ass?" Jenni counter offered.

Mr. Hallaman shook his head, like her choice had disappointed him, and it irked her to no end. He removed his gas mask to speak. "Miss McGuire, I have no argument with you. None. We can do this the hard way, or—"

"Oh for God's sake, shut up." Jenni pivoted her body to keep Nekoka far away from this man, and with a closed fist, struck.

The man's lip split under her strike, blood bubbling from the cut. Shock splashed across his face, then a resignation that caused Jenni to scramble back. He gingerly felt the cut, looking down at the blood on his finger. In the next instant, he reached out, grabbed her arm, and dug his bloodied fingers into the cut there. He was fast, not superhuman fast, but she hadn't expected him to target her wound. She should have known better.

Then, he rubbed his bloody fingers back over his lip. A shiver ran over his body as he spat on the ground. This wasn't good. Whatever this was, it wasn't good.

Jenni took a step away. The man replaced his mask, smiled, almost sadly, and said, "Perhaps you didn't understand me. Put her down."

Jenni set Nekoka gently on the ground.

In the next instant, her heart pounded in her chest. What just happened?

"Thank you. I've a problem, and I need your help. You see, the Director of this compound is blackmailing me, and I don't feel my survival once I've left the compound and the organization is guaranteed. You need to come with me. You must serve me. You must protect *me*."

Mr. Hallaman walked towards her. He did not have pale eyes. They were dark blue.

Why would you do this? she asked him as he drew closer, hoping he'd leak more information if she asked him telepathically.

"We've all found a cage, Miss McGuire," he said out loud, while his mind flashed a jumble of images, an Asian man and a younger woman being prevalent within them. With Nekoka and those she was close to, Jenni gleaned emotions, but strangers only presented cold images and words. "Sometimes it's of our own construction, often it's built with the help of outside hands. Now, let me tell you about how your life will continue in the future."

Unable to move, the man told her of how she would help him leave this compound. Protect him against her allies. Help him against the Asian man from his memories, whom he called Director Jeon. And once he was safe, she would be free.

Why are they doing this? she asked. She tried to wiggle her fingers, her toes, but she only got minute twitches.

Letting, came his immediate, unintended response.

"Why, Miss McGuire," he said aloud, plainly unaware he'd given an answer, the meaning of which she didn't quite understand, "they are harvesting something from us." He laughed bitterly. "Apparently, *they* put it there, in our heads, and now they wish to take it out." The man's face morphed into a feral gnashing of teeth. "No matter the cost."

I will not help.

The man was nearly chest to chest with Jenni now.

"Not them, certainly. Their agenda is not mine. Just protect me until I no longer need it. You cannot deny me," he said.

She was locked down, a statue of protesting muscle and attitude, her gaze always on his dark blue eyes. Action, she was all about action, and here she was, unable to move, unable to exert her will. Completely disarmed. She glared, she hissed through clenched teeth, she tried to distract herself by images of mountains, or flames, of a simple star, but her mind kept coming to Nekoka's furless face, her even, blunt teeth, those almond-shaped, black eyes.

I will deny you.

The flames from the office fire were eating their way towards them, the smoke clogging the air. Berlin's body was banging against the floor. In an instant of distraction, Mr. Hallaman narrowed his eyes, attention drawn to the flames and Berlin's convulsions. The rigor in Jenni's body weakened. She jumped for him. He commanded, "Stop."

No! Jenni psychically roared, but her body stilled before her fist slammed into his perfect face.

Mr. Hallaman flinched and briefly touched his temple. "You will do as I say. We are leaving." He turned his back on her, the pompous, arrogant jackass, and began walking down the hall. "Come."

The fire crackled as it ate along the walls, feeding on the plaster, scorching the whitewash.

I can't leave her.

But she followed her puppet master, anyway, leaving behind Nekoka and Berlin to the burgeoning inferno.

No!

Without turning his back, Mr. Hallaman said, reasonably, "I learned a lot from working at Minidoka. The biggest lesson is to make plans upon plans to protect yourself. You should know, Miss McGuire, that you are weak because of your attachment to that woman." He stopped and looked behind Jenni. "Someone took my most precious person from me, and I was freed."

A feral scowl twisted his handsome features.

"She's been neutralized. A feeble, simple human now. She will be no help to you and has not long to live. Do you want to kill her, Miss McGuire? It would be a mercy."

Fuck you!

Mr. Hallaman bared his teeth and roared, "You cannot save them all!"

Jenni took a step forward. And another. Towards this brutal man, away from Nekoka. *No.* No, she would *not* do this. This would *not* happen. She gasped, her body jerking, legs stilling an instant, but then he looked at her, eyes widening as he pushed his power into her.

Jenni couldn't breathe. Nothing was working; her muscles were not listening. Like an outside observer, she walked away from her best friend. Could hear the flames crackle and feel the sweat streak down her temples, between her breasts and shoulder blades. No. No. She could not abandon them to the fire. Never.

Behind her, she heard Nekoka's soft whimper over the roar of the flames.

Jenni took one step. Another. And slowly, struggling, she walked away.

CHAPTER 49

Thomas

Jenni McGuire. Fiann. Top tier, but certainly no Samantha Fontos or Zackary Silversmith. But still, she was fighting against Thomas' mind control.

Nobody withstood his mind control.

Thomas wanted out, out of this trap, out of this tomb. He harbored no expectations that the flash drive holding the truth of Thomas' Seeded nature and key to the deposit box would ever land in his hand. These people wouldn't want any proof to remain. He wouldn't be allowed survival. Or they had backups, and their constant threat would hang over him. He needed this person to fight for him. But she wasn't giving in to his influence.

He had to break her.

If he dug down inside himself and fished out the truth, he didn't want to do this. He had no grudge against the shapeshifter. But Fiann had to work for him and for her to be fully his, he must *break her.*

And the way she looked at Nekoka, Thomas hoped that woman's death would tear the roots from her stalwart conviction.

He'd made a mistake joining the Minidoka Project. He knew how men of power worked. He understood the grand schemes and the bright dreams. Understood the thrill of having others do as they were told. He, himself, thrilled under such power, but he valued true power, not this crutch of alien delivered abilities. As a professional, he never allowed himself to rely on his mind control. Only weak men bent others without having earned such respect or fear.

But now those far more driven than he threatened him, offering the empty promise of continued anonymity. Thomas was not naïve. He still planned on leaving it all behind, starting anew, but he doubted he would make it very far if Jeon survived.

Someone was always watching.

And it made him angry. Being watched. Being lied to and tricked.

Jenni roared.

Second thoughts drove up a cloud of guilt. An image of charred, crisp bodies already haunted him, and the deed hadn't even been done. Part of his response, he knew, was immature. Childish. He was lashing out in anger, a jealous impulse that Jenni McGuire had someone still, someone she would do anything for. He'd had someone once.

But he did need her. Did need to break her, no matter how petty the root of his actions were.

A dull ache throbbed constantly in his temples; the alarms threatened to fan it into a ceaseless pounding.

Why? Why would you make me do this thing? she yelled into his head. *Let me go. I have to save them.*

"Stop that!" Thomas hunched over, propping himself up against his knees. It felt like Battle Axe was cleaving through his skull with his signature weapon. Such strength to defend against his command.

He straightened and turned to her. Though the poison seemed to have stopped, the air was getting thick with smoke; his eyes watered and he was thankful for his respirator.

Miss McGuire's pale green eyes narrowed, her entire face twisted, teeth bared. The tendons popped out along her neck and shoulders. He could feel her fighting back. Feel his power, normally smooth like a greased wheel, grind up against this woman's will.

She no longer followed him. Had planted herself on the tiles.

Despite the fat drops pooling in her eyes, her expression masked authentic grief. Instead, it hinted at simmering fury. The throbbing ratcheted up in his head, now a jackhammer drummed away inside.

"Would you just give in!" he demanded, fighting. Fighting.

Red color swirled through the woman's light green eyes. Bright, incandescent, full-on fire-alarm red. Then Fiann's face shifted. Morphed. Cheekbones sharpened as a demon's visage looked back at him, a wicked grin full of pointed teeth. A lance of pain sliced into Thomas' brain, as she threw her head back and screamed.

CHAPTER 50

Jenni

Why? Why would you make me do this thing?

When Mr. Hallaman had suggested she kill Nekoka, Jenni's fingers had flexed and images of her hands giving in, sinking into Nekoka's neck, twisting and squeezing, stabilized Jenni's fortifications against the man's power.

Let me go. I have to save them.

She sent out another plea to Minnie before she abandoned that idea as folly: Minnie would have to face this demon as well. So, Jenni once again dug into his mind. There had to be something, something here that would help her win, some hidden secret, some weakness to be revealed, because it couldn't end like this. This was not her fate.

In an instant, pain ignited in her skull like a lightning strike, plunging her mind into an abyss of ice.

"Stop that!" Mr. Hallaman roared.

A voice. Another voice spoke in her head. *Hello, my capall.*

An inky cold sensation writhed within Jenni's consciousness. The words, they weren't from outside. They did not come from without like Nekoka's mental voice or anyone else she had communicated with before. "Hello, my capall" came from within her own head.

Lend me thy reins and release my power.

The man was facing her now. He would make her leave, abandon them to the flames and to the guards and force her on anyone he had a sick urge to kill and torture.

Together we will teach this mortal man deference for the will of the gods.

Who are you? Jenni asked, seeking the internal voice even as she continued to fight the imperative to follow the businessman away from Nekoka.

A low chuckle, a sound so seductive a heated shiver shook Jenni's body. She ground her teeth.

Your marcach. Your voice of Rage. The one who knows the Names and can sing the Songs. I am Durrachan. Durra. The *vengeful spirit.*

The words swirled like blood through Jenni's veins, sending trails of ice to every cell of her body. But deep in her head, at the back of her skull, heat flared.

These words, in an innate sense of awareness, Jenni understood their origin was the Seed.

Can you help me fight this monster? Save Nekoka? Jenni's eyes burned in her frustration and terror. What would this voice require in exchange for aid? Could Jenni even pay the price?

"Would you just give in!" Mr. Hallaman commanded, the words taking over Jenni's body. Her fingers closed.

Never! She thrust the word at Mr. Hallaman as she opened herself to the Seed.

CHAPTER 51

Thomas

The screech coming from Fiann's throat was not human. Thomas stepped back, his pulse shifting into overdrive. It took him just seconds, a mere span of a few breaths, to realize what was happening. Before his very eyes, Jennifer McGuire's Seed was evolving. A new power was growing. Though her body did not transform like Scratch's, it embraced a remarkable visage shift. It wasn't something he had any time to examine, though, before she completely shrugged off his compulsion and threw herself at him, screeching like a devil.

This new form, this...Banshee, went for his throat. It was alarming how swiftly the tables turned; suddenly, he was in for the fight of his life. He had no physical enhancements like Fiann. He did not stand a chance.

He dug into his pocket, stumbling backward as her fingers—claws—brushed against the skin of his neck. Then a fist sank into his gut.

Everything left him. His air, his awareness, nearly the contents of his stomach.

She screamed again, and for a moment, Thomas' sight blanked out. He blinked furiously, backing away, until sight returned, the edges still dark and grainy. Finally, his fingers landed on the emergency spray canister of Nutrix.

Bear spray for Seeded.

A claw sliced across his face, catching his gas mask. Another punch to the face shifted the mask enough to break the seal. He yanked his hand from his pocket, aimed the canister, and released it.

A jet of Nutrix coated the frenzied woman in a forceful spray. The reaction was nearly instantaneous once a certain percentage of body coverage occurred. To Thomas' surprise and relief, instead of just cutting her off from her power, shifting her from this Banshee into a manageable Jennifer McGuire, the woman collapsed to the ground, a bundle of bones and unresponsive muscle.

Thomas touched his face. His nose might be broken. Blood trickled along a stinging cut across his jaw.

He had failed to tame her. He kicked her in the gut, the air huffing from her lips, then turned to evacuate.

He would face Jeon and the Chief on his own.

He had plans to leave the country. Bitter laughter burned his lips. Knew this would happen. The moment he'd discovered the dark secret, he knew there was no exit strategy. They had trapped him.

Still, he had prepared for this. The documents. The plane ticket. The new life in the Caribbean awaited him. A new life meant new opportunities. Perhaps he could save the Caribbean like he was trying to save America. Make it safe for everyone.

First, to deal with Director Jeon.

As he fled down the hallway, away from the escalating fire, movement speared his attention. The woman was crawling towards her friend. They would hunt him too, if they survived. He hoped they would never make it out of those flames, but knew he wasn't that lucky.

CHAPTER 52

Nekoka

When Nekoka first became aware, a plethora of beeps and electronic buzzes greeted her. All around her, computers were talking to each other and sending messages to receivers farther away. Messages like blood pressure rate and sugar levels and brain activity. She was in a hospital.

Bundles of data communication zoomed from the watchful equipment in a kaleidoscope of information. Data she couldn't quite access but sensed streamed from phones and other equipment that had electronic data exchange. But without Whisker, she couldn't capture it. She couldn't talk to anyone. *Kokogyo* reached out, strained to gather information that was just beyond reach.

Jenni?

Someone squeezed her hand. She tried to open her eyes. Some goo was spread over them, blurring everything into a muted mud Edvard Munch painting.

"Nekoka?" Jenni said, soft and heavy, like every one of her worries clung to that word.

Nekoka licked her lips. Her tongue was dry, a slab of cardboard in her mouth.

Thirsty.

Nekoka tried to send her *kokogyo* senses out to Whisker.... She still couldn't find it. The monitor beeped as her heart rate increased. Whisker had died again. Maybe that was it. Jenni was charging it somewhere. All that data. All those secrets. All that hand-constructed computing power.

Jenni helped Nekoka lean forward, and a cup was placed to her lips. Nekoka drank, little sips because she didn't want to make a mess. It took time before she felt sated. Jenni didn't complain. Nekoka purred in thanks.

"How—" she had to stop and swallow. "How is everyone?"

Two hands took up hers. Nekoka blinked against the goo.

"Not okay. Not everyone," Jenni said.

You? Nekoka couldn't voice such a question out loud.

Jenni paused, and Nekoka's heart rate monitor began to sing quickly again. "I'm okay," Jenni said. "Listen, Nekoka...we saved a lot of people."

But not everyone?

"No. Not everyone made it."

Nekoka blinked again. She needed to see Jenni's face. She needed to see everything.

"The gas?" Nekoka asked. The gas, the fire, or the guards. Take your pick.

"Some, yeah. A lot of the prisoners were already sick and weak, and the gas killed a few." Jenni'd never sounded so hollow. "But all of them would have died if you hadn't found that place and called us in." She tried to force some perkiness into her words, but Nekoka knew what a false perky sounded like in Jenni's voice. "And most were taken to local hospitals and got treatment. But...there were those guards. They were focusing on the rescue teams."

Nekoka knew this already. Not everyone had made it, but at least her friends—

"Anyone I know?" Nekoka asked, her voice a tiny mouse. Of course, it was people she knew, that's why Jenni was dodging even answering the question. Was it Grace? Oh God, she hoped it wasn't Grace. But Nekoka didn't ask. Just waited, wishing she didn't have this goo in her eyes.

"I can't see," she said, to fill the air.

"The gas wreaked havoc on your eyes...others, too. I didn't get much, but my eyes still burn. It degraded lung capacity as well. It was meant to liquefy the lungs, but something stopped most of it from coming through."

"I tried to shut down the HVAC, but I didn't have time to figure it out and I was too tired to dive in. So, Berlin did it." She remembered that gray mass, like smoke, but with substance. "He did it with his ghosts. I saw them, Jenni." Then it hit her. Berlin had already been badly affected by the gas, had been letted by that needle. "It's Berlin. Berlin is dead."

Jenni squeezed Nekoka's hand harder. *Yes. And Minnie. She's gone. She saved Starburst's life. She was almost killed. And Trior lost an arm and a lot of blood. Thankfully, he'll live. Others were severely injured, but they'll live. But Minnie and Berlin. They're...gone.*

Nekoka went numb. Minnie. Berlin.

A small, hollow gust of air escaped her.

Nekoka had known Minnie almost as long as Zack and Jenni. She was too sweet. Too nice. She was Nekoka's friend, the sweetest of them all.

Nekoka sobbed. "Minnie shouldn't have been there."

"No, probably not. But she wanted to. She wanted to help people. Remember, she died helping people."

She died with her lungs turning into slush, is what she did, but Nekoka didn't need to salt Jenni's wounds. Nekoka would remember, though. An image of Minnie's last minutes, her pain and struggle, building in Nekoka's mind brick by brick into a giant tower. She would remember what they did to her friends. She would remember.

And they would pay.

When she blinked at the goo, her mind stirred up Berlin's smiling white face, his innocence lending his pale skin a certain glow, a kind of luminescence that drew her in. Forever, now, it was extinguished. A dark patch in her heart.

Berlin and Minnie.

Another sob, and she couldn't quite swallow it. She squeezed her eyes shut, brought up her arm to cover her face scrunched up in anguish.

"Whisker.... I had information on Whisker." Her voice broke.

"I couldn't find your computer. You went human, and it had to be somewhere, but I didn't see it. I was busy dealing with someone else." Jenni's voice softened again with a hollow lostness that Nekoka didn't like.

Her eyes burned. Let them sting, burn for days and days, but still no tears could come. She wasn't built like that. Cats didn't cry.

"Sparks has some of the info." She remembered. "They've other compounds like this. We need to find out who was doing this." Nekoka wriggled herself to a sitting position. She couldn't allow this to continue. These places that collected the Seeded and drained their Seed of praena. What exactly was that? Nekoka would find out, and she would take them down. All of them. "We need to get everyone on board and wipe them all away."

"Nekoka..." Jenni pressed her hand to Nekoka's chest, pushing her gently back down into the hospital bed. "First, you need to get better. Starburst, Pablo, and Chandler are badly hurt. And then Trior lost his arm. Sepia is out for the count. Battle Axe has some new scars, but didn't seem too phased. The gas hurt him, but he's recovering well."

"Sally?"

Nekoka barely discerned shapes through the goo; Jenni shook her head. "No idea. She was gone by the time we were counting up our survivors and tallying our dead."

Nekoka wasn't surprised. The little deviant was probably out finding some other ways to vent her bloodthirst.

"Sparks was pretty much out of the battle, so she came out okay. If it wasn't for Starburst's armored suit, she'd be dead. Thank god for pheno-aromatic-whatever-you-call-it."

"Phenylene terephthalamides. Poly-aramids," Nekoka said dully.

A pause, and then Jenni continued. "So, Berlin, Minnie, and Trior's fighting for his life." Why was it her friends, the people she knew? She'd promised to protect them. She'd promised to look out for them. Nekoka wound her fingers in with Jenni's and pulled her forward, tugged her onto the bed.

Jenni came willingly and cuddled up beside Nekoka, wrapping her up in her arms.

There was too much goop in her eyes. She couldn't cry.

SHE WAS OUT OF ST. Luke's Medical Center the next day, taking an auto-taxi with Jenni to a bar for a group meeting. Group. What remained of the group, anyway. Boise, Idaho, was a mid-sized city, absorbing all the smaller farming communities and single homes once the corporations bought up the land for farms. The streets were filled with buzzing drones and a striking absence of street people. Maybe the Minidoka thugs had scraped these streets of homeless with a front-end loader first before they moved onto the other cities. Maybe its winters were too harsh. Maybe they had taxes and funding to provide more services.

Many other survivors had been sent to St. Lukes and a few other city hospitals. After the aftermath, two other captives died of complications. Nekoka didn't even want to think of how everyone must be feeling. Nekoka felt like a litter box herself: if only she'd been faster. Stronger. Smarter. If only she'd known more.

Berlin and Minnie. Both were a black spot on her heart. Damn it, this is what happened when she cared.

When they arrived at Roadster, a kind of western style biker bar on the south end of town, she was a little relieved to see the faces she did. The main room had several large tables with chairs surrounding them, but one corner had the tables moved around and the chairs clumped together in threes and fours. Most of the gathering stood around, but a few sat. Grace looked gutted. Pablo, and she assumed Chandler was around, Battle Axe, and Sparks. John was at the long wooden bar with Eugene, talking to the bartender. Zack was speaking closely with Starburst, Mozart, and Devana of Guardian Alliance around two tables pushed together. Sepia was sitting off to the side, separate, but still close enough to the group. She looked like shit. Her body, her face, her expression. Wasted away, torn apart. Her very soul appeared battered.

Nekoka pulled away from Jenni and sat at Sepia's table. Jenni went to visit Grace. Sepia's eyes were heavy lidded, her mouth frowning. All the metal had been removed from her face; her hair hung loose. When she glanced at Nekoka, no life lit up that gaze.

Nekoka stared at Sepia, and Sepia didn't even seem to care.

"I'm sorry," Nekoka said.

Sepia nodded. "Everyone is."

Nekoka thought of Minnie, and her throat constricted. Remembered hugging her and laughing with the warm and supportive woman. A healer. Someone who only wanted to help. Shot by a guard. All it took to end her was one bullet. And Berlin. His upbeat nature was a gift to the world. She hadn't known him long, but he was still hers and she had been going to protect him forever.... Nekoka coughed, caught her breath.

"Trior is strong," she said. "I hear he did some amazing things to get his group in there. He was pretty awesome. He's going to survive. Just remember that."

Sepia's eyes narrowed, but she didn't say anything.

Nekoka patted her on the shoulder, squeezed, and returned to Jenni who was helping Eugene organize some tables and chairs.

"Okay everyone." Eugene clapped his hands once. "Vent sessions first. Anyone wanna bitch or boast?"

The group gravitated together.

"So, what happened with Minnie?" Nekoka asked, pulled up a chair and sat hip to hip with Jenni, needing to be close.

Starburst, looking like an average woman out to teach kids reading, writing, and arithmetic, tucked her curly hair behind her ears. "It was my fault." Her accent made her words softer, almost delicate in the sudden silence of the crowd.

"It wasn't anyone's fault," Pablo growled.

"Well, I was sprayed with that chemical, and I went norm." She blinked her eyes, glancing at her hands curled on the table, then looked at Nekoka, eyes glossy with emotion. "Someone had shot me, and luckily, my body armor stopped most of the bullets. But some got me. Minnie came from somewhere, I don't know, I couldn't see with all that smoke. And she saved me. Actually turned my powers back on."

Nekoka swallowed, nodded. Minnie would put herself in danger to save someone else. It was in her base makeup.

"So, she counteracted the Nutrix?" Jenni demanded.

Nekoka blinked, yes, that was important. Focus!

Starburst nodded. "I think it must have been her, or maybe I only got a light spraying of it, or it wasn't as effective with me with my armor. I've no idea."

"Something we need to examine more closely," Mozart said, making a note on a pad of paper. He seemed like a take charge kind of leader, which Nekoka completely supported.

"There is evidence of another of those compounds, but I'm not sure where, but they referred to it as Jade Road," Sparks said.

"That's pretty sick," Chandler said. Yep, he was there. "Jade, Seed.... Egh."

"I still have the packet of info you gave to me from your own computer, Nekoka, but not all of it. Also, all the information on the Myroi we have."

In that following bundle of silence, John approached, setting down a tray laden with drinks. Nekoka grabbed the only creamy looking drink from the tray. He sat in a chair next to her, and she felt warm and supported by her friends.

"What is a Myroi?" Starburst asked. She held herself stiffly, and Nekoka wondered where she'd been shot. She was so disconnected without Whisker and the constant influx of information from SPYme. Blind and dumb. "Is it a Seeded? An alien?"

There, she said it. Nekoka knew someone had to. She examined the reactions of the others to Starburst's question. Nods and blank expressions. Nobody denied it.

"I think it's an alien, or at least, not something earth bound," Nekoka gave her two cents.

"What do you mean by that?" Jenni asked, rolling her glass between her hands.

"Well, Berlin talked about them...said they were like ghosts. So, maybe they were similar to a spirit—here, but not fully here. Half in our world, half in their own." It was so hard to talk about him, her friend no longer here. So hard to think that he wasn't here, white eyes wide and spooky, expression earnest, offering his own report.

"Yeah...I sensed something different," John said, leaning his forearms against the round table. "Not like animals or plants. I wasn't sure what it was, but I could sense something alive that wasn't like anything I'd sensed before."

"Berlin could see them." Everyone jumped, turning to face Sepia. "Now he's dead. John, you're the only one we know of who can find them, now."

Another flash of Berlin's white face, his shy smile, the delight in them when he realized he was accepted, all tumbled through Nekoka's inner vision. John squeezed her shoulder. She gave him a soft chirrip.

"Maybe we can develop some device to sense them," Sparks said. "We know they are there. There are ghost chasers, maybe they have something that actually works."

Jenni growled and looked into the face of each of the survivors. "It will take some work and effort, but we have to find them. They are harvesting humans...Seeded. They are preying on us. Perhaps they are the ones who put the Seed in our heads in the first place. We can't stand by. We must equip ourselves. We must prepare to fight back."

Nekoka's ears perked forward. Jenni looked over at her, her pale eyes ringed in dark, like a shadow from a tower of worry blotted out her light. But there was steel there. Strength. Nekoka leaned towards it like a flower to the sun.

Feeling the energy of the moment, Nekoka said, "I can see about a device that does what Berlin did. Or John can do."

"Perhaps other Seeded have the same capability. I'll see what I can find in my database," Sparks added.

A round of agreement fluttered within the group, even Sepia showed interest. Nekoka figured vengeance would pull her out of her dark abyss.

"We'll find the Jade Road," Eugene said, firm and sure.

"Bottom line," Nekoka added. "This is bullshit. We won't stand by and let these aliens milk us and toss our rotting corpses into a pit." She wanted to throw their rotting corpses in a pit, that was for sure. If they had corpses.

They made plans, full of optimism and spitfire. Nekoka left notes on Jenni's phone, which was a sad mockery of what a *real* computer was.

After the meeting, Nekoka asked Jenni, "Where to now? Back to New Orleans?"

Jenni, super, amazing, lovely Jenni, simply looked at Nekoka, that dark shadow still ghosting around her green eyes. Then she smiled, a weak and hollowed-out substitute for her usual wry amusement, but it was a start. "Or Portland. They might need us. And you need to remake Whisker. I have lots of footwork to do, calls to make."

Demons to slay.

Nekoka tilted her head. "Demons?"

In a flash, a wash of red smoked over Jenni's green eyes, then it was gone. Nekoka's breath caught. Was she seeing things now? Had that mix of gas and smoke inhalation and going norm done something to her brain?

Jenni shook her head. "Nothing. Just thinking out loud. Sorry."

"So, set up a new base, find the Jade Road, rally the troops, prepare ourselves for the next wave."

Jenni smiled, showing more teeth than her last weak expression had offered. "Yep."

"You and me," Nekoka added, brushing her shoulder against Jenni's. "On this rum run."

"Always."

Always. Nekoka purred at that. Together, with Jenni, they would stop these Myroi and send them packing back to their own dark hole.

CHAPTER 53

Evolution

It watched the enriched praenletta gathering, the ones that tore down the compound built for the praena collection. Something within it recognized individuals. Singularities. A zing of heat shot through its form.

It moved towards one that had a different appearance. The ears were odd, and the praenletta had an appendage off its back. It wanted to be closer to that one. There was something warming about it. Something more intriguing.

The Myroi watched. Its moiety were gone. It was alone.

Alone.

Inside its head, thoughts bubbled into words. *Stay. Together we can watch. Watch her.*

Together? The single Myroi felt thin, pounded into a layer. The Myroi had a praenletta inside it, infesting it like a breeze. The white praenletta didn't understand. How could it? The Reeli horde was ever hungry. The Reeli harvest decimated the Myroi, destroyed them. The praneletta didn't understand the preana was necessary for the Myroi's survival.

Her. We will watch Nekoka, the praenletta infiltrating it thought.

Nekoka. It had a name. So many names. The thing inside, it had a name too.

It was called Berlin.

Acknowlegements

Ah, superheroes. They have a special place in my heart and have since watching the X-men and Spiderman cartoons after school as a kid. But these heroes in my story come from other places, have other origins. Many of them are characters of mine or friends' from years of roleplaying games. From college on, I've been playing rpgs and even did my stint LARPing. Though abilities and skills are modified, the personalities have come through, and it's with love that I bring them to life on the page of this epic story.

So, I want to thank my gaming friends who have helped people this story and build the framework for my characters to come alive. Joe Jones, Russ Needham, and Eric Hayden are standouts. Joe, as my storyteller, was instrumental in the evolution of Nekoka. The Knight Force crew and the Weaklings gang helped flesh out and spark ideas for other minor characters or cameos.

I also want to thank my beta readers and critique partners who have helped shape this novel. Mark Fraser, Joe Morreale, Carolyn O'Doherty, Sonja Thomas, Fonda Lee, Curtis Chen, Audrey Danals, and Deborah Kaminski. Also to Jean Thomson for military help, Clayton Callahan for help with weaponry, and Eriko Otsuka for guiding my hand with the Japanese. Thanks to Shelley Mann for the helpful thoughts and amazing edit, and for Khalid20 for creating this dynamic and fun cover. If I have forgotten anyone, it isn't with malice, it's just a scattered mind.

Vanessa Maclellan is an internationally selling poet and author. She's had short fiction published in a variety of publications from middle grade superhero to horror. She writes, hikes, camps, and bird watches in the Pacific Northwest, USA. You can find her at vanmaclellan.com.

If you enjoy heroic fantasy, please check out her other books available at retailers everywhere.

www.ingramcontent.com/pod-product-compliance
Lightning Source LLC
LaVergne TN
LVHW041107080826
845145LV00007B/1713

* 9 7 8 1 7 3 7 7 1 5 7 3 3 *